ADVANCE PRAISE FOR
Drive Me Crazy

"*Drive Me Crazy* is fun, fast-paced, and swoon-worthy! I was rooting for Chloe and Matt as they traveled from race to race in the high-stakes world of Formula 1, overcoming obstacles and finding that life-changing love everyone dreams of. Their electric chemistry on and off the track make this the hot F1 rom-com you won't want to miss."

—Annabel Monaghan, *New York Times* bestselling author of *It's a Love Story*

"Lizzy Dent delivers! *Drive Me Crazy* is a perfect blend of heart, heat, and plot in this fast-paced F1 romance."

—K. Bromberg, *New York Times* bestselling author of *Off the Grid*

"*Drive Me Crazy* is the sexiest possible introduction to F1 for those who haven't yet gotten the memo, and it's sure to please those who are already fans! I was hooked on Matt and Chloe's chemistry from page one and loved every twist and turn of this fizzy, fun, fast-paced ride. Lizzy Dent delivers everything I love in a sports romance—high stakes, big passion, and underdogs you can't help but root for—and she grounds it all in layered characters with wounded, yearning hearts. This book is a total triumph!"

—Melanie Sweeney, *USA Today* bestselling author of *Take Me Home*

"*Drive Me Crazy* had me laughing out loud and feeling the nerves in the pit of my stomach at every turn. Lizzy Dent serves both a lovable found family and a leading couple to root for. She meshes the thrill of the will-they, won't-they with equally nail-biting action on the Formula 1 circuit. Chloe—determined, intelligent, and finding her footing in the good ol' boys' club that is Formula 1—had my heart immediately. I found myself zooming through *Drive Me Crazy* in full Grand Prix fashion. In very few situations are you sad to reach the checkered flag, but this was one of them: you won't want this season with Chloe, Matt, and Arden to end!"—**Esha Patel, author of *Offtrack***

"*Drive Me Crazy* explodes with heart-racing, romantic sizzle. Readers will root for Chloe's ambition and Matt's comeback as Dent pushes the pedal to the floorboards, revving up the sexy tension until the tires smoke. I lapped it up!"

—**Ilana Long, author of *Pickleballers***

PRAISE FOR
The Summer Job

A *Real Simple* Best Beach Read

A *Marie Claire* Ultimate Summer Beach Read

A *New York Post* Best Book on Our Summer Reading List

A *Country Living* Can't-Miss Beach Read for This Summer

A *Cosmopolitan* New Book to Feed Your Wanderlust

A *Parade* Book You'll Want to Read This Sizzling Season

A *Fortune* Entertaining New Book to Read This Summer

"With a gorgeously picturesque setting, an utterly charming cast, and a hilarious protagonist, Lizzy Dent's *The Summer Job* is my perfect summer read! Sure to be one of the sweetest, funniest, and sexiest books of the year."

—**Emily Henry, #1 *New York Times* bestselling author of *Great Big Beautiful Life***

"This novel is what happens when you combine *Sweetbitter* with *The Princess Switch*, place it in the Scottish Highlands, and throw in a whole lot of wine."—***Entertainment Weekly***

"A rom-com-esque adventure in which a girl steals her best friend's identity to spend the season at a luxury Scottish Highlands resort. Lol, same."—***Cosmopolitan***

"The secluded Scotland setting makes it easy to immerse yourself in Birdy's world. . . . Plenty of bad decisions and dramatic disasters, a cast of supporting characters to love and hate, and a sweet and tender romance despite all odds. But through it all, you can't help but root for Birdy!"—***PopSugar***

"If you're a fan of *Outlander* but want an adventure in the Scottish Highlands with a little more Wi-Fi, this is the read for you."

—**Shondaland**

"Dent hits a home run with her first novel. . . . This witty, banter-filled novel seems frothy at first, but aptly balances the humor with darker subjects. Lovely descriptions of Scotland, quirky supporting characters, and a thoroughly lovable heroine make this a sure bet for fans of Jenny Colgan."

—***Library Journal*** **(starred review)**

"A frothy story reminiscent of late 1990s chick lit . . . It's escapist fun with surprising emotional depth; fans of Emily Henry and Katie Fforde should add this to their summer read list."—***Booklist***

"It's witty and funny and it packs an emotional punch, too, which is really tricky to pull off. . . . Loved it, I'm in the queue for more Lizzy Dent."

—**Josie Silver, *New York Times* bestselling author of *One Day in December***

PRAISE FOR
The Setup

A *PopSugar* Best New Book

A Motherly Buzziest Book

A Love to Know Must-Read Book

"An adorable rom-com packed full of nostalgia and Dent's trademark wit."

—**Sophie Cousens, *New York Times* bestselling author of *This Time Next Year***

"I fell in love with Lizzy Dent's writing with *The Summer Job* and have been waiting with bated breath to see what she does next. . . . With Dent's usual humor, wit, and warmth, and a spectacularly charming cast of weirdos, *The Setup* is exactly the kind of summer read I'm constantly on the hunt for. I love astrology-obsessed, hot-mess Mara, I love the crumbling little Broadgate lido she's out to save, and I love, love, love Lizzy Dent."

—**Emily Henry, #1 *New York Times* bestselling author of *Great Big Beautiful Life***

"[Lizzy Dent] is back once again with another witty story filled with love and lighthearted humor."—***PopSugar***

"[A] sweet and funny tale of a woman who has been barely scrapping by as she opens herself up to new friends and new experiences. For fans of Abbi Waxman and Emily Henry."—***Booklist***

"Grab your SPF and your carry-on because we have the ultimate beach read for your summer getaway. *The Setup* is a laugh-out-loud story. . . . You can't imagine the twists and turns [it] takes."

—**Love to Know**

PRAISE FOR
The Sweetest Revenge

A *USA Today* Summer Must-Read Romance

An *Entertainment Weekly* Best New Book to Take on Your Summer Vacation

A *Library Journal* Best Fiction Book of the Year (So Far)

A PureWow Book We Can't Wait to Read

"My favorite kind of story—one with an irresistible premise that delivers in a way I never imagined possible. It is at once funny, poignant, and deliciously satisfying. I had to force myself to slow down and savor the end. I absolutely loved it."

—Annabel Monaghan, *New York Times* bestselling author of *It's a Love Story*

"Equal parts hilarious, heartbreaking, and swoon-worthy, Dent's addictive novel isn't here to make sweeping philosophical statements about the morality of vengeance. In fact, it actually delights in how delicious getting petty retribution can feel in the moment (so relatable)."—*Entertainment Weekly*

"Dent writes quirky yet relatable characters, and her protagonist in this latest novel is outstanding. . . . Readers will love the fast-paced wit of both Amy and the supporting characters while she discovers who she is, where she wants to be, and what is truly in her heart."—*Library Journal* (starred review)

"The perfect storm of a rom-com—the chaotic, hilarious entanglement of a kickass heroine, her hot AF neighbor, and a very unwelcome ex. As intoxicating as a cocktail on a summer's day."

—Beth Morrey, author of *The Love Story of Missy Carmichael*

PRAISE FOR
Just One Taste

A PureWow Best Beach Read of the Summer

A *Kirkus Reviews* Book That Offers Pure Escapism

An Eater Food-Filled Beach Read for Your Summer Vacation

"Follow Lizzy Dent to Italy and you will smell the oranges, feel the sunshine, and taste the first perfect kiss. *Just One Taste* is a deliciously romantic and emotional exploration of love and loss, with Dent's signature humor and sense of fun."

—Annabel Monaghan, *New York Times* bestselling author of *It's a Love Story*

"Dent's cozy, slow-burn romance is a heartfelt journey through Italian cuisine and culture. Readers will delight in the rich descriptions of food and dream of a summer holiday in Italy."

—*Booklist*

"If you're a foodie and love vivid detail in writing, *Just One Taste* by Lizzy Dent is the book for you. You'll fall in love with the characters most of all."—*New York Post*

"Dent easily balances rom-com tropes with grief. . . . Leo and Olive have serious chemistry that simmers slowly on the back burner as they explore Italy, and the lush descriptions of simple foods like tomatoes, cherries, and oranges will make readers want to book a trip (or at least book a reservation at an Italian restaurant). A delightful, sexy summer read for foodies."

—*Kirkus Reviews*

ALSO BY LIZZY DENT

Just One Taste

The Sweetest Revenge

The Setup

The Summer Job

Drive Me Crazy

LIZZY DENT

G. P. Putnam's Sons
New York

PUTNAM
— EST. 1838 —
G. P. Putnam's Sons
Publishers Since 1838
An imprint of Penguin Random House LLC
1745 Broadway, New York, NY 10019
penguinrandomhouse.com

LIBRARY OF CONGRESS CATALOGING-IN-PUBLICATION DATA

Names: Dent, Lizzy author
Title: Drive me crazy / Lizzy Dent.
Description: New York : G. P. Putnam's Sons, 2026. |
Identifiers: LCCN 2025013090 (print) | LCCN 2025013091 (ebook) |
ISBN 9798217045204 trade paperback | ISBN 9798217045211 ebook
Subjects: LCGFT: Fiction | Romance fiction | Novels
Classification: LCC PR9639.4.D45 D75 2026 (print) |
LCC PR9639.4.D45 (ebook) | DDC 823/.92—dc23/eng/20250602
LC record available at https://lccn.loc.gov/2025013090
LC ebook record available at https://lccn.loc.gov/2025013091

Book Design by Shannon Nicole Plunkett

Printed in the United States of America
1st Printing

The authorized representative in the EU for product safety and compliance is Penguin Random House Ireland, Morrison Chambers, 32 Nassau Street, Dublin D02 YH68, Ireland, https://eu-contact.penguin.ie.

To Carolyn Burke—for buying me Stephen King's *On Writing* about fifteen years ago and encouraging me every day since. I feel your support always. ♥

CHAPTER 1

Chloe

Singapore Grand Prix
Qualifying

"I'm just very keen to sign the contract before we do this," I say, picking up my pace to keep up with Arden Racing owner Barry Arden as we stride down the hallway, followed by the pitter-patter of his two greyhounds. "Because once we announce, we can't take it back."

That's the most I'm going to push him, because oh my god, I would not take this moment back. I am fizzing with excitement. Or is it anxiety? *Anxitement?* Either way, I feel so high, I'm virtually levitating as I follow behind him.

My dream was always this, to be among the very best in the fastest, most advanced motor racing sport on the planet—Formula 1. And now it's happening. It might not be perfect, but it's happening.

There will be no take-backs. Not a chance. I spent most of the summer working with Barry and the team to get to this moment, and now *it's time.*

"We've agreed to the deal terms, love. Plus, there's no time with qualifying in just a few hours," Barry says as we reach the door to the pressroom, where a handful of the team are waiting. My friend Keyla always says I can trust a man who loves flowers, animals, or children, and Barry has two dogs, so that's something, at least. I nod at him, swallowing a frustrated sigh. Fine.

"Okay, soon?"

"Stop worrying. This is your moment," he says, beaming at me with too large teeth, his ruddy complexion dewy with sweat. Barry Arden also has this slightly performative cockney-gangster accent, which makes him sound like something from a Guy Ritchie movie.

"Okay. But one other thing, Mr. Arden. It would be great if you could call me Chloe. Especially in public," I say, clearing my throat as I do.

"All right, love."

"Chloe," I repeat, as evenly as I can.

"You got it, darlin'," he says, cocking his head as his eyes move down to my green pantsuit and then back up to my mop of red curls. "You ready? Want to fix your hair or something?"

Ouch. I thought I looked quite tidy and well put together in my new Bottega suit. Not my typical vibe, but that's the point. Today, I have to look elevated, professional, like I deserve to be here. Because . . .

I do. Don't I?

I think back to the bug-eyed, flame-haired kid with skinny legs and braces, interviewing herself in the bathtub after she'd placed third in her first ever go-kart race. ESPN, Graham Norton, and even Oprah would bring me on to rapturous applause. I practiced remaining cool, humble, and thoroughly impressive.

"Oh, stop. *Really.* I'm no wunderkind," eleven-year-old me would say to my mirror, smiling coyly. That kid quietly believed in herself. This *woman* is not so sure.

Am I truly cut out to compete at this level? Can I make myself heard? Will people listen? It is such a big jump up to F1. I put my hand on the wall to steady myself as I feel the anxiety wrap around me like some kind of giant python, starting to squeeze.

No! You are not going there, Chloe, I tell myself, burying the train of thought before impostor syndrome overtakes my body and I start to hyperventilate.

I steady my voice before answering Barry. "The suit is new," I say, while I force my dark red curls into a low ponytail. "And it's our team green."

"No offense, but you look a bit like a Christmas tree," he says, guffawing.

I fake a chuckle back at him.

"Don't look so uptight, love. You've worked hard for this. And besides, it's good you came dressed as a Christmas tree." Barry Arden grins mischievously. "We've got a present for you."

Before I have a chance to ask what the fuck that means, the doors to the hotel conference room fling open. Cameras, lights, and boom microphones line the back wall, and journalists, dozens of them, turn their excitable expressions in our direction. So many eyes, is all I can think. *So many eyes on me.* I'm not sure I'll ever get used to this attention.

For a moment, we stand frozen in the doorway. Just two greyhounds, both with a single paw lifted—tiny me and the man mountain that is Barry Arden side by side, and behind us, the team, all wearing Arden Racing kit.

It's an entrance, all right.

Lights burst on us almost immediately. Shielding my eyes, I notice everyone is here. The BBC, ESPN, DAZN, even Eurosport. I feel my chest constrict and I force an even breath. My appearance next to Barry is the reason the press corps are murmuring and fidgeting with anticipation.

"Showtime," Barry says, and we're quickly on the move, past the rows of journalists with their big-eyed excitement and on to the long table with the FIA-emblazoned tablecloth at the front of the room. I remove a short preprepared speech from my pocket and take my seat behind the little tented cardboard name card: Chloe Coleman.

Finally. I think about all the things I'm going to say, all the people I need to thank. And then, I close my eyes briefly and speak only to myself, to that eleven-year-old girl. *You did it. You fucking did it. I'm so happy for you.* I glance down at my prepared statement. *You got this.*

As I look back up, I notice an empty place next to Barry with a name card I can't quite see. "Who's sitting there?"

"Your present," he says, grinning, tapping his lecture cards into a uniform stack as he waits for the room to settle so he can begin. A camera flash startles me, and I swing my head forward again.

My eyes sting from the bright lights, so I create a visor with my hand to see more clearly. Who else could be coming to sit up here with us? A head of aerodynamics? We need one. Or is it someone else?

Along with the press, I can see team principals from Ferrari, Rossini, McLaren, even Mercedes, ready to do their various team updates too. I spot Jack Sheppard from *F1 Daily*, a driver turned journalist who I know from my old racing days. I smile nervously at him, and he winks back. *A friend.* I breathe out. *If I freak out, I'll just look at him.* By the far wall, I can see a couple of drivers too, before my eyes catch on a very familiar profile. . . .

Wait. Is that Matt Warner?

My eyes widen as he comes fully into focus. He's leaning back against the wall, arms folded, eyes on the floor like he doesn't want to be here. He looks so different after all this time, even at this distance. Older, wearier, somehow, though still admittedly attractive in that classic cocky Matt Warner way. His dark hair is too long, falling forward, hiding his eyes. Honestly, I'd be hiding too if I had burned out as spectacularly as he did at Rossini. Once their big hope, he's had a season—so far—of failing form, then a huge crash at the Italian Grand Prix, which took out his teammate and best friend, Stavros. The Chloe from our teenage racing days might have had some empathy for his rough run, but those days are long gone.

I sit up a little taller in my seat and turn my gaze anywhere but in his direction. That too tall, arrogant asshole is about to witness my ascension.

"Good afternoon, ladies and gentlemen. I have a short statement to make, and then we'll take questions," Barry says.

Click. Click. Click. He waits for the sound of the cameras to quiet, and I feel a smile creep across my face, a coy heat rising in my cheeks. I can barely contain myself.

This. Is. It.

"Welcome to everyone on this hot day in Singapore. The

qualifying will begin here at Marina Bay Circuit in just a few hours, and we have a lot of teams to get through, so I won't keep you," he says, before clearing his throat. "As you know, Arden Racing has been without a team principal since the end of the summer break. But we're very happy to announce Chloe Coleman will be filling that role, effective immediately."

I absorb the gasps from the press corps, feeling my chest swell with pride. That's right, I'm going to be leading Arden's F1 racing team for the rest of this season. The boss. The head of all staff and drivers and the ultimate decision-maker.

Even though I really, really shouldn't, I can't help but look at Matt. I have his attention now, his hazel eyes in my direction, mouth slackened.

I'm surprised by how sharp the pleasure of his surprise is. *See, I made it too.* I turn to the press and paint on a smile, trying to remain calm and professional.

"Chloe has a wealth of experience. Not only is she an immensely competent driver, but the work speaks for itself. Last year in Formula 3, she turned around the fortunes of Visor Racing, teaming up with Honda and raising capital to improve the engines. Her decisions ultimately delivered the biggest improvement of any team on any of the circuits."

I'm surprisingly impressed with Barry's statement, which is very competently drafted, and has not contained any derivative of the word *fuck*, yet. He's made me sound utterly worthy of the role, and for that I'm grateful.

I knew when he asked me to be team principal of the

worst team in F1 he was chasing a reputation clear-up as much as anything. It's bound to help improve the image of Arden Racing to have a woman in charge. A team that this year alone has been embroiled in a sexting scandal concerning the now sacked, very much married team principal and his personal assistant. And to make matters worse, there was a gender pay gap dispute that Arden ended up losing in court, resulting in a forced-groveling public apology, with Barry acknowledging that team Arden needed to "do better" when it came to ethics and diversity. It was honestly delicious to watch.

So yes, I'm a chance for Barry Arden to polish his team's murky reputation. But there is politics behind so many decisions in F1, and besides, I am the queen of making lemonade out of lemons. I've worked with the scraps I've been tossed my entire racing career, and look where it's got me. *Here.* Hopefully paving the way for more young women to break up this boys' club.

"I know you'll have a lot of questions for Chloe, but I just have another announcement to make before we unleash the hounds." Barry pets one of his greyhounds, Ginger, and chuckles to himself.

One of the female journalists in the front row tips her head toward me and grins. "Good for you," she mouths. I bite my lip, my cheeks warm with delight. All the work. All the hard fucking graft, it all comes down to this.

Barry clears his throat. "Now for the other big news . . . As you know, our first driver position has been empty since the departure of Jose Diaz. And so, we're excited to announce we've taken on a new driver."

I swing my head around to look at Barry. Hiring new drivers is really the team principal's decision, and I have ideas of my own. I feel the little groove between my eyebrows deepen as I cover the mic on my desk and lean in toward Barry, trying desperately, out of the corner of my mouth, to shut the guy up.

But he completely ignores me.

"I've just finished talks with Rossini about the immediate release of Matthew Warner from his contract there."

If I thought the news about me delivered gasps of shock, they paled in comparison to the breathless puffing and wheezing of excitement from this surprise announcement.

"What?" I say loudly into my microphone, causing feedback to squeal across the room.

Barry taps the table in front of me, his way of telling me to calm down.

Then he continues, a toothy grin on his round face. "As if he needs any introduction, Matt Warner has spent the last ten years at the top of the very best team, with over seventy podiums and one world championship under his belt. I know the last few months have been rough for him, but Rossini have agreed a fresh start for Matt here at Arden is best for everyone."

All eyes are on Matt, and he looks *furious*. He immediately cranes his head in the direction of the Rossini team principal, who is already picking his way through the crowd to make his escape. Barry glances toward the commotion, and I wonder if this announcement is a little premature. I wonder, briefly panicked, if Matt and Rossini are also missing a final contract.

Matt looks back in our direction, now frozen in horror,

and I'm surprised to find my first emotion is a wave of compassion. For him. For Matt fucking Warner. This massive bomb was just dropped on me, but was it dropped on Matt also?

I collect myself and feel a fury of my own start to bubble up. I put my hands on the table, and as I'm about to stand, I feel Barry's hand on my shoulder holding me down. "Trust me," he says, quietly but sternly.

"Matt, would you come up and join us onstage?" Barry booms.

Matt is still frozen stiff until he's slapped on the back by way of congratulations by another driver from McLaren. And then a small handful of the press awkwardly clap, more out of pity than anything, surely? Matt has just been forcibly moved from the top Formula 1 team to the bottom one. This is no moment for congratulations.

"Matt? I'm sure the press would like to see the new team all together?"

Matt looks like someone winded him, and yet he moves toward the stage, slowly.

The frenzy of clicking is so loud it starts to sound like white noise, and in the cacophony, I realize why Matt is going along with this: He's trapped. He can't force Rossini to keep him, and if Arden have bought him out, his ass now belongs to Barry. He has no choice, and the world is watching. What else is he going to do? Run?

The camera clicking evolves into shouting. They have questions. Many questions. The shouting from the journalists is so loud, the dogs have started to howl, and Barry has to lean down and run a hand over their little heads to soothe them.

"Matt, can you tell us when you found out about the transfer?"

"Matt, BBC here. This is not unprecedented, but exceedingly unusual. Why Arden?"

"Hi, Joe from *Racing Monthly.* Has this got anything to do with the crash, and your struggle to recover your previous speeds?"

"Has your teammate Stavros recovered, Matt?"

"Why won't you talk about the crash?"

"Can you look in this direction for a photo, please?"

But Matt isn't replying. He's just sitting with his arms folded, his mouth fixed firm, and a look of pure fury on his face.

This could have been the best day of my life. It should've been. It was supposed to be the moment when my career headed into the apex and emerged at full speed onto the straight. Me, poised to fly across the finish line, finally a winner in a sport I have battled for so long to do well in. Instead, my day in the sun has been completely overshadowed. And by, of all fucking people, Matt Warner.

"I think maybe it's best if we pass on questions today," Barry says now, holding his arms out to calm the room. "After all, we have a brand-new team and a Singapore qualifying to prepare for."

I crumple up my prepared speech, briefly glancing sidelong at Matt.

"Of course," Barry is saying to one of the photographers, who has pushed his way forward and is pointing his enormous lens in our faces. "Yes, we can get a team photo."

Barry Arden drapes an arm over my shoulders, and then over Matt's shoulders, squeezing us both in toward him. He is beaming. I'm pretty sure I look like I just saw a ghost. And Matt wants to punch something.

This ridiculous image of the three key members of the new Arden Racing team will no doubt appear in the sports news of every major paper tomorrow.

Barry squeezes us both closer. "So, darlin'," he says to me out of the side of his mouth. "How do you like your present?"

CHAPTER 2

Matt

It feels like a ten-truck motorway pileup in my head.

Fired from Rossini? Hired by . . . *Chloe Coleman*?

I escape the press conference without a word, leaving Chloe staring ahead, almost catatonic, in her seat. Barry has moved like lightning, ushering the remaining press into the corridor. As I slip past, I can hear him shamelessly boasting about how great the rest of the season will be with me in it.

"You're not worried about his form?"

"We'll get Matt back on top again," he crows. And then he starts to sing. "All he needs is love. Love is all he needs." A roar of laughter follows from the press corps.

Barry Arden brings the chaos. He's unconventional and, more interestingly, he's an outsider in a sport built on dynasties. And the press sure laps it up.

"Matt! Come with me," says a familiar, booming voice from the far end of the hall.

Archie, my older brother and my Rossini race engineer, my now *former* race engineer, is striding toward me like a bouncer. Thank fucking god. He's big and brash and permanently sweat stained and, right now, the only person I want to see. He yanks me quickly down the corridor, shaking reporters off left and right as he hauls me into a waiting lift.

"Take a breath. We can talk in private," he says, a reassuring hand on my shoulder as the lift climbs to the top floor.

But my private suite is not the calming refuge I was hoping for. Gone is all my slick silver-and-bloodred Rossini paraphernalia, and in its place, a new, forest green hellscape.

A cameraman and lighting crew are setting up for interviews in the lounge area, in front of a large Arden Racing banner, while a producer and her assistant who *were* draped across the sofa, sipping on espressos, spring up when we enter. Everywhere I look, another Arden logo, inexplicably bigger than the last. There's no escape from this nightmarish reality.

"Ten minutes?" says a cheery young woman clutching a clipboard.

"He'll be there," Archie says, shoving me into my bedroom, where I drop to the edge of my bed, my head falling into my hands.

"What. The. Fuck," I mutter into my clammy palms.

Archie pokes at my untouched breakfast on the little silver tray at the end of my bed.

"Is this caviar on the fucking scrambled eggs?" he says, forking the little black balls atop a congealed yellow mound. "Gross," he concludes, shoving it into his mouth, and then picking up a slice of bacon. "Why do you order this elitist junk? I hope the nutritionist at Arden is on your ass."

"What the hell just happened, Archie?" I say, looking up from my hands.

"Well. You just got sold to Arden, my guy."

"I need to speak to Miles."

"That so-called agent of yours should have been fired a long time ago," Archie says, knocking back my freshly squeezed orange juice. "What's he actually done since 2002?"

"Archie," I say, my voice thin. My mind is reeling.

He stops eating and his body slackens. He brushes the crumbs off his hands and pulls up a chair opposite me. "I mean, it isn't surprising, Matt. You were warned."

"I was warned I might drop to reserve, not . . . this."

"Would you have been happy with reserve?"

"No."

"Then . . ." Archie raises his palms upward, as if this isn't the worst outcome when it patently is. I scoff.

"And working for Chloe Coleman? Where the hell did that come from?"

"Well, she's been amazing in F3," Archie says, shrugging. "She's just what Arden needs after their bad press this year. A surprise, sure, but it makes sense to me. She's a rising star."

I frown. "Right."

Archie's eyes narrow. "You didn't know." He shakes his head. "Dude, you were pretty good friends growing up. Practically inseparable on the track until you left for F1."

I bristle. "Friends? She was more like a kid sister."

"Yeah, I guess. But you were still friends," says Archie.

"I hung out with her because Dad asked *us* to look out for her."

"Admit it. You liked her."

I glare at Archie. I don't need this right now, especially

with everything else blowing up around me. "Whatever, man. Does she still live in Brackley, or . . . ?"

"Her family is still there," Archie says, then he leans forward, looking me straight in the eye. "I know life has been a bit of a fucking circus, but you'd know that if you came home more."

I take it with a slow nod. "I need to speak to her."

"You sure do."

I look at my big brother, pleading with him. "Archie. I don't know how to move forward." My eyes sting a little, and I blink a few times, the weight of everything finally crashing down on me.

He grabs my shoulders and pulls me up. "Dude, something had to change," he says as he squeezes me lightly. "You don't train. You eat shit. You've been drinking too much."

"Say what you really think, asshole," I mutter, laughing weakly.

"One thing at a time, Matt. Pick yourself up. You need to or it's over, for fuck's sake. Maybe a new team, a new *car*, will help with all the problems from the—"

"I doubt it," I say, cutting him off. *I don't want to talk about that.*

"Well, a familiar face running the show just might. Someone you can trust. You can't deny Chloe always gave you good racing advice."

Archie is right on that, at least. As I recall, she did have this uncanny ability to spot minor imperfections. She helped me improve my race on more than one occasion.

I think about her back then, picturing her in her scuffed trainers, with the oversize T-shirts and wild red hair, sticking her tongue out as she raced ahead of me in her go-kart.

Those big brown eyes always wide with energy and nerves. What did I used to call her? Bug-eyes? *Bug?* The memory makes me smile.

"Fine. I get your point."

Archie knows better than to push. Instead, he ruffles my hair like I'm still five and he's fifteen, and turns away, scanning the room.

"Have they delivered a new kit already?" He finds the two zip bags hanging over the back of an armchair, liberating a new racing suit and undershirt. "Is this it?"

"It's so . . . green," I murmur, pulling off my white T-shirt.

"Come on, mate," Archie says, tossing me the undershirt. I look at the little logo. No more iconic silver wolf of Rossini. Instead, I see what looks like a barking yellow dog above off-the-shelf Arial font reading ARDEN RACING. Below that, a big silver square of gaffer tape covering a sponsor patch. I try to peel the edge of the silver tape.

"Don't pull it off," says Archie. "Could be a reason it's covered."

"Christ," I say, recoiling. "Save me."

"This is what you're gonna do, baby brother," he says. "You're gonna go out there and do the stupid little social media clips talking about how excited you are and whatever the fuck. Then you're going to head to the track and make the best of the rest of this season. Success is revenge."

"Okay," I say.

"We could build something there, you know," Archie says, heading toward the door.

"*We?*" I stop following him, aghast.

"Yes." He beams at me, motioning for me to hurry. "I was always more of a dog than a racehorse."

"Christ, don't willingly leave Rossini, Archie."

"Of course I'm coming. I'm your race engineer. You think I'm going to stay and work with someone else?"

"But for fuck's sake. It's Arden."

"We started this together. Where you go, I go," he says firmly.

I stare at the ceiling. "Promise me you won't do anything right away."

"I won't," he says with a grin. "Now get out there and be your handsome, charming self."

I sit impatiently as the makeup artist dusts a light film of powder across my face. I hate this part of the job. The press and publicity. Or the "media," as they call it now. I've always hated it, despite the fact that I'm good at it. It's such a big part of the gig now, because it keeps the sponsor money flowing and the fans talking. With F1's international growth, the sport has lately been as much about the personalities and the off-track antics as it's been about the racing. And I've had some pretty juicy off-track antics over the years.

The producer takes a seat next to the camera and taps the edge of the lens. "Straight down the barrel, if you don't mind."

I force a smile, trying not to come off too petulant, even if it's exactly how I feel.

"Hello, Matt. Just a warm-up question to test sound. How are you enjoying being back in Singapore?"

"I just got here last night." What does she think I've been doing? Clubbing? Sightseeing? I could be in Peru right now for all I know—having seen the inside of a private jet, the airport tarmac, the lights of the city through tinted car windows, and the cookie-cutter luxury hotel room. *God, I'm angry. How am I going to get through this interview without coming across as a megawatt asshole?* I look at Archie, who nods at me encouragingly.

"The sound is fine," confirms a voice from the back. The producer smiles tentatively as I blink a couple of times, trying to get my eyes used to the ring light.

"Great. Straight into it, then. Matt. How are you feeling about your move to Arden?"

I clear my throat. "I'm um . . ." Shit. My mind goes completely blank. How do I feel about it? I feel furious. Blindsided. Confused. Devastated. I pluck through the negatives until I find one tiny kernel that I can cling to. I glance at the producer, who is starting to look panicked, and I decide to just fucking do this.

"I'm excited for a fresh start at a team based closer to my hometown, Brackley. It will be good to be back in England."

"Is it okay if you say *I'm excited for a fresh start at Arden Racing*? Just to be really clear for our fans."

"Sure. I'm excited for a fresh start at Arden Racing. I'm happy to be on a team based closer to my family in Brackley. I've really missed the weather."

She smiles merrily. Archie gently pumps a fist in encouragement.

"And what about your new team principal? Brilliant, yes, to be working for your first female boss and only the second ever in Formula 1's history?"

"Er . . ." I try hard not to frown, conscious that the camera is on me.

This is an annoying question, directed, I suspect, by Barry Arden. Archie is right. He wants to maximize the cachet of this men's club having a woman as a team principal. The producer didn't even use her name, for fuck's sake. My hesitation is not because she's a woman; it's because I've had about thirty minutes to get used to the idea of that woman being Chloe Coleman.

It feels like a lifetime ago when I actually knew her. I think back to the eight-year-old with the braces and the vintage racing shirts who outpaced half the dudes on the track in our tiny karts. The teenager with the goofy smile and the wild hair who I looked out for because, as my dad explained, "the circuit can get tough for girls." But what had started as an annoying chore from my dad *had* turned into a friendship. Archie was right. She *was* my friend once.

I was about twenty when I left for Rossini. She'd just finished her first year in F3 at what—seventeen? And then we drifted apart.

I feel the clock ticking. I'd better answer something and fast.

"It's great." It's all I can manage.

"You mean, 'It's great to be at Arden Racing working for my first woman boss,'" says the producer. I summon all my chill. Then I parrot the line back, trying to smile as I do.

"Barry Arden has declared that Arden has been grafting hard in the garage and is ready for its fairy-tale finish. You were off pace at Rossini, can you come back?"

I want to reply sarcastically, "With the shittiest car on the grid and a team more famous for its partying than its pit performance?" But instead, I take a deep breath and roll out a list of PR classics.

"Nothing I like more than the chase. I drive at my best when I'm on the ropes. Sure, there's gonna be challenges ahead, but that's motor racing." I wait for something to stir inside me, but I feel nothing. Not even a faint hint that maybe, just maybe, the driver I was before the crash is still inside me somewhere. "I'll be taking my Rossini points with me, and I want to keep adding to that total. As always, I'm here to win. I'm never happy unless I'm standing on the podium."

"That's great, Matt," she crows. "Can you give us an update on your old teammate Stavros?"

"I ahh . . ." I tip my head, holding a hand up to cover the light shining into my face. "Sorry. I don't want to talk about Stavros."

The producer grins apologetically. "I know, Matt. It's just, you haven't spoken about it publicly, and we think it's contributing to the . . . ah . . . lack of goodwill toward you on the paddock, and among the fans."

Because they blame me for Stavros ending up in hospital after the crash. And of course they do. It was my fault.

"We'd love to get those Rossini fans to come to Arden with you," she continues, and then she gives up beating around the bush and comes out with the financial heart of the matter. "It helps so much with merch sales for you to be popular. You know, like Daniel Ricciardo. Everyone loves that guy."

"Fine," I say, sighing. The producer taps the lens again.

"Stavros is on my mind every day, and it won't be the same without him." I have to dig deep to keep my voice even. I see a flash of his car, in my mind's eye, flames licking out the front of the engine. I clear my throat. "But Stavros is a great competitor, he understands the sport, and I'm sure he'll be happy to see me back on the track."

I imagine my best friend watching me from his hospital bed and my stomach contracts like I might be sick. It's my fault he's there. And it's fucking unfair I'm back and he's not. I think about all the messages I've sent him over the past few months. All the times I've tried to reach out. But he doesn't want to speak to me. He's made it clear.

I stand and yank the battery pack free from the back of my shorts and unclip the little mic on my collar. "I'm sorry, I can't do this. You've got enough footage?" I ask the producer, who looks momentarily panicked before painting on a big smile. "We'll make it work, Matt," she replies eagerly.

I turn to Archie, the only person in the room I can truly trust, and he motions for us to escape. I move toward him, palms sweaty, chest tight.

"What's with the silver gaffer tape across the chest?" Archie asks the producer as we head to the door.

"Oh. Um. We lost a sponsor earlier," she replies, blushing.

I turn to Archie, my face expressionless.

"Come on," he says, grabbing my arm with one hand and the racing kit with the other. "We need to get you to qualifying. And you need to talk to Chloe."

CHAPTER 3

Chloe

I shrug off my stupid, expensive green blazer, feeling the sticky sweat already pooling between my shoulder blades and making its way down my spine. There is a reason Nico Rosberg described Singapore's street circuit as being like a two-hour spin class in a sauna. It's humid and hot as hell.

The cavernous garage is ready, doors about to open onto the Singapore pit lane. The interior is set like a stage show, plastered with Arden Racing forest green signage and sponsor logos. Along the sides of the garage are our custom-built engineer stations, rows of monitors detailing and transmitting every imaginable scrap of data to and from the team in Singapore and our headquarters back in North London.

In the heart of this cutting-edge technological theater sit the two Arden Racing cars. Multimillion-dollar machines, the black-and-forest-green livery shimmering under the bright lights. Through the back, away from view, are a set of rooms for testing, building, spare parts, and naturally, plenty of coffee.

I glance up at the digital clock that is counting down to start time.

Two hours to go. I desperately need Barry to leave. In the weeks leading up to this race, he has been standing over me, second-guessing all my decisions. He's like a manifestation of my own self-doubt and I need him to fuck off already and let me do my job.

"Where is he?" asks Barry, his eyes darting around for Matt. I watch the guy in a white boilersuit hastily painting *Matthew Warner* in big white lettering above one of the garage doors.

"Maybe he's firing his agent," I joke.

Barry laughs, slapping me lightly on the shoulder. "You're funny, you know that?"

I silently count to five. "I'm amazed we could afford him," I say dryly, recalling the tiny figure we have remaining on the spending cap for the year and the even tinier figure on my own deal terms. Barry looks at me sheepishly.

"I'll have to adjust *some* numbers," he says evasively.

On the way back from the press conference, I made the decision to deal with Barry and his "surprise," a.k.a. Matt Warner, *after* the Singapore Grand Prix. Or rather, my only friend on the circuit, McLaren strategist Keyla Kato, made the decision for me. As I stumbled through the sea of waiting reporters, she yanked me into the women's toilets (a famously quiet space in F1) and pep-talked me out of my shock.

"Welcome to the F1 disco," she said sympathetically.

"What in the name of Senna just ha—"

"There's no time to take you out for fucking cocktails to debrief."

"I'm just . . . Matt? I can't be his boss, he's—"

"*No.* We don't have time for that. Pull yourself together, Chloe," she said, squaring up to me, trying to catch my eyes. "This is Formula 1. You're not in Little League anymore. Matt is just a driver. *Your* driver. Okay?"

"Okay." I said the words, but I was not and am not *okay.* Matt isn't just a driver, to me, at least.

He is my aching, desperate, unrequited love from childhood. A nightmarish one-way infatuation only a teenage girl can have, made infinitely worse by the fact that Matt seemed to like hanging out with me.

I overanalyzed everything endlessly. *Of course I did.* A grin across the garage after a close race. Those long shared drives home head-banging to Queen after training. A gentle hand on my lower back as he pushed me forward, urging me to speak up in that room full of dudes.

The hometown connection felt special to me. Made us feel meant to be. We were the same working-class kids with fathers who were mechanics and F1 fanatics, and our families knew each other from the circuits. I could see Matt resented the rich kids. So many F1 kids were from big wealth, and while we didn't have the ski holidays and the five languages and the high-end kit on the track, we had Brackley grit, and that was something. To me, at least.

I eventually accepted Matt would never see me as more than that frizzy-haired, zany young girl who loved F1 as much as he did. So, I settled for friendship. I was his occasional confidante. Someone he could talk to about racing. About his string of short-term girlfriends. I was someone he called *mate* in a way I loved at the time, but in hindsight I know it was probably a pointed reminder.

I feel like I debased myself now, waiting around for years,

hoping he would wake up and realize I was *the one*. What a dumb waste of time.

And if I was in any doubt at all, after Matt got his offer at Rossini, I never heard from him again.

Of course, I knew I was going to bump into him regularly now that I was on the circuit. I'd readied myself. I'd role-played my nonchalant "Oh, hi. It's you," in a sexy dress holding a martini at some pre-race party. But I was not prepared for *this*. To be teamed up with him. I felt numb with shock, and Keyla brought me back to earth by grabbing my hand and squeezing it.

"Come on, Chloe," she said, as our eyes met. "Fuck your history with Matt Warner. Eyes on the damn prize. You can do this."

"I can do this," I repeated.

"Good. You've got your professional pants on," she said, glancing at my green pantsuit with amusement. "Now it's time to professionalize. Go!"

Looking around the garage at the crew now, I realize Keyla was right. No matter how furious I am, I need to focus. The eyes of the FIA and the whole racing community are on me. The very public Matt situation? I have to suck it up and pretend this is all part of *my* plan.

Then tomorrow I'll unleash hell on Barry fucking Arden.

"Just waiting for the star of the show. We'll give you a shout," Barry explains cheerfully to the team, who have been standing obediently for the past five minutes. The pit crew drop their heads and move quickly, livery polishing, rear jacking, tire wrapping, and rolling under the chassis to do final checks. I glance worriedly over to our second driver, a young Australian by the name of Noah Blacklock, who looks positively lacerated by Barry's description of Matt as *the star of the show.*

"What am I, chopped liver?" Noah says to Barry, sulking.

"Nothing wrong with liver," Barry replies, stroking one of the two dogs who are permanently at his feet. "You'll have your time, Noah. When you're out of nappies."

I shoot Noah a reassuring nod, which he seems to appreciate with a half smile shrug, before returning to his neck stretches. He's young, twenty-one years old, with all the talent in the world, wasting away at Arden Racing. I had hoped to bring in someone who could help mentor Noah, and instead I have Matt.

Where is Matt? I glance at the clock, nerves starting to pique.

"You should be out there romancing the beasts," Barry says, nodding at the press out on the pit lane.

"I will, I promise," I say, recoiling at the idea. "Let me get through this first qually."

Barry isn't listening. He is already scrolling his phone. I glance at the screen and watch his mouth curl into a big grin, as he revels in the drama of an earlier racing headline.

ARDEN STUNS F1 WITH NEW HIRE(S)

Below, a close-up photo of Matt Warner from his glory days, atop a podium, colorful ticker tape falling around him, a magnum of champagne in his hands.

I suppose I made the story. *Sort of.* That's me in the headline, the *(s)* in *hire(s).*

There is a thud and a slow crank as the main garage door onto the pit lane rolls open.

The sky outside is darker now as the sun begins to set over the waterside track. I can see the press, bloggers, and those famous enough or lucky enough to get a ticket outside starting to mill around on the grid. Above, the first of the crowd makes their way into the towering pit lane grandstand and unfurls their flags, drinks full and anticipation bubbling. There is simply nothing like the thrill of a night race.

And while I watch those first fans, giddy with excitement, the grid floodlights spring on, and I remember why we do this. We come to win, yes. Of course, everyone is here to win. But also, we're here because we love the thrilling, high-speed show of Formula 1 racing. We live for it. And so do those guys over there in the stands.

I feel a little of my earlier excitement return.

"Chloe Coleman in the flesh," says a husky voice behind me. I know exactly who it is before I spin around to see him, but the suddenness of his presence still makes me jump. I quickly take in his unzipped Arden Racing suit, the arms hanging from his waist, his black Nomex undershirt tight against his hard chest, with a crudely cut stripe of silver gaffer tape covering an ex-sponsor's badge. He's still got that imposing, magnetic presence that he's had since we were teenagers. My head has to tilt upward to meet his eyes. He seems taller and leaner than he used to be, but his forearms, which are now tightly folded across his chest, have thickened. Racer's arms. Firm. Strong.

It steals my breath to see him like this again.

Be cool. Be cool. Be cooooooooool.

"Matt," I say, hand to my chest. "Shit. Hello."

Well, cool Chloe crashed and burned before she began.

He hesitates for a moment, a curious *something* passing

across his face. A brief softness in his gaze toward me. But before I have a chance to reach out to shake hands, he leans in and kisses the air next to both my cheeks. I get a nutty, caramel hit of coffee and some kind of earthy cologne as his warm breath skims my cheek. It is almost instant, my body's reaction to him, a pulse of heat that rushes straight through me and travels all the way down *there*.

Damn my traitorous body.

I stand perfectly still until he has pulled back. "I can tell you've been living in Italy," I say loudly, as though explaining the kiss-greet to him, or myself, or anyone watching. I fight the urge to touch my cheek, which is still tingling. *Oh, this is not a good start, Chloe.*

"I have," he says. The right side of his mouth curls up in a half smile. "It's um . . . it's good to see you." Instinctively, I find myself examining his face for evidence of teasing but find none.

Instead, I find a different Matt. His once sun-kissed golden skin is paler, and that sallowness in his cheeks tells me he's not eating properly. By the look of those dark circles under his eyes, he's not sleeping much, either. Still, the depth of his attractiveness is undeniable: piercing hazel eyes with green flecks, surrounded by impossibly long lashes. His black hair is seriously in need of a tidy, but irritatingly, that, his lazy stubble, and the grown-up age lines around his eyes only add to the all-around rugged sex appeal.

Of course he was voted one of F1's sexiest drivers multiple years in a row.

"Yes. Good to see you too," I say, forcing myself back into the moment.

Matt takes me in with a subtle eye drop to my feet and

scans all the way back up to meet my eyes. Part of me wants to make a joke about how now that I'm a team principal, I have sensible pants instead of baggy jeans. But instead, I blush under his overfamiliar gaze with the speed and intensity of a thermonuclear blast.

Because it's the way Matt is looking at me, right now, that used to upend me all those years ago. The way his gaze intensifies, with a barely there smile that seems to radiate mostly from those hazel eyes. It's like he's waiting for me to catch on to some mysterious joke and I am not sure I ever will.

I clear my throat. "Welcome to . . ." I wave a hand around the garage.

"Hell?" he says, with a sideways tilt of the head, finishing my exact thought for me. Although his pointing it out so sneeringly only serves to irritate me. This may be hell, but it's *my* hell.

"Welcome to . . . your new team, I was going to say."

"Sure you were, *Bug*," he quips back, a knowing grin creeping across his face.

"Chloe," I snap back at him. "Not *Bug*."

"Still got those big eyes, though," he says.

"Stop," I say firmly, imagining the dark red of my cheeks deepening to a nice purple.

Matt frowns. Point taken. "Sorry. Where can we talk, *boss*?"

I look pointedly at the clock.

One hour and fifty-five minutes to go.

"We don't have time. I have a hundred things to do. I have the FIA breathing down my neck about the changes to the team, I need to get to the paddock presser, and Noah's race engineer is sick. . . . But *after*, definitely," I promise, sensing Barry's attention shift from his phone. I'd like to at least talk to Barry before I speak to Matt. "I promise."

"Matt!" Barry bellows delightedly. "How's my golden guy?"

Matt turns to Barry, readying himself to protest about something, probably *everything*, but Barry never seems to wait for the toss of the ball before he's on defense. He takes one look at Matt Warner's face and lifts both his palms as if he's been on the run for some misdemeanor and is finally handing himself in to the police.

"Look. I'm sure you're feeling a little blindsided—"

Matt and I scoff in the same petulant, teenage way, at precisely the same time. He cocks his head in my direction, raising both his brows in surprise, like he's the only one who is allowed to feel outraged by all this. The big main-character energy. The arrogance. There it is. There *he* is.

"*Everyone* is feeling a little blindsided," I explain.

"You didn't know?" Matt raises one eyebrow at me.

"Nope," I shoot back at him.

Oh, he looks deliciously surprised.

"Whose idea was it?" Matt pulls back, confused.

"His," I say, thumbing in Barry's direction.

Barry is watching us like a spectator at a particularly stressful tennis match, eyes darting side to side.

"All *my* idea," he finally says, puffing his chest up with ill-placed pride. If I were Barry, I'd be bracing myself for Matt's next shot.

Matt wastes no time. "What kind of fucking hack hires a driver without a phone call first?"

"Would you have picked up?"

"I might have."

"Bullshit," Barry says, laughing.

"You know what's bullshit? *This.*" Matt nods in the direction of the vehicles, the pit crew, the entire garage, in fact. While I agree everything needs work, *once again*, I'm irritated Matt is the one pointing it out.

I glance at the clock for what feels like the hundredth time. On the one hand, this argument needs to play out, and part of me is happy Matt is saying all the things I'd like to say to Barry. On the other hand, we only have one hour and forty-five minutes until the timer begins for the first round of qualifying and still no idea if Matt can even fit in that fucking car.

"Rossini were done with you. You were less popular than a shit in a kid's ball pit," Barry says.

"And yet *you* bought the shit," Matt points out, in a murky mix of gotcha and self-own, which he grimaces at when he realizes.

"Nobody here is *shit*," I try to interject.

"What else are you going to do, Matt?" Barry presses.

"NASCAR," Matt replies evenly.

"Gentlemen," I try, a little louder. "There's no need to bring NASCAR into this."

One hour and forty minutes to go.

"You won't leave," Barry says. Then he taps the silver tape on Matt's chest with a chubby pink finger. "Because there's still some bite in the old dog."

I watch as Matt's face ever so slightly softens, and I grab my moment.

"Okay, everyone. Can I have your attention?" I call out, my voice tight and high. One mechanic turns his head briefly, but no one else responds.

I feel Matt's eyes on me.

"You'll need to be louder than that, Bug," he mutters.

I ignore him, feeling the heat in my cheeks.

"Hello, everyone! Attention, please!" My voice lances through the garage, and everyone stops, the noise of banging and drilling and chatter falling completely silent. Out of the corner of my eye, I even see Matt flinch.

"Right, listen up," I say, tapping my watch. "We need to move. Guys, can you do the seat checks with Matt? We don't know how he fits the car yet. Do the best you can, and let's talk about getting a clay molding done before the next race in Austin. Noah, since this is his first time inside the AR21, can you sit with him and talk through the feel, give him any tips? Whatever you can do. I need to see the results from testing." To my delight and surprise, the crew springs into action, and I feel awash with relief.

"Barry. I'm sorry, but please. You need to go," I say, swinging around to face him, trying to stand a little taller in my sensible black loafers. "We have a lot to prepare."

Just as he's about to argue, he stops himself, reaching down to pat one of his little greyhounds. Sensing that he might convince himself into a fight, I add, "I'm sure Piero Rossini isn't debasing himself down in the pits with these grease monkeys."

Barry hesitates but seems to be pleased with the excuse I'm handing him. "Fine. I'll leave you experts to it," he says, skulking off through the back door with a final thumbs-up for good luck.

I spin back around, and just as I'm about to head off to speak to the strategists, Matt gently grabs my arm. "Chloe," he says, tugging me backward toward the driver room, but I resist, pulling my arm back from his grasp like it's made of hot iron.

"What is it?"

"You don't want to talk about this clusterfuck first?" he says, looking puzzled by my reaction. He motions toward the back, but I stay firm. "Come on, Bug—*sorry*, Chloe."

"If it's about our qualifying strategy today, then yes."

Matt pulls back now, his face suddenly impassive. Maybe even with a hint of anger. One of the young strategists shoves a printout in my hand and I glance down, flicking through the plans. "Soft tires?" I shout after him.

"Yup," the strategist says, nodding toward the tires, which are wrapped in blankets.

"But the race director just declared the track wet," I say, looking outside at the sky, suddenly completely overwhelmed by such a small thing. "Are we sure? Forecast is patchy, I don't want to get stuck out there on slicks."

"We think it's going to dry up . . . anyway, we can hold him back and wait," he says as if I'm stupid, nodding at the paperwork in my hands.

"I think he should take the full session. It's his first race," I say uneasily. I'm off-kilter. Second-guessing myself—and my team, who I feel are ready to pounce the moment I make an error. Fuck this nightmare, I need to focus.

"Chloe," Matt tries again, stepping in closer still, dropping his voice because he's just inches away from me. I can smell that heady mix of coffee and expensive cologne. "I need to talk to you. Privately."

I hesitate, narrowing my eyes as I try to subtly step backward.

He looks over at the strategist and then back at me.

"Aren't you supposed to be *team principal*? I'm your first driver."

I get that he's annoyed. I get that he's just left a legacy team to join this tin can rodeo, but the way he's putting that question to me feels undermining. And arrogant.

"Chloe, the officials are here!" calls another strategist from across the room.

"Coming!" I call back. I turn to Matt. "Please. If it's strategy you want to discuss, then yes, we can walk and talk," I shoot, deciding to stand my ground. "But otherwise, Matt"—I glance up at him, his eyes dark, *stern*—"I don't have time. *You* don't have time. You are about to head out to qualifying in a car you've never driven before and you weren't even here for testing. You're under a new management team and the whole world is watching."

"Yeah. *Exactly*," he says, holding his palms up like that's the point. "That's why I need to talk to you."

I feel the blood pulsing in my ears as the pressure rises. Excitement? Anxiety? Actual imminent stroke? Hard to tell. All I know is this "talk" with Matt Warner needs to happen later. When the pressure is off. When we have *time*.

One hour and thirty-five minutes to go.

"*Please.* Noah's waiting for you," I say, begging him to listen.

After a moment of worrying silence, I can see his body sag as he steps back and heads slowly, reluctantly toward a waiting Noah, whose eyes light up with awe and delight as two-time world champion Matthew Warner joins him for a pre-race briefing.

CHAPTER 4

Matt

I look Noah up and down. He seems okay. Better than the reserve driver at Rossini, who listens exclusively to Peruvian electro-industrial aggrotech and, although he speaks several languages, refuses to speak French on the basis that it's "overhyped."

Rossini drivers are famously coddled, most of them coming from legacy racing families, rising through the ranks in a trajectory promised almost from birth. But I've heard enough about Noah around the circuit to know that's not the case with him. Everyone in the field likes him—a driver who didn't come from money, had to push extra hard, and had parents who invested more than was sensible to keep him in the game. He's a rare breed on the grid, in a business riddled with nepotism and founded on dynasties.

Still, I don't want to get too close. After what just happened with Stavros, I think it's best I keep my distance.

I steal a glance over at Chloe as Noah leads me toward the rear of the car, but she's already busy with someone else. I'm trying to square the determined young driver I knew with the woman who is now my boss. A boss who apparently can't make time for me.

"This way, Matt," Noah says shyly, nodding toward the rear of the car. I can't help but feel an instant warmth toward him as he awkwardly points at the car's more eccentric features, muttering that "Rossini is probably a bit further ahead." He slicks his blond hair back with his hand before waving at the rear of the car. "The, um, wing is um . . . well, it has that flap tip, which is only semidetached, and see this? It's the old-style mainplane."

I stare hard at him as he fidgets. "How vintage," I joke.

Noah laughs, his cheeks reddening. "I know. They're working on it."

"I'm messing with you," I say. "What else?"

I nod toward the car for him to keep going, as I follow him around it. He's *so* young. Stavros and I were equals. Just a couple of years apart. Friends. Contemporaries. I'm not sure I know how to work alongside a driver this much less experienced.

"Oh, one thing . . . there is um, still crazy amounts of porpoising on the straight. All the other cars were fixed months ago," he says. "And like I said, they're working on upgrades in line with the new rules. Chloe is finalizing them with the team back home. Everyone is hyped about it."

"Well, that's good to hear," I reply, smiling. "Upgrades can really make a difference."

"McLaren 2009," he says.

"You definitely know your history," I shoot back. *Okay, that's impressive.*

Noah beams, then continues his tour of the car. But my attention is pulled back to Chloe, who has just removed her green blazer to reveal a tight white singlet and has let down her hair.

Wow. She has changed. A lot. She looks . . . super fucking beautiful, honestly, with that dimple on her right cheek, those huge brown eyes, and those pink, pouty lips. She was always kinda cute, but back then that wild dark red hair was either shoved into a baseball cap or knotted at the top of her head, her body hidden by boyish clothes. Now she looks older, curvier. Sexier.

But she had serious confidence issues back then, making herself smaller in all the wrong moments. As bright and mouthy as she was with me, she struggled to assert herself in that arena. So, I looked out for her when I could. Supported her. Stood up for her.

That is, until we moved out of karts and into Juniors. By the time Chloe joined me in F3, she was an absolute encyclopedia of knowledge and starting to shine. She knew more than anyone about car control, situational awareness, race craft, engineering competence, patience, balance, and on and on it went.

I was only focused on driving, and I was under serious pressure of expectations. It wasn't a case of *if* I'd make it into F1, it was with who and for how much money.

But then I got lazy. I stopped improving, the wins came less easily, and eventually I started to fall behind the other guys. One day, I was beaten on the track, badly. I remember Chloe found me in the garage after the loss, head in my hands, smashed helmet on the oil-stained concrete next to me. I wanted to quit. Then she put her hand on my back and said exactly what I needed to hear, as usual.

"You don't get it, do you?"

"Get what?" I asked her.

"We all need to work twice as hard to be half as good as you," she said, wise beyond her years as a young teenager. "Imagine what would happen if you stopped relying on sheer talent and put the work in too."

I didn't listen right away, but it woke me up a little.

One night she spotted my left peripheral reaction issues before my performance coach did. "When you knocked that saltshaker over, you couldn't catch it," she shouted over the music at some divey karaoke bar we used to visit. "You should have caught it."

I remember I laughed at her. Reminded her I'd had four shots of tequila. Told her to have a fucking night off. Leave me alone.

But she was right. That summer I trained with her. She taught me to juggle, we did ball drills to help with my reaction times, I got fitter. I honed my skills. And a year later, at just nineteen years old, I got the call from Rossini. Only the second person in history to jump from F3 to F1.

"Forty-five minutes," Chloe calls out. Our eyes catch briefly, but she looks away coolly. *What the hell is going on with her? Why does she seem so unhappy to see me? And why won't she talk?* She's clearly not happy about Barry hiring me.

It comes as no surprise she's battled her way up to team principal. While the other juniors were sneaking into nightclubs, dousing themselves in Allure Homme Sport and showing off their newly frosted tips, Chloe was sneaking into her dad's garage to pull apart car engines. The other drivers hyped up pre-race to deafening drum 'n' bass in their Bose headphones, while Chloe was reading up on strategy. She knew she needed a plan B, way back then.

It was fucked she never got picked up as a driver, and though no one says it out loud, it was obviously because the old men with the money just don't invest in women. "The risks are just too big," people would say, tutting and shaking their heads as if they all thought it was a big shame, without being self-aware enough to say out loud why *she's* more of a risk, despite her being faster than the boy with the rich dad, who just got a contract with Haas.

"How's the new team principal?" I ask Noah, as casually as I can. Though her hire was just announced, she'd have already started working with the team to get adjusted.

"Heaps good, mate," he replies, beaming like a goofball. "She's only been around a few weeks, though."

I look back at her, gesticulating calmly to her team, and feel angry she wouldn't make time to talk to me. She's the team principal, and she couldn't find five minutes to speak to her new driver? She's seen my recent performance, and *must* know what a bad bet I am. Still, no *How are you doing?* Nothing? After all this time? Last I checked we'd both moved on with our lives, and despite this strange new situation, I'm happy to see her again. Is she not happy to see me?

I need to catch up with her alone. Just a proper hello, yes, but also, I need to explain what's been going on at Rossini. Right after this qualifying shit show.

Thirty minutes to go.

"They need you to go sit in the car and check the fit," Noah is saying.

"All right. Cheers, mate. Good luck out there."

"Don't waste me too hard," he says with a wry smile, his entire neck and cheeks turning a subtle pink. "Mum's here."

I shove him gently on the shoulder. "I'm the one that should be worried."

My old boss at Rossini used to say, "Qualify first and you've got one foot on the podium."

And it's true. Qualifying is about setting the fastest time, to earn the best possible starting spot on the grid.

The day takes place over three rounds.

After Q1, five drivers are eliminated.

After Q2, five more are eliminated.

In the third round, Q3, the fastest ten get one final shot at placing as high up the grid as possible. The goal? Pole position. Pole position in F1 is everything. It's the front row. The clean air ahead of everyone else is a huge advantage when your foot goes down. Especially here in Singapore, where it is tough to overtake.

All the other teams are over half a season into the process of incremental improvements, working with their drivers and their engineers to smooth, refine, and rebuild. Arden, however, are starting from zero today with a car that has been the butt of a million cruel headlines and opinion pieces:

Why No One Has a Hard-On for Arden

How Arden's Clown Car Inspired My Decision to Buy a Bike

And my personal favorite:

A Fisher-Price Car, Owned by a Discontinued Muppet

I'm scanning the cheat sheet Chloe and the team have pulled together for me, which lists all the tips for my first race. *Watch pace management turn 4. Watch rear instability snowballing through the lap. Don't check fuel unless instructed. Two hot laps.*

I hand the printed pages to one of the pit crew, then I slide my feet down the chassis and settle into its imperfect grooves. It's too small and tight, as I knew it would be, but I can make it work. I fix the steering wheel into its slot and stretch my neck side to side. Across the garage, Noah slides into his car. He salutes me, grinning, and I salute him back. Then I glance up at the clock.

Time to go out.

"Good luck, Matt," says one of the team, his eyes full of hope, as he removes the last of the tire blankets. I feel a creeping dread as I gingerly drive the car into the pit lane.

And then I hear Chloe's voice over the radio.

"I'm on comms for today," she says, her voice crackling into my ears. "Just until we get your team reassembled."

"One way to finally talk, I guess," I shoot back.

The radio is open for the whole world to hear—the FIA loves it that way—and I've been caught out saying the most unholy shit on the open radio. But if this is the only way I can talk with Chloe, so be it.

"We'll debrief *after*," she says coolly.

If Chloe is simply stressed, she doesn't sound it. Instead, she sounds scathing.

Well, two can play at that.

"Your place or mine?" I shoot back, baiting her.

There is a long pause as I start to crawl down the pit lane toward my out lap, and I find myself grinning as I imagine her squirming in her seat.

"Let's focus on the lap, *Matthew*."

I exit the pit, picking up the pace a little, swinging the car side to side, getting a feel for the steering, the tires. In front of me is Ferrari, then farther up, Red Bull, and behind me my teammate Noah. Farther back in my rearview, I can just make out the silver-and-bloodred flash of Rossini and feel a surge of bullish anger. I breathe in deeply and glance at the sky, trying to calm myself. *Just fucking focus.* Try not to let the thoughts penetrate. I can do this.

"How's she feel, Matt?" Chloe's voice crackles in my ears.

"Like a tin can on training wheels."

I just catch the click of Chloe's tongue on the roof of her mouth as the radio is cut.

I look up at the stands and spot Rossini shirts and flags from France, the Netherlands, and Mexico. Orange rises from a stand in the distance. Arden Racing support is sparse up there, yet I can feel everyone's eyes on me. I can almost hear the commentary: "And here comes Matt Warner, his shocking transfer to Arden Racing announced just hours ago, and the talk of the pits here in Singapore today. One thing for sure, if he lacked pace in a Rossini this year, he's going to struggle in the Arden."

"Ready?" Chloe says.

"It seems to have started raining," I say coolly.

Chloe sighs. "I can see that. Let's try for one lap on the soft tires, then we can change."

Her instincts were right and she looked weak in front of

that strategist. If she's going to be the boss here, she's going to need to assert herself.

I put my foot on the gas and push her a little more, round the hairpin, the g-force light, the car moving better than I expected, and as the out lap draws to a close and I see the starting line ahead, I ready myself just as the first light droplets hit my windscreen.

The adrenaline surges, and my heart rate kicks up as I hit the throttle.

People wonder what it feels like to drive one of these fifteen-million-dollar machines, and you can't even begin to imagine, honestly. It's as different and as hard as flying a fighter jet. Hundreds, sometimes thousands of people work to get us to this point. It feels nothing like a normal car. Everything is built for 220-mile-per-hour speed. So, when your foot hits the floor, your heart is in your mouth, you pray to the racing gods that everything works as promised.

Let's fucking do this. I cross the starting line and head into turn one.

The force of that first bend hits me like a truck to my rib cage, and I have to fight to stop my vision from blurring as I steel myself against the pressure.

Then my thoughts start to swirl.

I blink away the images of Stavros being pulled from his burning car, but there they are. Again. I feel myself pulling back on the gas, as I gasp for breath out of the turn.

It's still happening. Everywhere I look, the crash replays over and over, like someone's trapped me in a virtual reality headset. I squeeze my eyes shut, and he's still there. When I open them, I've slid out of bounds. The guttural vibration of the tires as my car taps the wall rouses me briefly, and I course-correct. But as soon as I think I'm clear, the images are back. High-resolution horror, everywhere I look. I can't breathe. The muffled sound of the engine begins to seem like white noise.

"Shit."

"Go ahead, Matt."

"Car's all over the place."

"Understood," says Chloe. "Come in and pit. Let's change those tires."

"Fucking car," I spit.

"You okay in there?" she says.

My chest tightens further as I round the final turn and cross the line. Slowing immediately, I feel my chest start to expand, the air flowing in suddenly like a valve got switched on.

"Pit. Pit," I gasp.

"Okay. We'll switch the wets," says Chloe.

"No. I'm done."

"You're not on pace, Matt. We *need* another go."

"No."

As I hit the next bend, I make room for one of my replacements at Rossini, who barely glances at me as he flies past, likely making the fastest time of Q1.

As the crew rolls me backward into the garage, I avoid their eyes. Eyes that held so much hope a few minutes ago. I climb out, unhooking the steering wheel and tugging off all the various cords between me and the car. Those cords feel like chains right now.

The first face I see as I pull off my black fireproof face mask is Chloe's.

"Place nineteen, but one of the McLarens was a DNF," she says calmly. "There's still time for another hot lap. Please, let us change the tires."

Outside the rain starts to pour down, the crowd in the stands huddling under ponchos and umbrellas.

"No point, car's a donkey." I'm pouring sweat like I just did fifty-six laps, not three, and I wipe at my forehead with the back of my sleeve.

"The team can hear you, Matt," she warns.

I want to talk to her. I want to explain that when I drive now, I am haunted by visions of my best friend and the near-fatal accident that happened just a few months ago, I want to tell her how I begged Rossini to give me time to recover and to let me visit Stavros but they refused. Their plan to get me back in the silver wolf as fast as possible, to make me "man up" and move forward, failed. I want to explain to her that I'm a liability and that Barry hiring me was a huge mistake. That I'm going to bring her career down with my own.

Chloe steps a little closer, those dark eyes round with a mix of concern and frustration, maybe even a little anger. She drops her voice to a shouty whisper. "What's going on with you? And stop blaming the car."

There is the Chloe I remember.

"I . . ." I can't look at her; if I do, it's all going to come out right here on the garage floor. I drop my head.

"Yes?" she says, softly now.

I glance back up at those big brown eyes and open my mouth to try and find the words. Our hands are close, and if I wanted to, I could reach out and touch hers. Then suddenly we're startled by a whoop and a round of applause from the strategy team. Both of us swing our heads.

"News?" Chloe asks.

"Noah. He got sixteenth!" one of them shouts, with a thumbs-up. "Nearly made Q2."

Chloe turns back to me. She drops her voice to barely a whisper, shifting her stance, trying to shield us from the eyes of the team. "Come on. Let's talk," she says.

But I shake my head.

"I need to make a call," I say firmly, then I turn to one of the pit crew, who is assessing the fuel. "Don't forget to feed the donkey before the next race," I say, an attempt at a joke, which, by the looks of that wide-eyed mortification on his young face, I'm pretty sure didn't land.

I need to get out of here.

"Matt!" Chloe says, her voice sharp now.

I hand him my helmet and stride out of the garage without looking back.

CHAPTER 5

Chloe

In the quiet of the long bar at the Singapore Grand Prix, I wave the bartender over for another drink.

The post-qualifying debrief was a hot mess. Nobody understands what happened to Matt out there. I certainly don't. My heart was in my throat when he hit the gravel after a crude error out of turn six, too much understeer sending him careering off-track. And despite what he says, it wasn't the tires. I've analyzed the data. His pace was all over the place, and his vitals were too. I watched in horror with the team as his oxygen levels dropped, a sure sign of stress beyond what we would expect from a driver at his level.

But Matt is not answering his phone.

And he's not in his room.

And I'm worried that I have royally fucked up by not talking to him when he practically begged me to.

"Singapore sling?" The handsome bartender slides it in front of me.

"Xièxiè. And a chili crab with rice? I might take it to my

room. Is that okay?" I ask. It's just after one a.m. but the kitchen is open all night on race weekend.

I find a seat at a quiet, cozy table and quickly work through some emails. Key qualifying data from the strategist. An update on regulations for next season. A sale at Saint Laurent, which distracts me for five minutes as I fantasize about a *team principal* look. Then, I spot one from Barry, who always puts the entire message in the subject line.

To: CHLOE
From: BARRY
Subject: What in the name of fucking Hamilton happened to Matt out there? I thought you were better prepared. Don't make me come back there.
Message: [blank]

I sigh. Barry does not trust me at all, and after I failed to intervene on that tire choice, he probably has a point.

The next email is from the media producer. A brief hello, plus several attached clips—rushes, apparently, of Matt doing his first publicity stint. I look at the time stamp. Jeez, Barry had that ready to go fast. And right before qualifying, no wonder he was in such a mood.

I click open the first short film. It's a banal cookie-cutter response from Matt about how he's "glad to be racing with Arden." It's the second clip, however, that makes me want to throw my phone against the wall.

The producer asks him what he thinks about working for me, *a woman boss*—I hate the question, the question *sucks*—but it's Matt's response that is so . . . disappointing. There is a long, pregnant pause as he appears to squirm in his seat, his mouth straightening into a tight line. It takes several seconds for him to pull himself together, and then he answers as though he's being held hostage: "It's great."

I hit pause and place my phone on the table, picking up my drink and downing half of it in one gulp. It's sickly sweet and churns my empty stomach, but it's nice to have something cool in the relentless heat.

"Shithead," I mutter. "Stinking turd bucket. Misogynistic asshat."

"Hey there!"

I look up to see my old racing friend Jack Sheppard. "Who are you calling a turd bucket?" he says, nodding at my phone and the image of Matt frozen mid-expression, one eye shut, his mouth gaping. I start laughing, mostly out of embarrassment.

"Mind if I sit?"

"Sure. Hi! Go ahead," I say, quickly turning over my phone and gathering up my paperwork to make room for him. I wave toward the bartender, but in a bar full of nobody, he's already on his way over.

Before I have a chance to protest another round of drinks, Jack points at my cocktail and says, "Same." He smooths his cropped hair back with both hands. I see a few sprinklings of gray at his temples. He's still that long, lean, elegant handsome. A gentleman who crosses his legs and moves his body with slow intention. Like a sloth in a Panama hat.

Looking at him now, it's hard to believe Jack was a racer back in the early go-karting days. The son of Mick Sheppard, a two-time world champion and the stuff of legends at now-defunct Honda Racing, Jack had the pedigree but never the killer instinct. I've always liked him, though. He was a fun gossip and a hilarious drunk. In a paddock full of bullish alpha males, Jack was reassuringly self-effacing.

"How have you been?" I ask, glancing at the press pass around his neck. "You're at *F1 Daily* now?"

"Yup," he says, turning the plastic card to look at it. "Living the *other* dream."

"Ah well, we all had to pivot."

"Quite," he says, motioning toward my paperwork. "How is it all going?" Jack holds his hands up as if to say, *I'm not here as press*, then he pulls off his FIA lanyard and shoves the pass into the pocket of his linen slacks.

"It's been a day, all right," I say, grimacing.

"Well, congratulations anyway."

"On the bad qualifying run?"

"On the new gig, stupid," he says, chuckling. "*Really.* I know it isn't Mercedes or whatever, but it's F1. You're in the fucking room." He smiles a broad, earnest smile and lifts his glass. "Be proud of yourself. It's an incredible achievement."

I feel a little warm glow flow through me at this kindness, which I realize I've had virtually none of today. The only message I got from my family after the press conference was from my dad, who was thrilled about me working with Matt.

Matt Warner! Great news. Tell him hi from me. Love Dad.

Dad could never get over the end of my driving career. I suppose after all the years, all the money, all the sacrifice on his part, he felt he'd failed or lost something too.

"I loved what you did in F3. I followed the whole season,"

Jack says as he takes a sip of his drink. "You were always going to do the best out of everyone in our era."

"Stop it," I say, as feel-good hormones flood my every cell. God, I needed a bit of this. *Fuck it.* I'm having a third cocktail. I deserve to revel a bit in my achievement after a day that feels as though it was purposefully designed just to undermine it.

"There's a double-page profile on you in *F1 Daily* tomorrow. 'Arden Racing's New Leading Lady.'" He chuckles. "I hate the headline, bloody editors, but the content is great. Your background, your rise through the ranks. Barry says surprisingly coherent stuff too."

"Thank you, Jack. *Really.*" Blushing with pride, impostor syndrome be damned, I pick up my drink and take another swig. "I absolutely hate talking to press."

"I know," he says, chuckling. "You looked nervous as hell at that press conference."

I grimace. *Damn it.* "Ugh. How embarrassing."

"I take it you didn't know about Matt?" Jack asks.

"Nope."

"How is he?"

I scoff. "He continues to meet my expectations," I say, with mock magnanimity and a wry smile. Jack laughs, stretching back into his chair.

"All the likability of a global famine."

"All the charm of a dishcloth," I say, enjoying myself more than I should.

"What a pain. I'd hate to be forced to work with him."

"*Nobody* wants to work with him."

Jack and Matt never liked each other much. The jealousy,

I suspect, worked in both directions. Matt had insane raw talent that Jack coveted, and Jack had money and deep connections in the industry. But we waste time being jealous of the wrong things; Matt made it without all the money and the connections, and now he has both in abundance.

"I don't think he's happy working *for* me," I say, sighing. "I'm no Ron fucking Dennis, but it's pretty annoying." I pause for a minute, calculating the risk of sharing the video with Jack. I suppose since they're going out on socials anyway, it doesn't matter. I hand him my phone and hit play.

"Christ," Jack says, as he watches Matt squirm on camera. "Sorry, but I can't stand the guy."

I laugh, shaking my head at his brazenness. "Well, we can rectify the situation at the end of the season. I'm not sure I understand why Barry spent all that money on someone so out of form."

"It's panic-buying," he says, shaking his head.

I laugh feebly, but then think on his comment. "What do you mean *panic-buying*?"

"Well," he says, tipping his head, his eyes narrowing a smidgen. "Seems like he's making a final play, don't you think?"

"Final?"

Jack puts his drink down. "Maybe it's just rumors."

"Are you gonna keep me hanging? What rumors?"

He scans the empty bar and then lowers his voice. He looks so fucking serious all of a sudden, the hairs on the back of my neck start to prickle.

"The word is Barry is running out of money."

"Explains my modest hotel room," I quip, as my heart starts to sink.

"You didn't hear it from me, Chloe, but word is if Arden isn't in at least the midfield and Matt doesn't attract a major new sponsor before the Vegas Grand Prix, he's going to need to fold."

"Vegas? That's four or five races away," I say, aghast. "No. It's not possible."

"You know what this sport costs. Barry's been trying and failing for five long years. He struggles to attract sponsors because, well . . . who the hell is Arden? And who the hell is Barry, really? He's not one of us."

I cringe a little at that. Jack, like many in this sport, can come off really fucking elitist sometimes. I sigh. "We actually lost a sponsor less than three minutes after Matt was announced," I admit, but then I dig deep, sucking in a breath.

"You'll need more," Jack says, squeezing his lips together with a pity that embarrasses me. "But I'm sure if anyone can turn it around, you can."

"There's only so much anyone can do in a handful of races." And with a driver who is seriously out of form and unlikely to court any sponsors the way he's driving. And frankly, the way he's behaving.

"Maybe it's not that bad," Jack offers.

I sit for a moment, looking at my drink, my gaze softening as I zone out. A disorienting mixture of alcohol in my veins and the reality of what Jack is telling me makes me feel dizzy. Even if this is an exaggerated rumor, it's still deeply worrying. I get this big break, and then . . . what? The team folds before we finish the season? What kind of legacy would that be? Could I ever recover? Everyone knows you only get one shot.

The bartender arrives with my plate of chili crab, and the spicy, fishy mix hits my nose and makes my stomach growl with a confusing mix of hunger and nausea.

"It's just been one thing after another today," I say, standing, gathering up my things. "Sorry, Jack. I should wind down. Race tomorrow."

"Let me walk you to your room," he says, picking up my crab dish and knife and fork, and nodding toward the lift. "What floor you on?"

"Seven," I say, and he thumbs the button as I hold my card to the reader. I am swimming, exhausted suddenly. "Thanks for writing about me, and for being so kind."

As the lift rises slowly, I start to dream of crawling into my bed when Jack says, "Just being nosy here, but do you know if Matt has spoken to Stavros since the crash?"

"No," I say, yawning. "Not heard."

"Probably not, then," he says.

"That would be ice-cold, but also another example of Matt blissfully ignorant of the impact he has on people."

The doors open with a ding, and suddenly, in the quiet intimacy of the hotel hallway, I realize allowing Jack to walk me back was probably ill-advised. Not that he fancies me or anything, but I really shouldn't have a journalist walking me to my hotel room.

When we get to my door, there is an awkward dance where, because I have no room in my full hands to take the crab from Jack, he slips inside my room and slides the plate on my dresser for me while I lean on the door to keep it open. My room is dark, with only the small lamp on next to the bed, and it feels uncomfortable having him in my space.

"It's not a *terrible* room," he says, grinning as he quickly exits into the hallway.

"Stay in touch, hey?" I say lightly.

"I'd love to," he replies, his eyes darting down the hallway, toward the sound of another door opening. "See you around, Chloe."

I watch as he pushes through the door to the stairwell, a little relieved to be alone. But just as I step back to let the door swing shut, a large, socked foot inside a red-and-green Gucci slide appears in the doorframe to block it.

"What the hell are you doing?" says that familiar husky voice.

I drop all the paperwork and my purse onto the side table and pull the door back open, looking up to see Matt Warner standing there—towering, really—his palm high and flat against the doorframe, a black sleeveless T-shirt hanging loose around those strong racer shoulders. My eyes drop to his black cotton boxer shorts and the short tufts of curly hair on his hard thighs. I linger on the taut athleticism of those legs just long enough to make my own feel a little weak.

NO. This isn't undeniable attraction talking. It's the three Singapore slings on an empty stomach. *Please let it be the booze.*

"What are *you* doing in the hallway, with no pants on?" I ask, snapping my head back up to meet his glare. "Sneaking in and out of hotel rooms seems a little crude, even for you."

"I'm not . . . what?" Matt snarls at me.

"Aren't you supposed to be resting?"

"The better question is why was Jack Sheppard in your room?" he barks.

"Er . . . none of your business," I reply, my eyes grazing his stubbled jaw, which is grinding with irritation.

"He's a reporter."

"He's a friend."

"He's a virus in plimsoles," Matt snaps, and in my slightly woozy state, I struggle hard not to laugh.

"It's only Jack. *Jesus.* Nothing happened."

Matt's eyes dart down the corridor as a couple fall out of the lift, drunk, and make their way down the hallway toward us to their room.

Matt pushes past me into my room.

"Quick, shut the door before I'm spotted," he orders.

Oh, because he's *such* a celebrity. I should say no, but instead, I step forward, letting the door close behind me as we are plunged into the dim golden glow of my bedside lamp. The suite, with its rich dark furnishings, feels suddenly very small, and so I shrink myself back against the wall, trying to create as much space as possible between us. Matt peers out the window, then yanks the curtains shut and begins to pace the room.

"We just had a drink. He wanted to congratulate me on my new job. It was nice, you know, to have someone notice that today was a big day for *me*," I grumble, kicking off my shoes. *Why am I explaining myself to him?*

"Jack fucking Sheppard," he says, before he stops to face me. I feel my heart kicking up a gear under his scrutiny. "You're not dating him, are you?"

"What? *No!*" I let out an involuntary laugh, but Matt's expression remains deathly serious. The little hairs on the back of my neck begin to tingle. He seems so . . . *bothered* by the possibility.

"He's an old friend," I protest, all the anger and upset of our past in very real danger of bubbling up inside me. "Remember those?"

I swear I see him flinch; something uncatchable passes across his face before he regroups and crosses those strong bare arms across his chest. My god, those thick forearms and rounded biceps. It should be fucking illegal to wield them in public.

I shake my head. *I'm more tipsy than I thought.*

"Don't be so naive, Chloe." He takes a step toward me, and I suddenly feel pinned by his unwavering gaze.

"Fuck you. I'm not naive," I reply, forcing myself to straighten up, step forward, and meet him. I mirror his stance, arms folded. "Don't talk down to me, you asshole."

He tilts his head. "You don't know what it's like in this league." His voice is quieter now, as he takes another step closer.

"I don't need you to help me."

Matt doesn't reply, the corner of his mouth twitching uncertainly.

"I'm not that kid anymore, Matt," I remind him, taking a final, unsteady step closer, head tilting up, defiant. I'm just inches away now, close enough to see those green flecks in his eyes catching the dim light. God, he is so beautiful. *I hate him.*

Matt's jaw moves as he drags his eyes across my face. Scanning me.

"No. You're not that kid anymore," he replies slowly, his voice deep and gravelly as his eyes trail to my mouth, and then everything stands completely still. The room is silent, except for the shallow hitch of my breathing.

It's too much.

I close my eyes, feeling my cheeks on fire. *It is hopeless.* My body is reacting to Matt's presence like I'm seventeen all over again. It doesn't matter what happened in the years between, I'm back there, begging for him to notice me as something other than *that girl*. He can see it, I'm sure of it. I can feel myself starting to shrink back toward the wall and away from him again.

When I open my eyes, Matt is watching me, his eyes narrowed in what looks like concern. Then he drops his arms to his sides, and his body relaxes.

"Everyone watches everything. Just . . . be careful, Bug," he says, more softly now.

"Don't call me that," I say, my voice barely a whisper. "Or I'll call you fucking *Dials* in front of everyone."

Matt's face immediately breaks into a grin, a twinkle returning to his eyes. He steps back just once, and I allow myself to breathe out, as space finally appears between us.

"See, I never knew why calling my mum was so damn funny to everyone."

"I think it was the sheer volume of calls," I say, my body starting to relax. I eye my crab on the dresser. I sure don't feel hungry anymore.

Then he turns away from me and wanders to the window. He pulls back the curtain a little, the sky outside a midnight blue, the twinkling lights of the Singapore skyline reaching out into the distance. He needs to sleep, I realize suddenly. But I can sense he isn't done talking.

"Matt, it's late," I say. "I know you didn't come to talk about Jack Sheppard."

"Yeah. I tried to find you earlier," he says quietly.

"I did call you at least five times after qualifying."

"It's this situation." Matt puts his hands in his hair, sitting back on the windowsill. I want to feel bad for him, I truly do, but after watching him fumble through that press clip earlier, and now barreling into my room, throwing his weight around like he still has the right, and then calling me *naive*?

"You hate it," I say plainly.

"Yes. I mean, no," he says quickly. "It's my driving." He looks suddenly overcome with a different kind of stress. "I need to be able to talk to you. And you've been avoiding me. You can't do that, Chloe. You're the boss."

"I *am* the boss," I say. I can't help but take a jab at him. "You want to talk about that? I saw your interview."

Matt's face is frozen as it quickly dawns on him what I might be talking about.

"I was hijacked."

"Gun rammed into your rib cage?"

"Felt like it," he says.

I cannot help but smirk at him. "The time it took you to answer . . . Wow. You could have done several laps of the circuit. Even in the Arden."

He stands abruptly. "*You* being my boss is the least of my worries right now," he says impatiently.

"You being my driver is the *biggest* of mine," I shoot back, and I immediately, *completely* regret it, as I watch him stiffen.

"I didn't mean that," I say quickly. "I don't."

"You do mean it. And honestly? You should." He moves

past me and back toward the door, pulling it open, the light from the hallway spilling into the room.

"Wait." *Bad, bad, bad management, Chloe.* I need him. I need Matt to drive tomorrow. I need him not to think I'm awful. "Don't go, Matt. Come on, let's talk."

I rush to the door before it closes but he's already walking down the hall and toward his room. I watch him pat himself down and then kick the door, as he realizes he left his key card inside.

I contemplate calling out to him again, but he pulls out his phone and walks toward the window at the far end of the hall, entering almost mid-flow into conversation with someone.

And so, I step back from the door and let it swing shut.

CHAPTER 6

Matt

Bro," Archie calls out across the lot outside the pit building. It's hot. No, it's fucking hot. I'm in shorts, I've rolled the sleeves of my T-shirt up, and I'm still sweltering, waiting for my lunch from one of the little food trucks dotted around the area.

"You shouldn't be talking to the competition."

"Competition?" He chuckles, slapping me on the shoulder. "You wish."

I collect my double cheeseburger and curly fries from the food truck, with a quick thank-you, and then turn to Archie, my arms filled. "I'm carb-loading."

"Christ, mate, you'll end up like me," he says, wobbling his stomach and laughing. Archie glances at the empty bench tables and nods his head. "Got a minute?"

I climb over the bench seat and sit down opposite him, unwrapping the greasy paper from my burger and ripping open the paper bag of curly fries so Archie can have some, but he declines with a wave of his hand.

"I watched your lap," he says, his big fingers rapping on the tabletop.

"Car's a piece of shit." I tear into my burger with my teeth, just as I spot Fernando Alonso striding across the lot clutching a green smoothie, back from his track walk. Who the fuck does a track walk at his level? Does he seriously still walk around to look at the condition of the track ahead of the race? And then I wonder if Noah is out there on his own and feel guilty.

Archie tips his head. "It's still happening, isn't it?"

I shoot him a look. "How'd you guess?"

"No one *slows down* coming out of turn seventeen. Even in the rain. Even on this bumpy-ass street circuit."

I put my half-eaten burger down on the bench and pick up my Coke. Archie is almost recoiling at the amount of grease running down my chin. I roughly wipe at it with a napkin. "Yeah, it's still happening."

Archie frowns, then glances around to make sure we're alone. "Dude, you should—"

"What? What should I do?"

"Maybe it's time to speak to . . . you know . . . um . . ." He struggles, clumsily, in a field he wasn't designed to navigate, like a seal trying to ride a bike.

"A therapist, Archie?"

I put my drink down, lean back, and stare up at the clear blue sky, streaked with long milky-white jet streams, and contemplate telling him that I already *am* speaking to a therapist. A really fucking expensive sports therapist who specializes in recovery after trauma.

And thank god, because yesterday was a mind fuck, and his advice after qualifying is the only thing keeping me from running to the airport and catching the next plane home.

"Speak to Chloe about your problems on the track," Archie says. "You knew her well once. You said you could trust her."

But when I tried to speak to Chloe and caught her with that gurning sleazebag Jack Sheppard, I lost my way. It bothered me. A lot.

I know Chloe doesn't need or want me looking out for her anymore, but it's hard not to. That guy cannot be trusted, and I don't like him sniffing around her, especially when she's finally made it to the big league. His sly confidence only thinly veils his desire for status and desperate need to feel in the middle of things. It's a dangerous mix. He's the perfect tabloid reporter, actually.

I picture her standing in the low light of her suite last night, her back flush against the wall. Her cheeks pink, lips red, that small waist curving in just above the band of her trousers. The rise and fall of her breasts with every shallow, anxious breath. Everything about her was just so incredibly . . . sexy. I wasn't expecting that feeling, and I did *want* to protect her.

And she hated it. In fact, she seems . . . to hate me.

When I relayed all this to my therapist last night, there was a very long, uncertain pause, before he said, "I see. Matthew, maybe just get through the weekend and then we can make some decisions."

So that's what I'm doing. *Getting through the weekend.*

"Maybe I should just retire. I'm thirty-four," I say, looking back at Archie.

"Lewis is forty."

"*Eight*-time world champion Lewis Hamilton? Never heard of him."

Archie chuckles. "If you're retiring, can you let me know? I'll need to line up another gig."

He puts a finger up to his headphones as a radio message comes in. *One sec*, he mouths at me.

"I gotta go. Pre-race meeting," he says, standing. "Don't you got yours, bro?"

I shrug. "Maybe I'm already retired."

"Finally, you're here," Chloe says, wide-eyed. She's clutching an enormous water bottle in one hand and a clipboard in the other as she slips out of what is supposed to be the driver room, tucked away at the back of the garage, but appears to be also used as storage for parts.

At Rossini I practically had my own suite. This is going to be a long season.

"Yeah, I heard there's a race. Thought I may as well show up," I reply, as I strip off my T-shirt and pull my fireproof underclothes off the hanger, readying myself for the shit show.

But when the cooling gust of the air conditioner hits the bare skin on my chest, I open my arms toward it to feel more of that icy air in this sweltering heat. I run my hands down my chest to my stomach, where a few months ago, I had a really well-defined six-pack, and now it's a little less taut. Maybe it *is* time to ease up on the burgers.

"Matt?"

"Sorry, I'm fucking hot."

I turn back to her, letting the cool of the fan hit my back, as I cover my bare chest with folded arms, stretching my neck side to side. Chloe looks away, a little color flushing her cheeks. The Chloe I remember wouldn't have even flinched at a half-naked dude in a changing room. She's seen enough of them over the years.

Today, her hair is braided down her back, black cap pulled down, headphones around her neck. She's in a black Arden Racing polo, and when she turns to glance back at the garage, I see the curve of her ass in tight blue jeans. But when she looks back, my eyes trail to that mouth of hers, and I have to look quickly away to kill the stirring feeling in my stomach.

"What is it?" I say, quickly fishing for my fireproof shirt and pulling it over my head to cover up. There are four crew in the changing room, almost two dozen out in the garage, and nowhere we can speak alone, though it's clear as day that's what Chloe wants.

"I'm sorry about yesterday," she says, eyeing the crew around us, who are moving much more quietly now, clearly listening in while they gather gloves, tire wraps, and screws for a loose jack. "I'm sorry about what I said. Can we talk, please?"

"*After*," I say pointedly, and she sighs.

"Is it the crash, Matt? Are you—"

I cut her off abruptly. "No," I lie.

"Matt. You clearly have *feelings*. . . ."

"Oh, I have feelings, Coleman," I say, laughing as I pull my shorts down so I'm standing in my underwear. Chloe looks everywhere but at me, and I hastily pull on my long fireproof pants.

Two of the pit crew try to slide out unnoticed, and I watch Chloe make herself small so she can let them through, muttering "sorry" no fewer than three times as they pass. She's going to get eaten alive if she doesn't learn to take up space in this garage.

"You don't like the car," she says matter-of-factly.

"It looks like someone designed it blindfolded."

"Oh stop. It's not that bad."

"That Arden car is the Formula 1 equivalent of a circus car."

Chloe's mouth twitches like she's wrestling away a grin. "*That Arden car* is only two seconds slower in a single lap than McLaren. One point nine seconds slower than Rossini. *You* could be some of that difference."

"It's so sad it could make an onion cry," I snap, as the last two pit crew creep out and I attempt to put a leg into my racing suit, losing my balance and nearly toppling over as I do.

I'm sure I can hear one of them mutter *karma* as they slip out of the room. I'm certainly not winning friends at Arden, not that I really care. Retirement is feeling more and more like the right move.

"Enough. Let's be frank with each other."

"Who's Frank?" I smirk.

"You don't want to work for me."

I stare at her, annoyed more than anything. Have I *ever* said I don't want to work for her? "No, not true at all. I'm not sure I want to be here . . . *generally.*"

"At Arden?"

"*Racing.*"

"You want to quit?" Her mouth curls up at the edge.

"Retire," I shoot back.

"*Quit,*" she says again, grinning this time. But I'm in no

mood for this ribbing. I feel absolutely sick with worry about this race, and what I'm going to do next.

"Retire," I counter slowly, zipping up my racing suit, turning to face her.

"Then why did your brother call me sniffing around about a transfer if you're thinking about retiring?"

"Because he's a big idiot." I really have to speak to Archie about that.

Chloe tips her head to the side and folds her arms. "I know you don't think I'm up to the job."

"I don't know anything, Chloe. It's been less than twenty-four hours."

She laughs and scoffs at the same time. "Is there some version of this"—she points between us frantically—"of you and me, that we can make work?"

"You and . . . me?"

Chloe's cheeks go darker pink, and despite my irritation, there's something so distracting and adorable about watching her try to push on through her embarrassment. *There* is the Chloe from our childhood. *There* is that fire-hot blush that I could bring out so easily in her. I'm momentarily distracted by it, studying the flex of her jaw as she tries to wrestle back control.

"Meet me half-fucking-way here," she says, sighing theatrically. "Or is that too far around the track for you?"

I almost laugh. Chloe startles at her own words, her eyes growing rounder and larger.

Then, she lets out a guttural groan of frustration before regaining composure. I'm pretty sure the entire garage can hear it.

"Are you okay, Coleman? Too many sherries with Jack Sheppard last night?"

"Grow up, Matt," she says, and this time when her eyes lock with mine, I see not *anger* flicker across her face, but disappointment. And I don't like it.

CHAPTER 7

Chloe

There's something very wrong with Matt, and I've been too wrapped up in my own bitterness toward him to see it. It was fine, I suppose, when I silently loathed him in the privacy of my own brain, but that loathing has spilled out like a backed-up and overflowing toilet and now everyone has to deal with the shit.

Still. *What a petulant motherfu—*

"Chloe?" The cocky young strategist who made the wrong tire call from yesterday approaches, his face sour enough to curdle milk.

"Hiya," I say, as cheerfully as I can.

"We've agreed on a one-stop. Soft tires, then hard," he says, handing me his tablet. The sunken gray eyes and whiff of stale cigarette smoke tell me he was out enjoying the town last night.

I feel the same nagging as yesterday. "Softs? In these conditions? Those tires degrade quickly here, and Matt is not known for his tire management skills."

"I know. We've run all the options," he says plainly, scratching the back of his head, his eyes anywhere but meeting mine. He doesn't want to have this conversation with me.

I frown. "Okay. If you've run all the options."

The strategist hesitates. "Yep," he says, tilting his chin up. I watch him saunter back to the other strategists, and they all quickly fall into some kind of private joke together. I narrow my gaze on him. I've not felt ready to let anyone go since taking over, but I *am* watching.

I look over the line of computers that sit opposite the pit lane facing the track and see Matt fucking Warner standing out at the back of the grid, an ice towel around his neck, headphones on, drinking an electric-green sugary slushy. Press occasionally move into his orbit and he moves away quickly. He *looks* like he wants to retire, honestly. Like he's done.

The crowd is deafening already. As the music blares from the speakers over the grid, I feel a tap on my shoulder.

"Everything okay with you and your handsome new driver?" It's Keyla, shouting over the noise, as she pauses her walk across the pit toward McLaren.

"Hiya!" I pull my headphones off. "Mostly . . . why?"

"That's not convincing. You got a handle on things?"

"Nope," I say, dropping my voice as much as I can over the noise. "He's so *infuriating*, Keyla."

"Oh no. I know that look. I've been that look. You still want to fuck him," she says, tutting. "You can't fuck your driver, Chloe."

"Shut up. I do not," I shout back, mortified, and hugely grateful that no one is paying attention to us in the pre-race chaos.

"The rumors say otherwise," she yells back with a knowing stare.

"Rumors?" *Oh god.* At this point, can anything get worse?

"You can't go back to that place, Chloe," she says, wagging a finger at me. "You'll regret it. If people get wind of it, it's going to make you look—"

"I know, I know," I say bitterly. "Pathetic. Tacky. Ridiculous."

"Your words, not mine," she says with both hands up. "I'd hate that for you after you've worked harder than anyone I know to get here. I also can't go around beating up *every* gossiping loser who tries my best friend."

I laugh and nod at Keyla's classic ride-or-die attitude, glad to have someone around here who has my back. "Thanks for the straight talk."

She grins at me. "Good luck tonight, Chloe. I'm rooting for you." Then she spins back around, her braids swinging as she skips off toward her team.

I glance down at my team, at the glum faces—Noah's race engineer, technical director, and strategists, and at the far end, an empty seat that Archie will fill soon enough. His transfer is in the process, even though it's unprecedented to let go of someone like Archie without a period of time when he cannot work for a competitor. Rossini were just so keen to move on from Matt, they agreed, which works better for us.

I look back at Matt, watch him fidget for a moment and then examine the tarmac and saunter down the straight, away from the lights and the cameras and the rest of the drivers.

Has he even done warm-ups? Where are his earbuds? He used to love to listen to music, but now he just looks completely adrift. Unfocused. As my eyes trace the lonely figure, I feel my heart clutch a little. Which Matt are we going to see today?

"It's lights-out in Singapore," the loudspeaker booms as twenty Formula 1 engines growl and roar into action. I take a deep breath, glancing up at the numbers on the screen in front of me.

This is it. The main race we've been waiting for.

Come on, Matt, I find myself whispering. Willing him to find something. Anything.

As the cars hit speed on the straight, he is surprisingly aggressive. I feel a little thrill as I watch his speed dial up even more out of turn one, and he moves quickly past the lagging Haas.

I turn to my team and give a hopeful smile.

"He's in eighteenth," says the strategist.

Then there is a tussle into turns three and four, where Matt finds a little space on the bend, cutting underneath a Williams. Up one more place. He's now trailing Noah.

"Two places in half a lap," says one of the strategists and then she points at the screen. "He's on pace with the midfield."

"Noah next," I say.

The excitement starts to fizzle, and I suck back a deep, calming breath as he comes up behind his new teammate. The radio crackles.

"Matt's behind?" Noah says.

"You know what to do," says his race engineer.

The radio crackles again, and I feel a tug of guilt. But Matt was always going to be the first driver, and if there was a chance to get him into the middle of the field ahead of Noah, we had to take it.

"You got it," Noah says, utterly compliant. The perfect teammate.

We watch as Noah pulls to the outside of the lane, and all Matt needs to do is slip through and he'll have gained three places.

Except he doesn't.

Something happens as he hits the throttle careering into that sixth turn. Matt suddenly slows, losing his line and coming off the track again. The team runs their checks on the car data.

"Suspension's fine."

"Tires are good."

"He looks stressed again," someone says, pointing to his heart rate.

"Only time it should be peaking like that is overtaking Lewis Hamilton," says another.

There is something going on.

Noah and Matt drive almost side by side for three bends.

"Matt, push," says Noah's race engineer. "You've got the spot. You're slowing both of you."

The radio crackles. "Let the kid drive," Matt says.

And then to our astonishment, we watch him drop back, forcing Noah to pull in forward, ahead of him.

"Matt, strategy was clear," I say over the radio.

"Oh, hi, Chloe."

I swear, loudly, off-mic and the race engineer puts a hand on mine to calm me.

"He's dropped another place," says someone. "Back at eighteenth out of twenty."

"He doesn't listen to you," the strategist says, turning to glare at me as though it's not completely clear.

"He's finished," I mutter to myself, banging my forehead on the screen in front of me. "I'm finished. We're finished."

I walk through the emptying lot to wait for my ride back to the hotel, hiding twice behind parked trucks to evade the press. Jesus Christ, they never give up.

I slink round the back of the Rossini trailer and finally find a spot to wait. Then I get an email notification on my phone and open a long rant from Barry.

To: CHLOE
From: BARRY
Subject: You & Matt at the garage tomorrow morning, 10:00am. What the hell is going on? FYI I have a sponsor meeting with a company that builds water slides. Unsure about the powder pink of their logo.
Message: [blank]

I'm blithely wondering if I should encourage Barry to use a phone messaging service when I spot Rossini team principal Matteo Borelli standing across the lot with two of his team. Our eyes meet, and he stops mid-conversation, striding over to me, a pitying look on his face.

"Hi, Mr. Borelli," I say, a small thrill coursing through me as he approaches. Despite it all, despite this legend of F1 holding the same position as me, I still feel like this small racing superfan who is lucky to be on the lot. "Congratulations on the podium."

"Podiums," he says, grinning, holding up his fingers in a V shape. "Two." I smile as he smooths back his wiry salt-and-pepper hair. I suspect he didn't come here to gloat at me.

"Matt's still struggling," he says after a moment.

"Your drivers didn't need to lap him," I say, attempting a joke, humiliating as it was.

"He's in his own head since the crash."

"He was driving badly *before* the crash," I remind him.

Matteo tips his head sideways, scratching at the scruffy regrowth on his chin. "He was impatient before. Driving too fast, too recklessly. But since the crash, he doesn't drive at all. He's a lame horse."

"What are you saying? I should shoot him?" I quip.

Despite my attempt to seem jovial, I must look stricken, because Matteo dips his head, lowers his voice, and puts a hand on my shoulder. "Cut him loose. He's going to need too much time."

"Well. Time is what I don't have," I mutter.

Something passes over Matteo's face, and he nods as though he understands.

Because he probably knows the trouble Arden is in.

Jack was right. This team is on the brink of financial collapse, and everyone here knows it. I'm about to press Matteo, to see what he knows, when we are approached by a girl, can't be more than eighteen or nineteen, her long blond hair back in a ponytail, stuffed under a cap.

"Sorry to interrupt," she says shyly. I glance at the phone she's clutching in her hands. "Can I have a selfie with you?"

Matteo smiles warmly, standing a little straighter, making room for her to stand next to him. "Oh," she says, glancing between Matteo and me, flushing red. "I meant with Chloe Coleman."

"Ahh. Of course," he says, hands up good-naturedly. "I'll leave you to it."

She looks back to me and grins, and at once I feel a giddy sense of pride, misplaced though it may be right now.

"It's just so cool having a woman at the top," she says, giddy, as we lean in together and she takes several shots, moving her head into multiple positions as she does. "Thank you!" she squeals. "I'm at the academy. If things don't work out, I hope I can go into management like you."

I try to swallow a sort of embarrassed yelp.

"We're all cheering for Arden. For *you*!" she calls out, and I watch as she skips back to a group of young women, all drivers, I suppose, from the FIA's new woman-only racing academy, designed to help improve representation in the sport. I watch as they crowd round her phone to look at the photo, hooting and giggling.

Christ. I'm clutched by a nightmare worse than fear of failure.

Collective responsibility.

Barry is right. Tomorrow, Matt and I need to figure this out one way or another, or we're both finished.

CHAPTER 8

Matt

Thirty-four minutes and counting.

That's how long Chloe and I have been trapped in this tiny damn box of a room.

Barry told us to meet him here in the garage at ten a.m., packed and ready to head to Texas. I thought we were going to debrief, and was awake half the night planning my retirement speech. But instead, Barry lured us into this little room on the promise of those doughnuts over there on the small table, the strong black coffee, and an honest "chat." Okay, the venue seemed a little strange, but the neutral territory of the garage, away from the prying ears of gossipy reporters, made some insane sense at the time.

As Chloe and I stood there awkwardly exchanging glances, Barry asked for our mobile phones, to "keep us focused." Then, before we knew what was happening, he was on the other side of the door, locking it from the outside with a key.

"Come together, you two. If you learn to work as a team, you'll get out," he said as he grinned, before running off on his tippy-toes like a teenager mid-prank.

"It's like a PG version of that movie *Saw,*" I said, looking around the empty room as Chloe rattled the door for the hundredth time.

"At least there's no dead person in the room," she said dryly. "*Yet.*"

"Just a dead career," I muttered to myself. Chloe's head spun around so fast it nearly did a 180. "*My* career," I said quickly as I took in her mortified face.

"Are you really done?"

"You didn't watch the race? *I'm done.*" It came out uneasy, my voice hitching slightly. Chloe's eyes narrowed on me, and she folded her arms across her chest.

"I'm afraid I just don't believe you, Matt," she said.

"Believe what you want. As soon as we're out of here, I'm on a plane back to England."

"Going back to Brackley? *Finally.* Gracing your family with your presence at last."

"What's that supposed to mean?"

Chloe didn't answer, she just pulled on the door for the hundred and first time.

"It's locked," I said slowly, irritated, dropping my head into my hands. "I think we've established that."

Chloe rolled her eyes and tossed her hands in the air. "Fine. Let's wait for a janitor. Or maybe next year's circuit? Perhaps there *will* be a dead body or two in here by then." She shoved at the door, before shouting, "Barry, you are a monumental shit stick!"

Then she blew hot breath onto the glass window that looked out across the garage, steaming it up and writing *HELP* before kicking the wall and then whimpering like an abandoned puppy.

Now we are trapped in this box until such time as Barry decides to let us out. I accepted that half an hour ago, and now Chloe finally has, stubborn as she is.

I'm sitting on the floor, elbows resting on each knee, head in my hands, flight-ready in my chinos and Lacoste tee. Chloe is against the opposite wall playing with a discarded screwdriver she found among a sea of construction junk littering the room. The sweet smell of the doughnuts and coffee is tempting, but I've cornered myself into a one-way silent standoff with Chloe, so I'd rather starve than move first. I hear only the sound of a low electrical buzz and a vacuum somewhere in the distance until Chloe breaks the silence and taps the glass with the screwdriver.

"Shall I smash the window?"

I sit quietly, waiting for her to come to terms with the fact that she's not going to do that. Her shoulders slump.

"Never ceases to amaze me how quickly they pack down the garage and get everything into the crates ready to move on to the next country," she says, her whispery voice trailing through the silence.

"Especially if they lose."

Chloe looks at me and tips her head, raising an eyebrow. "Are you speaking now?"

"No," I say quickly, trying not to grin as I look away. "Thinking aloud."

She huffs. Then she slides down the wall and lands on her bum. I glance sideways at her; she's in coffee-colored soft cotton joggers and a matching T-shirt, her hair down and still damp from the shower. Traveling clothes, I suppose, for the jet we're due to catch after lunch. She's casual but there's something about the soft fabrics that adds to *her* softness, her effortless beauty. I suddenly want to be closer and feel her for myself, but then I quickly snap out of my unexpected daydream and back to reality.

"Is he even coming back?" she says, finally seeming to lose her temper, tossing the screwdriver against the wall and glancing up at the coffee. "Fuck it."

She pulls herself back up and walks past me to the box of doughnuts on the little table, a cloud of sweet-smelling perfume trailing in her wake. The light catches on a thin gold ankle bracelet sitting just above her left trainer. I let myself imagine holding that ankle for a moment, sliding my hand up her bare calf. *Fuck.* Why am I even having these thoughts of her? Where is this coming from?

"It's still kinda warm," she says, nodding to the coffee after she takes a sip. "Tastes like a punch in the throat, though."

I want to laugh, but I'm also stubborn.

I push myself up the wall and swipe the other coffee and a chocolate-glazed doughnut with all the visible reluctance I can muster. Then I struggle not to spit out the coffee.

"Was this filtered through Barry's underwear?" I say, and Chloe laughs, a high, fluttery giggle that warms me through. I'm hit by this sudden wave of nostalgia, recalling that sweet laugh when it was so easy to extract from her, way back when we were kids. I smile at the thought, and our eyes meet for the briefest of moments before she looks swiftly away, her grin vanishing. Just as I catch her, the old Chloe, she slips through my fingers again.

"We need to talk, Matt," she says, serious now, biting into her doughnut, then removing the sugary glaze from her lips with a finger. I narrow my eyes on that finger, as something begins to uncoil in the pit of my stomach. *Jesus.* One minute she's that teenage girl I grew up with, the next she is a very adult woman who is doing very adult things to my body.

"I know," I concede, my eyes firmly on the floor now. *I have to get a grip.*

"We should have talked earlier." I watch as she pulls out one of the chairs and drops herself heavily down into it. "You wanted to, and I fucked up."

"It's doesn't matter."

"It *does* matter," she says. "Please. I should have made time, even if you really want to retire. . . ." Her voice trails off as she eyeballs me. "Do you *really* want to retire, Matt?"

I meet her eyes, but again, they slide back down to her coffee, pretending it's the most fascinating thing in the world.

"No," I say, truthfully.

I can't quite tell if this has pleased or panicked her until her mouth stretches into a smile, her eyes still on that coffee. "Well, then."

"Are we still friends, Chloe?"

I watch her body go still, almost imperceptibly, before she replies, "Sure."

"*Convincing,*" I say wryly.

"We've known each other since primary school, maybe even before because of our dads," she says.

"True, but there's a difference between someone you once knew and someone you're currently on good terms with." I lean in, smiling at her, trying to understand where she's coming from. "You seem to dislike me, if I'm honest."

Chloe squeezes her eyes shut for a beat. "That's not . . .

not true," she says, stumbling over the words as she clears her throat.

"Even more convincing." I raise an eyebrow.

"I'm sorry if I gave you that impression."

She still hasn't denied it. I watch her closely as she pulls herself together, placing the coffee on the table and tossing the half-eaten doughnut into the box.

"Was it the press video?" I push her.

Chloe tips her head, turning to face me now. "It didn't make me feel great, if you want the truth."

I need to clear that misunderstanding up, at least. I slide in opposite her at the table, tilting the coffee cup side to side as though it's a glass of whiskey. I wish it was a glass of whiskey.

"When she asked me if I was happy to be working for a woman, I didn't hesitate because it was a problem," I say slowly and clearly. "I was thinking about how amazing you'd done and how dumb the question was, if you really want to know."

Chloe tips her head, her face curious, her cheeks pink. "You were not."

"It's the truth."

"Really?"

"Yes. And I'm proud of you, if that's not a weird thing to say now that you're my boss."

She says nothing for a while, but I can see the flush in her cheeks deepening a little, and I feel glad I told her. I should have said it yesterday.

She lets out a little *huh*. A half laugh. "I've wanted it all my life, and the word *boss* doesn't sit well on me," she says finally, picking her coffee back up.

"It should. By all accounts you really deserve it."

She ignores the compliment, pushing her hair back from her face.

"I don't know how to do this, Matt," she says finally, quietly. "Please just be honest with me. If you don't want to stay, I can work with that. I can look for someone new. But Arden Racing is on its last legs. The money is running out. The sponsors are jumping ship. I have heard from two people now that we have only a few races left before this is all over."

"I heard it too," I say quietly, nodding.

"You can retire now; your career has been incredible. But I'm just now getting started, and I've come too far for it all to come crashing down this soon."

My chest tightens with guilt.

"If you want to go, please just go. The crew can see there's tension, and it doesn't help my bloody fear that I'm not cut out for the job," she says, her eyes misting a little. "I'm very well aware I'm a PR exercise, but I thought, maybe stupidly, that I could prove them all wrong. That I am good enough." She drops her head into her hands, and I reach my hand across the table, my fingers outstretched toward hers.

She ignores it.

"Chloe," I say gently. "You do deserve this. You are cut out for it."

"On the one hand I know that's true; on the other, I feel like the impostor I am," she says, shaking her head. "I need time to settle. Find my feet. Fire that wanker of a strategist. But time I don't got."

The honestly from Chloe is arresting.

Tell her. You owe her at least the truth.

Her head is still in her hands, her gaze fixed on that damn coffee. I steel myself.

"Chloe," I say quietly.

"Yes?"

"I'm getting flashbacks," I tell her finally, pulling my hand back across the table. "At night and on the track."

She turns her head back to me. "The crash?"

"Yes. I have these physical reactions. Tight chest. Hard to take a deep breath. I have to slow down. I get worried I'm going to . . . well, crash again, I suppose."

I watch Chloe absorb the information. "Shit, Matt. I'm so sorry," she says quietly.

"Anyway. Now you know. That's why I think it's time to quit. Even if I really don't want to. Even if, as Barry says, there is still some bite in the old dog. If I can't drive, who am I? What use am I?"

"Is there really?"

"Really what?"

"Bite in the old dog?"

"Dunno. Sometimes I still feel it. For a second."

"Really?"

"I think so," I say honestly. "I think so."

"We can work with this, Matt. If you want to drive," she says. "You have a whole bunch of training and discipline issues. You need a pre-race routine, one that helps you focus. A therapist to work on the mental blocks."

She blinks a few times, worried, I think, that she's said too much. But I just laugh. To myself mostly, because no matter what, Chloe has been and will always be an optimistic fixer.

"What's so funny? There's nothing wrong with therapy," she says quickly.

"No, it's not that," I say, shaking my head, not ready to share with her that, in fact, I have been seeing a therapist. "I'm just remembering how you always know what to do. Remember when you whipped me into shape back in Juniors?"

I grin, but Chloe doesn't. Instead, her eyes flicker to the back of the room. "That was a whole lifetime ago," she says, with a laugh that sounds *almost* bitter. "But really, I can help you get back to the driver I know you can be. What do you say?"

"If anyone can do it, it would be you," I say, tipping my coffee cup at her.

She stares hard at me, scanning my eyes, searching for something.

"I'm serious," I reassure her.

She finally nods. "Okay. Great. We can focus on those things, while you work with a therapist. We can get more help for you if we need to. We can claw back some pace in other ways." Chloe is awake, suddenly. Excited, even. She springs up and starts to pace.

"I guess so."

"The car has a range of upgrades coming. And we need a new head of aerodynamics, for sure—I have to pressure Barry on that. But there are whispers of promise here." I watch her move into full leader role, right before my eyes. "We have Austin next, then Mexico. Then Brazil. Then back for Vegas. That's four races, around two months . . ." Her voice trails off as she stops pacing. "We can get a lot done. Maybe we can claw to the middle of the field. One top ten would be incredible. We could really get points, Matt. We really could."

"You make a good case," I say.

"Arden suffers a lot of problems, but the worst one is the lack of belief. In this fucking game of tiny, incremental improvements, you need a motivated team. Small gains beget small gains."

I shoot her a wry smile, but her enthusiasm is infectious; her excitement is rubbing off on me. "Do you believe?"

"In the team? Yes. In myself?" She laughs. "I'm working on that."

"Okay," I say.

"Okay?" she replies, those eyes big and round.

"You help me, and . . ."

"And?" Chloe asks, looking impatient.

"I'll help you with your *impostor syndrome*."

"Oh, that," she says, grimacing.

"You know, I've worked for two of the best ever team principals—"

"I know your impressive résumé, Matt," she says with a huff. After a long pause, she throws her hands up. "Fine. What am I doing wrong?"

"You need to stand a little straighter. People can smell fear. In the racing world, you get scared, you die."

"That bloody strategist," I say, nodding.

"Be the boss," he says. "Matteo Borelli will happily overrule a strategist he doesn't trust. And eventually, everyone will learn how you think, and you won't need to overrule anyone. You can let go of the micromanaging and be team principal. Talk to the press and schmooze the sponsors."

"I hate dealing with press. I feel like it's obvious I'm only here as a PR thing and they're going to say it to my face. On camera."

"Fuck it. You just focus on yourself, and your job and the respect will follow."

Chloe nods, turning back from the window to face me.

"I'd appreciate a person by my side. Someone who has my back. Someone I can talk to if I'm unsure."

"I can do that."

She smiles gratefully. "Are we really going to do this?"

"We're going to try."

"Shall we shake on it?"

"I think a couple of old friends can do better than that."

Before I have a chance to think it through, I am across the room, pulling Chloe into my arms. She is stiff at first, like a board, as I wrap my arms around her small frame, but then she sinks a little into me, and I can feel her body flush against mine. Breasts to chest, her head just at my shoulder. It isn't a hug like we used to. Not a slap-on-the-back kind of hug. This feels more intimate somehow, and at the same time, I'm completely at home.

Chloe sighs into my shoulder, squeezing a little harder as she does. I tighten my grip on the small of her back with both my arms. *Did we always fit so perfectly together?* She smells like fresh shampoo and sugary doughnuts, and I allow myself to drink that smell in, just for a moment. I stay incredibly still for as long as she needs. And *I* need.

Finally, Chloe's head moves back, and as she looks up at me, our eyes lock, and for a beat, for a flicker there is something more in her gaze. Something vulnerable. Something sad. Something . . . like . . . and before I catch it and myself leaning closer, she stiffens and looks away, springing back from me.

Whoa. What was that?

"Great, that's great," I say, quickly and very stupidly, looking at anything and everything but Chloe. "Just two old friends helping each other out."

"Yes. Old friends," she says, starting to pace. "We can do this."

"We can."

I realize how silly we're being and grab both her arms and catch her eyes to try to reassure her. *Everything is okay.*

"Right, Bug. If we're going to work together, first thing we need to do is get out of here."

"Right." Chloe looks around the room and settles on something. "Fuck it," she says, in a hoarse whisper. "Get that screwdriver. If Barry isn't coming for us, we're taking down the door."

CHAPTER 9

Chloe

I want to get decently drunk, in this dive bar, with you."

"You got it," Keyla says, her face lighting up with a huge grin.

We're at Donn's Depot, downtown Austin, Texas. A frantically busy little dive bar with very cold beer, live music, and most important, a degree of anonymity from the F1 world, most of whom will be holing up in the big five-star hotels on the east side of the city near the circuit.

"You look like hell," she says, motioning for me to sit.

Whereas Keyla looks gorgeous. Her braids wound in a bunch on her head, faded Rolling Stones T-shirt falling stylishly off her shoulder, her dark skin positively shimmering under the dim lighting above the bar.

"I've just traveled for twenty hours, after Barry locked me in a hot garage *with Matt* and we had to remove the hinges from the door to escape."

"Barry locked you in a room?" She drops her voice. "With Matt?"

"Yes, and it gets worse. He's on his way here." I look sheepishly at the floor.

"Hold up, what the hell's going on?" Keyla cackles and slaps me on the arm. "I can't keep up."

"He saw me leaving the hotel and asked where I was going, and like the idiot I am, I word-vomited and told him. Then, in the spirit of us getting along and this new arrangement we made in Singapore, I invited him to tag along and he said yes. I've officially lost my mind."

"Oh, girl, you better start at the beginning," she says as she motions to the bartender for two shots of whiskey to go with our beers.

"Bring them on," I say, rubbing my palms together.

We clink glasses and both down the whiskey on one, then I wipe my mouth with the back of my hand. Keyla slams her glass on the bar. "Now. Matt Warner. Sexiest driver in F1. *Spill.*"

"Yes. Right. Okay. Matt Warner." I breathe all the stale, boozy air into my lungs and blow a massive, overexaggerated raspberry. Because what exactly is going on? Was there something there in That Moment, with Matt? He looked just as rattled as I was, or did I misread it? I groan into my beer because I've been going round on this carousel since we boarded the jet in Singapore.

"Well, we had a rough start. The team noticed. Barry noticed. And there's no doubt about our history being a little awkward, but we talked."

"And . . ." Keyla squints at me, as though disbelieving.

"And we both agreed to try to make this work. He needs my help. And I could sure use his support."

Keyla tips her head to the side, studying me hard. "Are

you sure you can put all your past feelings to bed like that? I know how much he meant to you way back when. Those feelings don't just disappear."

I feel a rush of emotion sweep through me, and like the mind reader she is, Keyla puts a hand on my arm and squeezes. "Okay. Let's think positively. You probably just need to get used to being in each other's orbits as adults. I mean, do you even really *know* him anymore?"

"I'm not sure," I say, truthfully.

"Maybe once you get to know him again you'll think he sucks now," she suggests, taking a sip of her beer.

Maybe. The Matt I knew could be so unexpectedly sweet. A surprise lunch on a busy day. Sharing headphones while we waited trackside, when I forgot mine. And if any of the other guys ever said anything disparaging or, in later years, vaguely sexual to me, Matt could silence them with just one look. His attention made me feel so special. And so very confused.

Keyla leans in, a little tipsy now, and I realize I'm right there with her. "Maybe, Chloe, after a while you'll wonder what you ever saw in him."

Imagine that freeing feeling. No more reading into everything, wanting to believe the feeling is mutual. My chest relaxes just thinking about it, my body takes in the first full breath in a week. I wave to the bartender for more drinks.

"That would be the best scenario for everyone involved," I say, pushing away the niggling feeling that I'm simply bullshitting myself.

"As long as he feels the same way."

"Meaning?"

"Well, look at you. You're hot. You're a fucking team

principal of an F1 team. I'd be more worried *he* might have feelings for you, these days."

I slap Keyla on the arm and laugh. "Thanks for the ego boost, but he's still Matt fucking Warner, *GQ* cover model."

She tuts loudly. "You looked in the mirror lately?" She holds a finger up to the bartender for one more shot.

I think about Matt and his struggles on the track, and the promise we made in that locked room. I think about the incredible strain he must be under. I force myself to picture him back in training, trying to find his focus again. I've helped him before. I can help him again. *This relationship is for work, not personal.*

"Well, anyway, I told him I'd help him get his confidence back."

"The crash," she says, the way everyone talks about it.

I nod. "If I can get him back up to speed, we could be vaguely competitive with the upgrades we've got coming," I say, resting my elbows on the sticky countertop. I can feel the booze thrumming in my veins now, the music a little louder, my stress feeling a million miles away.

"That's your focus," she says, throwing her arms around me in a surprise hug, which nearly topples me off my stool. "I just want you to give this everything, Chloe. The job. You have so much potential, and I know this Matt thing is a shock, and there's feelings to process, but you cannot let it distract you."

I pull her a little closer into the hug and squeeze. "Yes. I need to just keep my eyes on the prize."

The bar is starting to get rowdy already, and as Keyla pulls back, she has that unmistakable look of mischief on her face. She nods toward the pool table.

"Wanna go challenge those frat boys to a game of pool?"

"Can we do it for money?" I ask. "Like old times?"

"You bet, baby," she says, grinning.

■■■■■■■■■■

An hour later, Keyla and I are both well on the way to being certified drunk, *and* have still managed to pocket around a hundred dollars from the group of young men.

On the jukebox, "Sex on Fire" by Kings of Leon starts playing, and in one of those drunken-bonding-of-the-whole-bar moments, suddenly arms and pints are thrust toward the ceiling and painfully loud wails fill the humid air.

"When's Matt coming? I promised I'd meet some friends soon and go dancing, which you have to join," Keyla whines, finishing her beer in one big slug. "You think he bailed?"

"Maybe. I'm too tired for clubbing though, Keyla," I say. Lining up the white ball, I shoot the black into the corner pocket. "That's another win."

"You girls are real fucking hustlers," says our new friend Micky before handing Keyla a twenty and the last of his pride.

"Not really," Keyla says casually. "We're just a couple of gals in town for the F1 race."

"I love F1," Brad or maybe Chad says. "I got tickets to the qualifier."

"Qualify-*ing*," I say, wagging a finger. "Not qualifi-*er*."

"Whatever," he says, shrugging. "You going?"

"Might make an appearance," Keyla says, catching my eye and hiding her laugh with the back of her hand.

"Got to say, nothing better than watching Red Bull."

Keyla eye-rolls. "Isn't Red Bull a drink?" she replies in her most girlish voice.

"Chicks say they love F1," he says, laughing. "But y'all just want to bang the drivers." He pulls out a packet of cigarettes and pats himself down, looking for a lighter.

"Who wants to bang a driver?"

I'd know that husky voice anywhere, which makes me really bloody angry and excited all at once. I spin around so fast, I nearly impale Matt with the pool cue.

"Whoa, tiger," he says as he steadies me with his big hands. *Were they always that big?*

"Matt!" I shout over the music as I fight the tipsy urge to hug him. I have to remind myself that I'm his boss. This is a professional hangout. Well, as much as dive-bar drunken hangouts can be.

But Matt stays cool and casual, one hand in his pocket while the other shakes Keyla's hand as he introduces himself. Keyla gives me a sideways look that says exactly what I'm thinking: He unsurprisingly looks *hot*. Shower fresh, hair still damp, chocolate hoodie and loose-fit jeans, black baseball cap pulled down low.

It's infuriating.

"Holy shit, you're Matt Warner," Micky says, glancing back at me and Keyla.

Matt lifts his baseball cap a little, grinning. "Yeah, but keep it down, would you?" he says, nodding round the crowded bar.

Micky grins back. "Good luck on Sunday, bro." Then, shaking his head, he saunters back to his mates with a wide smile.

"I didn't think you'd show this late," I shout over the music, steadying myself with one hand on the pool table.

"Sorry, took a minute to get ready and then was stuck in traffic," he replies, looking sheepish. "Damn, looks like I missed all the fun."

"I'm afraid so. I'm actually ready for bed," I yell back. "And I'm hungry."

"And you look a little drunk," Matt says, as I attempt three times to stand the pool cue up against the wall, before giving up.

Keyla takes the pool cue from me and, with almost the same lack of coordination, manages to return it to its catch. "I can go meet the team if you want to head back? They're going clubbing." She glances between me and Matt and narrows her eyes at me. "If that's what you want, Chloe?"

I slump down into the seat, waves of tiredness sweeping over me. I'm so exhausted I can't tell where the jet lag begins and the whiskey ends. "Yes, please."

"I'll take her back," Matt says to Keyla without missing a beat.

"Text me when you get home," she says to me before squeezing my hand and disappearing to keep the party going.

I watch Matt scan the bar, probably to close out my tab. The whole place is swaying and shouting in unison, engrossed in their own drunken business of off-tune singing and sweaty dancing.

And then, Matt pulls his cap down low and reaches out his hand to pull me up.

"Come on, Bug," he says, half grinning at me. "Let's get you to bed."

I can't help myself. "I bet you've used that line before."

"Oh, she's playful tonight," he says, chuckling as he gives up waiting for my hand and folds his arms across his chest. "You want a water instead? Food?"

"I want all three of those things, but I don't want to move," I say, and hearing the slight slur in my voice, I pull a face. "Shit. I *am* a little drunk."

"I don't have a teleporter shoved down the front of my pants, but I can get you back to the hotel with my car," he says.

"The hotel?" I say, sighing, wishing I was already there.

"Where there is food *and* there is water," he says.

"And you have a car?"

"Yes, I drove myself. You know, I have a driver's license," he says, grinning. "I passed my test and everything."

"Fine. Take me home," I say, lifting up my hand to accept his help. His big hand clasps around mine and jerks me up, and before I lose my footing and catch the side of the pool table he wraps his arm around my waist and pulls me close.

I immediately feel the electricity between us that sparked in the room back in Singapore. I slowly trace my eyes from his muscular arm holding me, up to his broad chest, and finally into those piercing hazel eyes. Am I that drunk, or did I just imagine him leaning in even more? Or maybe it's the crowd of people pushing us toward each other.

Fuck. This is so not appropriate. Before I can snap us out of yet another Moment, Matt thankfully does it for me.

"Sorry, let's get you out of here. It's too crowded." He takes a step back toward the bar, handles the bill, then grabs my hand and guides me toward the front entrance.

Matt and I step out into the night, sobered up from whatever *that* was.

"Oh yes, take me to bed now," I mumble as I follow him through the virtually empty streets. "I seriously can't wait."

"I bet you've used that line before," he says, clicking a set of keys as a green Maserati unlocks on the street next to us. He looks back with a mischievous smile. I slap him playfully on the shoulder, before realizing we're still holding hands, so I tug mine free, wiping it inconspicuously on my jeans.

"A Maserati?" I touch the side of the car, its green coat shimmering in the blinking light of the bar.

"I have a soft spot for them," he whispers, leaning in. And then, as his body moves past mine to get to the passenger door, I get a whiff of his aftershave. His freshly washed hair. I stand back, stumbling a little with the shock of it. This night is pure torture.

Matt goes to grab me, but I jump back. "I'm fine. Sorry. Damn shoes," I say.

As the door shuts and Matt makes his way around to the other side, I realize I can hear my heart beating hard in my chest.

"You came all this way just to have to take me home," I say.

"It's okay. I'm glad I witnessed it, Bug," he says, starting the car, which roars to life with that deep growl from the V-8 engine.

"Witnessed what?"

"You being a cheeky fucker," he says, laughing. "I missed it, actually."

I feel the heat in my cheeks as I reach for my seat belt and yank it across my body, but it jams, and the harder I tug, the more it jams. "Damn it," I mutter.

Matt reaches over to help, and our hands touch again,

sending another shock through my body. *I'm in no state for this.* I need to get to the safety of my room.

"There you go, Bug. Safety first."

"Can we go?" I say, hugging myself and shifting my body away from his.

"Sure. How fast do you want to get there?" he asks, sticking his tongue out as he grins.

"The speed limit," I say dryly.

"Come on, Bug. That's no fun," Matt says as he pulls onto the street, then hits the throttle.

CHAPTER 10

Matt

I tap on the door to her room and wait.

And then again. "Chloe?" I say sternly. I bite my lip to stop from grinning as I imagine her clawing her way out of bed.

The door creaks open. She has her hair pulled back into a rough bun, her hotel-issued robe clutched together with one hand at the neck, black smudges under her eyes.

"Matt," she says, almost angrily. "What is it?"

"I brought you a coffee," I say, thrusting the large cup toward her. "Black, right?"

"Yes, yes, a thousand times yes. How did you know?" she says, confused. Then she reaches her free hand through and rests her forehead on the edge of the open door. "God. About last night . . ."

"Forget it," I say, trying but failing to stifle a laugh. "Didn't mean to disturb your beauty rest . . . but I've been waiting at the world's worst hotel gym for our eight o'clock session and . . ." I glance at my watch and look up at her mortified face.

"Shit," she says. "Shit, shit, shit."

"See you in fifteen?"

"Five. I'll be there," she says, slamming the door.

I pause for a moment, before hearing her shout another "shit," and then hear a muffled scream, followed by the sound of a wardrobe being flung open.

"No stress, boss," I call through the door.

"Fuck off!" she shouts back.

Down in the gym, there is one bike, one ancient treadmill, and a free-weights area that has a bunch of mismatched dumbbells, kettles, and a vintage squat rack that rattles like it's held together with tape.

Chloe takes all of her promised five minutes and several more, but to be fair, I knew she'd be late after drunk Chloe came out to play last night. It's worth the wait, to be honest. She was so funny.

I got her back to the hotel room, and she invited me in for late-night beers and burgers. She said we should watch the 1984 Monaco Grand Prix. Although I wanted nothing more than to sit in her room and eat and drink some beers, it felt . . . not quite right after our talk. I got the sense she would have regretted it in the morning.

And I really didn't want that.

While I'm waiting, I jump on the treadmill, flicking through my phone to find some good workout tunes, and then turn the knob that increases the speed. It springs to life with a grunt and a moan.

"Piece of shit!" I grumble, slapping the screen to get the lights to stop flickering.

"No need to assault the equipment," says a voice. Then I feel a gentle hand on my arm.

"Fuck!" I nearly jump out of my skin before realizing it's Chloe.

"Your reaction times could still use work," she says, grinning. Her smart-ass tone makes me smile as the treadmill comes to a stop with a loud bang.

"Morning, boss," I say, turning to look at her.

Chloe is in a tight, body-hugging gym outfit. A pair of black leggings and a matching sports bra hug her in all the right places, and her wild red hair sits in a loose bun on her head. My eyes skim back up from her waist to the curve of her breasts as she tosses a towel over her shoulder and cocks her head. I can't help it; my eyes linger too long on the little beads of sweat on her chest.

Shit, I'm staring. I pull my earbuds out, step off the treadmill, and swig on my water bottle as casually as I can.

"What?" she says, narrowing her eyes at me.

"Just ah . . . nice kit," I say coolly, fumbling for an answer. "Who's the designer?"

"H&M. Not all of us have a closet full of free Lacoste training gear," she says, jabbing a finger toward the little crocodile logo on my bright white T-shirt. Then she laughs. "I miss those old Adidas shorts and the Brackley United shirt you trained in."

"Well, I'm really fucking rich now," I reply, "so . . ." I shrug playfully.

"You are," she says, grinning at me, that little dimple appearing in her right cheek. "Proof you can't buy taste."

I shove her shoulder lightly with my hand, laughing, and she nods toward the free weights. "Let's get on it."

"Yes, boss," I reply, following her, trying not to stare at her ass.

She glances back at me over her shoulder. "And . . . sorry once again, for last night. I was drunk. It was embarrassing."

"The team can't ever see you like that."

"I know. No more whiskey shots," she says sheepishly.

"I meant going home with me."

And that makes her blush, hide her face in her pale hands, and groan in abject humiliation. I can't help but cackle at her. "Forget it, Bug. We all gotta cut loose sometimes. Though . . . maybe not *that* loose."

"I said I was sorry," Chloe mumbles, reaching for a kettlebell.

Okay. Enough teasing. I watch her push the squat rack tentatively and it creaks on its hinge, tipping slightly to the right. "I think it will hold."

"You know how I was going to help you with your impostor syndrome?"

She quits setting up the bar and turns to me. "Yes?"

"Lesson one. Quit apologizing all the time."

She rolls her eyes, fighting a smile, and I enjoy watching her trying and failing to look annoyed. "Quit toying with me, then."

"But it's so fun," I shoot back, and at this, she doesn't laugh; instead she stands up straight, puts her hands on her hips, and nods at the weights. I drop my eyes down her body, and then, catching myself, keep going until my eyes are on the kettlebell on the floor.

"Enough. We're here to start you training again. Squats. Kettle swings, dead lifts, sumos, um, *thrusters*." She clears her throat, and I try not to laugh. "Lunge press . . . yada yada yada . . . core and then we'll work on your neck."

I clear my throat. "You're working out too?"

"Until we get your trainer over," she says, nodding at the rack. "Squats."

"You have to show me how to do it. I can't remember."

Chloe narrows her eyes at me. "I won't be bullied," she says, moving toward the weights and ducking her head under the bar. "Forty on each."

"You can squat eighty pounds? Impressive," I say, joining her by the squat cage and resting my hand on the bar. Our eyes meet, and for a split second, I find myself wanting to bury my nose in the crook of her neck. She takes a breath and drags her eyes quickly away. "I remember when you could only squat the bar. No weight at all."

She doesn't reply at first, but then she ducks her head under the bar, and I step back to watch.

"It's weird the things you remember," she says, dropping down into a low squat, and I move around the front to face her, so I'm not staring at her ass as she squats. *I have some restraint.* But then I spot the mirror along the back wall, where I can see it anyway.

"I thought you forgot the old days," Chloe says.

"Not everything," I say.

"Most things, though," she replies.

"I remember you drown everything in hot sauce."

She heaves the bar upward.

"You used to listen to those romance audiobooks, like, all the time," I continue, grinning at her. "And I was thinking this morning about how you never showed up to my leaving party."

Chloe drops the weights onto the rack with a bang.

"Your turn," she says curtly. "And *no*. I didn't. Come on. Focus."

"All right, all right," I say, holding my hands up. "No more reminiscing, then."

She steps back and holds her hand out. "Get to work," she says firmly. "Three sets. One minute rest."

"Bossy," I murmur.

"I'm not going to apologize for getting you to work hard."

"Would you look at that," I say, holding two thumbs up. "You're *not apologizing*."

"Fuck you," she says, sighing, half-amused, half-furious. I want to keep prodding her, but it's starting to feel a little bit like I'm flirting. *Am* I flirting?

I put my head down and work hard, and within an hour Chloe has me lying on the floor, arms burning, begging for mercy.

"You need work," she says, collapsing next to me as I peel off my sodden shirt, and we lie side by side on the stinky old training mat, breathless.

"That was great," she says, sighing.

I roll onto my side and look down across her sweaty body. The softness of her pale belly below her ribs, her hips rounding out her leggings, her delicate hands by her sides on the floor. I try not to imagine her looking like that draped across my bed naked. I try my hardest.

Chloe is looking at the ceiling, but I can see her eyes flicker in my direction once. Twice.

"You know, you got really strong, Bug," I say quietly. *And really pretty.*

"You're no string bean yourself, Dials," she says, finally looking at me. Right as we're getting comfortable, she abruptly pulls herself up. "But I asked you not to call me Bug."

Then the universe really kills the moment when Barry

suddenly bursts through the glass doors. He has two mobile phones on the go; one is tucked under his chin as he furiously texts on the other. One of his dogs is at his feet, the other with a nose in the garbage can by the door.

"I've found them!" he says into his phone. "Matt. Chloe. I have news!"

"Hi, Barry," I say, pulling up to standing, wiping the sweat from my brow with the bottom of my T-shirt. Barry glances at the strip of skin above my shorts and then ends his call.

"You need to work on your core," he says, touching his own rounded belly, before he looks mock offended. "What? I don't gotta race. I'm allowed a keg instead of a six-pack."

I can't help but chuckle. For all his ridiculousness, I'm kind of warming to Barry.

"Come on," he says, motioning toward Chloe. "I got some promising news."

"You do?" she asks, as warily as I feel. It honestly could be anything.

"Sponsors, my friends. Sponsors."

"Oh, that's great. Like . . . who?" I am bracing myself as I join Chloe, who has dropped onto a bench, sucking on her water bottle, her eyes firmly on Barry.

I look back at Barry. I'm half expecting him to reveal the big financial savior is some scammy crypto exchange. But instead, he folds his arms and turns to me looking triumphant. "Hot sauce."

"Hot sauce?"

"Hot sauce!" he says again. "Big Ronny's Ring Burner, to be precise."

"What?"

Chloe lets out an awkward laugh, before swiftly checking herself. "Ring Burner?" she says, biting her bottom lip. Wait. He's not having the name of a hot sauce called Big Ronny's Ring Burner painted on the side of a fifteen-million-dollar car . . . is he?

"Car, kit, and, um . . . helmet?" he says, looking at me sheepishly.

"No," I say, shaking my head.

"They're paying a damn fortune."

"I'm not having Big Ronny's Ring Burner on my helmet," I announce emphatically, with a sweep of my hands. "Forget it."

"Well, actually, you'll have their catchphrase," Barry says.

"Oh, this will be good," says Chloe, biting her lip as a giggle escapes her mouth.

"Mind My Hot Rear," he says evenly. "Right across the back, inside a little fart cloud. It works with the whole driving thing. I think it's a nice matchup."

"Mind My Hot Rear," Chloe repeats, wrestling the grin from her face.

"Chloe likes hot sauce. She can wear it."

"You're the one with the hot rear," she says, biting her lip again to stop from laughing. "On the *car*, I mean."

"I used to be sponsored by Bulgari," I say pitifully, and at this Chloe actually turns away from me, her hand to her mouth, her shoulders shaking in laughter.

"Hilarious, is it?" I shoot at her.

"You can think about it," Barry says, raising both hands. "But not too much. We've already ordered the changes to the livery. But the helmet branding is worth more, so try to get on board with it. *Fast.*"

"I won't," I say, rolling my eyes.

"Oh, and I have some even better news for you, Matt," he says, ignoring my irritation.

"I'm all ears," I reply dryly. "A photo shoot for a hemorrhoid cream, perhaps?"

"Nope," Barry says, not missing a beat. "We've signed the deal with Archie. He'll be here soon."

My mouth drops open. *Shit, that was fast.* I never spoke to him. Never begged him hard enough not to leave Rossini. "Oh, fuck," I mutter, rubbing my chin. As if I can take the pressure of having anyone else's career in my fucking hands.

"This is a really good thing, Matt," says Chloe quickly. "It will be good to have someone you know and trust running your races. Gets me out of your head, in any case."

If only she knew.

One of Barry's dogs lets out a whimper by the door.

"Nature calls," he says. "Have fun, you two. I like this." He waves a finger between Chloe and me as he backs out. "You fit well together at the top of my team. It pleases me to see you bastards getting on."

Chloe and I glance at each other, and I feel an inexplicable rush of shyness, and by the looks of her, so does she. Barry studies us both for a moment, his bushy brows coming together in one long, concerned line.

"Just don't get on too well," he adds, as the gym doors close behind him and Chloe and I are once again alone.

"I need a shower," she says, picking up her towel, fumbling her water bottle; it drops to the floor with a thud. I reach down and pick it up, handing it to her, but she doesn't meet my eyes. "Can you continue this routine across the week? And let's speak to the team trainer about your warm-up, okay? I want to see some reaction work."

"I will follow all orders," I say, saluting her.

"You did good today," she says, looking at the door and then back to me. "But it's time to cool down now."

Yes, I think as I watch her walk toward the door. *I sure as hell need to do that.*

CHAPTER 11

Chloe

"You're out of your fucking minds," Barry says, tearing the end of a burrito as the crew begin to assemble our Austin garage around us. The garages here are roomier than in Singapore, but right now, there's very little but a bunch of crates stacked in one end, a few of which still include the disassembled parts of our cars, and about six of the pit crew taping out the floor in front of us. *We're* also literally on the floor, paperwork everywhere, iPads and computers on laps, coffee in various unfinished states around us.

Weirdly enough, this is what I love. Sitting with my team, deep in the weeds. I don't want to be the kind of team principal who wines and dines celebrities and prances around on the pit lane taking every interview on offer.

I love the science of racing.

"We just want to improve, Barry," I press.

"But a head of aerodynamics? I thought that was your job," he says, flicking his head toward a data analyst. The guy who has the PhD in data science and analytics couldn't be less in charge of aerodynamics. I spot Matt sauntering in, fresh from another workout, another kind of hideous green drink in his hands.

He's looking better already. I know it's only been just over a week since we touched down in Texas, but his face is less red and puffy, his skin clearer. He's even cut his hair.

Matt grins at me, straw in his mouth, one hand in the pocket of his charcoal shorts. He looks so *handsome* today. And the way he keeps looking at me is really fucking distracting. I have worked hard to keep out of his way, and it has offered some respite in these past days. I just hope I can keep my resolve up.

I turn back to Barry to continue arguing.

"If you want us to climb up a few places, we have to think about what to improve on," I say firmly. "This is where we should focus. I'm telling you."

"I'm not a bottomless pit. Even billionaires need to watch their pennies."

"My heart bleeds for you," Matt says.

I glance at the pit crew, embarrassed by the tone of the exchange.

"Then wear the fucking sponsor helmet," Barry shoots back. "And try to do better than eighteenth place so we can get more sponsors," he says.

"I can't do any worse," Matt replies, shrugging playfully.

"Who can't do any worse?" says Noah, who has also just arrived, box-fresh cowboy hat on, which he takes off and frisbees across the room, landing it perfectly in an open bin.

"*You.* Seriously, man, you can't do worse than that hat," Matt says with a slight smirk. Noah's face splits into a grin as he joins us. If this is Matt's attempt at comradery with Noah, it might just work.

"All right, let's try to look forward," I say, holding both my hands up to try to keep everyone focused. "There's no point in going over and over things."

I hear a scoff half-heartedly disguised as a cough from one of the pit crew, then a snigger from that damn strategist. Now it's my turn to shrink a little inside. An angry owner who doesn't listen to me, two drivers who need to gel, fast, a crew who doesn't respect me because I'm a PR hire—how am I going to manage it all?

"Chloe is absolutely right," Matt cuts in loudly, in a deep, commanding tone, which triggers even Barry to adjust his posture. "We should be focusing on the race ahead. I know *I've* got work to do. And . . . um . . . sponsors to attract."

I glance at him gratefully, but his eyes are on the crew, shooting any unrest down with a pointed glare in their direction. I am almost loath to admit it, but having Matt tuned in, focused, and on my side is *a godsend*.

I turn back to Barry. "We have the upgrades coming next week, but we really need someone who can approach the entire car with that holistic view on drag to keep developing into next year and beyond," I say, tipping my head, slightly widening my eyes. Fuck it, I'll use all my resources to get what I need, even the girlish pleading puppy dog look. "It really would impact our results."

Barry is onto me right away, and half grins at the audacity of me trying to sweet-talk him. "More, more, fucking more," he says, sighing.

"You can hire him outside of the budget cap," I remind him. "We are allowed to have three people outside the budget cap, and we only have the two right now."

"So out of my *personal* money," Barry says, scoffing. "The *audacity*. Meeting adjourned. I'm going to get some air."

Matt sucks his smoothie loudly through his straw, watching Barry leave, then he looks back to me.

"We need sponsors to take the financial pressure off Barry," I say pointedly. "He's not the bottomless pit of Rossini. He's one guy."

"One billionaire," he shoots back, unsympathetically. But I can see a hint of sheepishness on his face. So much hangs on his performance and his ability to attract sponsors. He tosses the rest of his drink in the bin. "Kale, cucumber, avocado, wheatgrass, sea algae, hemp powder, and *vegan* protein powder. I'm doing enough today."

"*Matt*," I scold, trying not to smile, as two of the garage technicians tut away behind me. He might be showing me some support, but he's going to have to work hard to undo the damage of his behavior from last race weekend.

"I'm doing my job, happily drinking the damn pond slime," he says, raising both hands in the air. "No worries." He shoots me a cheeky grin, his eyes sparkling.

"Well. I'm pleased to say your seat molding arrived," I say. "We can do some checks and make sure you're a good fit."

"About fucking—" Matt stops himself, appears to take a breath, turns to the crew, who look braced for more criticism. "Sorry. That's great news. Can't wait to check it out."

Three hours later, we've made some great pre-race progress. Noah and Matt are on an iPad watching some of the footage from Singapore, whooping and groaning intermittently. The pit crew are doing drills and Barry has mercifully left for a seven-course dinner across town with *Vanity Fair*. A dinner he wanted me to attend to shmooze, but I declined.

Around seven, I get a call from the reception of the pit garages.

"Ahh . . . Did someone order dinner?" I say, holding my hand over the phone. "There's a dinner delivery?"

I turn to the pit crew, who don't hear my small voice as it's swallowed up by the sound of drills and crashing metal. "Guys!" I shout louder.

They stop their drills and turn to me. "Anyone order dinner?"

"Nah, we're going out for tacos," says one. "Last night of fun before we got to knuckle down for the race."

"Thanks for the invite," I joke, and when they look incredibly shamefaced, I wave a hand. "Don't worry. I'm just joking. Have fun!

"Matt?" I say, turning to him.

"Oh yeah," he says, closing the iPad and looking a little flustered, as he springs up, patting his trousers down looking for his wallet. "That's my dinner."

"Do you mind if I take that as our cue, chief?" says Noah. "I got a date."

Noah glances at Matt, looking for some bro-to-bro nod of approval, which Matt reluctantly gives. "Better not wear that cowboy hat, though."

Noah beams back at Matt. "See you tomorrow, Dials," he says and scurries out of the garage before Matt has the chance to strangle him.

"Let's all call it a night, then," I say to the room, folding down my laptop and arranging all my belongings into my tote. "Everyone! Same time tomorrow?"

The rest of the crew start to clear up their things. It was a slightly lighter mood in the garage today. Matt even tried to act like a nice, normal human being, coaxing some laughs out of the crew. We might be the shittiest team on the circuit, but there is a little hint of hope with the upgrade. Let's just pray it does well in testing.

As everyone clears out, a guy in a bright orange delivery driver outfit walks in with several paper bags filled with food and two six-packs of beer. His eyes brighten as he spots Matt Warner moving toward him with a crisp hundred-dollar bill, and it becomes quickly apparent that this wasn't dinner just for Matt.

I hesitate. *He bought the crew dinner?*

"Matt, what is this?" I say, my voice dropping, but he ignores me, posing for a selfie with the delivery guy, before they slap their hands together in an enthusiastic shake.

"Well," Matt says, pausing as the last member of the crew leaves through the side door, and we are suddenly, despite all my best efforts, alone once again.

"I thought I'd get dinner for everyone, but I guess I forgot other people have lives." He laughs, but the smile never quite reaches his eyes. "Got room for a bunch of ribs and an ice-cold beer?"

"Ribs!" I jump up and examine the insides of the bags to find enough ribs, slaw, and warm bread to feed half the pit lane. My stomach rumbles. I look back at Matt, whose mouth is fixed in a straight line, a hand in his hair, and my heart bruises for him. I can't run off and leave him alone with all this barbecue, which smells, frankly, insanely good. I hesitate, as we catch each other's eye, and I make the call.

"You know what? I have enough room for ribs."

You can do this, Chloe. This is a good way to normalize things.

I put my purse down and pull a foil pack of ribs from one of the bags, tipping my head for Matt to join me. "Come on, then. Is there any barbecue sauce in there?"

He grins gratefully, knocking the cap off his beer with his palm on the edge of the wood crate. The motion brings a heady wave of nostalgia, watching Matt do that on a fence post at Silverstone. We'd snuck in for MotoGP and F1, the first time hiding in the bed of his dad's truck. Then later, the two of us took a wire cutter to the chain links and slid in free, drinking our own beers in the stands as though we were paying customers. We did it each year until Matt got invited by Rossini as a guest. I couldn't get the clips off the fence posts by myself, so I sat in a tree, alone, able to make out about ten meters of track.

"Still don't have a bottle opener, huh?"

"I'm just having the one," he says, mistaking my nostalgia for concern, nodding at one of the six-packs.

"Race day is five days away," I say, awkwardly smiling at him before I tear the rack of ribs in two. I look back up at him and grin. "You can have one and a half," I say mock sternly.

"You got it, boss." He shoots me a cheeky smile and hands me an open can.

I stare out across the brightly lit garage, then turn to him. "Actually, shall we take this outside?"

"Good plan, Bug," he says, lifting his food as we wander out into the mellow light of the pit lane and settle on two closed crates. It's quiet. There is some activity in the McLaren garage a few doors down, but otherwise it's empty out there. The heat has been cooking the track all day, and there's that familiar thick smell of baked tarmac, mixing with the sweet smell of barbecue sauce.

"*Now* I feel like I'm in Texas," I say.

"That heat. That smell," he says, nodding.

"And the pork," I reply. "This is exceptionally good shit."

"I go there every year," he says, chugging his beer.

"Yeah?"

The small talk. The pleasant chitchat. We can do this.

Matt lifts his beer and hesitates, before he says, "Stavros found it." The comment sits out there in the night air, as I wait quietly for him to elaborate, but he doesn't. He drinks. He sits quietly.

"He was a bit of a foodie, wasn't he? Didn't he have a restaurant in his hometown in Greece?" I remark, trying to keep him talking. He nods, looking like he's deep in thought.

"Did you ever go there?"

"In Kefalonia? Of course I did. I was at the launch. Wouldn't have missed it for the world. We practically lived there during the offseason." His smile at the memory fades as soon as it appears.

"You miss him."

Matt blows out a long breath. "Yup," he says softly.

"That's why you don't let Noah in."

"I'm trying with him."

"I know. I can see that," I say, frowning at him. "But it's all banter. You keep him at arm's length. Haven't you ever wanted to guide a younger driver?"

"Not really," he says, but I can see his eyelids flicker as he swallows. He's *so* lying.

Matt reaches for the coleslaw, fishing around in the bag for a plastic fork. "It's not Noah's fault. I worry about getting close to another driver, you know? Stavros practically haunts me on the track," he says.

"He does?" I ask, turning my head to him. "The flashes?"

"Yep. My best friend. In a blazing fire *I* caused. Doesn't get more nightmarish than that."

I try to suck in my breath inconspicuously, covering my mouth with my beer, but Matt catches me.

I want to ask him if it's true he hasn't been to visit Stavros. But it simply couldn't be, could it? That he could abandon his best friend like that? I get that I was delusional about how much *our* friendship meant, but Stavros and Matt's bond seemed legendary.

"It's okay, Chloe," he says, reaching up to scratch the back of his head. "I'm ah . . . I'm already speaking with a therapist. We're working on it."

"You are?"

"I am."

I shake my head in disbelief. "I'm so glad to hear that. Why didn't you mention this sooner?"

"I know, I should have told you already. I wasn't planning on telling *anyone*, except my brother, of course." He turns to face me, eyes narrowing. "You know, I forgot how easy you are to talk to. I missed this."

I mentally feed the half-baked compliment into a shredder, a new trick I've employed to survive the torrent of sweet things Matt has said lately. I look out to the pit lane. *He's just being nice. It doesn't mean what you think it does, Chloe.*

"You didn't miss this?" he prods when I don't reply. "It's a shame we lost contact."

The lack of self-awareness is truly stunning. Stunning enough to make me spit out my beer, laughing. "Oh, okay, Matt."

"What?" he shoots me a confused look. "I'm serious. I

was lying in bed the other night, and I remembered your pet rabbit Senna. What happened to Senna?"

"He's dead," I say, though I can't hide my surprise that he remembered. "It's been, like, ten years, and rabbits only live to about nine."

"I'm sorry," he says as he pours out a little of his beer. "Rest in peace, little Senna. It's shame I wasn't there for the funeral."

I laugh at the absurdity of it. "Yeah. You were really missed at my pet rabbit's funeral," I say, playing along.

"If I'd known I would have rolled up in my black suit and sunglasses to pay my respects."

I roll my eyes. "You met him, like, once. And he was a bunny."

"So?" he asks, grinning. "You talked about him so much, I kept forgetting he was a rabbit."

I cannot help but laugh. "Wait. Did you think I had an invisible friend, Matt?"

"You were the type," he says.

"I was *the type*?" I say in mock outrage.

Matt's face scrunches up and he laughs so hard, no sound comes out until he gasps for air. He reaches for a napkin to cover his face, and his laughter is so infectious that I find myself joining in. "I'm kidding, I'm kidding," he splutters.

"Fuck you," I say. "At least I *had* friends."

He tips his head now, his laughter subsiding. "Well, we both struggled a bit on that front. It was slim pickings in Juniors. Such rich wankers. Like that Jack Sheppard."

He tosses his napkin to the ground as he says Jack's name. For someone as rich as Matt is now, he acts weirdly jealous of the guy.

"You know what *was* fun?" I say. "Those times we snuck in to watch the racing at Silverstone."

"Oh yeah. And remember when we snuck in *offseason*?" he says, laughing, and my face breaks into a huge smile as the memory floods back in.

"Of course I do. You stole the Bambino karts," I recall, laughing. "And we raced them for hours. You couldn't fit your feet inside the car."

"That's the only reason you won," he says, shaking his head as the laughter subsides. "Fucking hell, those days were a laugh."

"The best," I say, standing, reaching out a hand to pull him up. He glances at my fingers for a moment before taking my hand.

"Share an Uber?" I suggest.

"Guess we better," he replies, crushing his second beer as I quickly order the car. "I enjoyed that, Chloe. Really. It's so nice to be working with you. Even if everything else about this sucks."

"*Obviously*," I say, rolling my eyes.

"It's true," he replies, and I can feel his eyes on me as I pack away the food mess. "I'm glad to have you back in my life. I'm lucky, actually. Really lucky."

I glance back up him, his skin shimmering in the golden glow of the last of the daylight, his eyes sincere, and I have to summon all my strength just to nod in reply. He was always so handsome, but these were the moments that sealed my fate all those years ago. These quiet, private moments, with a Matt only I knew. Sensitive. Thoughtful. Surprisingly funny.

"Just like old times," I say, bittersweet nostalgia sweeping through me as I stand to face him. I can't seem to look away from his gaze, which only intensifies as our eyes meet.

"We should do this again," he says quickly. *Seriously.*

"I'd love that," I reply, despite myself, and Matt's face softens into a warm smile. Then his eyes narrow a little on me, like he has more to say.

But un unmistakable buzz comes from the phone in my hand. "Five minutes," I say, looking at the screen. "We better go."

Matt gathers all the food mess and tosses it into a black garbage bag by the track exit. We touch our passes to the gate, wander outside, and wait for our Uber in a heavy silence. The crickets are deafening, the sun setting in the distance, and it will be dark before we are back at the hotel.

Matt is quiet. He's not standing too close, but I can feel his presence radiating like a warm fire. I've *always* been able to feel him. In the car back, we barely speak, staring out our respective windows, the gap between us as wide as I can make it. Is this companionable silence, or is there something else going on?

I can see, out of the corner of my eye, Matt turn toward me a few times as though he wants to say something. But then his body shifts, and he looks back out the window. When we're just five minutes from the hotel he seems to spring to life.

"Let's walk the last few blocks," he says suddenly.

"Without security?" I scan the sidewalk; it's a busy street. No way Matt won't get recognized.

"It's only a few blocks," he insists.

"It's not a good idea. You'll get swamped."

"Not in Texas. Come on, I need to walk off these ribs."

It doesn't feel like that's why we're stopping, but still, I follow his lead and climb out of the car. We move through the foot traffic, both with our eyes on the ground. I sneak glances at him while scanning the people around us. I get the feeling he's trying to delay saying something.

And then, on this warm Austin night, the skies open above us and it starts to downpour. "Oh god!" I say, ducking for the awning of a nearby antique shop as the streets clear, with people clamoring into cars and under other dark and dry awnings down the street. We stand in silence for a moment, watching the rain pour, clawing our damp hair out of our faces. My shirt is soaked and clinging to my skin.

"Bit of a dumb idea to walk," Matt admits. "My trainers are soaked."

"Well, look," I say, thumbing at the window. "We picked a good place to wait out the rain."

He turns and we both lean in against the glass to get a better look at the F1 memorabilia display in the shopwindow. Vintage Rossini gloves, a brake disk signed by Mark Webber. A Ferrari helmet worn by Kimi. Danny Ricciardo's Nomex shirt from his time at Red Bull.

"Jesus, is that a leather jacket worn by Senna?" I say, gasping.

"He probably only wore it once," Matt quips. "Everyone's used shit is here."

"Except yours," I point out.

"I can offer a private sale of my now wet socks if that's what you're after, Chloe."

We both chuckle along, but then there is a heavy silence.

The clapping of shoes on the sidewalk as the rain starts to ease from a downfall into a light shower. The purring rise and fall of passing traffic. Sirens in the distance.

"So . . . if you're not dating Jack Sheppard, who *are* you dating?" Matt asks, his eyes still on the window display.

Where did that come from?

"No one," I say. "Are you dating?" I shoot back, unable to help myself.

"Not recently," he replies coolly.

"It's hard to keep up," I tease, enjoying the dig.

"I was only seriously dating Maria Colenso."

"The daughter of the Rossini engineer?"

"Yep. Made things a bit awkward on the track for a couple of years after that imploded."

"And there's yet another example of why you should never screw the crew," I say, as though I've been keeping a mental checklist.

Matt turns to face me and stills, leaning against the glass of the storefront. I risk a glance at him and the intensity of his stare pins me to the spot. His hair, like mine, is wet and hanging slick against his forehead. His shirt is damp and clinging to the muscles along his arms, slightly transparent. The warm light from the streetlamp hits his face perfectly, bringing out the green flecks in his eyes. He flicks his hair back out of his face, and the corner of his mouth turns up in just a hint of a smile.

I look down at my hands, then adjust my tote on my shoulder and turn my attention once again to the contents of the storefront. In the distance is the wail of a siren, like a warning not to go any further.

Matt finally breaks the silence. "I know it's not ideal, but

I gave up trying to have anything normal. It's hard with this life."

"Truth."

"You never met anyone, Chloe? Never fell in *love*?" he asks, and although the delivery of this question is light, I can detect the awkwardness in his tone.

I do not take my eyes off the contents of that store.

"Sure," I say.

"When?"

"Oh, way back." I take a breath, facing him again. On some level, I guess I want him to know the truth, humiliating as it is. I bravely hold his gaze and his jaw twitches, those hazel eyes dancing side to side, scanning me for the truth. A bead of rainwater trails down his temple, and I have to resist the urge to wipe it away. Instead, I tuck my own wet locks of hair behind my ears. And I breathe. *Slowly.* My heart seems determined to unsettle me with heavy thuds against my chest.

"Who?" he pushes. And then I see that little curl at the edge of his mouth and the crinkle in the corner of his eye, and I feel unsure I can trust him with this deeply personal fact.

"Why are you asking me this?" I shoot back, folding my arms, backing away from the storefront and from him. I feel Matt's hand on mine as he tugs me away from the curb and under the awning into the darkness. His hand is warm, and gentle.

I hear his breath catch slightly as he waits, but I don't respond.

I don't really need to. I'm angry with him. *Why is he badgering me? What is he looking for from this conversation?*

Before I have a chance to walk away, he reaches toward

me, his hands grazing slowly up my arm. He touches me *so* gently, it tickles, and my body twitches against his fingers. I feel so fragile under his touch. Like thin glass. Like I might shatter if I move.

"It's still raining," he says quietly.

"Mm-hm," I barely reply, my voice thin as his fingers move down my arm again, and I try not to sink into the delicious friction against my damp skin. He's never touched me like this before. It's tentative. This is no friendly arm draped around my shoulder, or bear hug after a race. This is different. This touch is filled with longing, with *intentions.*

I don't blink, I barely breathe, until he gently lays one hand on my cheek, and then I let out a small breath. He smiles tenderly at me, as the rain intensifies against the awning. Then his thumb moves slowly toward my mouth and he traces my lips lightly.

Is he going to kiss me? Is . . . is this happening?

The tension between my anxiety and my desire makes me feel like I'm levitating.

"Matt . . ." I whisper, as his eyes move from my mouth to meet mine, and he looks at me in a way he never has before. A whole new Matt. Gentle. Determined. And maybe, just a hint of vulnerability too.

"You're so beautiful," he whispers.

The response from my body is instant, my nipples tighten against the thin, wet cotton of my T-shirt, and I hate that my desire for Matt is, in the end, so instinctual.

Before I have a chance to reason with myself, or think about anything but the million little sparklers that are currently firing across my skin, my lips part for him and he dips down toward me and presses his lips against mine. So gently. So tentatively.

Matt tastes delicious—like barbecue and beer, sweet and fragrant. His lips are just as soft as I've imagined all these years.

His hand barely moves on my face, and in a single heated breath, the gentle kiss moves from something sweet and nervous to ravenous, as my mouth opens wider for him and he kisses me hungrily, his hand curling around my waist and yanking me closer.

So much longing fills my body. I love him. I am angry with him. I want him. I have always wanted him.

I find no way to stop as I find myself reaching up and clawing at his hair. I'm rough. I want *more.*

Matt's hands are all over my body, roughly tugging at my T-shirt as he snakes a hand underneath, fingers searching for my breasts. He's gentle but single-minded, and I find myself arching into him as his palm grazes my nipples through my damp bra.

I moan into his mouth and bite him gently on his lip. He laughs, and moves in closer, pulling me toward his hips as he presses into me. Jesus fucking Christ, he's hard, and the thought makes me feel as though I'm drowning, my body falling limply into him.

Suddenly, I'm pushed up against the glass, and with expert ease, he slips his hand down the waistband of my skirt. I am aching for him to touch me, but he pauses, his fingers so close, and he stares at me, searching my eyes for permission.

"Please," I say, my voice gravelly and hoarse. His hand fans out, his fingers curling between my thighs as that whisper of a smile returns. "Don't tease me," I say, pushing forward into his hand, hungrily.

Matt seems to take a moment, closes his eyes, and buries his face briefly in my hair, inhaling deeply.

"Please, Matt," I say again. "I want you to."

He obeys with a groan into my ear, his fingers pushing aside the elastic of my lace thong and moving expertly to find my clit. I gasp, stiffening under his touch, but he just groans again, this time into my mouth, as he kisses me hard.

"Fuck," he says. And then his other hand moves from my breast to my lower back and his head drops onto my shoulder, his breath hot on my neck. I want him to move his fingers. To fill me up inside with them. I want so much that release that I always felt only Matt could give me.

His first stroke is soft, and I cry out, with the intensity of the pleasure and the sensitivity. *It's been so long since anyone has touched me like that*, I think, and then I push the thought away.

"Please," I say again. *Before I think too much.*

His second stroke is long and I hear his breath hitch as I move against his finger.

I can feel how wet I am as he continues to stroke me gently, rhythmically, and I cling to his neck, hanging there in delicious pleasure, my body giving away my desire completely. I want more. I want all of it right here. Right now.

He moves his finger down and teases my entrance, moving the tip of his finger against me, while never sliding it inside. My body is flooded with heat, my mind swimming. I move against him again, tugging at his hand, pulling it toward me.

"You feel delicious, Chloe," he says, pulling back to kiss my neck as I feel the cold glass on my back, his breath moving to my ear, my chest heaving. "You're so hot."

Speech isn't something I can manage right now, but I do manage to let out another strangled growl as he circles my clit again. He's driving me crazy with this teasing game.

"I want to do this properly. I want to take my time," he whispers, between kisses. "Let's take this to the hotel."

His words immediately cut through the frenzy and I'm alert again. Suddenly I can hear traffic, and people's voices, and footfalls, and even though we're out of sight I'm seized by a fear of being caught. I pull at his wrist, and he hesitates, before sliding his hand up and wrapping his fingers around my waistband, tugging at me to come closer.

"Matt," I whisper into his mouth, against my lips. His hands move back to my face right away, and I can see his pupils have dilated. His eyes look almost black in this lighting, his desire for me undeniable. It's enough to almost make me change my mind. *Almost.*

"We should stop. People will recognize us." I say it so quietly, so gently, and so at odds with my body I can barely get the words out.

"But," he says hoarsely, almost as if in pain, "I don't want to stop, and I have a feeling you really don't either."

"You're right, I don't want to. But we *have* to."

I feel him stiffen in my arms, and he pulls back to look at me. He is ravaged. His hair tousled, his lips red and swollen. An unmistakable bulge presses into my hip, and I try not to imagine him sliding inside me, taking me to the brink again. I'm still clutching him hard, so I loosen my grip a little. Matt's eyes are resolute.

"This is a mistake," I say, my breathing heavy.

He looks like he's just been slapped. "Do you really think that?"

I don't know how to answer. Part of me doesn't think this is a mistake. Part of me, the romantic, whimsical girl inside, believes this is what always should have been. But *all of me* knows this can't end up anywhere good. It's a no-win feeling that can't be figured out between Matt's sheets tonight.

When I don't respond, he takes a small step back and puts his hands in his jean pockets. "Okay. You go to the hotel first, then I'll follow. No one will see us," he says.

He takes a moment, looking frantically at me, and then he smiles sadly, dropping his head so our foreheads touch and we both try to slow our breathing.

"But who gives a fuck if it's a mistake? We're adults," he whispers.

I step back. "We have to go," I say. Unable to find any other words, I try to smooth the creases in my T-shirt where Matt's fingers bunched it up just moments ago.

I look in the reflection of the shopwindow, stepping slowly back. My hair is damp and wild, my nipples still hard under my shirt. I'm desperately unsatisfied, and by the look of Matt, he is too. That kiss will never be enough. *Never.* And yet.

"This can't ever happen again, Matt," I say, feeling tears of frustration prickling in my eyes. "For the sake of the team and our careers." *And because it'll completely undo me.*

I turn in the direction of the hotel, my stomach churning. And I hear Matt call out to me. "You think you can just turn this feeling off?"

I don't respond. I already know the answer.

CHAPTER 12

Matt

United States Grand Prix
Qualifying

Security strides alongside me on the paddock as I head over to the garage, my lanyard swinging, eyes to tarmac, avoiding any potential interruptions. It's busy already. Press. Sponsors. Rich fans with VIP tickets milling around for a glimpse of their favorite driver. Plenty of the team principals are out here too; I spot my old Rossini boss and pick up the pace.

All I want to do is see Chloe. The clouds overhead have cleared, and the bright blue Texas sky beats down on my skin. I feel like a vampire, shrinking from the light. I didn't sleep. My mind has been swimming.

"Good luck today," says the security guard, as I disappear into the cool darkness of the hallway.

I'm about to quip back, "I'll need a miracle," but I catch myself.

"Thanks, man," I say instead, squeezing past two crew members as I make my way down to the garage.

And there she is. The first face I see across the brightly lit room. Our eyes meet briefly and she nods, her face impassive as though I'm just another member of the crew. But the little darkening of her cheeks tells a different story. I smile to myself.

"Little brother." Archie tips his Arden cap toward me and I shake my head.

"You look a fucking mess," I say, throwing my arms around his hulky frame and giving him a big squeeze.

"Your driving is the fucking mess," he says, grinning, then he turns to the team and booms, "How do you pricks work with such a useless wanker?"

Laughter fills the garage, and Archie slaps me on the shoulder. If there's one thing Archie knows how to do, it's bringing a team together at my expense.

I finally talked to my brother three days ago. He was at some country music festival outside Dallas and was readying himself for the move. We argued, as we always do, but Archie was adamant he was coming. And besides, he told me, "The deal was fucking inked" and I had to "get the hell used to it."

Now that he's here, I'm mostly happy. An uncomplicated friend with whom I can be almost entirely myself with.

I watch him walk over to Chloe and bear-hug her next, lifting her whole frame off the ground as he does. Her smile stretches across her face, and her cheeks flush pink with a mix of embarrassment and delight. I force myself to look away. It is nearly impossible to look at her now without wanting her. I can't get that damn kiss out of my mind. I can't get *her* out of my mind.

Where the hell did it come from? She was . . . well, she was like a kid sister. You could play out my life a million times over and I'd never have guessed I'd end up *wanting* Chloe Coleman. *Never.*

I've felt the shift between us these past couple of weeks, though. Getting to know Chloe again after all these years—her fiery, smart, sexy self—it was just a matter of time before that spark turned into something real. Then we lit the match.

But she was clear. "This is a mistake." She doesn't want to get entangled with me, and she's right that it would be messy. But damn, how am I going to push aside these feelings? Whatever this intense thing is between Chloe and me has been snatched away before we've even had a chance.

It's been a really, really long time since I've been able to let my guard down like that, just talking, hanging out. And then having this intense desire for her too? It's practically intoxicating.

"Let's go!" Archie booms across the room. "Qualifying is just around the corner."

I chuckle, glancing at Chloe as Archie pushes her toward the pit lane, but she waves him away. "Later, later," she says.

I keep watching her pacing the room as she talks to someone on the phone, stopping only to point at data on-screen, and then she looks over and catches my eyes on her. She knows when I'm watching. Just like I can feel her eyes on me. How long can this go on without relief? I turn to the car and employ some of the visualization tricks my therapist recommended for when I'm out on the track.

I need to get my head in the game and off Chloe Coleman.

■■■■■■■■■■

The difficulties don't begin until I'm around the third bend and on to the chicane, but when they do, I lose just enough time trying to readjust and focus on the track to drop out of the first round of qualifying. In the end, I'm seventeenth.

"It's better than last qualifying," Chloe says as soon as I get back to the garage and climb out of the car.

"Better than nineteenth. Wow," I say, pulling out my earplugs.

"Better is better," she says firmly. "We only need better every day and then the good part comes. Noah got sixteenth."

"Good for him," I say sharply, as someone drops an ice towel around my shoulders.

Chloe frowns at me.

"Sorry. It *is* good for him. I'm happy for him," I say quietly. Then I raise my voice across the garage. "Nice one, Noah."

Noah looks delighted and shoots back a thumbs-up, while Chloe whacks me in the arm with her iPad. "That just sounded sarcastic," she says scoldingly.

"I can't fucking win," I say.

Archie comes bowling across and he grimaces as he pulls down his headphones. "Chicane?" he guesses.

I nod. "But only there," I say.

"Chlo, mind if I take little bro out back for a chin-wag?" Archie says, covering the mic on his headpiece.

"She knows about the *issues*," I say, nodding toward Chloe.

Archie looks around; some of the pit crew are listening in. "Fuck it," I say, pulling my gloves off, deciding then and there not to make a secret out of it anymore. "Everyone else may as well know. At least then you can all work with it."

"Brave of you," says Chloe quietly.

I tip my head a little in thanks, avoiding those eyes in case I see pity. I don't want to see pity from Chloe.

"Well," Archie begins. He pulls out his iPad and starts to swipe through some of the numbers. "Before that, we got a pretty good gauge of the car speed. You were fast in turns six through nine. In fact, third fastest."

"Third fastest!" Chloe can barely contain her delight.

"I was?" I frown in disbelief.

"Yeah, but ahh . . . on the straights the speed just falls apart," Archie says. "And it isn't because of your . . . troubles. We really need to look at the drag," he says, turning to Chloe.

"What we need is that head of aerodynamics!" Chloe says, raising her voice a little so it's loud enough that Barry can hear. "Someone to bring in all the ideas and make them cohesive."

"Tell your driver to accept the fucking sponsor!" replies Barry from the back of the room, feeding his dogs strips of chicken from a paper bag and then stroking their heads.

"I'm not wearing a fucking hot sauce logo on my forehead."

Barry waves us over, and after a brief glance between me,

Archie, and Chloe, we head to the little desk at the back of the garage to join him.

"I don't know really what a head of fucking aerodynamics does," he says, throwing his hands in the air. I roll my eyes toward Archie like, *Why the fuck does this guy even own a racing team?* "I can take a guess. But I trust Chloe when she says she needs one."

"Thanks, Barry," Chloe says, looking surprised by the frank admission.

"See these beautiful little guys?" Barry says, stroking the head and neck of Ginger and then Roger. "You know where I found them?"

He looks at me, pointedly.

"No," I say slowly. "Where did you find them, Barry?"

I cross my arms over my chest, ready for some grand and pointless tale about god only knows what.

"They were racing dogs. Ginger there was kept in a cage. Too timid, they never let her race. And Roger? He was lame. Front leg was septic after an injury no bastard saw to. He was about to be shot," Barry says, wiping his hands on his trousers and looking over to me. "I snuck into the yard with my mate Reg, and we stole both of them."

"You rescued them, Barry?" Chloe asks, looking at Ginger and smiling. I have to admit, I'm surprised by this.

"You're fucking right I did," he says. "My parents raced dogs. And horses. My grandparents too. But I hated it. It was a cruel sport. But I had the racing bug. So, I broke from my parents and bought a dirt bike to race instead. I couldn't be in the business of racing animals."

Archie and I exchange a look, both of us seemingly wondering where this is going.

"I'm not the smartest of blokes, Matt. I don't really know how the hell your team makes a fucking multimillion-dollar road-ready spaceship. But I want to give you what you need. I want you to do well. I want you to win."

"I'm not a dog," I protest.

"Oh, but you are, Matt. You're lame. And someone was going to eventually pull the trigger. And like Ginger, Chloe is afraid to put herself out there."

"Good grief," Chloe mutters under her breath as the analogy becomes crystal clear.

"I don't want *rescuing*. I want to race," I counter.

"You want to race?" he says, with such ferocity I nearly jump backward. "Great. But I've taken all the risk here on a dog with a limp, so what are you going to do for me?"

I drop my arms and nod slowly. "The sponsor."

"I can't do this if you don't," he says, the most truthful I've ever seen him look.

"And if I do, can we look into bringing in a drag expert?" I say, glancing over at Chloe for the briefest of moments.

"Sure." Barry stands up, slipping a lead around Ginger's neck and then doing the same to Roger. "Yes, Matt. You wear the helmet, and Chloe can go find herself a head of aerodynamics."

"That's the one," says Chloe, looking thrilled.

"Fine," I say. "I'll wear the damn logo."

"Yes!" Chloe blurts out, standing up. "Thanks, Barry. And Matt."

"I'm not giving you much," Barry says. "You'll be able to afford a fucking grad student, but it's not nothing."

"It's a start," Chloe says. "*Thank you.*"

"Let me know if I can help with my helmet design or anything," I say, unable to stop my smart-ass mouth.

"I gotta go," Barry says, then he shoots me a wry grin. "Helmet's already done." He kicks a large crate under his desk.

After Barry leaves, Chloe pulls the box out and drops it onto the desk.

"I never thought to ask about the dogs," Chloe says, using a wrench to force the lid of the crate open.

"Barry has hidden layers," I say, grinning.

"Guys, I'm going to fire up the team," says Archie, thumbing toward the strategists. "Looks like there's some press waiting for you, Chloe?"

She glances over his shoulder toward the waiting crew, and then shakes her head at Archie. "No. Tell them to go away. *Nicely.*"

"You're going to have to get out there and do these press interviews, Chloe." I pause for a minute, then continue, "Think of it as the next step to overcoming *your* 'issue.' And by the sounds of it, you need a fucking agent."

"I hate the press stuff, though," she says, lifting the lid and pulling out the helmet. "I'll tell you what. I'll do a press interview, if you finish above fifteen tomorrow."

"Unfair," I say, laughing.

"There it is," she says, spinning the helmet around so I can see "Mind My Hot Rear" emblazoned across the back.

"I can't believe he already went ahead and approved it," I

say, snatching the helmet from Chloe. "That whole speech was just to remind us to be grateful."

"Nah," she says, smiling. "I think he wants us to know he actually cares." She holds the helmet toward me. "You gonna wear this for the race tomorrow, then?"

"Yes," I say, rolling my eyes.

"And are you speaking with the therapist later?"

I nod and take the helmet from her, turning it around to inspect the bright yellow-and-red logo.

"Here," she says, tearing the plastic seal off the strap. "We better make sure it fits." She grins.

I let her do it. I let her move in close to me and reach her arms up toward me. I try not to watch her breasts rise as she reaches above me and then pulls the helmet down hard over my head.

She flicks up the visor and we stare at each other for a moment. Chloe quickly smiles, but I can see the worry behind her eyes.

"Are you okay?" I whisper through my helmet, and then quickly add, "About last night? I've been trying to get in contact with you."

She nods quickly, her cheeks coloring a little again. "I'm sorry. I can't open that door, Matt. This job is too important to me to throw it away on something that's just too . . ." She stumbles, her big brown eyes burning into me as she clears her throat. "*Disruptive.* To the team." She was going to say *dangerous*. She's afraid of what would happen between us, and I'm not sure I understand why.

Still, she's making it clear she wants me to bury it. Keep things professional. "Are *you* okay?" she says, her eyes hopeful.

I'm no liar, but I tell her what she needs to hear in this moment to keep going.

"Focusing ahead," I reply.

Chloe nods, looking to the floor. Is she sad? Relieved? What I wouldn't give to be in her head right now. Then one of the strategists calls out to her, and she's off to join Archie.

On my way back to the hotel, alone, I decide to send what feels like the hundredth text to Stavros over the past few months. All of which have gone unanswered. It takes several versions of *Hi again* and *I'm sorry* before I settle on what feels like another empty message.

How are you getting on?

It is read right away, but by the time my head hits my pillow six hours later, there is still no reply.

CHAPTER 13

Chloe

United States Grand Prix
Race Day

After two weeks of preparation, it's race day. I glance up at the screen, where the Sky Sports hosts are walking the pit. "*This* is it. The Circuit of the Americas, in Austin, Texas, set in the five hundred acres of rolling hills outside the city. We have just six races to go before the end of the season, with Rossini's team riding high. This year only one team has failed to get any points . . . the black and green of Arden Racing still unable to finish higher than their season best of fifteenth place way back in Monza."

I groan, pulling my headset off. Yesterday, Matt qualified in seventeenth, and Noah just ahead of him in sixteenth. And with a track this fast, I hold little hope we could see improvements today. But we only need a little, tiny step. Just an inch here and there. Just a few seconds.

As the race gets underway, I listen to Archie guiding Matt. They have famously sparky communication, and this race is no different. Archie's legendary line to Matt as they crossed the finish line first in Monaco is now part of F1 lore, memed and repeated endlessly.

"You're gonna be a fucking nightmare," Archie said, his words broadcast out across the world and played back on every sports channel for a week.

Not *Great work*. Or *Congratulations, you just won your first Monaco Grand Prix*. But "Christ. You're gonna be a fucking nightmare."

It still makes me laugh when I think about it, and I hope that having Archie here will be a lift for Matt.

But as the race progresses, I feel a knot tightening in my stomach.

The crew are sloppy with a pit stop. Noah comes off the track and damages his front wing. Matt seems unable to push past anyone, his once-famous killer instinct completely vanishing as soon as he is within striking distance.

I had allowed myself to hope that Matt was going to somehow pull off a miracle, but my heart sinks as he crosses the line in sixteenth. Just ahead of him, our rookie rider Noah takes fifteenth. When Matt crosses the line, Archie pulls his headphones off and looks at me.

"Let me see the data," I say.

Back in the garage, there is little joy. Despite his best effort, Noah is frustrated, kicking his helmet across the garage and accidently smashing a computer screen. One of the younger mechanics is in tears. The strategist, who has become my nemesis, is playing *Candy Crush* on one of Arden's iPads as I walk in. I snatch it out of his hand and toss it on the bench. He looks at me, defiant.

"Everyone, let's huddle," I say, calling the team into the garage. "Doors down."

The smell of burned rubber and gasoline fills the space. The heat of Noah's car radiates in the already stifling hot air.

"Can we get the coolers on?" I say to no one in particular, just as the pumps start to blow. "Right. Better today. We have taken a step up from last race, and that's all I ask."

"I suck," Noah says, plonking down on the floor as he peels off his balaclava and gloves.

"No. You showed some real class on turn three to take the Williams."

"Fifteenth is terrible," Noah says, petulantly kicking away his sponsored water bottle.

"If fifteenth is terrible, then how about sixteenth?" says Matt, pulling off his own balaclava and nodding grimly in my direction. "It's the pits of fucking hell."

Noah looks mortified, but Matt drops a hand on his shoulder and course-corrects immediately. "You did great today. We should grab a beer and watch it back."

"Anything to see in the data?" Archie asks me hopefully.

"Yes, actually," I say, scanning the numbers and the summary evaluation that's come in from the data team. I feel suddenly energized. "In lap thirty-six, and I almost can't believe this, Matt clocked the fastest time out of the turn-one hill. And sixth fastest during the sweepers in turns seven to nine."

Matt looks across at me, surprise on his face. "That's not nothing, I guess."

"It was a promising moment," I say, smiling broadly, barely believing it myself. "We definitely have problems on the straights, but we can improve that. We know we need to work on drag."

Archie chuckles, and I glance at Barry, who seems pleased as he grins at me while stroking Roger's fur. "Look at my little rescue dogs starting to heal."

I steal a glance at Matt, who looks different; there's a small glimmer of something I've not seen in a long time across his face. Barry is right. Maybe he *is* starting to heal. But before I get too swept up in encouraging Matt, I elbow Noah's race engineer gently in the ribs.

"Oh. Right," he whispers, fumbling around on his iPad. "Noah, you moved up one place from qualifying. Hit a sixth-fastest time, right behind Matt on that turn one."

Noah looks up, smiling shyly. "Wow. That's cool."

"Guys. These numbers *show* we have a little something. That what we're doing, if we can stay focused, will work," I say, clinging hard to this scrap of hope. "We have to believe a lot harder than we do right now. Because we *can* claw up that grid. I know we can."

But I *don't* know. I don't know at all. I glance across at Matt, who nods at me encouragingly.

"I don't think anyone should go home tonight," I say, raising my voice so it fills the room. "Whoever can, should come out for a meal. Let's try to get to know each other a little better. Bond as a team."

"Great idea," Matt says quickly, before anyone has a chance to groan.

"Are you celebrating one good turn in two hundred and thirty-six turns? Let's not over-egg the pudding," Barry says, frowning. "We placed fifteenth and sixteenth. And two cars crashed, so that's basically third and fourth last."

"Also one of the Williamses had a broken wing," mutters that awful strategist, and I have to fight myself not to snarl at him. I need to get rid of him if I ever get settled.

"It doesn't matter. Come on. Who's in?" I raise my hand and look around the room.

Matt's hand shoots up, and then Archie's. I breathe out, looking gratefully at Matt. Thankful that despite everything, at least he has my back.

▪▪▪▪▪▪▪▪▪▪▪▪

In the end, there are seven of the core team who make it out. Archie, Matt, Noah, a young strategy assistant called Michelle, two pit crew members, and I feast on a hastily organized dinner at a karaoke bar. It's the only place we can find that will take us all at the last minute, and, conveniently for me, the same place Keyla and some of the McLaren crew might be heading, per her text.

Archie is in charge, ordering trays of fish and pulled-pork tacos and endless frozen margaritas. Some girl in Daisy Dukes is already on the microphone doing a rendition of "Sweet Home Alabama," much to Noah's delight.

"I thought you were dating someone," Matt says, spotting the thirsty look on Noah's face.

"She bought a new fucking handbag on my room service," Noah shouts back.

Archie and Matt look at each other and laugh.

"Live and learn, my dude," says Matt, holding his beer up to cheers Noah, before grinning my way, as if to say he can't help but banter with the kid.

I mock-scowl back at him before flicking through the

karaoke list, my sloppy fish taco in my other hand. I actually swore I'd never do karaoke again after The Last Time, but it's the perfect bonding exercise for all of us, so I suck it up. We need some fun right now.

A huge gloop of fishy taco juice lands on my white shirt. "I'm filthy." I dunk my napkin into my glass of sparking water and try to wipe off the splodge, but it's no use.

"We have matching stains," says Matt, pointing at his own T-shirt and the trail of black beans on his front.

"Were you raised in a fucking barn?" asks Noah in his poshest accent, while pretending to eat his taco with a knife and fork. Matt finds this hilarious and starts to cut his buffalo wing with a fork, catching the bone and sending the wing flying across the table to hit Noah in the middle of his brand-new Gucci T-shirt.

"We need more shots," says Michelle, before giggling wildly at something one of the two pit hunks has said.

"To not quite coming last," says Matt, who like most drivers saves his drinking for just after a race, and only needs a couple to get any kind of effect. He holds a shot of tequila aloft.

"To the best rear end on the grid," teases Noah, his margarita slopping over the sides of his glass as he toasts Matt.

"You know, he's got a sponsorship coming for an adult nappy," says Archie. "They're getting the spot across your ass."

"Fuck you," says Matt, tossing a deep-fried pepper at him.

"Finish up, you drunk idiots. It's time for a last nightcap. I'm spent," I say, not wanting a repeat of the last time I saw Matt in a bar.

"A nightcap?" Archie roars. "We're just getting started, Bug."

"She doesn't like Bug anymore," Matt says, wagging a finger at Archie as he leans across the table, grinning at me.

"But look at those eyes," says Archie. He uses his thumbs and fingers to stretch his eyelids apart. "Permanently startled. Like a baby deer."

"Cute as hell, though," says Matt, and I shoot him a look: *Stop it.* So he reaches forward and grabs the song list in its plastic folder, leaning across the booth as he pats the cushion playfully. "Sit here and let's choose a song, Chloe," he says, eyebrow raised.

I'm stuck. On the one hand, if I don't move, it will look weird to the others. On the other hand, I don't want to be next to Matt when he's looking at me like he is.

"He won't bite," shouts Archie above a searing rendition of "Total Eclipse of the Heart."

"He might," I whisper under my breath, but I oblige, sliding in next to him. He immediately lifts his arm up and lays it on the back of the seat behind us, making more room for me, but making the space entirely too intimate for my liking.

"If I remember correctly, *you're* the one who likes to bite," he whispers into my ear. The little hairs on my neck start to prickle, but even in my loose and drunken state, I refuse to back down with Matt Warner.

"Matt, not here," I whisper defiantly, unable to stop myself from glaring at him. "We're with my fucking team."

"Later, then?" He gives me a cheeky grin, then quickly shakes it off. "All jokes aside, I want you to know I respect your feelings on the matter. If it's what you want, we'll keep our relationship strictly professional and friendly. But I have this feeling . . . Is that actually what you want?" he says, his mouth dangerously close to that little place just behind my ear as he leans even farther in, handing me a shot from a large tray in the middle of the table.

I don't think I can do this. Be this close to him. Hide how much I want him in this moment—and *any* moment, for that matter.

"I've had enough. Have to keep my wits about me," I say, pushing the shot glass away, starting to feel like I'm in dangerous territory. Drunk, flirtatious, and entirely sweet Matt is doing nothing to help hide the memory of what happened on the street a few nights ago.

"I'm sorry," he says, entirely serious. "Please stay."

"Probably best I go. I don't do karaoke anymore."

"Well, that's too bad, because I actually already chose us a song," he says, pulling an awkward face.

I snap my head around to look at him, his eyes a little glazed, a smile on his face.

"I hope you did not," I say.

"I certainly did."

"Jesus fucking Christ, Matt," I reply, trying to laugh despite the mortification. "Cancel it. Just let Archie do 'Addicted to Love' and let's all get out of here."

He shrugs, a smug look on his pretty face.

"I mean it. Cancel it," I say, hauling myself up. I wander through the club searching for Keyla, elbowing my way past throngs of drunk twentysomethings. I spot McLaren in the opposite corner to us, but no Keyla. *Damn it.*

My stomach knots as I push into the quiet of the bathroom.

I stare at myself hard in the mirror. It is now clear to me how deluded I was back then, because this Matt? The one out there? *He wants me.* I can feel it in every intense glance. In every touch of his hand on my arm.

Still, I don't trust it. What if I'm just some plaything? What if he only fancies me because I'm what's in front of him at this vulnerable point in his life? What if it doesn't mean something to him in the way it does to me? And yet, as I think it, I'm not sure I believe it.

"What have you gotten yourself into, Chloe?" I say to my reflection, and then I sigh, heavily, just as another woman emerges from the adjacent stall.

"Men, right?" she says, pulling out an eyeliner.

"Keyla!" I say, spinning around, pulling her in for a hug. "I looked everywhere."

"I saw you," she says, pulling back, laughing. "Was waiting for the right moment to slip across the aisle and party with the competition."

"I think I'm going home," I say, grimacing.

"Matt?"

"Matt." I don't say any more, but instead study myself in the mirror, looking for the answer in the purple shadows beneath my eyes. I'm exhausted. I cannot lose myself to Matt and whatever *this* is. *I can't.* I have to protect my fledgling career first and foremost.

"I saw it the other night," she says, turning to me, the music thrumming through the bathroom walls. "The way you two looked at each other."

"I gave it all away, didn't I?" I say pitifully.

"The way he looks at *you*, Chloe." She bites her lip as though she doesn't want to elaborate. Then she sighs. "Honestly, it's like he has real feelings for you."

"Oh god." I glance around the room and lower my voice. "I wish we could talk properly," is all I can squeeze out. "I'm really struggling."

"You wanna split?" she asks. "Give me, like, an hour?"

I nod. "Maybe. I might be gone before then with the way this night is headed."

Keyla slumps against the wall. "I just worry for you, Chloe," she says. "I want you to be happy, and maybe Matt is the person who can do that. It would just look *so* bad. Maybe when you've proved yourself, in time . . . but now?"

"It's impossible," I say, my voice almost a whisper.

"Imagine if the press found out."

"We already kissed, Keyla," I confess, my eyes dropping to the floor.

Her face sags as her eyes rake over me, sympathy radiating.

"Well, if you can't stop it," she says, sighing, "you're going to need a burner phone and nerves of steel."

I laugh wearily and we hug. "I'll call you in Mexico," I say as we push our way into the crowd and head in opposite directions. But right as I leave Keyla's side, ready to shut this night down, I hear the announcement of my nightmares.

"Next up we have Bug and Dials. Bug and Dials in the house?"

Did I hear that right?

Matt is craning his neck to look for me, and when our eyes meet, he waves cheerily.

I could run. Right now. I could go back and grab my handbag and run out of the club.

"Come on, Bug. You're up," Matt says, looking pleased with himself.

"Bug! Bug! Bug!" shout the team, fist-pumping the air.

"Bug? *Yikes*," Michelle says, showing me all her teeth in a smile that is 80 percent grimace.

"Great," I say, glaring at Archie and Matt. "How the hell do I get them to respect a boss called Bug?"

"I don't know, but don't leave your crowd waiting," says Archie, motioning that we need to hurry, as Matt pushes me toward the stage, his hand on my lower back.

"Come on, boss, your team have been waiting."

I know what the song is going to be before we even get to the stage, and I pick up the microphone and sigh loudly into it, causing it to squeal. Classic. Absolutely classic. I hold my hand up like a visor and peer around the room at all the faces staring in my direction. The memory comes flooding back, and when I look over at Matt, he appears utterly delighted with himself.

The familiar piano chords of "Don't Go Breaking My Heart" begin and I turn to Matt, who grabs my hand, and I snarl at him, yanking my hand back to hoots and cheers from the audience.

"Matt, you're a pain in the arse, you know that?" I shout over the music.

"Memories, Bug," he says, laughing.

I know he's a little tipsy, but it floors me that he remembers this song. Our song.

It was a karaoke night at the Star and Crown a few weeks before Matt was leaving for Rossini. He pulled a reluctant me onstage then too, and we laughed and squealed our way through this very tune. Matt was holding my hand. Archie was there. All the other drivers. I stumbled off the stage, deliriously happy, and smacked straight into Jack Sheppard.

“You’re so in love with him,” Jack said, rolling his eyes, laughing, as he draped his arm around my shoulder. “Don’t make a fool of yourself.”

I recall it so clearly now. The abject humiliation. Being called out so brutally. But still, I was grateful. It was the smack in the face I needed.

“Don’t go breaking my heart,” Matt sings, his voice warm and gravelly and *almost* in tune. And yet, here he is, a different Matt, in a different time, and now . . . *is it any different?*

“I couldn’t if I tried,” I say back dryly, the sarcasm dripping off my vocals. The room erupts in laughter, which eases the tension a little, and I glare between him and the karaoke screen as we continue to sing, as if I need any help to remember the lyrics to this song.

“Right from the start . . .”

“I gave you my heart.” I half sing, half speak the line and Matt grins at me.

He has no idea how loaded this fucking song is for me.

It’s enough. I stare up at the ceiling, purposefully singing badly off-key, willing the song to end. Matt tries to grab my hand again, but I edge away from him to the end of the stage.

I’m embarrassed as hell. With myself more than anything. I feel like everyone in that booth can tell exactly what’s going on, and they’re going to judge me for it. I shouldn’t be here. I shouldn’t be singing on a stage with Matt Warner.

I'm going home.

When I'm done singing, but before the music is even over, I head back to the table, forcing a smile and offering a little bow to the team.

They applaud and cheer as I fight the heat in my cheeks.

"Have fun!" I say as I grab my handbag and rush out into the heat of the night.

CHAPTER 14

Matt

I fucked up.

After our song, as Chloe heads toward our table, I head to the bathroom, slapping myself on each cheek in front of the mirror. "Pull yourself the fuck together, dude," I bark at my reflection. I look tipsy. I look bleary-eyed. I look ridiculous.

I'm not thinking straight when it comes to Chloe. I was hoping singing our karaoke song would ease the tension, but it was painfully obvious she hated it. And me. I'm not navigating my growing feelings for her very well, and all I know is I fucking *want* her. More than anything I've ever wanted.

The banter. The teasing her. The trying to make light of everything. It's bullshit. I'm just fucking flirting, and it's clearly making things worse.

"Chloe left. What's up with her?" Archie asks when I return to the table. "I thought she loved karaoke?"

"Times have changed," I say, dropping back down onto the seat next to him. "Is she coming back?"

"Dude, she looked upset," Archie says, leaning into me and dropping his voice as much as is possible in this cacophony. Someone on the mic is belting out quite an impressive cover of "Summer of '69."

"Yes, seems so," I murmur, pushing the hair back from my face.

"Matt," says Archie. "Wanna talk?"

"Not really."

"Is she still in love with you or something?"

"What do you mean *still in love with me*?" I shoot back.

"Come on, Matty," Archie says, folding his arms. "You're no fool, my dude. She has feelings for you. She always did."

"She didn't," I say, as the thought unsettles me. "She didn't even come to my leaving party."

"She did," Archie says.

"She told me she didn't."

"Maybe I shouldn't be saying this, but hell, since you both won't talk about it." Archie takes a swig of his beer. "She didn't come into the party that night, but I saw her loitering around outside. She looked really upset."

I turn my head to stare at Archie. I'm not sure I can absorb what he's saying. She came to my big send-off party to F1, but she didn't come in? What happened?

"No way," I say, picking up a shot glass and then tossing it back down. "Even if what you're saying is true and Chloe had feelings for me back then, I think it's definitely the other way around now."

"Either way, she's the fucking boss, isn't she?" Archie says, dropping his voice.

"I know, Archie."

Damn. This situation sucks. I thought that old song of

ours would be fun to sing. I thought that being playful and trying to have a laugh could be a good way to move on from it. Because lord knows I am struggling to move on from it.

"Buongiorno, gentlemen," a voice says, and I glance up to see Marco, my replacement driver from Rossini, with a few of the crew behind him. They're drinking champagne. Of course they are, they just got another podium. "We heard you were out *celebrating*," he adds with a wry smile. He's teasing, but I'm in no mood for it.

"We're masochists," I say dryly.

I sink into my seat as Archie stands up and hugs him warmly. Sometimes I wish Archie wasn't such a lovable guy and had at least one bad bone in his body.

"Matt, you taking up singing now?" Marco says in a beautiful, thick Italian accent.

"Matt's always been a bit of a singer," bellows Archie, cackling before downing another shot.

"You found a new talent at last, Grandpa?" Marco says, grinning, and Archie guffaws even harder. Behind him, a couple of statuesque girls hang off the arms of some of his team. I stare hard at one of the girls and she smiles coyly back, her eyelashes fluttering. Part of me wants to respond. To turn it on for her and take her back to the hotel with me.

She's not Chloe, though.

"That's right," I say, dragging my eyes back to the shot glass on the table.

I sink further into my seat. Not now. Not a gloating Rossini. It's the last thing I need.

I know he's just trash-talking. I know it's a bit of fun. I know that Marco is a nice dude, really, but there's a little sting in the tail. Everyone who leaves Rossini feels the loss. They're the greatest team in the world, legacy-wise. And when you're in, you're in. When you're out, you're out. It's heartbreaking.

I glance up and see the girl with the eyelashes looking like she wants to play. But as Marco slides into the booth across from me, I feel suddenly clear.

"Archie, I have to go," I say, standing up.

"Be careful, Matt," he says, shaking his head.

When Chloe isn't in her room at the hotel, I don't have to think hard to figure out where she could be. And so, here I am, at two a.m., back in our garage on the circuit, avoiding the eyes of the shipping crews and cleaners as I pick my way through the almost-empty lot and to the back door of Arden.

She's there, as I knew she would be. Sitting on a crate, playing with a carbon fiber engine part, looking so damn sad. And so beautiful. The garage is still thick with the smells of race weekend—fuel, burned rubber—but there's also a treacly hint of whiskey in the air.

"Chloe," I say quietly, making her leap.

"Fuck!" she says, clutching her heart. "Matt."

I spy a tiny bottle of Jack Daniel's on the floor just behind her.

"I took it from the hotel," she says, her face flat. "What are you doing here?"

"I came to find you. I wanted to see if you were okay."

I'm not sure whether to go sit with her or to keep my distance, so instead I stand in my spot, trying to force myself to look straight. She pushes herself up off the crate.

"No, you didn't," she says, rolling her eyes.

"I did. *Really.*"

"I saw what you were doing tonight. What are you getting at? What is your end goal?" she asks.

"With what?" I ask, taking a step closer to her. I'm dangerously, furiously close to grabbing her by the waist and pulling her into me again. For a hug. For more. For whatever she needs.

Chloe puts a hand on the crate to steady herself.

"With *this,*" she says again, gesturing between us. "You know *this* can't happen."

"I know. I know. I just . . . wanted to find you. Make sure you're okay," I say, studying her as she pushes her long hair over her shoulder and tips her head, fixing her bleary eyes on mine. *Wait. Has she been crying?*

"Are you mad at me?" I ask.

"Matt," she sighs, kicking the floor. "Please, just go."

"The karaoke," I say suddenly. "That's what upset you. Our song."

"*Our song,*" she says bitterly. "It's just a dumb song."

I can tell by the way her eyes dart to the floor that she's trying to be tough. I think about what Archie said back in the bar, that Chloe had feelings for me back then, and I try to reconcile it with my own memories. Is it really true? Was it serious? Did I feel it? Did I know?

I look at her now, and realize that somewhere in the depths of myself, I did know.

"You were sort of like a sister to me, growing up," I say.

Chloe looks up at me and sighs. "So?"

"Your dad called my dad and asked me to look out for you," I say, completely unaware where I'm going with the confession, but feeling like I need to put everything out there for her.

"Oh," she says, taking a step back, laughing to herself. "So that's why you hung out with me all those years ago." She picks up the bottle and tosses it into a nearby garbage bag. "Of course. Everything makes sense now."

"I'm just saying that my dad asked me to—"

"No need to explain. I get it. Sorry for the trouble," she says, sweeping her hands in front of her as if to say, *Enough*. "The humiliation is officially complete."

"Wait," I say. "What humiliation?"

She looks up at me, her eyes tired, and I feel a deep ache in my chest.

"What I'm trying to say is that you were someone I had to look out for, so I would never have . . . crossed any lines back then or whatever." I'm struggling to find the right words, too unsure to ask her outright if she had feelings for me back then. No. *I'm not going to ask that.* I can't demand that of her now. I just need to finally be honest with myself and her.

"And I'm really sorry I ran out on our friendship."

Chloe stills. She raises her hands to her face and becomes completely quiet, breathing into her hands.

I move toward her, pulling her hands from her face and forcing her chin upward. Close up I can definitely see she has been crying. Her big brown eyes are red and her makeup is smeared.

"Our friendship wasn't just a thing my dad asked me to do," I say. "You meant a lot. I loved that stupid song. I loved hanging out with you. And now I just keep thinking of you, and us, and how it feels like there is something special here. And I'm wondering if it was always maybe, potentially there, but I just didn't want to acknowledge it. I was leaving, you know?"

"You were an asshole," she says. I search her eyes, as I slide an arm around her waist and pull her closer to me. All I can do is show her I don't feel that way now. "You never spoke to me again," she says.

"I know," I say, rubbing at her streaky tears with my thumb. "I'm sorry. I worked so hard to get to Rossini, and I thought that was the most important thing in my life. I just had that singular focus. It's a dumb excuse, and I'm ashamed of it and know it doesn't fix what I did, but it's the only one I have."

We stare at each other for a moment, our eyes burrowing deep into each other. And then I lean forward and kiss her gently on the cheek, just below her eye, the taste of salty tears on my lips.

"I'm sorry. I shouldn't have just fucked off like that. I should have realized how special you were back then. I should have seen what was right in front of me. But, Chloe, I see it now. It feels real."

I kiss her once more on the other cheek.

"I don't want to cry over you again," she says. She feels so light in my arms, her body molding into mine the more we stand here. I kiss her again, this time on the lips, and when I do, everything around me disappears. My whole world shrinks into the soft contact of our lips. I hear the gentlest of moans escape her lips and I feel myself melting into her softness.

"I *am* sorry," I whisper into her mouth.

I feel so bad for hurting her, and I'm suddenly seized with the repercussions of it. She can't let me in now. There's no way she trusts me, even if we could somehow get past the working-together complication.

"I can do better. I can *be* better," I say to her, to *myself*, before kissing her top lip again, gently. But then she lifts her hands up and cradles my face, and pushes me gently back, shaking her head.

Even through those tears, she looks so beautiful. "I can't. I just can't," she says. "Because now it's my turn, Matt. I finally have this thing that *I* have worked my whole life toward. And I need to make it work, without distraction."

"But couldn't we just see—"

"No, Matt," she says, suddenly angry as she pulls farther back. "Besides, you're dealing with your own demons right now. If I help put you back together, will you still feel this way toward me? I really fucking doubt it."

I let go of her waist, feeling frustrated as I step back from her. She's so wrong, but I don't know how to convince her. Chloe lifts her shirt to blot gently at the dampness under her eyes.

"Let me do my job, Matt," she says, in barely a whisper. "Please."

I feel lost. I want her so much, but not this way. I know what it's like to forget everyone and focus on your dream. I want that for her too. I want to see her happy and for her to have everything she wants. So for now, this has to be enough.

"Yes, you're right. I'm sorry. Let's focus on work. On finishing this season strong," I mutter.

She sends me a knowing half smile in return, picking up

the carbon fiber part she was playing with when I arrived. "And on that subject," she says, swallowing.

"Yes?" My throat is dry too. I'm suddenly thirsty.

She turns the part over in her hands. "I was sitting here thinking of how we can claw back time, and I had an idea."

"What kind of idea?" I steady my voice.

"About a head of aerodynamics," she says. "You know, we can't afford the kind of person we need. I understand Barry is under pressure. But there is someone . . ."

The thought comes to me like a bolt out of the blue.

"Jasper Cox," I say, almost gasping. *What an idea.*

"What happened to him? Everyone says he was fired. A drunk?"

"He wasn't fired, but he was a drunk," I say, raising both eyebrows conspiratorially as Chloe stands a little straighter. "He went through some family stuff and Rossini waited as long as they could. But, Chloe . . ."

"He's retired. Living in Mexico now," she says, nodding.

"Apparently. So, what are you thinking?"

"Are you going home before the next race?" she asks.

I smile, catching on to her train of thought.

"No," I reply, pulling my phone out of my back pocket. "Due to fly to the Mexican Grand Prix day after tomorrow."

"Let's go earlier," she says. "Let's find Jasper and see if he wants to help us beat Rossini."

CHAPTER 15

Chloe

I'm really not used to private jets," I admit, rolling my trolley from the black Mercedes taxi toward Barry's plane the next morning. I'm tired as hell, and not sure how Matt is functioning.

"Yet," says Matt, laughing, as he nods toward the little stairs where we will board. "When you get used to them, you're ruined."

"Ruined?"

"Yes. It's very hard to go back."

I laugh. "I find them a little bit embarrassing."

"You'll find them amazing in a few hours," Matt says, laughing at me, his smile broad and relaxed. "But honestly? I always fly commercial."

"Aww, Matt, you fly economy. With all your millions? How sweet."

"I said *commercial*," he replies, laughing. He is a completely different person today. Good-humored, amiable. But he's also keeping his distance. And there is almost no eye contact. *Like a colleague.*

I've had so very little time to unpack everything that's been going on, but for now, having Matt keep himself at a bit of a distance is exactly what I need.

Barry is already on board when we get there, and I use his complete availability to corner him and go through the long, long list of issues I want to tackle ahead of Mexico. Matt heads for the back of the plane and straight into one of the small cabin beds.

"Shout if you need me," he says.

"What's so urgent you two needed to come on my flight today, then?" Barry asks wearily.

"Ah . . . we're just going to talk to a potential crew member."

"Matt said." Barry eyes me suspiciously.

"It's a long shot. I'll tell you if we pull it off," I say quickly.

"All right. Better show me where my money has gone," he says, nodding to the graph on my screen with a downward trend so sharp it could bore a hole through the plane's floor and all the way to Antarctica.

▪▪▪▪▪▪▪▪▪▪

When we land, Matt has a car waiting, and although he's managed to sleep, he still looks drawn and tired.

"What if he doesn't want to join us?" I ask for the hundredth time.

"Then we've lost nothing," Matt reminds me again.

We clamber into a waiting car, a purposefully low-key local taxi, and drive the four hours down the coast toward Jasper's house with Matt chatting away in terrible Spanish to the driver. It's my turn to sleep as my eyes grow heavy staring up at the big blue Mexican sky, my head against my balled-up cardigan and the window.

I wake hours later to the sound of the trunk slamming, and then Matt shouting something. I climb out of the car, and by the time I slide on my sunglasses, it's already pulling away, leaving Matt and me standing on the dusty earth in front of a gorgeous, but very small, villa perched right on a white-sand beach.

Oh god, a swim in the ocean is just what the doctor ordered.

"The Pacific," says Matt. "There is nothing like it."

I rub my eyes and follow him to the faded cerulean wood-slat front door, hoping and praying that Jasper Cox is the breakthrough we need.

But the minute we meet we realize he's going to require some convincing.

"I don't work anymore," he says, pushing back his wiry gray hair, stubbing a cigarette out in an ashtray. He holds his other hand toward the open terrace doors, which open onto the beach, palm trees framing the picturesque sandy shore and the turquoise shallow waters ahead. A hammock is blowing gently in the sea breeze.

No wonder he doesn't work anymore.

"I get it," I say, nodding.

"Jasper, you know me," Matt says, leaning forward, his elbows on his knees. He looks handsome today, in a loose-fitting cream linen T-shirt and tailored matching shorts, his feet bare inside a pair of dusty gray Birkenstocks. I watch him talk, calm, persuasive, and I get moments of giddiness in the pit of my stomach as I'm gripped by visceral memories of soft lips and hungry, searching fingers.

"I know you're driving like shit," Jasper says matter-of-factly.

"So, you've been watching the racing?" Matt folds his arms as if he's caught Jasper out.

"Not really," he replies, his eyes flickering to the TV, which is, in fact, currently showing a replay of Austin. Matt grins.

"Come on," Matt says. "Won't you at least talk to us?"

"You're a lame horse," Jasper says. "It's clear you're sitting around waiting to die. You'll never get Arden to the level you need."

"Well," I say, clearing my throat. "I mean, that's *my* job."

Jasper tips his head. "You always let him talk for you?"

"No," I say, my eyes darting toward Matt. "Of course not."

Matt looks as embarrassed as I feel. "Jasper," I say, leaning forward, clasping my hands together. "You didn't want to leave F1, did you?"

"I was a drunk," he says. "I deserved to lose my job."

"It was the worst time. Your wife had died. Don't you want another shot?"

Jasper's eyes narrow on me as he sits back in his chair; there is nothing but the whirr of the ceiling fans and a loud bird crowing by the back door.

"Maybe," he says, finally.

I hesitate. "We have problems with—"

"The downforce," he says, finishing my sentence. "But you got bigger problems than that."

"So you can help us?"

"Why would I want to leave all this to go back to that?" he says, lighting another cigarette. His knee jiggles up and down. "Besides, these cars are complex, and all the parts of the car are interconnected. Without access to the actual data I don't really have a good idea of what's truly happening."

"I can give you full access."

"Oh really," he says, not hiding his skepticism. "Why do you want to hire a drunk?"

"But you're ah . . . sober now, right?" I ask, grimacing, as I glance at Matt for help.

"Oh . . . I get it." Jasper laughs, slapping his knee as he does. The laughter turns slowly into a cough and then he cocks his head to the side.

"Barry's got no money left."

Matt cackles unhelpfully, and tips his head toward me, grinning as though the jig is up and we've been caught out.

"I mean, I wouldn't say that, exactly. I just got off his private jet," I say, forcing out a little light banter as I rack my brain for a way to put this delicately.

"You can't afford anyone else."

"Look. Jasper. You love racing. You didn't want to go, and everyone knew that. For what it's worth, I'm sorry about what happened," Matt says, clearing his throat as he glances around the beach house. "And couldn't you use the money?"

"You *really* can't afford anyone else," he repeats, laughing, as though everything has fallen into place now.

"But you are one of the best," I push, trying to appeal to his sense of pride, since I cannot deny the money issue. I glance at Matt, who is suddenly deep in thought, chewing the inside of his cheek as he examines his hands.

"Once upon a time," Jasper says, stubbing his cigarette out again, a trail of smoke filling the breezy room.

"Please, Jasper. I can beg," I say, holding my hands together in prayer.

"Don't you want to win?" Matt says quietly. "Don't you want to come back and win? And show them all?"

Jasper and Matt lock eyes, and I hold my breath, hoping like hell Matt has found a way in.

"I know what it's like to not get support when you're struggling. I know how shit it feels. I know how all the promises of family and loyalty fall away when you're not performing at your peak. When what you need is a bit of fucking sympathy."

Jasper seems to take this in, his eyes narrowing on Matt. "I tell you what, I don't have a lot on today."

I nod, looking out at the view, wondering if he ever has a lot on.

"Why don't you load up the tablet there with all the aero data, and I'll take a look."

"You got it, but I'll definitely need you to sign an NDA," I say.

"Fine. But I said I'll take a look. Nothing more," he says slowly. He picks up his tobacco and rolls another cigarette.

"How long will you need?" Matt asks, glancing down to the stretch of white-sand beach beyond Jasper's rickety fence.

Jasper stretches his neck side to side, and then cracks his knuckles. "You're not in a hurry, are you?"

The heat of the afternoon sun on my skin is divine.

Matt is in the water, and I'm on the sand, borrowed beach towel stretched out and a chocolate brown bikini hugging my body. My phone died about an hour ago, and I have made a decision not to plug the bastard in. I deserve these few hours to relax.

"You don't want to swim?" Matt shouts over at me from the ocean.

I roll lazily over and prop myself up on my elbows and look at Matt, whose entire perfect torso is above the water, the waves lapping against his back. "It's so warm!" he says, flapping those arms around in the gentle swell. So casually handsome, such a sparkling smile of childish joy as he dives under and comes back up a little closer. "Come on, Chloe!"

"I'm good," I say, grinning as he gives up and wades toward me. I settle back, sunglasses on, and close my eyes. When I hear his soft footsteps on the sand, I open them again to secretly watch him dry off behind my mirrored aviators, before he drops heavily down next to me.

"I could use a nap myself," he says.

"Tequila and travel don't mix," I say, sitting up and reaching for the sunblock. "You think this is going to work? With Jasper?"

Matt hesitates. "Dunno."

"We truly can't afford anyone else."

"Well then, it has to work," he says, shrugging.

I squeeze out the cream and rub my legs down as Matt just stares ahead and out toward the sea. "Pretty happy waiting around here, though. God, the peace and the distance from everyone and everything. It's great."

"It's definitely beautiful," I say, feeling awkward suddenly, as I finish applying cream to my chest, trying desperately to reach round the top of my back. I'm glad Matt has his eyes fixed firmly forward as I apply my sunscreen, but equally, I'd love for him to offer to do my back.

I imagine his broad hands touching my oily skin and I shudder involuntarily.

He'd just be helping a friend out. Nothing more.

"It really is beautiful," he says quietly, as he turns to me.

I narrow my eyes at him from behind my sunglasses, as he stares at the cream in my hand, and then up at the hand that's currently hooked over my shoulder.

He hesitates, as though thinking better of it, but then asks, "Want me to do your back?" He smirks as though it's exactly what I'm asking.

"It's fine," I say casually.

"I'd suffer through the chore if you wanted me to," he says playfully.

"I wouldn't want to force you."

I laugh and he grins in return as I hold out the sunscreen and he nods for me to turn around, and I do, sitting cross-legged and pulling my hair forward over my shoulders.

"It's a dirty task, Chloe Coleman," he says, "but with skin this pale, it shouldn't be ignored."

I feel the cool sunscreen hit my back and then the light touch of his hands on my shoulders as he rubs it in, casually at first, then a little rough as his hands glide down my back and he reaches my waist. I flinch at his touch on my side.

"That tickles," I say, a little breathlessly. His movements are slow, careful to stay precisely on my back.

His fingers run up the side of my spine and between my shoulder blades, turning into a half massage. I let out a long, deep *ahhh* at the pleasure of his firm fingers against my tight muscles.

"I'm going to book a massage for when we get to Mexico City," I mutter, almost slurring.

“A massage?” he says, his fingers hooking over my shoulder, his thumbs digging into the muscles at the back of my neck.

“Oh my god that feels so good,” I say, glancing back at the house, but there is no sign of Jasper. “But you really shouldn’t.”

“Lie down and I’ll do it properly,” he says.

“I somehow don’t trust you,” I say, grinning.

“It’s just sunscreen,” he says playfully, and I lie back down, face on my towel as Matt sits beside me, moving his hands expertly up and down my back.

“You need that sunscreen everywhere?” he asks, finally reaching the small of my back, as his hands slow and he slips just the tips of his fingers under the top of my bikini bottoms.

“Everywhere that isn’t under my bathers,” I say, laughing into my beach towel.

He seems to hesitate again.

He moves to my legs and feet then, rubbing cream from the backs of my knees down my calves to my feet. He spends a few moments on the ball of each foot, where I certainly don’t need any sunblock, and then moves his hands slowly back upward, and I squirm as they touch the backs of my knees, and then he slides his hands higher up my thighs.

“Matt, this is a bit . . . I don’t want to say . . . um . . .” I’m scrambling for words that are not *erotic* or *sexy.*

“I’m just applying sunscreen,” he says, running a hand to the top of my thigh now. He stops for a moment and moves his hand slowly over my ass and up to my lower back. I gasp at the intimacy of it. “Is that enough?”

“Um, maybe. . . . What on earth will Jasper say?” I try to be serious, but I’m also gasping into the towel.

"He'll say *yes*," says Matt. "He's just making us sweat."

"I mean if he comes down to the beach and sees this."

"*This?*" Matt says, teasingly. "I thought we were focusing on work?"

I flush with embarrassment. On the one hand, I'm pushing him away, telling him to focus on work, and on the other hand, I'm letting him move his hands across me in a way that would get most people sent to the human resources department. I'm the definition of a mess.

I'm aware now, although my face is turned away from him, that Matt is lying right beside me, and has propped himself up on his elbow. His hand doesn't move from my lower back, and I find myself sinking into the possessive, protective feeling of it.

"It's so chill to be with you, away from all the fucking paps and the press."

"Only the sharks and crabs to bother you," I say.

His hand moves up to my shoulders and then back down to my lower back, slowly circling as he finds my ass again.

"For the love of god."

"Yes?" he says, laughing. "I can't help it. It's such a great ass."

"Matt," I say, weakly.

"Also, you can never be too sun safe," he says.

And then his hand reaches between the tops of my thighs and stills, his finger just millimeters from touching the edge of my bathers. "Matt," I scold into the towel.

I freeze. I don't move a muscle.

If he moves it just a breath higher, he will be dangerously close to touching me in a way that cannot be explained by *sunscreen application*.

"Want me to stop?" he says into my ear as his fingers squeeze my thigh, slick with the oily cream.

I take a long pause. Maybe the longest pause ever.

"No," I say back to him quietly.

"Good, because it's impossible," he says, leaning in toward me, his mouth close to that sensitive spot behind my ear. "I'm trying to focus on work, but you're so touchable."

"You're too much, Matt," I say, hopelessly losing the battle between my head and my burning fucking desire. He squeezes my thigh again, moving his hand in and out, slowly.

"Okay," he says, moving his fingers higher so I can feel them on the seam at the edge of my bikini now. "Although . . ."

"What?"

"I'm not sure I can focus on work with you next to me. Looking like that."

"We're not doing this," I say, glad that he cannot see the tortured smile, my teeth clamped on my lip.

"Touching is allowed, right?" he says, almost pleadingly.

"Non-sexy touching," I say.

"So many complicated rules."

"Just like racing."

"I better be fast, then," he says, laughing.

He drags his fingers up along the edge seam of my swimmers and out from between my thighs, and then slides them down again. "Just massaging," he says, as his finger slips easily underneath the fabric of my bikini bottoms. I feel a coil tightening in my stomach, and fight hard not to move.

I grip the towel with my fingers as he moves very close to sliding a finger inside me. But he never quite gets close enough, stroking the softness in the crease of my thigh. It is dizzying, and just this one small movement brings so much pleasure I feel like I might explode.

I feel his finger suddenly slip under my bathers, and it emerges slick. Matt moans into my ear, as he feels it too.

"I didn't even touch you properly yet," he says.

"You're fired as a masseur," I reply, rolling over. I'm under him now, grabbing at his hand before he moves it back between my legs.

"Don't you want a happy ending?" he says, interlocking our fingers and pinning my hand to the side of my head on the towel.

"Of course I do," I say, staring hard into his eyes, making sure he understands all the layers of meaning I'm sending him. "But it will never be happy."

"I can give you a happy ending, Chloe," he says.

"Can you?" I reply, half in earnest and half testing these dangerous waters. Matt's eyes darken, and I can tell he's grappling with his desire and the agreement we've made.

"Can you trust me again?"

"Not really." Although, as I say it, I realize that somehow, I do. "Maybe."

"I want to make you happy, Chloe. That's all I want."

His one hand is still laced in mine, waiting for me to say the word.

It's a sink-or-swim moment. Scary and exhilarating all at once.

"Okay." I laugh, then bite my lip. "Then do it."

He lights up at this olive branch, this slightly open door I'm trying not to overthink. Before sliding his hand under the band of my bikini again, he leans in and kisses me softly on the side of my neck.

"How happy?" he says, as he inches closer, teasingly.

"Fireworks," I say. "Nothing less."

His hot breath makes my skin prickle, and I feel his mouth move into a grin against my neck. Then, in one move, his finger glides across me, and a moan escapes my mouth, my eyes clamping shut as pleasure blooms through me.

"Well, *I'm* happy," he says.

"That's not the job, buddy," I say, yelping with pleasure as he moves gently across my clit, rubbing slowly in small circles, and I arch my hips up higher so he can get better access.

"Happy yet?" he asks, as he pulls back onto his elbow and watches my body move against his fingers.

"Frustrated," I say breathlessly.

Matt leans forward, and through the fabric of my bikini top, he puts his mouth over my nipple, sending a bolt of pleasure, my back arching.

When I open my eyes, I see he looks delighted with himself, and he does it again, the pleasure almost too much for me to take. And so, I settle back into the groove of the sand, the breeze against my hot skin, and let go.

"Just a little longer and this will all be over, Chloe," he says, kissing my neck.

"Please," I beg him now, opening my eyes to catch him looking at me with such desire, and yet such tenderness. I have to squeeze them quickly shut again in case I start thinking about him, about this moment, about how much I've longed for it.

Heat pools between my legs, and finally, the pleasure is too much and I grab Matt's neck and pull him against me and come against his fingers in wave after wave, my heart racing, my head thrown back, my free hand grabbing at the sand for purchase.

"God, that was . . . amazing," I moan, as the waves begin to ease.

"You're so perfect," he replies. "I could watch you forever, Chloe."

"Stop it," I say, blushing. I come back to my body while Matt kisses me once on the lips, and shakes his head in disbelief.

He has a smug look on his face as he pulls his hand free again, but this time, he moves it to his own crotch. I glance down at the huge erection he's trying awkwardly to contain in his swim shorts, and I bite my lip.

"Sorry, but you were too hot," he concedes, burrowing his face into my neck, inhaling me. "And you smell so good. Chloe, I want to do that for you whenever you'll let me."

"I want to do that for you too," I say, allowing him to lie against me for a few minutes, as I catch my breath. "I wish . . . I mean, I really *really* wish—"

"Chloe! Matt! Where are you?" Jasper's raspy voice calls out from inside the house. "Vacation is over. Get your asses inside. I think I got some ideas."

"Coming!" I quickly shout.

"Again?" says Matt, eyeing me up as I stand and brush the sand off my thighs.

I grin at him as reality bites, and then I grimace. "We shouldn't have done that."

"If you say so," he says, raising his hands. "But I'm glad it happened. I can't resist you."

"You're going to be the death of me," I say, standing up,

legs weak. God, how I want to be back on that towel, letting him absolutely ravish me from here to forever.

"I'm glad it happened too, and I selfishly want more," I confess to him, which makes his eyes sparkle with mischief. I shake my head, irritated, amused, wanting to smack him in the mouth.

Instead, I lean in and kiss him hard. "Come on. We have a job to do."

CHAPTER 16

Matt

Mexico Grand Prix
Qualifying

She so completely has me wrapped around her finger. And she has no clue.

I watch Chloe walk around the back of the garage, and I have to work hard not to think about her splayed out on that sand. All mine. Almost.

She's in tight jeans, rolled halfway up her calves, new trainers, and a white dress shirt with a couple of logos signed into the breast. She's wearing her glasses today, looking so businesslike. So serious. *The team principal.* I wonder at the thought of the old Chloe seeing herself as she is today. She would be so proud, if she ever believed it.

Chloe and I were offered a room to stay at Jasper's house, but she put an end to that idea quickly.

"I want to go back, Matt," she said after Jasper had given us his thoughts. "Get our heads in the game and prep for the week."

As much as I wanted to stay in that room with her, to do things to her and watch her writhe with pleasure, I have to step carefully here. These are her rules, after all. Even if I want to break them every second I can.

We traveled back to Mexico City by car, and Chloe made her excuses and left me alone to fend for myself with the rest of the Arden team. She had *shit to do,* she told me plainly, in front of everyone. Clear as day she didn't want me to bother her.

So, I hung out with Archie. I trained hard. I spoke to my therapist. And I focused on the thing I know Chloe really needs from me now: a fast race.

And I'm not just being altruistic; I can't help but feel that any win on the track will be a win off it too. If I can get some good laps in for Chloe, if not for myself, then maybe she'll open herself up a little more to me.

I smile to myself at the thought of it as Jasper crouches down beside the car to talk to me.

"I've increased the cooling vents, and we've maximized the downforce as much as we can."

"Thanks," I say, giving him the thumbs-up.

"It's going to feel like Monza, Matt, despite the altitude."

"I wish," I say, grinning. Monza was my very last podium finish for Rossini.

"This car isn't the shit heap I thought it was," Jasper says, pulling out his tobacco pouch and looking around to make sure no one is listening. "The coming upgrades are sound. Team is good. I've been through all of it. Chloe knows her shit. There's some *now* stuff we could get wrapped up in, but she wants to look long-term. Smart."

"She's a total fucking rock star," I say, staring into my

mirror again to see if I can spot her. "Just really great to have a team principal who is still on the floor."

I see one of the pit crew smirking as Chloe's talking to him and feel an almost instant rage at the thought of him undermining her.

"Mate?" I call out. The crew member, a buff twentysomething with an unearned swagger, flicks his hair back, and tries not to look concerned at being caught out.

"What is it, Matt?"

"How about you give Chloe the respect she's fucking earned?"

Jasper raises an eyebrow at me, and then I hear the crackle in my earpiece and realize my radio has been live.

"I wasn't laughing at Chloe," he says, holding both his hands up. "It wasn't that."

Jasper leans in and switches off my mic.

"Maybe don't be so fast, and um, passionate in your defense of the boss," he says, nodding toward Chloe. "Don't want the others to get the wrong idea." Then he winks, putting the rolled-up cigarette between his lips.

I feel suddenly sick. "Shit," I murmur. I must be careful here, because it's one thing to fancy Chloe in secret and quite another thing altogether to have anyone find out. That's what Chloe is most nervous about, and I have to honor that. "Thanks, Jasper."

He chuckles like he's seen it all. Then he pushes himself up, using the halo as a brace as he wobbles unsteadily. "I'm too old for this shit."

I pat him on the forearm with my gloved hand. "Just give us a season, hey?"

"Good fucking luck, Matt. I always liked you. You puffed-up, arrogant piece of shit," he says, before he walks off cackle-coughing.

I take a deep breath and turn the radio back on.

"Hi, Archie," I say into my mic.

"Well, that was embarrassing," he says teasingly.

"Fuck off," I retort.

"You ready to get to the second qualifying round?" he says.

"I'm going to try," I reply, watching the two Rossinis slide out of the pit lane ahead of me. I feel the nerves churning inside of me, but then, suddenly, I feel a little spark. Not a heat—not that deep fire—but something. Something coming.

I picture Chloe next to Archie on that pit wall, and I take another deep breath.

"Let's do this," I say, rolling out of the garage and joining the queue.

■■■■■■■■■■

The Autodromo Hermanos Rodriguez is an old track, the original version built in 1959, with the first ever win here by a British Formula 1 driver. I've won here before too, a couple of years back.

I've always loved this track. The altitude brings with it some serious technical decisions, affecting the downforce and the grip level. While the track itself has changed a lot over the years, losing some of its most thrilling and dangerous corners, it still has one of the longest straights of any circuit, and with that comes plenty of chances to overtake.

The grandstand is packed, Mexican flags waving in

support of Red Bull's Sergio Perez, racing on his home turf today. Nothing for Arden that I can see.

I drive slowly out of the pit, pushing Chloe to the back of my mind as I try to focus on the lap ahead. One slow warm-up lap and then I need to drive my fucking heart out. Hopefully I can make it on to the second round of qualifying.

The sound from the stands is deafening, and I glance in my rearview to see Perez pulling out of the Red Bull garage just behind me.

I close my eyes briefly.

I'm just racing myself.

It was an accident.

Stavros will come around.

The first lap around and the car feels good—heavy in the turns and fast out into the straights.

"Keep it easy, Matt," says Archie. "We've got a few shots at it. Let's let the track warm up."

I launch down the straight, the force of the speed sending me back into the mold of my seat. The first corner comes fast—a tight right-hander. I brake hard, feeling the tires grip beautifully as I turn in, hitting the apex perfectly and powering out smoothly.

I am slightly stunned by the difference in feel. The car seems balanced, and fast. My mind is clear, fear replaced by focus. The engine roars as I push toward the Foro Sol stadium section. I love this stretch of the track; it actually *feels* like a sports stadium, with the towering grandstands on all sides.

I feel the crowd's energy surging, but I stay in my zone.

I keep my foot down, the car gripping the best line. As

the start/finish straight appears ahead, I floor it, crossing in what I can feel is a good time.

"Fast, Matt. Holding thirteenth place," Archie's voice crackles in my ear. "Box."

He wants me to come into the pit lane. Relief washes over me as I slow round the circuit once more and make my way into the pit. The crew blanket my tires, and we wait to see if I need to go again.

I glance up at the screen showing Sky Sports while I wait, listening to the commentary over the radio.

"That's Arden through Q1 and into the second round of qualifying with both cars. Noah Blacklock moving through in fourteenth and Matt Warner placing thirteenth with an aggressive drive and some serious pace in places. It's truly a surprise achievement this late in the season for a team all but written off. Can they get through the second round of qualifying and make it into the top ten? You'd have to think that's a hope a bit too far for the struggling team."

I grimace. A "hope too far" that we might finish in the top ten is something I'm simply not used to hearing, but it fires me up.

I have a seven-minute wait now until the next round. Time to collect our thoughts and prepare. With just fifteen cars left, the goal now is to finish in the top ten. An impossible task for Arden three weeks ago, but is it still? A finish in the top ten would give us our first points of the season. I try to calm my nerves, but I *really* want those points for us.

"Four minutes," says Archie, as I crane my neck to see if I can spot Chloe.

"Keep your focus, Matt," he says now, as if sensing my distraction.

"Good luck, my little puppy," another voice says. *Barry.* Jesus Christ, who gave him access to a microphone?

This time, the car feels perfect as I navigate the first few corners, but as I approach the tight right-hander, the fucking flashes return.

Stavros. I see him, and my stomach turns.

No. *Focus.*

My grip tightens, and I hesitate, braking a fraction too early. The car skids slightly, but I quickly regain control, pushing past the fear and refocusing.

It was a racing accident.

He'll come around.

My mind barely clears, but just enough for me to finish the rest of the lap. The car responds flawlessly as I power through the final corners and across the line.

My time. What is my time? Where am I placed?

Archie's voice crackles in my ear. "You didn't quite make it into Q3. But you got eleventh place, Matt!"

Damn it. I just missed out on getting through. Still, when we start on the grid tomorrow, I'll be in place eleven and breathing down the neck of the top ten. I'm actually in points contention for the first time for Arden.

"Well, that's something. Car felt great."

"*You* looked great, bro."

Relief, but also a long-forgotten sense of achievement washes over me. I haven't made it to the final round of qualifying in a while. I have a long way back to peak performance, but I've delivered a season best.

Archie chuckles. "Not bad for a . . . what did they call you? A lame dog?"

I grin as I pull into the pit. I can't wait to see Chloe, hear her thoughts on the run. I can't get the steering wheel out fast enough. I yank everything out and leap out of the car. Behind us, in the pit, I spot the cameras right on me, and I turn around and give them two fists in the air.

"Hell yeah," I shout, as Archie comes over and chest-bumps me, and then hugs me tight. I spy Chloe by the back with her strategists, and try to wave her over, but she has seen the cameras too and waves me away.

After being weighed and relieving myself of my helmet, I race back to find her, but she's not there. I push out of the garage and out into the paddock, where I spy her leaning against the trailer, head down, arms folded.

"Chloe!" I shout as I run across the lot to her, not caring who can see us.

She looks up, and for a brief moment I wonder if something has happened. But then a smile stretches across her face, and my heart squeezes.

"Eleventh place. The best we've ever done!"

"It's a start," I say, sheepishly.

"If you can follow that tomorrow, we can stay in this. You were so—"

"It was the car," I say, holding out my hand and pulling her up and into a hug, unable to control the excitement I'm feeling too. I forgot this. I forgot what it was like to fight your way up. To be outclassed in every way, and to scrape back, slowly, in tiny steps, until you improve.

At Rossini I was only ever there to drive. Just a driver. The brand was bigger than all of us. This absolutely feels more like a team. It feels damn good.

Chloe does a little jump up and down in my arms, burying her face in my chest. Then she pulls back abruptly, remembering herself, glancing around the lot.

"Your stats were good. Your vitals pretty normal. Was it okay?" She stammers around the words.

"It's not good still. Maybe a little better."

She breathes out with relief. "Better *is* good."

"Better isn't great, though. I've got a ways to go."

She stares at me like she's got ideas. Her brown eyes are alive in a way I've not seen before.

"Come on," she says, yanking on my arm as she pushes the door to the driver room open and tugs me inside.

"Wait! You have to go talk to press, Chloe. Everyone's going to be looking for you."

"All the more reason," she says, slamming the door shut and twisting the lock.

It's only seconds before she's unzipping my racing suit, and with the adrenaline still coursing through me, I do nothing to stop it. My undershirt is damp with sweat, and I must smell of burned rubber, and motor oil, and . . .

"Where did this come from, Ms. This Is A Mistake?" I say, laughing at her.

"I'm so amped up, and proud of us," she says hungrily, as she pulls me in for a kiss. I've not seen her like this, hot and greedy. I stop her for a moment, pushing her off me and holding her at arm's length.

"I don't want to stop this, obviously, but yesterday you were . . ." My voice trails off.

"Yesterday we weren't eleventh place on the grid."

The room is long, narrow, and tight. A small table to the

right of us, and a little sofa with a TV at the far end and a window overlooking the lot. Chloe doesn't seem to care, as she tugs at my undershirt, peeling it up and off.

She pauses for a moment, putting her small hands against my skin, her fingers tentatively dragging behind as she moves them down my chest. I allow her fingers to explore for a moment, as her chest starts to heave.

Damn. I reach under her and lift her up so her legs curl around my waist, and I push her up against the wall, pinning her underneath me.

"Hey, I was in the middle of something," she protests, as I cover her mouth with mine, kissing her. I feel almost instantly hard, the pressure inside my suit verging on uncomfortable as I grind into her, and she holds on to my neck, kissing me back.

This won't work.

"I want you too much," I murmur.

"I know," she whispers, as I lift her onto the little table and rest her ass on the edge, my hand on her lower back, pulling her into me.

Then I move quickly, unbuttoning her jeans. She has to lift her ass to let me pull them down, and then I put my hand on her bare thigh, and drop to my knees.

I look up at her, desire and a questioning look in her eyes.

"I should be doing this to *you*," she says.

"Doing what?" I ask, pushing her thighs apart.

She smells intoxicating, and for a moment I just lay small kisses on the insides of her thighs, pulling aside her lace knickers.

"Chloe," I say as I put my mouth against the delicate skin

around her clit, and she squirms, and her hand goes straight to my hair; she grabs at it roughly. I rub my nose along her, burrowing deeper inside with my tongue.

"Oh shit," she says.

I groan in reply, moving my tongue against her, reacting to her movements. I reach up and tease her with my finger, as I lick and kiss and bite at her. She drops her head back against the wall, allowing herself to enjoy the pleasure as much as I'm enjoying giving it to her. She deserves it. She should be with someone who wants to do this to her all the time.

I hear voices outside, the murmur of an energized crew hurrying past toward the press conference, probably, and I feel Chloe stiffen a little against my mouth.

"Chloe, it's okay," I whisper, putting a hand up to her belly to hold her in place. She grabs my hand and squeezes it.

"Don't stop," she says.

I move quicker now, reaching up and sliding my finger inside her. The feeling of her, wet and warm, squeezing tight around my finger . . . it is almost enough to make me lose it completely.

She comes so gently this time, a hand clasped over her mouth, her moans quiet and restrained. "Matt," she whimpers, softly.

I squeeze both her thighs with my hands, and trail kisses across them as I wait for her to calm and her body to relax. She reaches down and grabs at my hair.

"Kiss me," she says, and I stand up and oblige, but just as we ease into it, Archie's booming voice rings around just outside.

"I don't know where the fuck he went," Archie says. "No, you go back in. I'll find him."

"Shit," says Chloe, biting her lip.

"You need to go do team principal things," I say.

"I'd rather do this," she says, all coquettish and smart-mouthed.

"No," I say, closing my eyes as she digs her nails into my ass. "You should be out in the pit crowing about all the changes you've made. This is your moment to shine."

"I don't like that part of the job," she says. But I can tell from the tone of her protest, she knows I'm right.

"You *need* to do that part of the job," I say. "You have to promote yourself, Chloe. And the team needs to hear you talking about how good they did."

She sighs, stepping back. "Eleventh fucking place. And Noah in fourteenth. I can hardly believe it."

"Go out there and be loud and proud," I say, pulling up my race suit, and pushing her gently toward the door.

"Can I just go out there and be me, instead?" she says, and I grin.

"You *are* proud," I say. "Show them. Show the team."

CHAPTER 17

Chloe

Mexico Grand Prix
Race Day

Dude, you guys should be so proud," Keyla says down the phone, as I sit cross-legged on my hotel bed, a plate of fried eggs, freshly squeezed orange juice, and a strong coffee in front of me on a tray. "And you must be *especially* happy with Matt."

I fork some of the huevos rancheros into my mouth, trying not to think about Matt. "Yes, he did great."

"Look at you, on the verge of getting points," she raves. "You're on the way, honey. I'm getting jealous."

I laugh into the phone. "Oh yes, Keyla. It must be tough working for the best team on the planet."

"It's not *everything*," she says, but something catches in her voice.

"All okay?" I say, sitting up a little straighter.

"All okay," she says quickly. "I love McLaren. *Really.*

They're an amazing team. But I can't help but feel I reached my ceiling there, Chloe."

"Come work for me. You know we'd take you in a heartbeat," I say, throwing it out there.

"Tell you what," she says. "Get Noah or Matt on the podium today and we can talk."

I spit my eggs out in a roaring laugh. "Podium?"

"You can dream it," she says.

"Oh, I'm happy with just improving right now."

"Then you should try to look happier in these damn press clips!"

Keyla has been messaging me links to the various clips of me looking steely and completely emotionless as the camera is shoved in my face and pithy sound bites are sought by the ravenous press after qualifying.

"Big improvements for Arden, how are you feeling?"

"Good, thanks." Small nod. Smile that doesn't reach my eyes.

"Is it true Jasper Cox is joining your aerodynamics team?"

"Not sure yet." Shrug. Straight face staring off into the distance. Nothing giving away how fast my heart is racing, and how terrified I am of saying the wrong thing. I just look . . . bored?

And now I'm also the internet's favorite new meme.

A GIF of me, behind Barry's back, with a face so sour it could curdle milk. Barry's going on about eleventh place being "just the beginning," and there I am, rolling my eyes theatrically as if I don't agree.

But it wasn't Barry's speech that caused that reaction. It was Matt in the background, pulling the corners of his mouth up in a ridiculous attempt to make me smile. Assuming I was off camera as the press were talking to Barry, I gave Matt a look of unfiltered contempt, followed by an almost 360-degree eye roll. But when you play back the footage, it looks like this is directed at Barry.

So yeah. *Naturally*, I've become a meme. An eye-rolling meme that apparently captures mansplaining in one perfect GIF.

"It *is* kind of perfect," says Keyla, laughing.

"Jack Sheppard has put a good spin on it," I say. " 'Stone-Cold Arden Team Principal Is Nothing but Business.' "

"Stone-cold," Keyla cackles.

"That was nice of him," I say to Keyla. "Makes me sound formidable."

"Chloe, you're the biggest softie I know. It wouldn't hurt to show a little emotion from time to time."

"I know, I know. Matt's on my ass too," I moan. "I'm just afraid I'll say the wrong thing. And to be fair, I've said barely anything and managed to make the news. What if I actually *did* say something? What then? There are so many possible catastrophes."

Keyla giggles. "At least you look hot," she says. "That blow-dry. You finally spending some of your salary?"

"Yes," I confirm. "Got my nails done too."

She chuckles, and I down my orange juice, checking my watch. I have to leave for the track soon. "How's things going with Matt?" she asks lightly.

"Please don't ask if you don't want to hear the answer," I say.

There is a long pause, and I hold my breath. Part of me

wants to share it all, but another part wants to keep it close to my chest.

"Oh no," she says. "You've done it. You've slept with him?"

"Technically no. . . . But we're not exactly innocent co-workers either," I confess, grimacing as I wait to see how the news lands. Keyla is silent for a while and then she just sighs.

"You like each other," she says gently. "I could see it that night at the bar in Austin. I can hear it in your voice. It's just such bad timing, Chloe."

I throw myself back and stare at the ceiling. "We can't be the first team principal and driver who have had a fling, can we? What about Suzie and Toto?"

"Suzie didn't drive for Toto, and anyway, they're married. Also, I know you. You can't have *a fling*. Especially with Matt Warner. Can't you guys just cool it until the season's over?"

"We *are* trying."

"Doesn't sound like it," she says, laughing. "Oh, Chloe. I just really don't want to see this ruin anything for you. Or ruin *you*. You know I love you."

"I know, Keyla. I do know it."

She's right. He did hurt me once upon a time, and while I want to believe that he wouldn't do it again, I can't be sure. Still, I can't seem to stop the direction this is going. Neither of us can.

"I am afraid of being hurt, but this feels different. It feels grown-up, like we're on the same level, and I've never felt that before. . . . I feel so confused."

"Are you both going to be home during the break?" she asks.

"Well, I am. Matt doesn't come home much anymore, but he said he might this time."

"Try to have some time out. Work through your feelings."

"I will. You're right. It might be good to cool off a bit. It's so intense at the moment."

"That's F1," she says. "What happens on the circuit . . ."

"Stays on the circuit?" I ask, hopefully.

"Tends to end up in the paper," she says, laughing. "And you really don't want that, Chloe."

On the way into the lot, just hours before the race, I spot Jack Sheppard chatting away to a couple of the officials from the FIA, holding out his phone mid-interview. I watch at a distance for a moment, until Jack glances over and waves toward me just as the interview wraps.

"Hey you," I say, not inclined to stop, but eager to thank him for the good press. "Thanks for the piece this morning."

"Stone-Cold Chloe Coleman," he says, chuckling, pulling down his fedora and stepping away from his conversation. "Can we talk?"

"Talk? Sure," I say, glancing over at a coffee cart. "Flat white?"

"You're in Mexico," he says, laughing. "You're going to want a café de olla."

I nod my head toward the cart, and he follows me. "But put that bloody phone away," I say. "It makes me nervous."

Jack laughs but obliges, sliding the phone into his back pocket before ordering us each a coffee in perfect Spanish. I recall his stories of holiday homes near San Sebastián and Michelin-star barbecue in the foothills of the Pyrenees. Of course he knows Spanish. I grin at him. "How many languages can you actually speak, Jack?"

"German, Spanish, and Korean. And a little French," he says, laughing lightly. "You?"

"Seems I can barely speak English," I reply, blushing with embarrassment under his wide smile. "At least publicly."

"You should really get some training," Jack says.

I sigh. "I know. Keyla said the same. And Matt."

"Matt?" Jack raises an eyebrow, mockingly. "I thought you guys hated each other."

You have no idea. I suddenly blush, hard, unable to control it as I get a brief flashback to our time on the beach. Jack must notice something is up, given my beet-red face. It wouldn't take a genius, let alone a reporter whose job is to dig for the truth.

"Getting on better, then?" he says casually, handing me a coffee and indicating with his head we should walk and talk.

"Not really," I say quickly, sipping my searingly hot coffee and suddenly regretting the decision to talk.

"Same shit, then?" says Jack, shooting me a look of knowing empathy, like we share a secret. And I don't like it this time.

"Yeah . . . I guess," I say, feeling terrible. Horrible. Disingenuous. But the other option is far worse. What am I going to do? Tell him things are great now? That I've been pulling Matt into dark rooms to snog when no one is looking, while he's made me come harder than I ever have in my life? If I give him a whiff, he'll guess.

"I'm serious about the media training," he says now, reaching out to touch my arm. "You know I could help you."

"Oh, thanks, Jack, but I don't think that's necessary."

"You don't? You need to rewatch yesterday's press clips," he says, nudging me with his elbow, chuckling. I can't help but laugh along.

"Well, okay, maybe I'll take you up on it one day. I better go get the team ready," I say, nodding toward the back entrance to our garage.

"Wait," he says, reaching back around and pulling his phone out. "Could you give me a couple of lines? Something to make me look good to the senior editor?"

I nod. "A couple of lines?"

"Yeah. Something exclusive?"

I blow out air, racking my brain for something. "We're right on trajectory. I know exactly where this team is going, and with the new upgrade package we're aiming for points."

"Is it true Arden is finished if you don't get some results soon?"

I stare hard at him, feeling annoyed. Do I comment? Or do I use the chance to reassure my team, and quash the rumors even if they're true? Jack must see my panic, because he looks thoughtfully at me, and then hits stop on the recording.

"If I were you, I'd brush the rumors aside and reiterate your point about aiming for results."

"Good thinking," I say gratefully.

He turns his phone back on record and nods encouragingly. I clear my throat. "You know, I'm not interested in the gossip on the lot. I'm interested in results. And they will speak for themselves after this race."

I feel a flush of relief wash through me. Jack grins, switching off his phone again. "Perfect," he says. "See? I'm a good teacher. I can totally help you." He hesitates, dropping his head a little so his hair falls over his eyes. I smile warmly. I really don't know why Matt doesn't like this guy. He's been nothing but kind and generous to me.

"Thanks, Jack," I say.

"Or I could just take you to dinner," he blurts out.

I still, my hand clasping my coffee hard enough to crush the paper cup a little. Shit. Shit. Shit.

"Oh, Jack," I say, cursing myself for stopping to talk to him. "I don't think that's a good idea."

"An old friend can't take an old friend for dinner? As friends?"

I tip my head to the side, and my voice comes out shaky. "That's not what you're asking, though, is it?"

He nudges his coffee toward me, his face immediately impassive. "Can't blame a guy," he says, shoving his free hand into his jeans and stepping backward, readying himself to go.

"I'm always here for a coffee on the lot," I assure him, but he's already turned away.

The race is thrilling. Edge-of-your-seat, heart-stopping, blood-pressure-raising, I-need-a-fucking-beer thrilling.

I'm out on the pit wall, my body rigid in my seat, my mouth dry, as Matt moves with stealthy determination. He's driving like a predator, ready to pounce on the Williams in front of him, but the tires are shot and he really needs to pit.

I hold my breath, not wanting to interfere with the team's plans. I close my eyes and pray Archie is on the case.

Just then, I watch the Williams turn into the pit, and now I know for sure Matt will follow. I let out a slow breath.

"Box, box," Matt calls through the team radio as the crew behind me assemble.

"Softs?" the strategist bellows.

"Let's go," says Archie. "We need to come out in front of that second Alpine."

"No shit, Fuck-Knuckle," Matt replies.

He pulls into his spot, the waiting crew poised and ready, and I spin around to watch the lightning-fast pit and change of tires. I'm sure I see Matt's helmet turn my way before he's back in the pit lane and accelerating out toward the track, *MIND MY HOT REAR* emblazoned in all its ridiculous glory.

"Two point twelve seconds," says the strategist, to muted cheers. That was fast. "We can do this."

I hold my breath, watching the Alpine screaming down the straight, but Matt is out already, and after a little bit of defensive driving, he's done it. He's slipped out of the pit lane just ahead of the Williams, and now we're in ninth place. We're in the top ten, and with all cars having pitted, it's now a race to hold position and hold on to those precious top-ten points.

We have points!

I can scarcely believe it. All he has to do is defend his spot. But Matt, it seems, has other ideas. He takes an incredible swing into the apex, and cruises out onto the next straight. And he's . . . fast. Very fast.

I hold my breath. He can't be trying to get to eighth, can he?

My eyes skirt to the second screen as I watch Noah squeal past that very same Williams. My eyes bug. My heart is slamming against my rib cage. We have ninth and tenth now. This is incredible.

I turn to Noah's race engineer, just as Noah shouts into the radio.

"I got him!"

"Copy that," says his engineer. "Keep pushing, Noah."

Meanwhile, Archie is swearing like a sailor, "Push, you fucker!" at Matt.

But it's a Rossini in front of him. He'll never catch it. . . . Will he?

As they cruise out of turn five and into the chicane, Matt manages to gnaw off another half a second. I gasp, clutching my chest. The crowd is roaring.

Keep focused, Matt. Don't get into your head. You can do this.

He bears down on the red beast ahead. He is bumper-to-tail and as soon as he hits the drag-reduction zone he will have him, and we will have a car in eighth position.

My favorite part of racing are these special little strips on the track where a driver is allowed to open their rear wing flap to increase speed. This is where so much of the overtaking happens, but you need to be close enough to the other car to utilize it. I imagine the sweet sense of revenge Matt will feel overtaking that Rossini and I want it for him so badly.

I feel a little head bump at my hand and look down to see one of Barry's dogs has found her way onto the lane. I should send her safely back into the garage, but instead I stroke her head in soft rhythmic moves, which is soothing me as much as it is her. "I can't believe it," I say breathlessly. "We're going to get points."

I swing my head around to find Barry, who is pacing back and forth at the garage entrance, unable, it seems, to watch the screens.

"You can do it, Matt," I whisper.

The crowd swells, and someone sets off orange flares, which make the whole pit wall jump in unison. "Verstappen takes the lead," the commentary blares, but who gives a damn about first place? We're not racing for first. We're racing for our own best.

Matt moves into the DRS zone, and, off mic, Archie speaks for everyone when he screams, "TAKE HIM, MATT!"

We wait. But . . . nothing happens.

And then I see it. The ticking up of the numbers on the screen. *Matt's vitals.* Then the hesitation. The DRS fires, the rear wing flips open, and instead of flying past that Rossini, Matt drops back. The Rossini presses ahead, and now instead of overtaking and moving up into eighth, Matt has Alpine behind him inching closer and threatening ninth place.

Still. It's ninth place. I know Matt will be disappointed he couldn't close in on that Rossini, but it's our first points. As a team, it's a huge victory.

When the cars finally cross the line, Matt's anger and frustration are clear as he climbs out of the car.

"We got points," I say, although the words feel weak as Matt's eyes stay on the floor. He waits to be weighed and get out of here as quickly as he can.

"I'm never going to be okay," he shouts across the garage, as Archie bowls in and throws his arms around his brother.

"Points!" Archie says, as Barry joins us, a look of questioning confusion on his face as though he's about to start on Matt too. But Archie holds an arm up. "*Points.* The rest is noise."

I nod to Archie, and move to intercept Barry, grabbing his arm and pulling him toward Noah, who has just jumped out of his car, beaming with delight at his improvement.

"Eleventh place!" I shout, fist-bumping Noah, encouraging Barry to do the same with a nod of my head.

And then I look back at Matt and Archie. Archie's hands on Matt's shoulders, Matt's head dropped forward. The disappointment overshadowing today's incredible achievement.

Damn it. Poor Matt. My heart squeezes for him.

I need to talk to him about the crash. I thought Matt needed to see Stavros weeks ago, and now I feel so strongly, in the pit of my belly, that Matt needs to go *now.* He needs to skip the two-week break back home in Brackley and head to Greece to speak to his best friend. Stavros might be hurt. He might hate Matt right now. But Matt needs to make a massive effort to show him how he truly feels.

It's the only way to heal that hurt.

CHAPTER 18

Matt

It's ridiculous that Chloe is taking her own car from Heathrow to Brackley, but I'm not sure I'll be able to stop her. Especially after our fight, if you could even call it that.

After the race, she sat me down. I was still sweaty and frustrated, with half the bloody media watching me. She tried to calm me down and convince me I needed to go see Stavros.

"Stavros doesn't want to see me," I replied, wiping my brow with a towel and glugging down a good liter of water in seconds.

"How do you know that for sure, Matt?"

"I sent him loads of messages."

Even as I said it, I knew it was pathetic. Stavros, the man with the enormous Greek family, who once flew halfway around the world to attend his grandmother's ninety-third birthday brunch, who handwrites his own damn Christmas cards, deserved more than a few calls and text messages. But I'm a fucking gutless bastard and I can't face him.

And Chloe knows it.

"Get on the plane," she said. "Go to him."

But I didn't want to hear that. I just walked off, pushed myself up off the floor and left her there, standing on the lot with about a dozen eyes having witnessed what surely looked like a fight.

Since then, I must have checked my phone a million times. No message or missed calls from her, though. *I'll get in touch with her later to apologize.*

To make matters worse, coming home always makes me nervous. It's been a while since I saw Mum, and I know she's been missing Archie and me over the past few years. I'm not really up for seeing Dad at all, but I have no choice but to face him.

I drive the two-hour trip from the airport and am reminded how nice the countryside can be after being away for so long. I pass ancient oak-lined winding roads with huge, overgrown hedgerows. Everything is turning autumnal and beautiful and familiar. This I missed.

My parents' house is exactly the same when I pull up to it. The same climbing pink rosebush almost eating the whole of the redbrick facade, the garden wild and overgrown. The shiny black door with the number 7 in silver. I tried so many times to upgrade them, but they weren't having it.

Mum flings the door open before I have a chance to knock.

"We heard the car," she says, pulling me in for a hug, her body soft and comforting, her arms a little too tight around my body. "Dad's made room in the garage."

"It's fine there for now," I say, taking Mum in. She's the same, her gray hair dyed warm brown, clear-rimmed glasses.

"No, it isn't. Brackley isn't what it was, I'm telling you.

The Clarksons had their electric bikes stolen last month. And Gail saw a flasher at the station."

"I'll put your fancy car in," says Dad, appearing from behind her, reaching out a hand to shake mine. "How much did those cost?" He nods to the Gucci sunglasses on top of my head.

"Not as much as the car," I say sheepishly, taking his heavy hand in mine.

"Nice of you to turn up," he says with a wink, as I fish the keys out of my pocket and hold them up for him.

"Nice of you to tidy up for me," I say, nodding to the overgrown front lawn.

"It's about your turn, don't you think?" he says, folding his arms.

Dad. On the one hand, he's a grounded, salt-of-the-earth type, who has never liked the high-flying life of F1 and whose circle of friends make a sport of mocking rich footballers. And on the other, he's a massive F1 fan, a trained mechanic who cannot easily hide the huge pride he clearly has for me and Archie. And so, when I'm home, he prods and teases me about my clothes and my cars and my money—his way, I think, of trying to remain a mechanic from Brackley and not the father of Matthew Warner.

He'd never say it, but he's probably disappointed on some level that I've been dropped from Rossini.

Mum's laughter breaks the banter, and she tugs me inside the house. It's a strange snapshot of nineties England: huge old tube TV as deep as it is wide; wood-paneled kitchen cabinets. The hallway is a collection of celebrity autographs: signed photo of the Spice Girls (Mum), signed photo of David Beckham (Dad), and signed photo of the Wiggles (me).

Mum has scones laid out on the slate-topped kitchen island, with clotted cream and raspberry jam. Fresh flowers on the kitchen table. The radio plays Elton John softly in the background. Everything is the same as it always has been. Routine, constant, safe. The only thing that is wild and unpredictable in this room is me.

"There's tea too," Mum says, pushing the pot with the pink knitted tea cozy in my direction.

"There's something wrong with the engine in that car. I can hear a rattle when you move to third gear," Dad says, joining us, sliding onto the stool at the kitchen island opposite. His gray hair is more obvious these days. Still, his eyes are bright as ever, his steely gaze strong and penetrating like he's always got more to say. Because he surely does.

"You needed three gears to roll her into the garage?" I tease, laughing, knowing he would take her out for a quick run. What he really wants is to get her into the workshop and have a good poke around. It isn't often someone rolls into his workshop with a vintage Jaguar.

"Maybe you could take a look for him?" Mum suggests, playing along.

"If I have time," Dad says, reaching for the scones.

Mum gives me a look, rolling her eyes, and I laugh, reaching for the tea, and pour myself a cup.

I accept a scone piled high with cream and jam and take a greedy bite.

"I'm sorry I've not been back more," I say, frowning at Mum. "It was kind of hard to say no to the free holidays the company liked to send us on."

"That's okay, love. You're here now. We just love having you home."

"I like you at Arden, son," Dad says, crashing in like he can't keep the thought in his brain any longer.

I swing my head around to him, cocking it in surprise. "Really? I thought you'd be disappointed."

"He likes *Chloe*," Mum explains. "Even if her dad is the local competition."

"I like her family," Dad elaborates. "And it isn't just her, anyway. It's watching you have to fight again. To build up something. It's better for *you*."

"There's a lot to build," I say.

"Ninth is their best-ever result," dad counters, enthusiastically.

His delight lifts me a little. "True. It's not as bad as I thought it might be. I kind of like the battle."

"And Dad likes Chloe," Mum whispers again, behind her hand.

"She's good," Dad remarks, eyebrows raised as if I ought to know the truth.

"She's good. *Yes*," I agree, trying not to sound irritated.

"She's good for *you*," Mum says. "Always has been. What's it been like working with her again?"

I picture her climbing into the car a few hours ago, her red hair blowing in the wind. I wonder if I should just fucking call her. Maybe take her out one night while we're home. I imagine taking her on a date to a little English pub. I smile a little too wistfully and Mum catches it.

"Oh," she says, eyes wide. "So, it's going well?"

I feel a sting of embarrassment and shake my head wildly. "There are a lot of problems. Not with Chloe. With me."

My mum's face drops. Sympathy is radiating off her, and I really don't want to hear anything about *that* right now.

"Have you heard from him yet?" she asks gently.

"Don't push him," says Dad. "Stavros will call when he's ready."

"*Darren!*" Mum shoots back.

"Wow, that took, like, five minutes," I say, checking my watch dramatically.

I just knew she would bring up Stavros and the accident. She can't bloody help herself. How is it that mums know exactly where to jab you to get a reaction?

"You know what? I'm super jet-lagged."

"Honey, I only care about you," Mum says, reaching across the counter and gently holding my hand by the wrist as though I might try to escape. "Archie says you're getting better. That you're not thinking of retiring anymore."

"I am a little better," I say, nodding slowly. And then I sigh, dropping my head to my hands. "And yes. I do need to see Stavros. Chloe is on me about it too."

I catch Dad looking at Mum, and Mum giving him an I-told-you-so look, with a raise of her eyebrows.

"You've always avoided emotionally difficult things," says Mum.

I bank that little insight to share with my therapist.

"Not everything needs to be discussed endlessly," my dad counters, sighing heavily. "Another problem with today. Everyone is so self-absorbed. Better to get on with things rather than rake over them endlessly."

I bank that one for the therapist too.

"It's never as bad as you think it's going to be," she continues, ignoring my dad. "Stavros will forgive you, darling. You're best friends."

I nod, turning my tea around in my hands. And then I try to fight off a yawn.

"I'm going to go . . ." I thumb toward the upstairs.

"Take a shower," Mum says. "You just shut down, baby. Put your feet up. Dinner is at six."

"Six o'clock?"

"Yes, we're over sixty now," my dad mutters.

"We eat at six and fall asleep watching *EastEnders*," Mum agrees.

After my shower, I dry myself down and put on a fresh tracksuit and hoodie. I pull back the curtains in my room, which is also technically still shared with Archie when he visits too. At least Mum finally upgraded from bunk beds to two singles.

I can smell the roast chicken wafting up through the floorboards. I pull up the sash window, let the breeze blow in, and kick back onto my bed, when I hear a buzz from my phone.

And there it is. A message from Chloe. Even with the awkward way we left things, I still wish more than anything she was here with me now.

C: How's Brackley?

M: Scones. Tea. Roast Chicken. You?

C: Toad in The Hole x

I glance at my watch. Dinner is in an hour, not enough time to race across town and see her. Tomorrow, maybe?

M: Let's catch up while we're both home. Pint at the Fox and Oak?

C: Maybe . . . Mum has a lot planned.

It's enough of an opening. I sit back and listen to the sounds of the birds and their evening song as I contemplate asking her to meet me for dinner tomorrow. Or maybe a pint at the Fox and Oak *is* better?

A nightingale continues its jaunty song on a branch just outside the window. The breeze is cool and damp, a long way from the heat of the Italian summer.

Everything is so still. It could be like this, my life. *Quiet.*

I try to imagine leaving F1, making this my final year. I like the idea of it, but there is something so grating about going out on a low in my last year. It's a depressing time to walk. Like that tennis player who won't give up, even when half his body is strapped with tape and he can't chase down the ball.

I lift a hand up behind my head, feeling the call of sleep not too far away. I settle back, contemplating retirement, when my phone buzzes.

C: Do you still know where the holes in the fence are?

I grin. She's fucking perfect.

M: Can you get your hands on two go-karts?

C: See you around 9.

CHAPTER 19

Chloe

This might be a dumb thing to do, but fuck it.

It's a full moon, and the track is bright enough to race on even though there isn't a single light on anywhere in the vicinity. Matt and I have done this a million times before. I mean, sneaking into Silverstone as team principal of Arden and as a world-famous F1 driver is reckless. But at the same time, it feels like something Matt and I need to do.

There are two beat-up old go-karts at my feet, which I've hauled out of the trailer attached to my dad's truck. Although it's only slightly cool, I dress warm, wearing a denim Levi's racing suit emblazoned with McLaren logos. It was a Christmas gift from Keyla that I clearly can't wear publicly, but it's perfect for a secret night race against Matt.

It is a fast fifteen-minute drive to Silverstone, and despite attempts to fully close off this circuit to the public, I have always known where the gaps in the fences are.

And so has Matt.

I spot what looks like a Toyota Corolla pull up at the back

gate, and stiffen as the headlights pass over me. I can't be caught already, can I?

But as the driver emerges and Matt's familiar silhouette walks toward me, jingling his keys, I realize he's taken his mum's little hatchback.

"I thought it was more clandestine," he says, looking like he's about to hug me, but then he hesitates and it's immediately awkward.

"It's been a while," I say. "I hope there's no new security measures."

"Unlikely after a decade," he says, smirking.

"We're so going to get caught."

"Isn't that half the fun?" Matt grins. He looks so handsome, his eyes sparkling under the cool blue moonlight. I bite my lip and smile.

It isn't long before we've unlatched the karts and pulled them through the fencing. We're rolling them as quietly as we can to the starting grid. Matt can't stop laughing, and I'm frantically trying to shush him and wind up in a giggling fit myself.

"We're a disgrace," I chuckle, hauling my kart into pole position.

"Nothing changes, Bug," he agrees, dropping the front of his kart into second position. "Don't think I didn't notice you took pole position there, Coleman."

"You probably don't remember, but I won the last race," I shoot back.

He puts his hands on his hips and tips his head. "Actually, it was the late summer of twenty twelve or twenty thirteen. And *I* won that race. I remember because you threw a banana peel at me, which hit me in the face."

I am stunned into silence. I didn't think he would remember. The memory, his remembering, it clutches at my heart in a way I'm not ready for, and I look away, down to my kart.

"Cat got your tongue, Coleman? Your dirty Mario Kart tricks didn't work, did they?"

I take a few steps toward him and put my fingers on the zipper of my racing suit, unzipping the front slowly.

"That isn't going to work either," he says, as his eyes drop to my fingers. "Well. Maybe it will."

"Looks like it might," I say, unable to stop laughing as I reach inside the suit and pull out a ripe banana.

"You are the worst," he says, his eyes darting from the banana to my unzipped racing suit, which is showing off a hint of lace from my bra. I zip it back up and toss the banana into the back of my kart.

"You have to eat it first, you know. I'm pretty sure it has to be a skin, not a whole banana."

"I'm too full of the seventy-thousand-course dinner my mum just forced me to eat."

Matt taps his belly, laughing. "Same."

I glance over at the karts. "Shall we?"

I watch as Matt climbs into his kart, his knees jutting awkwardly up and his arms ridiculously long for the wheel-to-seat space. He's all pointy elbows and tight angles.

"You look like a pretzel made to look like Matt Warner," I say, climbing more easily into my own kart before I jam the ignition and we're off.

As we speed around the track, Matt hangs just behind me, as he always does. Looking back over my shoulder, I shoot him a mischievous grin as I move my kart in front to block any moves.

He's right on my tail, the delight of racing me all over his face. He pretends to make a serious move to overtake, but then eases off the throttle, allowing me to maintain my lead. *The little shit.* I grin as he pushes me, moving round so we're side by side. He sticks his tongue out and tries to push but I cruise ahead.

"Don't just let me win," I shout over my shoulder. "Fight, you bugger."

"You're too aggressive," he shouts.

After a bit of toe-to-toe down the final straight, I cross the line just ahead of him, my smile stretching wide. He pulls up next to me, laughing, and I shake my head at him.

"I'll take the win," I say, breathless and exhilarated. "Even if it was given to me."

"Best of three?" he says, and before I have a chance to respond, he's off again around the track. *The bastard.* I hit the throttle, ready to chase.

After three rounds, with me winning two to one, we've both finally had enough.

"We better get off the grid," he says, pointing to a floodlight that has been triggered by our movement at the far end of the pit.

We roll the karts back toward the gap in the fence, then load them into the trailer before I reach into the back seat of the truck and pull out a beer.

"Wanna share one?" I ask, holding it out toward him.

"Up on the mound," he says, nodding toward the grassy

hill that rises above the track. We wander together, the sparkly fun of our race still invigorating me, sweat on my forehead, cheeks inevitably pink from the thrill. I take a seat on the dry grass and Matt drops heavily down next to me. I twist the top off the bottle and hand it to Matt, who takes a thirsty glug and hands it back.

"Nice to be home?" he asks me.

"Yeah. Grounding as ever," I say, laughing. "My dad tells me he called your dad when you moved to Arden. They're talking about throwing a joint party for us when we get back at the end of the year."

"Oh god," he says, laughing. "Please, no."

"They're good. But my dad talks to me about F1 as though I'm not a team principal, or if I am, do I really know what I'm doing?" I say, swigging back the beer. "I can take the misogyny, but it's hard from your own dad."

"He must be a little proud."

"Oh, they are both so proud. I love them so much, don't get me wrong. But Dad has enough secondhand impostor syndrome for the both of us," I say, thinking back to his nervous face as he drilled me about all my decisions so far. Most of which I had to answer with "I don't know yet," because I genuinely don't know yet. I need more time.

"Dads have more impact than they know," Matt says, looking up at the full moon. "Sometimes it's what they *don't* say that you learn the biggest lessons from."

I'm not sure what he is getting at exactly, but I have my suspicions. His dad is a closed book, and as a young girl I found his quiet judgment a little scary. But Matt doesn't elaborate, and I don't want to push him after the Stavros conversation in Mexico.

The breeze is cool against my bare forearms, and I'm pleased to have escaped the vast heat of Mexico. We can see the finish line. The end of the season is nearing, and still we have so much to achieve. So much to do to keep Arden alive and afloat. Ninth place is fantastic, but can it be sustained?

And at the end of the season, what will Matt and I be to each other?

"I'm sorry for coming at you after the race," I say quietly.

He breathes a heavy sigh. "It's okay. My mum just did the same." His tone is even, maybe a bit amused at being ganged up on by two strong women in his life. "I'm sorry I snapped at you."

I take a breath. "Don't you think it's the missing piece of the puzzle here, though?"

"Yep. Probably."

I take another sip, wondering whether to push him as a team principal or as a friend. It feels like I'm not confident enough in either role to know what is best.

"But honestly, Chloe," he says, dropping his eyes to the grass, his elbows resting on his knees. "Even if Stavros forgave me. Even if he told me it wasn't my fault. I know it was. I did that. Years of overconfidence in the fastest car on the grid, and then a few months of frustration. I was reckless on the track that day."

"All good drivers have those days," I say reassuringly. "Verstappen, Sainz, even Hamilton."

"I scared myself," he says. "Do I know the difference between aggressive, determined driving and risk-taking? Like, for example, you know when you're normie road driving, and you have the chance to overtake a tractor or a cyclist or something? You learn when to pull out, after years of experience. You know where the risk line is. Where it's safe for you, but also safe for the person you're overtaking. It used to be my greatest skill that I could push that line to the limit. It's a driver's greatest instinct, really. And now, I'm not sure I know where that line is. The line is blurred, and it's killed my confidence."

I feel a tug in my heart for Matt and let him know with a gentle hand on his arm.

"So yeah, I need to see Stavros. To let him know how sorry I am for putting him in that position. But I also need the confidence to not think I'm going to kill everyone I overtake."

"Go and see him," I say. "Promise me."

He nods.

"It was one mistake, Matt."

"I should never have made it," he says, turning his head toward me.

"We all make mistakes," I say, feeling the air shift around me as our eyes connect.

"Yeah, and I seem to keep on making them," he says. "I'm so glad I can talk to you about this. I can't talk to anyone about it. Not Stavros, not anyone."

I search his face in the low light, looking for any hint of a double meaning behind his eyes. And then I curse myself for thinking about him, about *us*, in this moment. And yet, here we are. Back where we were over a decade ago, on this very hill, with Matt sharing his darkest thoughts and feelings with me, in a way he doesn't do with anyone else. And here I am, listening, caring, and wanting to kiss all those sad thoughts away.

"Chloe?" he says, frowning as he takes in my expression.

"I was just thinking about how I want you to be happy," I say truthfully. "But part of me is happy you're sad because I get to be the person you share that with."

Matt's face is overcome. His expression softens into something hopeless. His eyes round. "I don't want you to feel like that," he says, reaching out a hand to touch my face, his fingers gentle on my cheek.

"Matt, I have to be honest with you about something," I say, closing my hand over his, lifting it from my cheek, and squeezing it.

"Uh-oh," he says, his hand stiffening in mine, before he pulls it back.

"Don't worry," I say in a voice so small, it's almost a whisper. "It's nothing bad. Not really . . ."

I take a deep breath, and turn to look out over the silvery, shimmering track. I'm not sure where Matt and I will lead, but I know if I don't open up to him 100 percent like he has with me, if I don't take the leap and bare it all, I'll never know.

"When we were young, I had um . . . *big* feelings for you."

Out of the corner of my eye, I can see him smile into the darkness. "Yeah. I kinda got that from our conversation after karaoke in the garage. I can't tell you how sorry I am I didn't realize sooner."

"Thing is, Matt . . . after you left, I was in a bad place. I really liked you, maybe even loved you in that crazy first-love sort of way. It's scary to say, but it messed me up for years."

He says nothing, but I see his head tip forward a little.

"You talk about the risk line with racing, how you instinctively know where that line is? Well, I never knew where the line was with you. I mistook every kindness, every conversation, every arm around my shoulders for more than it was."

"That must have been confusing," he says quietly.

"It was torture," I say, laughing bitterly.

Matt starts to protest. "But my dad asked me—"

"I know. I get it now. I get why an eighteen-year-old fucking wunderkind didn't have time for a girl from home. . . . It makes sense you were doing it because you felt you had to."

"That's not the whole truth," he counters. "It's like I said before in Austin. I genuinely *liked* hanging out with you. We used to talk. Really *talk* to each other."

"Matt . . ." I say, sighing. "Just be real with me."

He turns his head sharply. "Here's what's real. I adored spending time with you. You were fun, and smart, and damn, you understood racing like no one else. You meant a lot to me, more than I was willing to admit. You still do, but now I see how crazy I was to let you go all those years ago.

"I was an asshole," he continues. "I ran out on everyone like a spoiled fucking kid."

"I get that you had this break none of us had," I interject.

"Sure, but I didn't get what was important. Maybe it's the crash, maybe I understand the stakes now," he says. "Chloe. Listen to me. If you had feelings for me once, please don't shut me out because of the past. Or work, or whatever it is you think is keeping us apart. We are adults. And now we have this chance to . . . explore this. No one is in the way. There are no obligations, just what we want. And I know without a shadow of a doubt I want you. I want to make you happy, Bug. Just how you make me feel."

I look at his pleading face and hear his urgent tone, and for the first time, I genuinely take in what Matt Warner is telling me. I feel the truth coming from him.

"No one is telling us not to, *but you*."

My breath catches, and it takes everything, all my steel, to calm my nerves.

"I'm just saying," he continues, his voice softening, "we can make this work. I know it."

The silence thickens between us.

"I hear you," I say quietly. "I really do hear you."

He smiles softly, his eyes taking on a wicked glint as he leans a little closer, his thumb stroking my cheek. "You better." His voice now has that gravelly edge.

My heart stops beating, and I'm pretty sure it's never going to start again.

As if conspiring in the moment, a cloud passes over the moon, covering us in near darkness. "I don't think you understand how I have *no* fucking control around you," he says, his voice suddenly tight.

Before I have a chance to think of anything other than how much I want him inside me, he grabs me around the waist and rolls over, pulling me down so I'm on top of him. I pull back, straddling him. I bite my lip, stilling as I look down at him, unable to make much out in the dark.

"No one can know," I say, unable to hide my amusement as I say it. I'm just repeating a mantra we both know has become a flimsy excuse. Like it's made of dust, one breath and it's gone into the wind.

"No one has to know," he says, pulling on my arms, trying to get me to lie down on top of him.

“My god,” I say, breathless, leaning forward, my hair falling around him. And then he pulls my hips down into his, and he lifts his head up, trying to catch my mouth.

“I want to—”

But before he has a chance to finish, I take over his mouth and kiss him, messy and hard and *needing.* His mouth is warm and wet and there is nothing tentative about it. I am suddenly frantic for him, all of him, and I pull at his T-shirt, lifting it up over his head, and he maneuvers out of it. His chest is bare. The fan of hair across it is invisible in the dark to everything but my touch.

“So little discipline,” he teases, his fingers fumbling at my zip, but when he can’t get purchase on the heavy ring to pull it open, he spins me over so he’s on top. Once I’m pinned under him, he opens it with one fast motion, revealing my black lacy bra.

“Beautiful,” he says, as he fans his hand across my belly, his fingers like fire against my skin. He leans in and kisses me hard, first on the mouth, and then in short, hungry kisses down my neck, pulling my arms out of the sleeves of my jumpsuit as he goes. The cool air makes me yearn for his kisses everywhere. “Christ,” he says, as his fingers reach the lace of my bra and his palm moves down to cover my breast, moving in soft circular motions against my nipple.

“Mmm,” I moan into the night air, as Matt pulls at my bra, reaching around to unclasp it and then tossing it far away across the grass.

“So you can’t get it back in a hurry.”

“They’re going to find that next year. When the groundsmen prepare for the race.”

“Lucky groundsmen.”

I'm naked from the waist up, splayed out on the grassy, stony earth, which is rough against my bare back, but I don't care. Matt looks down at my face and then my breasts, and closes his eyes as though trying to cool himself down.

"I don't want to rush. But also . . ." He opens his eyes, and his mouth comes down on my nipple and I arch my back into him, the pleasure flushing between my legs. He's expert. His hands are experienced, light, deft, and they know exactly where to move to match my desire. Just as I'm about to beg him to fuck me, he reaches down between my thighs and I help him by kicking off the legs of my jumpsuit and opening my legs for him. His hand moves quickly, and then he stops for a moment, staring deep into my eyes.

"I want to feel you come," he says, as his fingers move aside the lace of my underpants. His finger dipping in between my lips, stroking my clit. "You're so wet, Chloe. Always so wet for me."

The words send me, and my eyes roll back in my head as he rubs his finger up and down and around in expert circles.

I make all sorts of deeply unholy noises as he dips his finger inside me, and then buries his head in the crook of my neck, groaning as he moves his finger slowly in and out. I can feel myself stiffening against his finger, my body at war with itself, wet and slick and yet unable to fully open for him. It's nerves. After all this time. Am I enough? Will I be enough?

"So perfect," he says, sensing my feelings immediately. "So. Fucking. Perfect."

I clench around his finger, and he lifts his head, a look of devilish approval as he starts kissing my jaw and making his way to my mouth. My back arches as the waves of pleasure start to build, and all I can think about is how much I want him inside me. All of him.

I groan into his mouth, pushing myself against his finger as it slides in and up to my clit and then back inside me again. The pleasure is not enough. It's not enough. And yet . . . it's too much to take. My desire is pooling in my belly, and I'm starting to stiffen and then writhe against him.

"Yes, Chloe," he growls approvingly, as he moves so he can kiss my neck, just at the edge of my ear.

If it isn't his tongue against that spot behind my ear that finally sends me, it's Matt saying my name. *Chloe.* I clasp his wrist and let out a final moan as everything fades into darkness and I explode against him in wild contractions. Matt is moaning too, and although his hand slows against me, he doesn't stop as wave after wave shudders through me. It feels too good. *Too good.*

"Delicious," Matt says, kissing my cheeks, my eyelids, my nose.

I want more.

As I slowly regain my senses, I'm still ravenous for him.

"Now you," I murmur, as my eyes open and his silhouette appears above me, the moon moving from behind that cloud, and we are flooded with silvery light once again. Matt is relentless. His fingers don't stop moving inside me, even as the sensitivity makes me flinch endlessly. He looks down between our naked bodies, and then removes his hand from between my legs long enough to pull my panties off.

"I want you to do that while I'm inside you," he says, kicking off his Gucci tracksuit pants into the dirt. I can just see how hard he is. I reach down for him, but the way he's lying puts him just out of reach.

"Are you on birth control?" he asks, not a speck of awkwardness in his voice.

"IUD. We're covered, don't worry. Though I'm a little rusty," I say, instead moving my hand up to his chest as he climbs between my legs, forcing one thigh up slightly to make room.

Matt grins. "You didn't feel rusty to me."

"Filthy," I reply, smiling at him.

"Anyway, don't worry about it. I'm not rusty," he says, and I roll my eyes, slapping him gently on the chest.

"You're so arrogant," I say, and he laughs into my neck.

I feel his cock now, hard against my thigh, and I take a moment to feel his naked body with my fingers, his arms flexed as he holds himself up.

"I've been thinking about this for weeks," he says, nudging himself between my thighs. He's slowing. Making sure I'm present. I want to say that I've been thinking about this for years, but instead I say, "Did you also bring a banana?"

Matt laughs. "God, you need to be fucked," he says. He pushes in and I cry out with the sudden fullness of it.

"Too much?" he says, kissing my top lip.

"You wish," I say, grinning back at him, moving my legs slightly to accommodate all of him. He moves slowly, once, and then he leans forward and whispers into my ear.

"You feel incredible."

It is all I can take. I start to fall backward into the abyss as Matt moves inside me and I surrender completely to the moment. He seems to want to move slowly but loses the fight with himself, speeding quickly up. "Matt," I say, almost in disbelief at all of it.

All too soon, he's moaning my name back to me, into my

ear, holding me close to him as he comes. He stays inside me for a while, and we lie perfectly still, our skin slick with sweat, my thighs wet. I run my hand down his broad dewy back and across his backside and we both catch our breath in the darkness. "Gorgeous," Matt whispers, as he rolls off, runs his hand between my legs and then up my stomach, covering my body in our sex. It feels utterly erotic, and a little possessive. As if I hadn't dreamed of being possessed by him.

When I start to become aware of our surroundings again, I see the glow of a red light on his cheek and then a blue light. For a moment I can't work out where the color is coming from, but then I prop myself up on my elbows and spot the police car at the other side of the pit lane.

"Oh shit. Oh shit. Oh shit!" I whisper loudly, shoving Matt out of his sleepy daze. "We gotta run, Matt."

He sits bolt upright. "Fuck. We cannot get caught, Chloe."

"My god, the press," I say, giggling as I spring to life.

The two of us tug our clothes on as fast as we can, pants and T-shirts flying as we sort through our discarded pile and then sprint through the fence toward our cars. We're falling on the grass, tripping as we run, and laughing so hard tears stream down my face. As we hear the bang of the main gates being opened, Matt gently helps me through the fence.

"Go," he says, kissing me through the fence quickly. "You have the go-karts."

I don't wait to argue. I jump in Dad's truck and, driving with the lights off, speed away in the opposite direction from the police car and down the road back toward Brackley. When I get onto the main road, I turn on the lights, and my mouth breaks into a wide and wild grin. I feel like a teenager again. Like a wild and reckless teenager, only this time, I got the guy. *My* guy. And he had me. And it was perfect.

My stomach flips and turns as I fight back a manic laugh, covering my mouth with one hand, keeping the other steady on the wheel.

"Oh, hell, Chloe. You're in trouble," I say out loud, as I thunder home.

CHAPTER 20

Matt

I find Chloe in the British airways first-class lounge on the phone furiously pacing back and forth. I watch her gesticulating wildly, her hair down under a baseball cap, in soft-looking gray tracksuit pants and a matching skintight top. I can't stop thinking about those curves I finally got to touch. Such a delicious mix of innocently sweet and really fucking sexy, sprawled out naked on that grass. I'm getting hard again just thinking about it.

The police *did* catch me at my car that night, before I had the chance to escape. One officer shone a torch into my eyes, then down my dirt-covered tracksuit pants, and back up to my face.

"Yes, officer?"

"We had reports of some kids on go-karts on the track."

I pulled a face. "You don't say?"

"Hey, aren't you that F1 driver," said his partner suddenly, "Matt Warner?"

I quickly tried to hide the panic that crossed my face, but

the copper immediately saw it. Still, he seemed to decide an F1 driver visiting an F1 track at night was probably not too strange. He swept the light across Mum's car.

"You think Matt Warner would be seen dead in a Toyota?" said the copper as he eyed me with a grin, nodding for me to disappear. Sometimes being me has its perks.

"I'm not being a fucking princess." Chloe glares at me while on the phone and she nods toward the plush sofa. "I'm happy to fly with the team, but we're not with the team, are we? You've specifically put *me and Matt* in economy."

She listens intently for a few minutes, before she hangs up and tosses her phone onto the sofa in fury.

"Barry has decided we need to fly economy to Brazil today."

I chuckle. "I saw the boarding pass. Thank god we have lounge passes, eh? Imagine having to mingle away out there in the bull pit among the masses."

"It's not funny! I'll go pay for the upgrades myself," she says, picking up her handbag.

"Ohh . . . someone's getting used to the high life," I say teasingly, plonking down on the sofa as she strides back and forth. "Missing the private jet?"

Chloe tuts. "It's the principle of it," she moans. But I can see her starting to fight back a laugh as she clocks my amusement. "He wants to remind us that money is tight, he tells me. He says it's good to get a cold, hard reminder on that."

"Well, the press is going to have a field day. Did he think about that?"

"It's Barry. He runs Arden like he's running a school softball team," she shoots back.

"Maybe we need to have an honest conversation about what's actually happening instead of all this subterfuge," I say. "Sounds like you should be paid more than you are."

She sighs. "I was worried money was going to make Barry think twice about hiring me. It's still the most I've ever earned." She tips her chin toward me defiantly. "And I don't want to give him a financial reason to drop me."

"This sucks," I say.

Chloe stops fussing with her wallet for a moment and stills. "I just got the budget for this year. He doesn't talk about next year." She holds a hand up. "What am I going to do, Matt? Quit?"

"Definitely don't sign anything for next year until you have an agent," I say, folding my arms. "Just not my old agent. I fired his ass after the Arden surprise."

At that, she smiles. She's so flushed and big-eyed every time our eyes meet, and it's adorable. I close my eyes, trying not to think about making love to her again and again and again.

"I've got it under control," she says firmly.

"Maybe he's still trying to force us to *get on* better," I say with a wry smile. "Maybe I should call him and let him know we already did *get on*."

Chloe looks away, her cheeks darkening. "Shut up."

"Come on, Bug. Sit. You've been avoiding me since we went racing."

"I wasn't . . ." she says weakly.

She double-takes at my hand patting the sofa. "Sit," I say again.

She does, making sure there is plenty of distance as she

glances around the first-class lounge to see who might be watching.

"There's never press in first class," I say reassuringly, as I reach across the sofa and pull her hand into mine and give it a squeeze. "I hoped we might see each other again while we were in Brackley."

"I was busy with my family," she replies. I know her head was spinning after that night, so I let the excuse go and squeeze her hand again to let her know *I get it*. But I also want to tell her that it wasn't a onetime thing for me. That I like her, and I want to talk about *possibilities*.

"Matt. What the hell did we do?" she says, sliding next to me, her voice soft as a whisper.

"It was inevitable, and it was great." Her eyes flicker to mine as I say it, and a small smile spreads across her lips.

"It was Pandora's box," she says.

"Is that what you'd call it?" I lean in toward her, trying to put a hand between her legs.

"Jesus, Matt. We're boarding in twenty minutes!" Her cheeks bloom pink. It's a satisfying sight.

"I'm only sorry it was so dark," I say, pulling on my branded Big Ronny's Ring Burner cap and standing. "I would have liked to see your face when you were calling out my name."

"*Stop!*" she says, laughing, all flustered now, and she starts walking toward the lounge exit, pulling her own cap low.

We wander through the airport toward our gate. We're noticed everywhere we go. Some people take photos subtly. Some come right up and ask for a selfie. I'm trying to learn to be gracious in a way I wouldn't have been in the past. And grateful for this crazy job I love and hate and can't seem to walk away from. Chloe too is noticed, and I watch her, amused, as she awkwardly and apologetically signs a man's T-shirt.

I have to get her comfortable with her success, especially since I know there's more to come in her F1 future.

We're seated next to an elderly Brazilian lady who falls asleep during taxiing and remains asleep for almost the entire flight. The F1 fan across the aisle outright asks us why we're flying economy, and I explain that they were the only tickets available, and we had to change our times.

He seems to buy it. I hope I said it loud enough that someone will post it. No better way to spread a lie than to leak it to someone eager to spread it *for* you. I learned that little trick from the shit-hot Rossini press team.

"Can I ask you to dinner?" I say to Chloe as the meal service begins.

"I have no choice." She's so curt, ignoring me, flicking through the movie selection.

"Chicken or vegetarian?" I ask, unperturbed.

"Vegetarian," she mutters. "I'm going to watch a movie, then go straight to sleep."

"Ouch. Rough date," I retort teasingly. "What are you going to watch?"

"Something you hate," she says, grinning.

"*Really?*" I ask, my lip curling at the choice, as I unclasp her tray table as dinner arrives. "How do you know what I'll hate?"

"Because the only films we watched together were *Final Destination*, *Saw*, or literally anything in that horror genre—"

"I was a teenage boy!"

"Well, I'm going to find the opposite."

"What's the opposite of murder?"

"Love," Chloe says, her cheeks turning a little pink as she says it, settling on *Pride & Prejudice*, the 2005 film. I don't tell her I've seen it a few times already. It's my mum's favorite film.

"You know, you're a lot like the first-half Mr. Darcy," she says, eyeing me with amusement.

"But not the second half?" I say, queuing the film up.

"Not yet," she says, grinning. "Oh, come on, Matt, you'll hate it."

I ignore her. "Let's hit play at the same time, so we're watching it together."

She shakes her head. "Fine. It's your funeral."

After I enjoy a surprisingly tasty chicken and rice, some inedible bread, and a killer chocolate brownie, Chloe and I settle into our film with a plastic tumbler of red wine, blankets pulled up to our necks.

Mr. Darcy is standing at the back of the dance floor looking disgusted by everything, and I can't help but laugh. Chloe hits me on the arm and whispers, "Shhh," fixing her headphones on tighter.

When the cabin lights dim, I reach my hand under the blanket and try to find hers, but she squirms away.

"Stop it! Someone will see!" she whispers loudly.

"No one will see," I say, trying again. This time, I try to reach for the waistband of her pants, and she pulls my hand away. I see the man in the aisle opposite peer across at us, and I quickly give up.

Chloe eventually falls asleep as second-half Darcy begins

his mission to quietly win Elizabeth over with his hard work behind the scenes, sorting out the true scoundrel, Mr. Wickham. Man, I *really* know this movie. Maybe too much.

I glance down at Chloe's sleeping face as her head falls onto my shoulder. She really deserves a second-half Darcy. I reach my arm up and let her head lie against my chest and I sit very still, feeling her body rise and fall slowly as she sleeps.

I am falling for her. There is no denying it. To have her on that grass at Silverstone was one thing, but to have her completely is another. I've dated some cool women over the past decade, but none made me feel more grounded and yet more alive than Chloe. She knows my life, she knows my past, and she knows me. Really knows *me*.

But what she doesn't know is what it is like to feel safely cared for. And I'm worried—so worried—that I can't get that part right. She deserves an arm around her shoulder, a chest to lie on, someone she can really trust.

I wonder which Chloe would emerge under those circumstances. I wonder how much she could truly shine if I pushed her, believed her, and loved her the way she deserves.

As she moves slightly beneath my arm, I vow to stay here, completely still, and let her sleep the whole way to São Paulo. I vow to give her everything she needs to feel secure. That's the first step.

I gently kiss the top of her head and make that promise.

And I try to ignore the stiffening of my neck, and the prickling feeling in my arm, still for too long around her neck, like a thousand fire ants throwing a rave.

CHAPTER 21

Chloe

São Paulo (Brazil) Grand Prix
Qualifying

The hum of activity fills our garage—the clackity-clacking of whirring machinery, banging tools, and that constant murmur of a team hard at work as we prepare for this critical Rio qualifying. Above all, I'm delighted to hear the occasional burst of laughter. As though our team is *enjoying* this again.

Our mechanics, decked out in their green-and-black uniforms, dart around the gleaming Arden F1 cars, making those all-important final adjustments. We are almost ready.

I watch a shirtless Matt do bench presses while Noah lazily spots him with one hand wrapped around a green smoothie. I'm trying not to watch, but it's virtually impossible not to ogle Matt. And now that I've touched that chest, run my hands up those arms, I know what it feels like to have him.

I stare up at the ceiling, cursing myself and my shitty

self-control and the situation we've managed to get ourselves into.

But when I look back at him, my stomach flips. The way he looks across at me right now, sitting on the bench between sets, towel over his shoulder. Once upon a time when Matt looked at me like that, I felt as though there was a joke I wasn't in on. Now I know the joke—trying to deny what was between us this whole time. He's even more attractive to me than before.

That glint in his eye is just enough to send me back to the hill at Silverstone. He lifts the corner of his mouth into a wicked grin. I shake my head back at him. *Stop it.* We are going to get caught if he keeps looking at me like that, let alone constantly putting his hands all over me, every time he thinks no one is looking.

I look away, smiling despite myself.

"Barry, can we talk?" I say, calling him away from Matt's eyeline. Or maybe I'm mostly getting myself away. "Also, whose idea was it to bring the gym gear into the back of the garage?"

"Matt and Noah's," he says, as we walk down the hallway toward the driver quarters.

"I see," I reply, frowning.

"Feel like we have a new kid out there," he says. "He's stopped eating shit, he's training. He's climbing up the fucking leaderboard. He can have whatever he wants."

"It was a good start."

"Good start? We're heading to the top!" Barry kisses his finger and points to the sky. Or at least, the roof of the garage.

Climbing up the leaderboard? We have two points in eigh-

teen races! I admire Barry's belief in his choices and our ability to deliver, but he's in delulu land if he thinks one good race is going to change things. We have so much work to do.

"Barry," I say, ushering him to the back of the garage. "How are we doing with sponsors? I need to start thinking about next season."

"Let me worry about that," he says evasively.

I take a deep breath, reminding myself that it is *my* job, and not the owner's, to think about the strategy for next season. "It's my area to worry about it. To start planning for it. Even if you decide to replace me."

Barry's eyes drop to the floor as if he's looking for Ginger and Roger, and I realize it's the first time I've not seen them by his feet.

"Where are they?"

"Ginger was sick, so she stayed in England, and I couldn't take Roger alone."

He looks a little anxious as he says this.

"I'm sorry, Barry, you must be beside yourself," I say.

"Just don't take it the wrong way if I stroke your head during the race," he says.

I cannot help but laugh.

"But yeah, to your question, Chloe, we have some sponsors, some more *upmarket* sponsors, promising to come to Vegas if we can perform this weekend."

"Oh, that's good news. A bit of pressure, but good."

"If we can secure a really top sponsor . . ." he says, his voice trailing off as he catches himself.

"I know about the money problems, Barry," I say, hands balling in front of me. I don't want to embarrass him, but also, I need him to share these things with me.

"You do?" he says, snapping his head round.

I nod. "Just . . . try to share the full picture with me, okay?"

"The press was fucking good last week," he says, "but it isn't enough, Chloe. We need big motherfucking headlines. We need something to make people want to be with this damn brand. We will never be Rossini or Red Bull."

"We won't. But we can be Arden."

"Who the fuck is Arden?"

I suddenly hear the crash at the other end of the garage, which catches both our attention. Noah falls onto Matt after a failed chin-up, causing both of them to break out laughing. Noah's green smoothie was knocked over in the process and spilled all over the mat, and in almost comedy sketch fashion, Noah slides on it as he tries to stand, landing him back on Matt. I see the pit crew laugh together for the first time since I joined, and I see Archie rushing over with paper towels, also slipping and falling to the floor in the process. Three grown men, a salad of arms and legs, smothered in green goddess smoothie.

"That's our team," I say wryly, and Barry giggles. "And we're a family."

"You feel like that?" he asks, his big eyes round with delight.

"I do, actually," I say.

"And not just because you and Matt are, like . . . you know?"

I flame beet red. Holy shit. He's noticed?

"We're nothing. We're old friends," I say quickly. "Now, who is the sponsor? Shall we plan a night out with them in

Vegas?" I hope my speedy deflection moves the conversation on.

Barry grins. "*Finally.* You got something to wear that isn't a pair of jeans?"

But before I speak, just behind us, I feel the atmosphere shift.

The sound of footsteps marching across the garage floor and a door shutting firmly.

I spin around to see a group of stern-faced officials filing into the garage, led by the chief inspector—a tall man with terrifying villain energy, who looks like he could part the ocean with one downward glance.

"The Fédération Internationale de l'Automobile," I whisper to Barry. "The FIA."

"I know who the governing fucking body of F1 is," he shoots back.

The hum of activity stops abruptly, and I race over to protectively stand in front of the cars as a tense silence fills the garage. *What are the FIA doing here? What is going on? Is this an inspection?*

"Hi, all," the chief inspector says, his voice cutting through the silence, his German accent truly not helping with the villain energy. "We have received a formal complaint and are conducting a surprise inspection. I need all the crew to step back."

Matt, who is still paper-toweling the green goddess off his bare chest, spins around, eyes blazing with disbelief. "What? Are you serious? Qualifying is in a few hours."

I feel my blood pressure spike as my outrage matches Matt's. But I need to remain calm.

"Right, boys, you heard the man," I say, as they put down their tools and moan. Matt glances sideways at Jasper, who shrugs it all off as if this just *ain't no thing.*

As the FIA officials begin methodically disassembling the car, our team of engineers and mechanics watch on, frustration etched on their faces as their hard work is pulled apart piece by piece. The chief inspector's expression remains serious but impassive, as measurements and weights are cross-checked.

Matt paces back and forth like a caged tiger, the team behind us, his anger barely contained. He turns to me, his voice low but seething with fury. "This is a joke. Who the fuck complained?"

"We jumped several places. It's not unreasonable a competitor made the call," I say, trying to reason with my own nerves. "But it's fucking annoying."

Barry wanders over to join us, a broad smile on his chubby cheeks. His jolly presence is the polar opposite of the anxiety that grips the room.

"Well, well, well," he says, his voice brimming with amusement. "Looks like we've got everyone's attention now."

Matt and I turn to him.

"If we've got the attention of another team, we'll be getting the attention of sponsors. This is the kind of press I mean, Chloe." He grins, sweeping a hand across the air as he says, "Arden Under Surprise Fucking Inspection After Complaint About Huge Fucking Improvements."

"Wordy headline," Archie mumbles.

"We can edit out the swear words," I grumble back to him.

"Do you know how much pressure the team will be under to get these cars back and running for qualifying?" Matt seethes. "Fucking Rossini. It's straight out of their playbook."

"Relax. This is a good sign," I say.

Archie's outrage softens slightly. "I suppose that's one way to look at it."

"It's sabotage," Matt interjects, fists clenched just as Jasper joins us, rolling a cigarette with long, tobacco-stained fingers. "This feels personal, honestly. What if they find something?"

"They won't," says Jasper.

I nod in agreement. "Car's sound. Budget's tight. Let them look. We'll come out stronger for it."

The officials meticulously examine every component of the car, following their precise checklist. They measure the thickness of the car's floor. They inspect the front and rear wings. The bargeboards and diffusers are scrutinized for their dimensions and placement. They check the fuel system, the electronics, and the energy recovery systems to ensure they meet the strict standards set by the governing body.

Meanwhile, Jasper is back outside smoking, Matt is still pacing, Archie sits with arms crossed, poised to appeal any tiny suggestion of illegality. Our mechanics hover nearby, ready to answer any questions and provide documentation. I keep a close eye on the process, arms also crossed and expression stern.

"I'll lodge an objection," I say quietly to Barry. "We can play the game."

But Barry is enjoying it. He moves through the garage, offering words of sarcastic encouragement to the officials. "Found nothing? Oh, gee, I'm so sorry. We should do a better job of cheating next time, huh?"

The news of the surprise inspection spreads like wildfire through the paddock, and soon, the press begin to gather outside our pit.

Barry notices it before I do, taking a step toward them. Then he pauses, scratches the back of his head, and turns back to me. "You should probably do this," he says, nodding. "It's really *your* job, right?"

I glance sideways at Matt, who has stopped pacing long enough to nod encouragingly at me. I swallow the bile that rises up in my throat as I head out to the pit, ready to meet the scrum and answer a few questions.

Microphones are thrust forward and questions are shouted. There's a cacophony of curiosity and speculation, which sounds for all the world like a bunch of hungry yapping puppies.

"Surprise inspection? Anything to hide?"

"Absolutely not," I say, stone-faced. I spot Jack in the semicircle of microphones and smile at him, but am surprised to see him remain impassive in return. I frown. What is that about? *He's not still smarting because I didn't go to dinner with him, is he?*

"Chloe, is it true you've made illegal alterations to the rear wing?" says a reporter, jolting me back to the scene.

"What?" I say, caught off guard, and then I regroup. "Who told you that, Ian?"

Ian laughs. "My source," he replies, playing along.

"Not true, sorry. While we're annoyed at the timing of the inspection, we're confident this is a fishing expedition." I take a breath. "All I want to know is, who's afraid enough of Arden to make a complaint?"

Several of the reporters laugh, and I grin in response. I

hope, pray that I've given the impression that we're totally relaxed, have nothing to hide, and are in fact slightly amused by the whole thing. I spot Jack looking down at his phone among the group of reporters and feel a dark unease. There is nothing so unpredictable as a man who has been romantically rejected.

Nothing so *dangerous*, actually.

I make a mental note to send him a text later, and maybe even meet him for a friendly drink. The last thing I need is Jack hurt and turning on me in the press, just as I'm beginning to gain some confidence.

As I return to the garage, the chief inspector straightens up, face giving nothing away. He nods to his team, and they begin reassembling the car. "You're clear," he says simply. "We found no violations."

A collective sigh of relief sweeps through the garage. The mechanics spring into action, working triple-time to get the car ready for qualifying. Matt gives Barry a tight-lipped smile, still simmering with anger but relieved. I allow myself an internal "whoop whoop" of triumph before kicking into high gear for the race.

"See?" Barry says, clapping a hand on my shoulder.

"I have to admit, you're right," I say, grinning. I turn to the bustling garage. "Team, we got them talking," I say loudly. "Now let's make them cry."

CHAPTER 22

Matt

Seeing those inspectors in our garage really fired me up.

At Rossini, everyone pulls that shit on you. Complaints to the FIA on the slightest race incident, upgrades all scrutinized. Barry is right, it's a sign we've been noticed. It's a warning of what's to come. And we *should* be proud. Still, as I pull out onto that track, and the rain threatens from the dark gray skies above, I feel not just fired up, but *angry*.

I manage to breeze through Q1 with ease, not stopping to talk to anyone but Archie between races. I don't even look for Chloe. No distractions. *Just revenge.*

And now, as we move into the second round of qualifying, I'm fired up even more.

I want it—to start in the top ten, within sniffing distance of a podium. But on this track, the iconic Interlagos in São Paulo, it's not going to be easy. Famous for unpredictable weather, its undulating track, and its counterclockwise direction, it has plenty to challenge even a seasoned driver.

I tighten my grip on the wheel, glancing up at the absurd

Big Ronny's Ring Burner advert plastered around the stadium. My face, with an exaggerated expression of heat, tongue hanging out, eyes bulging, looks ridiculous. But instead of making me grimace, it adds to my drive. You want your luxury watch sponsor back, Matt? *You gotta drive for it.*

I take a deep breath, focusing on the damp track ahead.

I know this track. I love it here in Brazil. It was my first ever win, after all, so surely I can produce something here today. The roar of the Brazilian crowd grows louder as I head toward the long drag uphill past the pits, ready to start my lap.

The car feels good. So much better than even three races ago. I hold my breath as we near the starting line; I'm ready to unleash hell.

And boy, do I want to unleash.

"All right, Matt, let's do this," Archie's calm voice crackles over the radio. This track rewards bravery and precision, things Archie knows I need to work on.

Chloe's voice follows, softer and filled with encouragement. "You've got this, Matt."

She's on the radio too.

The memory of our night at the track surges through me. I think about our conversation about my fears on the track. My admission of everything that has been worrying me, and the way Chloe just listens.

I hit the throttle and leave the starting line in the dust.

Something hardens further in me; within the blink of an eye, I'm laser focused. I cannot hear anything except a whistling in my ear. I see nothing but what's in front. I feel nothing except the thump of my heart, which is so hard it feels like it's trying to break through my rib cage.

Ticktock. The imaginary clock spins in my head as I push, push, push.

I can do this. I can do this.

Every movement is precise. Time stops, even as I'm racing the clock. In the cabin of this car, everything feels like slow motion.

As I move through the turns, I catch a flash of red in my rearview mirror. Rossini way behind me. I grimace but push the thought away. *I'm only racing myself today.*

But it's unsettled me, and thoughts of Stavros return. My wheels come off the track, the car bumps the barrier, and I overcorrect. The error is almost negligible, but it's enough to lose a precious tenth of a second, and in this game, that's enough to knock me back.

As I cross the finish line, I glance at the time displayed on the steering wheel.

"Archie," I say breathlessly into the radio.

"You're in thirteenth," he says calmly. "Both Rossini to go. Stand by."

"Right, I'm coming in," I say, deflated. Thirteenth? Damn, that's the same as Mexico.

Still, the rush of adrenaline is overwhelming, and I can hear the joy from my team in the garage before I cut the engine and they roll me back into place. Thirteenth is still so good for Arden, even if it falls incredibly short for me.

I spot Chloe across the room grinning and holding herself to the back of the garage, allowing the team to celebrate together. I reluctantly high-five Jasper, and then Archie pulls me in hard for a hug.

"Noah?" I ask him, pulling back.

"He got eleventh again," Archie says with a grin.

I turn around and fist-bump Noah, trying not to let my own feelings of disappointment dampen the enthusiasm of the team.

And then, without thinking, I rush to Chloe and throw my arms around her, dropping my head into the crook of her neck.

"I can do better," I say. "I saw the Rossini and thought of Stavros, but tomorrow I can fucking get us some points, I know I can."

"Matt," she whispers, pushing me gently back.

For a moment, everything stills around us, and I feel a knot in the pit of my stomach.

Chloe is not smiling.

In fact, Chloe looks mortified.

She steps back, thrusts her hand out, trying to turn the hug into something professional, but it's too late for that. I glance around the garage and hope to god no one is looking. Thankfully, the crew are distracted in their own congratulations.

Chloe's body slackens, and she breathes out before aiming those big, brown, annoyed eyes at me.

"Don't do that again," she mouths.

"I don't care if anyone knows about us," I snap, irritated suddenly. Deep down I know she's right, but the rejection still stings.

"Well, I fucking care, okay?" she snaps back.

There's something in her eyes, a struggle against an undeniable force.

I lick my lips, which are dry from the sweat and exertion, and shake my head. "I'm going to find you later."

"You better not," she growls, eyes darkening on me as she

pushes me aside and shoots across the garage to congratulate Noah.

Press have gathered by the chain-link fence on the other side of the pit, and I can hear them calling my name. Fuck it. I'm going to talk.

I head out to the waiting microphones, feeling the sun on the back of my neck, the sweat pouring down my brow.

"Hey there."

"Matt, Matt! You looked good out there, until you hit the barrier."

"Car is much improved. Under Chloe Coleman things have really started to build."

"Is Jasper part of the team now?"

"You'll need to speak to the gaffer about that."

"Any regrets about not driving for Rossini today?"

I want to tell the reporter to fuck off, but instead I hold my gaze firm and say, "No regrets."

"How are you bedding in with Arden's star team principal, Chloe Coleman?" says a familiar voice. *Interesting choice of words*, I think, craning my neck to see who it came from. I spot Jack Sheppard then, just to the back of the scrum. *Oh, hell no.*

I don't respond and watch his jaw flex as I move my eyes to a young reporter from Sky Sports I recognize. "Yes, Sam?" I say, smiling.

"Economy flights, a hot sauce as a sponsor," she says, her voice light. "Would you say Brazil is Arden's last shot to remain in the competition?"

"Look, it's no secret Arden needed to improve," I say. "But we are. We'll get there."

"You won't get points with thirteenth place." Jack Sheppard again. "Do you think you'll get any more points on the board for Arden?"

"Yes," I say simply, without looking at him.

"Have you spoken to Stavros yet?" he asks, and I feel the blood start to pump through my temples, my chest tightening.

"Thanks, everyone," I mutter, turning on my heel and heading back into the garage. *Fuck that guy.*

"Is Chloe coming out?" says another voice as I disappear into the safety of the garage and head for the driver room.

"Chloe!" I call out to her as I pass. She's surrounded by the team, examining data, planning for the race tomorrow already. "The press want to speak to you."

She looks up and nods. But as she spots me, her expression changes to concern. I wave it away. "I'm fine," I mouth, nodding to the press scrum. "Go speak to them."

■■■■■■■■■

Later that evening, I sit on my bed, headphones on, trying to get myself back into the zone. Instead, I stare at my messages to Stavros from over the past few months. They start with me messaging him from our respective hospital beds. I was only in, really, for observation. Stavros had borne the worst of the crash.

Me: Hey Stav. Call me when you can. I'm sorry.

And then, as I scroll through my chat history, I see a bunch of calls from me to Stavros, none of which he answered. He was angry at me. I knew he was, and he had every right to be.

No one knows this, but there was one moment two or three weeks after the accident when I decided to go see him in person.

I arrived at the door to his rehabilitation suite and saw his mother and the Rossini doctor speaking in the lobby. His mum clocked me, and before I had a chance to speak, to plead my case, *to say sorry*, she marched toward me.

She bashed her fists against my chest and wailed at me in Greek. I knew enough key words to gather she was blaming me for nearly killing her son. I wanted to say sorry. Beg forgiveness. I wanted to say so many things, but she just shouted at me to leave.

"Go! You've done enough."

I turned and walked back down the corridor, fighting tears as I went.

That was my window to make things right. When I walked away, I felt like it closed.

I messaged him later that day, hoping I could catch him before they discharged me from the hospital:

Me: Sorry. I've been calling and calling. They're sending me home tomorrow. Can you message when you get this?

Me: I'm back in Monza. I hear you gave the nurse absolute hell about the food yesterday. Sounds like you're on the mend. ☺

Me: Hey. Are you ok? You don't want to talk, I get it. But I'd really like to speak to you at some point.

I should have tried harder. I should have spoken to his mother again and again. I should have come back the next day, and the next. But I didn't.

Now what was there to do? What *should* I do?

My fingers hover over the call button. Is there any point in calling him? I throw my phone down on the bed, annoyed that Stavros is back on my mind when I'm right here on the cusp of getting my confidence back. *Fuck Jack Sheppard for bringing it up.*

I'm showered, in my T-shirt and tracksuit pants, and about to order some room service when I decide instead to stretch my legs and head down to the bar to order something light to eat.

I don't expect to see her—she said she had to work tonight—but Chloe is there, in the corner of the bar, paperwork, computer, and a ridiculous tall iced cocktail in front of her. Her hair is up in a topknot, some thick clear-rimmed glasses on her nose, head in the books. I can't resist.

"Hey you," I say, looking down at her. She looks up, flushed, hand to her chest.

"Oh god, I thought you were someone else," she says, almost relieved.

"Expecting someone?" I ask.

"No." She puts her pen down.

"Not a certain charmless snake in a fedora, perchance?"

"Jack?" she says, shaking her head at my tone, disapprovingly. "Well. Maybe. Last time I snuck down for a night-before-the-race drink, he joined me. That night you saw us, in fact."

"Did you see him in the media circle?" I ask, lip curled as though even talk of him is like sucking on Bigfoot's toe jam.

"At the press conference too," she says, pushing her glasses back on her head. "I think I should talk to him. He's getting jittery. Cutting off his access—"

"No fucking way," I snap.

"I can handle him," she replies, eyebrow raised. "He asked me out to dinner. So it's an ego thing."

"He *what*?" My god, the ferocity with which that riles me up is a shock, even to me.

"Listen, buddy," she interrupts, tapping her finger on the table. "You're not the boss here. Of the team. Or of me."

I smile. I think fiery Chloe is my favorite. "Fine." I hold my hands up, willing myself to calm down. "Can't a guy who likes a girl get a little possessive from time to time?"

"Shush." She tries to contain a smile, then looks around the room. "Can you get me another drink?"

She pushes her empty glass toward me and I do as I'm ordered. I head to the bar for another cocktail for Chloe, a large ice water for me, and a plate of rice, beans, and chicken.

"I'm eating," I say, sliding the drink toward her.

"Can't you do it in your room?"

"You're so paranoid, Bug," I tease.

She flicks her eyes up to meet mine and grins. "How are you feeling?"

I sigh. "I'm okay." I want to add that I'm thinking too much about Stavros, but I don't want to worry Chloe just as we're on a high.

"I see," she says, glancing at every single person who enters the bar. She's so jumpy.

"Pass me some papers," I say, watching the way a lock of hair falls in front of her face. I fight the urge to pull the rest of her hair down too. I point, instead, to a stack of paper-clipped notes. "That pile there. Then, Chloe, it looks like we're having a meeting. We are allowed to do that. *We work together.*" I speak slowly, teasingly, as I keep my eyes on her, watching her every nervous twitch.

She scowls again, her grin widening, despite her attempt to appear fierce. She hands me a stack of paperwork.

"What the hell even is this?" I ask, flicking through the numbers, the charts. I spy the next season in small writing at the top of one of the pages. "Are you planning next year? Did Barry confirm you?"

"Just in case," she mutters, her cheeks flushing. "Can we talk about something else? Just literally anything but work."

"Anything?" I raise a single brow, leaning forward, elbows on the table. The music is jaunty—some kind of Brazilian jazz—and the bar is otherwise pretty quiet.

She breaks then, her face lighting up as she laughs hard. "You are *relentless.* I'm trying my best to keep things discreet, and you're not helping."

But the mood has softened, and the conversation finally lightens up. For a moment, it feels like it's just the two of us in the world, sitting in a bar, sharing a drink.

As the time hits eleven p.m. I try to hide a yawn, and Chloe spots it and yawns in return.

"Bed," she says, gathering her things. Then she pauses and looks up at me. "Alone."

"You've only got one thing on your mind, Coleman," I say, standing.

I walk her back to her hotel room, which, as luck would have it, is on the same floor as mine.

But just as I stop to say good night, hoping for a sneaky kiss out of sight in her doorway, we hear the ding of the elevator. Roles reversed from that night in Singapore, I spot Jack Sheppard exiting the lift.

"Hi, Matthew," he says, eyes darting between us. "Chloe."

"Matt was just going to bed," she says, shoving me, but I stand firm against her hands like a tree trunk and don't move an inch. Jack watches the exchange from twenty feet away.

"Lost your way?" I say, my voice impassive.

Chloe tries to subtly elbow me, but I move slightly in front of her as if trying to hide her. Or protect her. Or I'm just pathetic, alpha-male-ing out in front of this fool because he might fancy Chloe.

"Nah, I'm staying down the hall," he says, thumbing toward the rooms with a view of the car park. His eyes flick back to me and they are filled with contempt.

I narrow my eyes at him, wanting to make some dig about family money, but I resist.

"Can we catch up tomorrow, Jack?" Chloe asks, her voice light. "Maybe grab a coffee before the race?"

"Yeah, maybe," he replies, evasively. I watch his eyes drop to the floor as he searches his pockets for his room card.

I hear Chloe tut under her breath. "Can you go, please?" she says to me, before calling out to Jack. "Wait! I have been meaning to catch you."

I take a step backward. I have to let her do whatever the hell she thinks she needs to do here. Even if it kills me.

"I got a bunch of things to get done," Jack says, holding up his key card to show us he's found it, before stepping backward, turning on his heel, and heading down the hall.

"Damn you, Matt," says Chloe, when his door closes behind him.

"Did he get a room on this floor to be near you?"

"Now you're being paranoid."

"He works for a shit rag," I say, staring at his closed door.

"His parents are loaded," Chloe counters.

"I hate him."

"Shhhhh."

I do hate him. He was just suspiciously off with Chloe too. Is it because I'm here?

"You didn't have to be so obnoxious," she's saying now. "He's been good to me with the press."

"He's shady, Chloe. You should stay away from him."

"He's fine. I'll just call him," she says, tapping her card against the door and pushing it open. My eyes drop to her ass in her little shorts, but as I reach for her waist she ducks away.

"Not tonight, lover boy," she says, shaking her head. "Go to bed."

I nod, sighing heavily to let her know how hard it is to drag myself away.

Chloe places a hand on my arm, her touch warm and fizzy against my skin. "Matt. Get some rest. You've got a big race tomorrow." She then pauses and looks back at me with a newfound intensity. "We're going to do this, you know. We're going to build this team from the ground up."

I grin, and she tips her head, wondering out loud, "What is it?"

I lean my head against the doorframe and just drink her in. "Nothing."

"Then go."

"Okay, Bug. Sleep well," I say, glancing down the empty hallway to make sure it's clear before I reach in and pull her in for a kiss. One long, hard kiss on the lips. Her hands move to my chest right away, but she doesn't push. Instead, she digs her fingers in and kisses me back, her body slackening against mine. It's a different kind of kiss this time.

It feels like a promise. She reaches her hands around my neck and pulls back, smiling once, a flicker of something unsure . . . and so I kiss her again, this time more softly.

For a moment, it feels not like the kiss of mere lovers, but like a deeper connection. Trust. And maybe even . . .

She pulls away and smiles at me, warmly. *Tenderly.*

"Now. Get the fuck out of here," she says, pushing me playfully away.

I nod and laugh as I watch her disappear into her room. I stand there for a moment, battling the urge to knock, to say something more. Instead, I turn and walk back to my own room.

Tomorrow is a big day. Race day. And I have to focus. But as I lie in bed, my thoughts keep drifting between Stavros and Chloe, and what I have to do tomorrow on that track.

CHAPTER 23

Chloe

São Paulo (Brazil) Grand Prix
Race Day

I can't breathe.

There is a knock on the door, but I can't answer. I just stare at my computer screen, heart in my gut, willing the words I'm reading not to be real. But they are. And they're *my* words.

"Chloe, it's me, Keyla. Let me in."

I rush to the door and yank on her arm, slamming it shut as though reality is outside and I'm somehow still protected inside this room.

"I came as soon as I saw it," she says, pulling me in for a sturdy hug.

"I've fucked up so badly," I say.

"So, you really did tell Jack Sheppard those things?" She pulls back, hands firmly squeezing my arms, searching my eyes. I tear mine away, and skim through the article again.

Arden Team Principal Spills: Arrogant Warner Has Abandoned His Ex-Teammate Stavros Aetos

No sooner has Matt Warner been booted out of Rossini for underperforming than he finds himself in hot water again on his new team.

Principal Chloe Coleman has branded Warner arrogant, and as "charming as a dishcloth" and the driver "nobody wants to work with," as she rails against the decision to hire him without her say-so in an exclusive interview with F1 Daily.

But perhaps most shockingly, Coleman revealed Warner has not been to visit his critically injured teammate Stavros Aetos after their crash, a fact confirmed by Aetos's camp in Geneva. The drivers had been close on and off the track for over a decade, but with Aetos's career finished in a fiery crash at Monza, it looks like Warner has no use for his old friend. According to Coleman, Warner called the friendship "a bullshit Rossini thing" and jokingly referred to him as "burned-out"—literally and figuratively. Warner even went on to complain about the impact the crash has had on his own driving.

Allegedly, the two-time world champion is reluctantly seeing a therapist now, but there is little indication it's working. Rumors abound of substance abuse, with endless nights out drinking and womanizing. Warner also called his new young teammate, Noah Blacklock, weak and unimaginative, "lacking the killer instinct," and said he is only driving F1 because Barry can't afford anyone decent. Coleman confirmed Warner had pressured her to let him go.

My eyes are glued to the floor, shame crawling up my face. "I mean, some of it I said. Not all of it."

"About Stavros? About him not visiting? That quote is

really, really bad. I don't think anyone will forgive him. Joking about Stavros's burns? Fucking hell."

"He never said that to me," I say firmly. "Matt misses Stavros."

"But he's never been to see him. . . ." Keyla's voice trails off. "So it becomes easier to believe he might say something like that."

"Matt would never," I protest.

"It doesn't matter what you think. It matters what everyone else thinks. What about Noah? Did he really pressure you to drop him?"

"He said it one time," I say. "But he wasn't serious. He was lashing out."

"Jesus. And you told Jack?"

I rake over our conversations and try to remember. "Well. Matt has *not* been to see Stavros, but he never said those horrible things about him being 'burned-out.' *Never.* And the part about Noah is stupid. They took a while to gel, but Matt respects Noah. I certainly didn't tell him Matt is in therapy. He only told me, I'm not even sure Archie ever knew. . . . He's clearly found that out some other way."

"Shit." Keyla lays her bag, room key, and baseball cap on the dresser by the door, and nods for me to go sit on the bed. "Problem is that some of it's true, and you said it, so it's hard to defend the parts that Jack has made up."

"It's a disaster," I say angrily. "I could kill him."

"Fuck Jack Sheppard, Chloe. You need to think about Matt. Your team. *Barry.*" She pauses and takes a deep breath. "Have you spoken to the press team?"

"I'm too ashamed," I whimper. The tears that have been threatening since I saw this hot mess at seven forty-five a.m.

start to flow. But Keyla looks at me sternly, her dark eyes sympathetic but impatient. I take a deep breath and pull myself together. "But I will."

She nods approvingly.

And then just sits there.

"Now?"

"Now," she replies firmly.

I reach across to pick up the phone, and spot the message that has come through from Matt.

Tell me it isn't true.

"Oh god," I moan. "What have I done?"

I turn the phone around to show Keyla. She nods, takes a breath, and says, "Call your press team."

"I need to reply to Matt."

"I know, but first, call your press team."

The phone buzzes in my hand, a number I don't know, and I tap on the answer button before I have a chance to think.

"Hello?"

"Chloe. It's Daemon here from *Motorsport Monthly*. Just wanting to ask you a few questions about Stavros Aetos and Matt Warner."

"Arghh!" I shout, hanging up immediately, and tossing my phone across the room.

"Chaos Chloe needs to fuck off," Keyla says, pulling herself up from my bed and collecting my phone where it landed on the carpet. "We need Capable Kick-Ass Chloe. The woman who worked her way up through the leagues and is fucking smashing it out there as F1's youngest ever team principal. The girl I know and love. Can she come back, please?"

I smile pitifully, retrieve the phone from her, and then dial the media team. Of course, they waste no time with small talk.

"Hi, Chloe, this is Faye speaking," says a voice. "We met in—"

"I know you, Faye," I say, my voice shaky.

She grunts happily, and then launches into a plan. "As I see it, we have a few options. We sit it out, which is totally doable. Vegas is coming up, and we hear that Rossini are going to announce some changes to their driver lineup for next year, which should steal the headlines. Option two. We come out fighting. You deny the story—"

"But I said some of those things," I say, my voice as quiet as I can make it.

There is a beat of silence, and then a sharp intake of breath down the phone.

"It doesn't matter, Chloe," she replies sympathetically. "I know Jack. I know all the journalists. I know you guys are old friends. People chat. People say shit off guard. I know you didn't say this on the record."

"No, I didn't."

"So, we can deny the story," she says.

I look down at the headline.

My chest tightens further, and I start to find it hard to catch my breath. Keyla puts a hand firmly on my shoulder and it helps to ground me. "But I said those things," I say. "It was the day of the announcement. He put his phone away. Took his press pass off . . ."

I'm so stupid.

"We can still deny," she says plainly. "I've seen worse. I had to deal with the sexting episode with the previous team principal. Chloe, this is a walk in the park."

I shake my head. "I don't think I can deny."

"Fine. Then we wait it out. Wait for something else to grab the headlines. You play cool, Chloe."

"Okay. Really? I shouldn't say anything to the team?"

"Not today. We need to put on a show of unity for the cameras. You and Matt can maybe talk to the press together and laugh it off. Barry and you should have breakfast this morning."

"Have you spoken to Barry?"

There is silence on the phone for a beat.

"We'll get you through this," she says. "Someone in F1 will do something worse or more dramatic in a matter of days. Hours, probably." She chortles.

"Okay," I say, nodding.

"I'm serious. The real problem here—the long-term one—is internal." There is a pause as she takes in a deep breath. "And I can help you, but only to a point, with that part."

"Have you spoken with Matt?" I ask, my voice shaky again.

"We're on him," she replies. I can't ask her what he's said. I can't debase myself by whimpering down the phone and asking if he's mad at me. I can't do any of that.

"Good," I say, after I steady my voice. "Okay. I'm going to get dressed. Call me when you know next steps."

I hang up, and Keyla smiles softly at me. "They have a plan?"

"She is working so fast."

"There's a lot of women in this sport who will work fast for you," she says. "And hard."

I push away the overwhelming feeling of shame and try to focus on what she's saying.

"You can't crumble now, Chloe."

"I won't."

"Good," she says, staring at me, willing me to hear her.

I nod furiously. I have hardly spoken to her about any of this. She's always so wise, and if I weren't so ashamed about what's been going on with Matt, I would have seen more of her.

Oh, Matt. Is he ever going to forgive me?

I take a breath, suddenly galvanized. I shower, turn my hair up into a damp topknot. Keyla chooses for me a pair of black jeans and an Arden polo from the wardrobe.

"How am I supposed to be with the team, Keyla?" I ask.

"Honestly," she says, "they will have read it this morning over their cornflakes and then moved on to the next thing."

"Liar," I retort.

She laughs, pulling her hat back on, readying herself to slip out unnoticed. We can't have another scandal on our hands. "Say nothing, just as your PR team advised, Chloe. You can't control it anyway. And, honey." She looks at me. "You survived your first scandal? You've really made it."

I swallow the bile that threatens to rise every time I think about Matt. But first things first, I need to meet with Barry over a very public breakfast, as instructed.

I spot him across the floor. All eyes are on me as I walk through the enormous breakfast hall with its cascading hanging ferns and huge observatory-style windows. My stomach churns.

"Ms. Coleman," he says, standing up and giving my hand a shake with a light kiss on the cheek. He's all formal and smiles, which throws me.

"I'm furious," he says, grinning as we sit down, and he calls the waitress over to take my order. "I should fire you on the spot."

He belly-laughs, the fleshy rounds of his cheeks straining from the sheer force of his cackle, and for a moment I think he's joking. But then I realize he's putting on a show. Right now. And people are watching.

Shit. I can't sit here looking chastised. And so, I belly-laugh too.

"Hello," chimes in the waitress. "Can I offer you anything?"

I glance up at the waitress and gulp. "Sure. Eggs are fine." Like I can eat anything at a time like this.

"Scrambled? Fried? Poached?"

"Oh, she's all those things," says Barry, pouring lots of milk into his steaming percolated coffee.

"Fried," I say quickly. "Thank you."

I turn back to Barry, who pushes the small, ornate sterling silver coffeepot in my direction.

He leans forward, grinning widely. "You *are* fried. And you're *toast*, Coleman."

I blink. There sure are a lot of insults in a breakfast menu.

"I'm so sorry. Barry, it was a moment off the record, with

someone I thought was a friend. I was letting off steam after you—"

"Letting off steam?" He shoots me a look.

"It was indiscreet, and I was naive. It will never happen again."

The eggs have arrived with lightning speed.

"No, it won't," he says, looking down at his own fried eggs, spearing a bulbous orange yolk with a corner of thickly buttered toast.

I shudder, forcing myself to laugh, and playfully hit his hand so everyone in the room thinks he told me a particularly wicked joke. Before we have a chance to thrash things out, Barry takes a long call, and I sit sipping on coffee I don't want, poking at eggs that make my stomach turn. Eventually, I shut off the internal self-loathing monologue and start to hear the content of Barry's call.

". . . yes, Noah will be released. I'll announce in October. . . ."

It's Barry, doing my job yet again. Talking to someone—an agent?—about releasing Noah from his contract. Suddenly, I feel a tightening in the pit of my belly. I push my eggs forward, fold my arms, and wait for him to hang up.

When he finally does, I'm pissed. "You know what, Barry?" I say, fake grinning at him, keeping my voice low. "You claim to have uncaged me, to have given me a shot no one else would have, but you continue to clip my wings. I can't do my job unless you step back and let me fucking do it."

"If you *could* do it, maybe I would," he murmurs, chewing on his toast.

"I fucked up on this one thing. I did fuck up. But in every

other way, I've measured up and surpassed all expectations."

Barry sits back in his chair, folding his arms over his belly to mirror me as he considers my words.

"You hired me, and then hired a driver without asking. And yeah, I was angry about it. I have known Matt my whole life, and for personal reasons it was a gut punch when you announced it."

"I see," Barry says, reluctantly absorbing the information.

"And now you're . . . what? Letting Noah go? It's a mistake. He's good."

Barry sighs. "We can't afford him, despite what you said to that reporter. And Matt's comments have fucked him in the eyes of sponsors. Who wants their brand on a driver with *no killer instinct*? I would have talked to you about it today if I knew I could trust you."

"You *can* trust me," I say. "But can I trust you? I don't know the extent of our money problems, which I should. I heard that we are dead after Vegas if things don't improve. Is that true?"

Barry looks sheepish suddenly. "In the background things were slowly happening. . . ."

"What things?" I say, folding my arms. Point made. "Unless I know what's going on, I can't help you."

"Sorry," he says, looking at his eggs. "Matt was expensive and we just need more investors. More sponsors. I was delaying until—"

"Oh my god, until when?"

"The sponsors dinner in Vegas is our make-or-break. The dinner you're supposed to attend, though your absolute disinterest in working a room has been evident from day one."

I gulp. Okay, I deserve that. But in my defense, I didn't realize things were so critical.

"And if that doesn't work?"

Barry sniffs, looking out the window. "It would have worked after all the improvements you made," he says grimly. "Now who's going to touch us?"

"You should have talked to me. We were nearly a real team."

"*You* broke up the team," he shoots back. "You were a mistake."

I stand up and wipe the crumbs off my face with my napkin, ready to make a bold move. "Obviously I'll finish out the season, as per my very low-paid contract. But if you want to fire me now go right ahead."

Please don't fire me. Please don't fire me.

"May as well stay until Vegas," he says wearily. "We're finished anyway."

I feel the eyes of the room back on us, and so I turn on my biggest smile. "Until Vegas, then."

I strut out of the breakfast room. Next stop: facing the team and Matt.

■■■■■■■■■■■

Still running on the adrenaline of standing up to Barry, I push through the back door and out into the garage. The first person I see is Noah.

I will not let Barry sell him. The thought hits like a sucker punch.

But I have zero leverage. If he goes under, we all do.

And then I remember the article. Shit, this is going to be hard. I somehow cannot believe the professional advice is to say nothing and act like nothing has happened. Can that *really* be right?

"Race day," I say, trying to act chill, but feeling my cheeks burn hot.

"Yes, boss," he says, without looking at me.

"Give them hell today, Noah," I say, my voice serious. He's got to perform now either for himself, or so any other team will pick him up.

"Of course, boss," he replies.

"Matt values you a lot," I say. "He doesn't want you to go. And I don't either. You got real talent. And huge potential."

He looks at me, finally, and smiles. "Yeah? Really?"

"Yes," I say, hand on my heart.

Noah grins, momentarily buoyed. "Thanks, boss," he says.

"I'm fighting for you," I say to myself, just as I spot Matt out in the pit. He's already talking to press, the scrum the biggest I've seen in the three races since he joined. I walk slowly but purposefully toward him.

I make my way out into the bright sunshine and wish I'd worn sunglasses to hide the fear in my eyes. I know I have to act like everything is fine, but did Matt get the memo? Has the team told him the plan?

I swallow just as one of the reporters in front tears his flirtatious eyes from Matt long enough to spot me. "Chloe! A few questions, please?"

Matt turns his head and our eyes lock. For a split second—

just the briefest of moments—I see the deep hurt, but then he forces a spectacular, full-face smile.

"There she is," he says, holding his hand out and motioning for me to join him.

I hesitate, but Matt waves his hand to hurry me.

"What a beautiful morning here in São Paulo," I say, my mouth dry. More smiling. Keeping my voice even.

"Have you got any comment on the scoop in today's paper? Are you and Matt at war?" I can smell the warm plastic of the microphone that has been shoved in front of my mouth, but the faces of the press are shadowed, the sun behind them shining right into my eyes. *Good.* I can't see them properly.

I look to Matt, and we each pull a fake amused face at the other.

"Does it look like war?" I say, pointing a finger between us both. Matt chuckles, and I smile back at him.

"Did you really compare him to a used dishcloth?"

"Dish? I think Matt Warner has been called a dish many times."

The journalists laugh, and the cramping muscles around my lungs slacken a little.

"Are you denying the disagreements between you and Barry Arden? That you didn't want to hire Matt?"

I take a breath. "Look, it's true Matt's contract was unexpected, but to have someone of his caliber on the team is an honor. His improvement tells me everything I need to know."

"So, Matt, is it true you never went to see your old teammate Stavros?"

"Of course not," he shoots back, cheeks flaming.

I want to jump in, but he also needs a chance to defend himself. He can do this. He's really fucking good at this.

"Stavros suffered some burn injuries; did you really make light of those?"

"No," Matt shoots back angrily. "The story is bullshit."

"Do you deny, then, that you haven't seen him since the crash?"

Matt hesitates, and I quickly jump in with, "Stavros is still recovering," and before he can come back, I point to another reporter. "Jenny, any questions?"

"Did Matt pressure you to drop Noah Blacklock?" *Oh, brother.*

I falter, searching the depths of my brain to find another retort, and worse still, I spot Noah loitering just behind one of the reporters. But now it's Matt who jumps in.

"Noah Blacklock is a fantastic young driver," he says sharply. "He's hardworking and he's sharp. I think he'll be world champion one day."

"Are you denying the article? Chloe, you're quoted directly in it."

"Come on," Matt says, holding his hands up. "Are we really taking that filthy rag as the bastion of truth now?"

"And what about Arden's financial problems? Are you on the edge of collapse?"

"I sure hope not," I joke. And then I think about Noah, and the rest of the team, and I know I need to give more. "Arden Racing hasn't got the deep pockets of a Rossini or a Mercedes. We don't have the training programs, the legacy, or the luxury goods sponsors. But we have one thing. We have talent. All the way from the bottom to the top." I try not to think about that one awful strategist. It's true of everyone else.

I'm sure I can see Matt smile out of the corner of my eye.

"And Barry Arden is all heart. He loves this sport . . . *almost* as much as he loves his dogs."

Laughter waves through the scrum.

"Any other questions?" I ask, pointing toward the back of the crowd.

"Arden's car is looking faster. Reckon you can get more points today?"

"Reckon I can try," says Matt. And then we're interrupted by Archie in a move that feels perfectly timed, perhaps coordinated. He whispers something into Matt's ear.

"Duty calls," Matt says, pointing toward the garage with his thumb, while Archie nods for me to follow him. I move slowly with them, Matt striding ahead and Archie by my side.

"I . . . *Archie*," I say, grabbing his hand when we slip inside. "I fucked up."

He stops, puts a hand on my shoulder, glancing over at Matt to make sure he's out of earshot.

"Yeah, okay," says Archie. "You fucked up, and now you know how those rats take your words and twist them and pretend you said shit and invent sources."

I suck back breath, my eyes widening.

"I get you were just blowing off steam with an old friend." He pauses to shake his head. "Jack Sheppard is finished in F1. No one will talk to him again after that."

I sneak a glance at Matt, who looks completely deflated now that he's out of view of the cameras. His shoulders fall forward, eyes on the floor as he spins his new helmet in his hands. I feel my eyes mist a little, my heart squeeze, and then a wash of complete despair. *Please, God, please help him forgive me.*

I glance at my watch. One hour until we race.

"I have to speak to him," I say to Archie.

"After the race," he replies with a smile. "I'm really rooting for you both. You're one of the good ones, Chloe."

"Thanks," I whisper.

CHAPTER 24

Matt

"Keep pushing, Matt!" Archie's voice crackles in my ear. But I can tell by his tone he's worried. I came in late, I avoided everyone, and now I'm driving like I'm unhinged, and not in a good way.

I try to navigate each corner with as much accuracy as I can, but my scattered brain continues to distract me. The car is responding quickly to every precise turn, but every imprecise one too. She's really a beautiful car now. Incredible what Chloe and the team have managed to get done in her short spell here.

Shame it's wasted on a shit driver like me.

No sooner are my thoughts on Chloe than they pounce on her betrayal, and my body stiffens, as if bracing itself for the hurt. The car careens dangerously close to the barrier.

And then I remember that the whole world knows I've been too gutless to face my friend. That I let a few difficult moments scare me off from doing the right thing. That I should have camped outside that damn hospital until I could get in.

And Noah. This young kid who has fought his way to the top with no support, just his own hard work. I should never have betrayed him either. It's not who I am.

I suddenly snap back to the track, and as I approach turn twelve I realize I'm coming in too fast, my rear tires losing grip. I skid into the Haas, which has been threatening to overtake for the past lap, clip the front, then spin off the track, the gravel violently shaking the chassis as I struggle to regain control.

Stavros. I gasp as I'm transported back to that race, back to the thunderous clap as our cars clipped each other and Stavros was tossed into the air, landing upside down and skidding into the wall. Then came the flames.

"Matt, pull back!" Archie shouts, but it's too late. I veer onto the track, rejoining the race with several cars now ahead of me.

"We can still salvage this," he says, trying to keep me focused.

"I clipped my wing," I say.

"We're checking."

I grit my teeth, pushing hard to make up for lost time. The disappointment stings, but I don't have time to dwell.

"Come on, Matt! Eyes forward, let's claw back some places," Archie urges. But it's no use. My brain is just too jumbled. The despair and hopelessness I felt before I came to Arden, before I found my feet again, before I fell for Chloe is back with a vengeance. My heart not on the track, but off it, somewhere, feeling bruised. A little bit more damaged, just as I was starting to heal.

As I cross the line, having dropped five places and finishing in eighteenth, I drop my head into my hands.

"It's understandable," Archie says in my ears.

"I'm finished," I say, but the radio is off. I talk to no one. I do the postrace checks, and I hide away until I can safely escape from everyone and everything.

I know just what I have to do.

■■■■■■■■■■

The small villa that Stavros has been recuperating in the past couple of weeks sits on the edge of a bay in Cephalonia, a small island off the coast of Greece. I can imagine him a lot happier here than that rehabilitation place in the hills near Geneva.

I stand at the entrance to the villa, the cab still running, and look up through the iron gates toward the white-plastered estate with its wide balconies and stone walls covered in pink climbing flowers. This is it. I hand my cabdriver a hundred euros as I ask him to wait.

"I'll wait as long as you need," he says, folding the bills and shoving them into his shirt pocket.

My phone has been buzzing all morning.

Archie.

Then Chloe.

Then Barry.

I message Archie quickly.

Tell everyone I'll see them in Vegas

Each step up the driveway I get more nervous, a knot forming in the pit of my stomach as I imagine Stavros's face when he sees me. I've already made a deal with myself—if I get to see him and he tells me to leave, then I will walk away. The heat is almost unbearable; the trees on either side of the stone path seem to be buckling in the parched air.

I see a shiny black SUV with dark glass windows under a tree, and a second farther along poking out of the garage. He's not alone, not that I ever imagined he would be.

I reach the wood-slat door and knock.

Here we go.

But there is no answer.

I step back, trying to see up to the balcony above, but all I can see from down here are the railings. I pull out my phone and a hit the call button.

Come on, Stavros, pick up.

After a few rings, I pull the phone away from my ear, about to hang up, when I hear that unmistakable Apple ringtone, faintly coming from somewhere nearby. I look up, craning my neck. *Yes, it's coming from that balcony.*

"Stavros!" I call out.

Nothing. The phone rings out.

"Stavros!" I say again.

And that's when I hear the splash of water and the sound of a body heaving itself out of a pool. "Well, well, well," I hear above me.

I'd know that voice anywhere.

"Stavros?" I call out again, scanning the railing. *Surely he can't ignore me now.*

I almost jump backward when I see his face leaning over the railing. His black hair cropped short, the scar visible along his skull, though the hair will cover that soon. That was a surface wound; it's the injuries to his arms that I worry about seeing.

His face is blank as he stares down at me. "You finally came, motherfucker," he says at last, in his thick Greek accent.

"I'm sorry it took me so long," I say.

"You've got no balls."

"True." Stavros has always been good at calling me on my bullshit.

"Get the fuck up here, then," he says, nodding to the trellises nailed to the side wall, covered in climbing vines. He disappears behind the railing. "Hurry the hell up, Romeo."

I glance back down at the waiting cab, and then put my hand on the first beam and climb up. It's hot work, and the heat of the wood burns my skin. Once I get to the top, I pull myself over and find Stavros lying on a sun lounger, his eyes closed, his chest bare, and his red swim shorts barely covering the scar on his right thigh. Close up, the burns are just visible on his forearms now, still red and angry, but healed.

Not as bad as I've imagined in my nightmares.

"I wondered when you would show up. The longer I waited, the more I hated you," he says, opening a single eye and nodding to the sun lounger next to him. I do as I'm told, sweat pouring off my forehead and running down my back.

"Stavros," I start, sitting forward. There's so much I want to say, and I have no clue where to begin. "Dude. I'm so fucking sorry. I know it's no excuse, but I tried to come and see you but your mum—"

"Stop," he says, holding a hand up. "Just stop. Don't put this on my mum. Jesus. That was one time. It's been months."

"I know. I'm a fucking coward. I thought if I kept my distance and messaged you . . ." My voice is tight, and I swear to fucking god my heart is beating harder than when I'm driving the straight at Silverstone.

"You don't message someone to say *I'm sorry I nearly killed you*," he deadpans. "You get off your ass and you come to the house." He holds his hands out and I cringe. "At least you're here now."

"Stavros. I'm . . ." I don't want to say *sorry* again. It falls so terribly short of how I feel.

His eyes dart to the floor and then back up to meet mine. "It's probably better we waited to see each other anyway. I needed time to cool off and process," he concedes. "I saw your text messages and they made me really fucking angry."

I bunch my hands up in my lap, but I don't take my eyes off my friend.

"Sorry. I know," I say, chewing on my lip. "How ah . . . how are you doing?"

His smile is wry. "I'm better. But, ah . . . you sure you want to go there?"

I nod. Stavros looks surprised, but he shrugs, looking back up to the sky, his eyes closing again. "I was in a lot of pain for the first days," he says. "I was very confused after the operation. Twelve hours, the first one. Seven hours, the second. On it went."

My heart squeezes as he talks, more quietly now, dropping in and out of Greek as he details the days after the crash. His eyes glaze a few times.

"But yeah, I'm recovering and doing better now. I had some realizations as I've been away from the track. Out of the F1 world."

"But will you recover?" I ask, my eyes darting to his hands. "I mean, eventually?"

"Apart from the hands? Actually, maybe," he says, crossing himself, and then looking back to me. "I still struggle with headaches. But the fog in my brain is . . . clearing."

A woman emerges from the house behind us with a tray of lemonade and two pills for Stavros. Her long brown hair is wound in a bun on top of her head, a golden sheer caftan just hiding the bikini underneath. She's not a nurse, that much I can guess.

"This is Céline," he says, nodding toward her. "We met at the clinic."

My eyes widen as I notice the burn scars up her left leg. "Bonjour," she says, smiling wide. She follows my gaze and lifts her skirt a little. "Helicopter crash."

Then she leans over and gently kisses Stavros on the mouth. "I'll leave you two to catch up," she says before walking back inside.

"Take one," he says, nodding to the drinks.

I do, gratefully, downing almost all of it in one go.

"I had a little bet going with Céline," Stavros says, stretching out his hands and cracking his knuckles. "I said you would come. She said you wouldn't. And so, I win," he says, grinning. "I know you don't like to face your shit, so in a small way I'm proud of you."

I can't acknowledge the compliment. Not yet. I don't deserve it. And so, instead, I shrug.

"Stavros, *will* you race again? I read you can't," I say, my voice gravelly as I pray to the gods it isn't true.

"I think I *could* race again," he says, tipping his head to the side. "But actually, I don't want to."

"What? Really?" I'm stunned by this. "Why? Is it . . . are you nervous about—"

"Matt, I'm older than you," he says. "I was ready to move on a while ago."

"You don't mean that."

Stavros pushes himself up, wincing a little as he does. "Hip gives me hell," he explains. "But it's getting better. I just think an old man needs to accept when his time is up."

I stand too, unsure what's happening.

"Come on. Let's go open a bottle of something," he says. "You got nowhere to be today, right? How many days until Vegas?"

"Twelve."

"Great. Tell your car to go."

"Is that it?" I say, unable to move. "You have nothing else to say about what happened?"

"What happened? That's racing. That's the gig," he says, a hint of sadness in his eyes.

"But it was my fault," I say. "I did this to you."

"It's always someone's fault. In a different circumstance, maybe it's my fault."

I squeeze my eyes shut. "Stavros," I say weakly.

"Is it easier for you if I don't forgive you?" he asks. "Were you getting used to feeling terrible? Does it make you feel like there's been some kind of justice in the world, if you live in agony? Sorry, old friend, I'm not going to hold your hand in purgatory."

I laugh bitterly. "I guess maybe I thought I deserved it," I say.

"Well, if you hadn't got off your ass and come to me, I'd still hate you," he says, turning to me. "Do you still play very bad chess?"

"I do," I say. "Terrible."

"Great, because I'd like very much to beat you," he says, pushing the door to the villa open onto a large lounge room, plushly decorated in whites and cool blues. He drops himself down on a rattan chair, wincing again and touching his hip. And then he begins to rearrange the chessboard. "Sit, sit."

I join him, still a little stunned by everything, still watching him intently, hardly daring to believe I'm really here. And hoping—just pure hope—that I can have him back in my life for good.

"I want to hear about Arden. I read the little hit piece in *F1 Daily* from that prick you hate. Jack Sheppard, right?" Stavros grins. "I suppose you *had* to come after that was published."

"Reading in the paper that I had abandoned my friend certainly gave me the shove I needed," I say, feeling the heat in my cheeks. "But yeah. It was quite the character assassination."

"Did you really say I was burned-out? That was so cold I nearly laughed."

"Of course not."

"And your new codriver. Is he really shit?" Stavros puts his king down on the square and glances up at me. "You should be mentoring him, you know that?"

"Noah's brilliant. And I didn't say those things."

"Then your team principal made all of it up?"

When Stavros puts it that bluntly, I know it isn't true. "I don't think so. Some of it was definitely made-up."

"Then it *was* Jack?"

"Chloe is friends with Jack," I say, trying to unscramble my own thoughts on it all. "That's where it's confusing. I know she said at least some of it. I know she probably called me arrogant."

"Even I call you that," Stavros says, pointing a rook in my direction, before placing it on the square. The board is set, so Stavros reaches across to the sideboard and pulls the cork out of a bottle of red wine with his teeth and fills two tumblers.

"I think she off-loaded some stuff onto him that first night in Singapore," I concede. "But she's a hell of a team principal and a hell of a person, and I think she'll be eating herself up over it. She's too good. Too fair. . . ." My voice trails off as I think about her.

Stavros holds his glass in midair, his mouth open. "You *like* her."

I shake my head, knowing it's useless to fight him. "I do. More than like, even."

"Have you spoken to her?"

"She's messaged me, and I just can't face replying yet. She says sorry. She says it was a mistake."

Stavros laughs. "Well. Now it's *you* who has to decide whether to forgive a mistake."

I move the white pawn forward on the board and grin at Stavros. "Yes, I'm kind of seeing the irony here, thanks." I roll my eyes, but my mind is whirring.

"What about Arden?" he asks, ruthlessly taking my bishop on the third move.

"Arden?" I shrug. "It's been really great building something. Next year feels exciting."

Stavros nods, considering this. "Better than the reds?"

"Rossini?" I breathe out heavily. "It's got a kind of wholesome family vibe."

"I can see that," he says, sipping on his wine, moving his rook forward.

"Why?" I ask.

"I've been watching Arden slowly rise to the top. You all started as a shit show, but now you look like a real team with a lot of potential. Might be worth my while to invest," he says, winking at me. "One thing's clear, though—you have some things to figure out with Chloe Coleman. Both on and off the track."

"I do," I say, nodding.

I gaze out the little window toward an olive tree, perfectly framed by the white stone wall with the bright blue sky behind it. I think about her, and everything I feel about her, and how awful it was to read those words. I also think about how I wouldn't be here, talking with Stavros and figuring out my shit, if it weren't for her encouragement.

Can I forgive her, though? Trust her again?

"Another drink?" Stavros says, lifting the bottle. "You don't have to be anywhere tonight, do you?"

CHAPTER 25

Chloe

The next few days are a blur. Matt has jetted off to who knows where, and I travel to Vegas sad and defeated. My bones are heavy, my eyes permanently strained from tiredness. When I do sleep, it's patchy and dream filled.

On one hand, I think about the career I have flushed down the toilet because I was too angry, too hurt, too juvenile to move on from feelings about a teenage unrequited love. I lashed out, a little drunk, too stupid to focus on the professional gift I'd been given. *No. Not a gift.* A reward for my years of grit and hard work.

And on the other hand is the impossible reality I've found myself in. Falling back into those feelings with Matt and having him finally, deliciously reciprocate them. My heart overruling my head. My pathetic demands that we stop, cool off, overruled by my heart and my fucking insatiable desire for him. Then I went and messed it all up.

Of all the stupid things I've done, this takes the cake.

As I slide open the balcony door and look out over the strip, with its garishly bright, twinkling lights in one direction and the track visible in the other, I feel the tug of two lives—one where I'm team principal of an F1 team, and one where I'm happily in love with my first driver. Deep down, I know they can never become one.

My phone rings. *Barry.*

"You got my gift for the event?"

"Yes," I say, looking back inside at the dress I was sent to wear. In a couple of hours there will be a hosted party at some fancy mega-hotel on the strip. All the main sponsors will be there alongside potential new sponsors. I have to go with Barry and charm them, basically begging for money on the back of a terrible performance in Brazil. We've made the job so much harder than it needed to be with Matt's catastrophic placement collapse.

Which is my fault.

His already fragile state on the track was completely upended by that article.

"I'll be there."

"You'll be collected at seven," he says gruffly, before hanging up.

When you feel on the outs with everyone, it's easy to fall into a mode where you're happy just taking the shit. Like a dog with its ears flat and its tail between its legs.

My hair is blow-dried. Makeup perfectly applied thanks to the stylist Barry sent over. Feels a little over-the-top, but if this really is our make-or-break moment, I'll do anything to win.

"Nearly finished?" I say, looking up from my screen, trying not to sound desperate.

"Nearly," says the makeup artist, spraying my face with a mist. "There! Slay, you F1 queen."

"Thanks. It kills me that Barry will have had a two-minute shower and pulled on a suit," I say, grumbling as I head over to the dress bag and unzip it. I am almost blinded by sparkles. Oh, good god.

I unzip a little more tentatively, frightened of catching the fragile sequins in the zipper. Inside is a very short silver dress, which moves like molten metal as I free it from the bag and hold it up.

"Wow, is that a Stella McCartney?" she asks, gasping.

"It's beautiful," I say as I put it on. I glance at my face in the mirror and am shocked at the reflection.

I look *good*. The blowout is voluminous with soft bouncy curls, and my makeup is subtle with smoky grays and muted neutral lips to match the dress. My eyes pop out even more than normal. "Gosh. Thank you. You're a makeup wizard."

"I know." She grins a wide toothy grin. "What's the event for?"

"It's a pre-race mixer for sponsors and teams. A chance to woo new investment in your team."

"Will the drivers be there?"

I turn to her, and she flutters her eyelashes playfully. "I have a big crush on Lando, though my best friend is more of a Lewis girl."

I laugh. The first laugh in days.

"You probably find them all a pain in the ass," she says bashfully.

I raise my eyebrows and grin wryly. "Absolutely not."

I pull the dress down fully and it smooths like still water

against my curves. I turn to check out the back, and yank the hem down a little.

"It's immoral," I mutter.

"You're a long way from church," she says, thumbing toward the view of the strip.

Well, I think, sliding my stockinged feet into a pair of shiny silver heels, I'm going to go enjoy what might be my last night as team principal of an F1 team. I might as well go out there and schmooze my ass off.

There is a knock on the door, and then a gruff "Let's go" from Barry on the other side.

Ginger the greyhound is in a silver bow tie, Roger in a black bow tie, and I walk alongside Barry, who is not wearing a bow tie or even a tie, and has instead opted for something you might wear to a summer wedding in Spain: a pale blue linen suit and fedora.

We walk to the lift and I step in, feeling self-conscious and slightly uncomfortable. I don't think I've gotten this dressed up *ever*, certainly not for an F1 event.

Barry is quiet, for once, until the lift dings for the top floor, and we exit into the rooftop foyer. "You go out there and you be charming," he says.

"It's okay, Barry. I'll do what needs to be done for Arden."

"Good," he says, offering a slight smile, then reaches down to pet Ginger. I'm reminded that Barry is a man whose entire character is built on loyalty and trust. He saved those dogs, and he gave me a shot, and he needs to hear more than *I'll do what needs to be done.*

"Barry," I say, as he looks up from stroking Ginger's ear. "I want you to know that I am so grateful to you. And that I will never forget what you've done for me. And that I am loyal to Arden until the end. Whatever that looks like. Okay?"

He stands and shrugs, petulant, as if it's too late for all that. But I don't care. I want him to know. "Okay. Go get me a sponsor, then," he says. "You're quite the golden girl on the circuit now, it seems."

Sarcasm, I presume.

I nod, and push through the glass doors and out onto the roof terrace, walking as confidently as I can directly to the bar to order a martini. A drink that hopefully says, "I know I made my shit team the laughingstock of F1 but I'm a chic professional who's still here to do her job."

The terrace is spectacular with its fairy lighting, subtle F1 branding, complimentary bottles of champagne on every high-top. *I wish Keyla was here*, I think, as I clutch my drink, the liquid sloshing around in my unsteady hand.

I see the team principal of Rossini chatting in a circle, and the McLaren management a little farther down, looking across at the view. I should have done this more. I should have been brave and stepped out into the circus just as Matt had pushed me to do. I may have become more at ease with the press, but it's this room, full of these people, where the deals happen, where the teams are built. I owe my team that maximum effort.

"Hey there, Chloe Coleman." I turn my head and see two definitely not F1 men, suited and booted in matching pinstripes. One of them holds out his hand.

"This is Darryl and I'm Ali," he says, smiling.

"Am I under arrest?" They look like a couple of undercover policemen, to be honest. "You gonna pull out a badge?"

Darryl, the taller one with blond hair, laughs a warm,

open laugh. "I know, I know. We somehow bought the same suit," he says.

"Somehow?" Ali says. "You stole my motherfucking tailor."

"Excuse him," Darryl says, pushing Ali slightly, before turning to me and clearing his throat. He seems . . . a little nervous. "We wanted to meet you because we've been following your success at Arden."

"Oh?" I say, feeling the drink start to rattle in my hand all over again. I turn back to the bar to put it down.

"Yeah. We represent a few brands back in the UK, and one of them—Burberry—was interested in coming in."

I scoff. "Burberry? You're kidding."

"Not at all. A British gal at the top of her game in a men's sport? The dog logo? It's all very Burberry."

"I'm sorry." I frown, confused. "You're saying you'd be keen to sponsor the team, or me?"

"The team," Darren says quickly. "But we'd love to bring you into the press campaigns. Matt and Noah are strong, of course, but no one focuses on the team principal, and you're as much a part of the Arden story as anyone."

"You're actually the *real* story," Ali says.

"He's right. I don't want to take anything away from the boys. But the story is you."

"Especially with Matt's performance last race," Darren says, pulling a sympathetic face.

"He'll give it everything this weekend," I say, panic starting to claw at me.

"But you'd replace him for next season, anyway, right? I mean, you didn't want him."

"Are you referring to the article in *F1 Daily*?" I gulp. That fucking article. It's done more damage to Matt than I realized.

"Well, sure. Sounds like you want to take Arden in a different direction."

"But he's one of the best drivers of his generation," I say.

"*Was*," Darren says. "With all due respect."

"It would be great to see someone fresh, don't you think?" Ali says, before chuckling. "But you're the expert. Maybe he'll pull something out of the bag."

I glance over at Barry, who is deep in conversation. And then, one of the men steps sideways and I realize Matt is there next to him. I suck in a breath, my heart in my throat.

He looks beyond sexy, almost unreal in a black velvet dinner jacket and open black silk shirt, with a silver chain just showing against his tanned skin. But he also looks tired, drawn. I cannot believe I had him, really had him in my arms, and fucked it up so royally.

"He's a hot—I mean huge, experienced asset," I say, sipping on my drink. "But yeah. We need results. Every team needs results."

Darren exchanges a satisfied smile with his colleague. "Well, we don't want to keep you," he says, following my eyeline back to Matt, who has seen me now; our eyes are locked in an expressionless standoff. His eyes drop down to my feet and then make their way back up to my face, slowly, his gaze leaving sparks along my skin in its wake.

Please smile. Please smile. Please smile at me.

After what feels like an eternity, he does. There is some warmth there. Some thawing, I hope. He lifts his hand in a small wave before getting pulled back to his conversation.

"Oh, it's fine," I say, turning back to pick up my drink,

shaking hand spilling a little on my arm as I turn and take a sip.

"Well, I think you have a line," Darren says, pointing behind me, and I turn around to see a woman in a red suit waiting patiently for her turn to chat with me.

"I won't keep you either," she says, as the two men smile broadly and make their way through the crowd. She slinks in next to me and drops her voice. I can smell strong floral perfume and cigarette smoke as she leans in. "I'm just here on behalf of Haas."

I stiffen slightly.

"Not because of anything in particular," she says with a wink, handing me her card. "We'd love to take you for dinner sometime."

"I can't be seen—"

"It's okay, I'm off," she says. "Call me if you're intrigued."

I quickly slide the card down my cleavage and into my bra, glancing around to see if anyone has noticed. Then I look back to find Matt, but he's no longer in the group. In fact, I can't see him anywhere in the room. But before I have a chance to really pine for him, I am touched on the arm by someone else.

"Sorry to interrupt," says a Southern drawl. "Have you got a moment?"

I glance back at Barry, who tips his drink toward me in approval at the attention I'm getting. If only he knew I just got approached by Haas. That piece in the press may have ruined me inside my team, but it has raised my profile out of it. When Barry said that I was *quite the golden girl*, did he already know?

CHAPTER 26

Matt

When I saw Chloe across the room in that disgracefully short silver dress, everyone fawning over her, I knew I had to get out of her eyeline. She was literally shining. Sparkling. She's worked so hard, finally reached the pinnacle of her career. She deserves to have this attention all to herself. And so, I snuck over to the far side of the room, took a whiskey, and sat there alone, gazing out across the city, waiting as patiently as I could for a moment to go to her.

But now she's gone.

"Where did Chloe go?" I ask Barry, who is speaking enthusiastically to some advertising dude with a man bun.

He looks back over his shoulder to try to see her, but then shrugs. "I excused her a little bit ago. Dunno where she went, though."

"Can *I* go yet?" I ask, and he just cackles.

"Bringing in one extra investor, who is also your friend, doesn't give you a free pass."

"Guess I'll have to finish this scotch," I reply, tipping my glass. "Did Chloe make any impact?"

Barry nods emphatically. "Oh, yes. She did good tonight. She's outpacing us all. Making us all look like dumb, third-rate dudes."

"If she can pull a bigger sponsor than Ronny's fucking Ring Burner she'll be my hero."

I know Barry must be teetering on the edge here. He probably wants to release Chloe after all the chaos that has engulfed the team, and I don't want that for her.

I'm going to leave the team, I'm sure of that now. I have felt retirement calling all year, and this latest disaster is the final straw.

Barry is glaring at me. *What have I done now?*

"Why can't any of my team keep their damn mouths shut?" he bellows, tossing his hands in the air.

Suddenly I get a tap on the shoulder and turn around to see the guy with the man bun holding his hand out to me. I shake it, unsure who I'm actually greeting.

"I'm Ronny, from Big Ronny's Ring Burner," says the man. "And don't worry, I understand." He laughs enthusiastically.

"Oh." *Shit.* "Sorry. I love the helmet," I add meekly.

"Oh, that's just one thing I do. More of a hobby, really. But I also have a pretty big tech company. And we're looking to get in on sports marketing in a big way."

Barry shoots me a look. *I could die of embarrassment.* Of course the guy with the silly sauce company is also a stupidly rich tech billionaire.

"A crypto platform," says Barry.

"A crypto platform?" I say, grimacing. "Of course. Sorry again."

Ronny laughs, a sort of snort-laugh, and nudges Barry. "Lucky he's only here to drive."

"I'm an idiot," I say, shaking my head, grimacing. "Have I blown it?"

"Not if you place this weekend," Ronny Ring Burner says, chuckling even more. "I reckon there's a few sponsors here who are waiting to see results." He jerks both his hands up, beer sloshing out of the top of his drink as he grins. "No pressure."

"I'll see what I can do," I reply, and the man seems satisfied, patting me on the back.

"Good luck, Matt."

As I emerge from the lift and head toward the media scrum by the front door, I realize I can't wait anymore. I need to find Chloe. I need to hear her out. I need to see her.

Fuck the article. Half of that bashing I deserved, and the other half I'm sure Jack just conjured out of thin air. I know Chloe better than anyone. And I know I want to be with her whatever it takes.

On the car ride back to the hotel, I press my cheek against the glass and start to imagine what my life would look like if I quit racing. I've done no prep for it. No lengthy media training in hopes of a job as a commentator or contributor on the paddock. I have little interest in other ventures like opening a restaurant chain or going into the car business like other drivers have. I have enough money. Much more than feels fair.

I could move back home to Brackley, or the nearby Cotswolds. Buy an estate there. Get a couple of dogs. Maybe collect some sports cars.

I shudder.

I'm not ready for that.

But also, trying to claw back this career? And be with Chloe? That feels impossible.

The car pulls up to the hotel and as I get out and enter the lobby I know exactly where I need to go.

I ask the receptionist for Chloe's room number, but when I get there and knock she doesn't answer. I look at my watch: 11:09 p.m. She should be here. The bar? She does like a quiet, solitary drink.

I head back to the lift and then up several floors into the hotel cocktail bar: a deep blue furnished room with huge potted palms and floor-to-ceiling windows overlooking the city.

I motion to the bartender.

"A light beer, please?" I ask, and he nods, pouring my beer as I scan the room.

I check the seats in the perimeter by the windows, then look down the bar, and just when I'm about to give up, a man in the far corner sits back in his chair and I can see her.

Chloe. With . . . *Jack Sheppard.*

No.

The feeling shoots up me in a firestorm of anger. That absolute bastard, sitting there, chatting to her after all he's done. And why is she putting up with it? I push myself back against a pillar so I'm out of their eyelines.

I should go. I should leave. Did she leave the function to meet Jack?

Is this the truth of the situation in front of me? Has Chloe been playing me this whole time? The ferocity of that fear clutches me hard. And yet, even as I think it, I don't believe it. *Not Chloe.* She's too loyal at her core. Too good. Isn't she?

I watch her, her face completely even as Jack shakes his head. Chloe leans in and gesticulates wildly at him. She looks agitated, actually. My feelings switch from fear and hurt to anger and a protective urge as I watch her, still in that silver dress, her legs crossed, the fabric draping high on her thigh. My protective urge wins out.

Something in my gut tells me to approach with caution. I scan the seating near them. There is a wingback armchair just behind a huge potted palm that I could sit at. Take a drink. Pretend I didn't see them if I get caught.

I move quickly, sliding into the seating area adjacent to them, but hiding my body behind the oversize plant. I can just hear them, and it's clear from the tone that Chloe is on the offensive.

The bartender brings me my beer, and I stiffen slightly, hoping not to attract their attention, but the timbre of her voice is unchanged; she is too focused on whatever it is she's saying.

"Please, Jack." Her voice is exasperated.

"I'm just confused," Jack says. "I thought you hated him."

"I don't *hate* him."

I hold my breath, waiting to hear what Jack is about to say.

"You were so mad Barry hired him." He also sounds exasperated. "And you were right to be. He was holding you and the team back, surely you can see that."

"Jack, I want you to leave me alone," she says, her voice falling now.

"Why?"

"You don't get it? You hurt my team."

There is a long silence, before I hear someone stand up. It's Chloe, I think.

"If you won't go, I'm going."

"Chloe, wait."

She doesn't reply. She can't reply. She can't say anything that might end up in the newspaper tomorrow; she must know that now.

"You're not a good person, Jack. You took advantage of me, and unethically printed an off-the-record conversation and added your own bullshit to it."

I hear him scoff. "To be fair, you never said it was off-the-record."

"I was upset, and you exploited that for your own gain. That's not what friends do."

"For the love of god, Chloe, I did it for you!" he says, his voice loud and clear. "Look at the press. When you were appointed, they were laughing at you." I stiffen, my hand clasping my beer, as Jack continues. "Laughing at Barry. Matt was a disaster on the track and off. Arden was a fucking joke. Now, you're the darling of the circuit. I did that. That was because of me. And I can undo it."

"I didn't want you to do *anything*," she barks back, her voice strained and upset. "You hurt Matt and that's the last thing I want."

"Who gives a fuck about Matt Warner? He's an asshole. Everyone who works with him thinks he's an arrogant prick."

There is a long pause. I can feel my blood pump, my body tense, ready to spring up to protect her if I need to. But then I hear Jack laugh a pitiful, almost sadistic laugh.

"Oh my god," he says. "You're in love with him. *Again.*"

Chloe says nothing in response. I can picture her giving him a look, but then I hear her groan. "I'm going to bed."

"Of course you are," he says, sardonically laughing, and my fingers flex. I want to smack that guy in the face. "That's pathetic. Just like when we were kids. He's going to cast you aside like he did back then. He does to everyone. I thought you were better than that."

"Good night, Jack."

"You're a fool, falling for him," he says, sounding desperate now. "It's going to ruin you. You'll look ridiculous. Falling for a driver? It's so fucking tacky."

"I'd rather be a fool than a soulless snake," she snaps.

Go, Chloe. I try hard not to cheer. *Soulless snake?*

"Have a lonely life, Jack."

I hear her short, hurried paces as she crosses the bar and heads off, leaving Jack sitting exactly three feet behind me, with nothing but a high-backed armchair and a potted plant between us.

Fuck it.

I stand and walk around to the seating area to see a fidgeting, flapping Jack, playing with his phone, a recording app open on the screen. Concentrating hard on whatever the fuck he's doing in there, he doesn't look up and see me, and so I reach down and snatch the phone out of his hand.

"I'll take that," I say curtly.

"Hey!" he says, springing up.

I delete the latest recording, assuming it's Chloe. And then in a fit of rage, I smash the phone against the pillar, shattering the screen and almost splitting the phone in two.

"What the fuck? Have you been listening?" he says, frowning, looking back toward the entrance, expecting, I think, to see Chloe there.

"Chloe didn't know I was here," I say quickly, handing him back his destroyed phone and then crossing my arms over my chest. "Did she know you recorded her?"

"That's none of your damn business," Jack says, standing and sliding what's left of his phone into his back pocket while picking up his waxed messenger bag and hitching it over his shoulder. He slicks his hair back from his forehead, and then stares at me, pointedly. "What?"

"Why do you hate me so much?"

Jack's eyes are steady, his face impassive. "I'm just doing my job, Matt."

The anger inside me hardens, and my right hand starts to twitch. I want to hit him. So bad. Punch him in his slimy mouth.

"That article was a stitch-up."

"It was worth burning the source for."

"You need to leave her alone," I say, standing up a little straighter. Jack's on the skinny side of lean and clearly stopped working out some time ago. I could take him. Easily.

"You don't know what Chloe needs," he says, and then his eyes narrow.

I steady my breath. "What you did? It's really fucking unethical."

Jack scoffs. "You want to lecture me about ethics? How's Stavros?"

I tip my head back and stare at the ceiling, my hand balling into a fist.

"Jack," I say quietly, in warning.

"Oh, you still haven't seen him?"

I take a step forward, drop my head, and stare him down.

"You gonna hit me? Ever the intellectual, Matt," he says, laughing. "Remind me. Did you actually finish school in the end?"

Don't do this. A voice inside my head pushes all of it aside, and then Chloe's words come back to me. She didn't deny being in love with me. She didn't flat-out deny it. And there would be no reason to lie to Jack. *Unless she simply couldn't lie.*

"I'd rather be a fool." Her admission to Jack that she had fallen for me was there in what she didn't say. Could it be true? I feel my anger disperse a little and I relax my fist, deciding to let it all slide.

"Off you trot, Jack. Print your little stories about how awful I am. You are . . . what did she call you? A soulless snake?"

"Oh, I've got another, more interesting story now," he says.

I don't falter. I don't change my expression. "Yeah?"

"The team principal of Arden and her first driver having an affair."

Now, that one *would* hurt Chloe.

But he has no evidence of it. No one has seen us. Except . . . maybe me standing here, about to punch him in the face, is enough proof.

"Yeah," he says, a smarmy little smile crawling up his face.

I do what I have to do. What Chloe would want me to do. I do what's best for her and the team.

I laugh. Then I lie.

"Chloe Coleman?" I pull a face. "She's like a fucking sister, Jack. Don't be disgusting."

■■■■■■■■■■

When I head back to my room, I see Chloe standing outside her door, fighting with her room card, red-eyed, grunting and eventually kicking the door.

God, she's adorable. Those legs, that dress, her hair. That feisty temper. Could she really care for me? Could I drag her into that room and talk it out with her? Now?

Chloe snaps her head around as I walk toward her. I know now that we need to be careful. I glance up at the camera in the hall, and then keep walking, the smell of honey from her perfume filling my senses as I near.

"Chloe," I say, my eyes dropping down to meet hers.

"Matt," she says, her voice barely a whisper, her eyes round and full of shame. "I'm so sorry. You have to—"

"Shhh," I say, taking the plastic room card from her hand. I push it into the slot and open the door. "Not now."

"I'd like to explain," she says, as I take her by the hand and lead her into the room. She closes the door behind her and for a moment we stand looking at each other, her eyes nervous and searching. "I don't think those things about you. I promise."

"Well, that's good to hear," I say, and then I take her face in my hands and kiss her hard on the lips. Her lips part in return and I hear the faint moan that escapes her as she wraps her arms around me. *She wants this just as badly as I do.*

I quickly scoop her up and walk her over to the bed. She

lands with a gentle bounce, her hair fanning out, her dress shimmering as it catches the low light of the lamp.

I run my hand up the length of her stockinged leg, catching my fingers on a lingerie suspender belt near the top of her thigh. She tentatively grins, cheeks pink, as I curl my fingers around the edge of the silk fabric.

"You're not mad at me? Or hating me for what happened?"

"Do you want me to be?" I say as I rip the stockings off the clips and pull them down her perfect legs.

"No, but—"

I don't give her a chance to finish that thought, as I reach my hand between her legs, push her lace panties aside, and rub my finger across her clit. "I can't get enough of you," I say, feeling her arch against me right away.

"We have qualifying tomorrow," she reminds me, groaning into my ear.

"It's a night race," I say, feeling her hot breath quicken against my neck as she smiles. I inhale her scent, my nose buried in that mass of curls.

"Matt, I'm going to—"

"I know," I say, feeling her body stiffen against my hand.

I stop moving my fingers and Chloe's breath hitches; she turns her head to me. "What are you doing? Why are you stopping?"

"Not stopping," I say. "Just taking it slow."

She reaches down and tugs on my hand. "Of all the times to take it slowly," she says.

I sink my teeth into the fabric of her dress just on the shoulder, as I pick her up and push her against the wardrobe, obligingly taking her to the very edge again, feeling her come against my hand.

I pull her relaxed body into me, moving her back toward the bed, leaning down to kiss her on the mouth as we fall into each other, peeling our clothes off slowly. I lift the dress carefully over her head and she lies back in her black lace underwear. "Beautiful," I say. "You're just beautiful."

Chloe reaches up to slowly unbutton my shirt, as I unbuckle my pants and kick off my trousers. For the first time I have her somewhere quiet.

I kiss her everywhere I find skin, and she runs her fingers across my body; her soft touch is electric, and I flex in response.

As I slide inside her, I feel her body shudder against mine. She pushes the hair out of my face and kisses me gently on the mouth. I want to tell her I love her. It feels without any doubt that I do.

I have to rest my head on the pillow for a moment, just to hold on to this a little longer, because I'm not going to last. Not with her looking like she is. Not with me feeling like I do about her. But she reaches her arms around my neck and moves her hips just so, and I move deeper inside her.

"I . . . Chloe," I stammer. I want to tell her how I feel, how much I adore her.

"I know, Matt," she says. "Me too."

CHAPTER 27

Chloe

Las Vegas Grand Prix
Qualifying

I think about one hundredth of a second per lap," Jasper says, wiping the grease from his hands as he reaches into his cigarette pouch. "Impossible to know until we see her race. We're not going into the wind tunnel for testing any-time soon."

"I see." I try not to grin too much, or get too excited. Jasper has made so many minor adjustments—everything he can actually do to improve this car short of a complete re-build. Now it's up to the drivers to execute.

"Wanna smoke?" he says, holding out the rolled tobacco in my direction.

"Still no," I say, laughing. "I think I'm going to part-walk the track." I spot Alonso and his team out there already, sauntering past, chatting, laughing. Just like a team ought to be. "Take in the sights from the safety of the circuit."

"Your drivers should be doing that," says Jasper pointedly.

"Those puffed-up, spoiled peacocks?" I reply.

"Careful," he says. "You're still on thin ice, little lady."

"That's boss to you," I reply, punching him in the arm.

I head out onto the pit. It's busy as you'd expect for a street circuit with plenty of teams about. The officials and staff set up stands, erecting barriers along the wide boulevards. I wander along the winding tarmac to the edge of the lane and look up at the bright lights of the Las Vegas strip, starting to sparkle its famous colors against the sunset.

My god, I love this sport. I love the night races. I love the street circuits. I love it when we can bring our game so close to everything.

I find a crate where some workers are erecting the stands, and I decide to take a seat, pulling out a stick of gum, and drink in the pre-race atmosphere. Tomorrow, there will be three hundred thousand people in these stands, with more peering out hotel windows onto the strip. There will be sponsors too, looking at the next season and beyond and wanting to hitch their brands to a rising star. It feels so close at Arden. So many fragile, tentative, human threads that need to braid perfectly together to work this beast of a machine.

We could have been such an incredible story.

We could be going into qualifying today with another top-ten win, if it weren't for my stupid mouth.

My phone rings in my pocket and I pull it out.

I stare down at it, almost dropping it to the street with the anxious excitement of seeing his name.

"Matt," I say breathlessly into the phone. "Where are you? You snuck off early this morning, and we never got to . . . well, *talk*." I feel my cheeks heat at the memory.

"I know. I need to talk to you too. I'm walking the track," he says, his voice light. "With Noah and Barry's dogs, actually. We can see you. Wait for us."

I turn back down the track and see them picking up the pace, heading in my direction, the two greyhounds trotting in front on long leads as they come.

"Barry asked us to walk Ginger and Roger," Noah explains as they catch us up. "Matt's been giving me some really great tips for the circuit."

My eyes scan over to Matt, who offers a small smile.

"Come on," Noah says, enthusiastically being tugged ahead by Roger and Ginger. "It's a long fucking walk! At least we can see the whole strip."

And then he's off, racing ahead with the dogs, and Matt and I are left standing alone. Matt starts walking right away, slowly, following Noah and motioning for me to walk alongside him.

The sounds of the strip float across the barriers and onto the road. Above me, I can see the twinkling lights of the Flamingo and ahead the broad, brightly lit Caesars Palace. The air smells like heat, and tarmac, and the filth of the city, but I drink it in, Matt at my side.

I turn to look at him, and he glances sideways, grinning. "Well, we can talk now," he says playfully. "I have to keep my distance."

I ignore the warmth his teasing brings. "I'm sorry about what happened. I failed you," I say. "I failed at my most important job as team principal and that is protecting my team."

Matt stops, his eyes darting around cautiously.

"No one can hear us," I say, the point seemingly proved by the huge, thunderous crash of machinery from the construction crew nearby. I jump suddenly, jittery and anxious. I wish to hell we were somewhere private.

"I need to tell you some things," he says as we continue walking. "I went to see Stavros."

I halt and a small gasp escapes my mouth. I turn my head to face him. "When? Is that where you went after Brazil?"

"Yes," he says gravely, nodding for me to keep walking. "I went to see him in Greece."

"Oh, Matt. How did it go? Are you okay? How is he?"

"It actually went well, considering. And yes, I'm okay."

"And Stavros?"

"He's getting there. He looked okay. Still some visible healing," he says slowly. "God, he was so um . . . forgiving. It was really humbling."

"How do you feel? I have so many questions," I say, indicating that he should wave at some supporters who have spotted us on the track. He does a quick salute in their direction.

"I feel stupid that I didn't go earlier. You know, Stavros was ignoring me on purpose to force me to come see him," he explains, shaking his head in disbelief. "No text in months and now he's texting every five minutes. He's got plenty of advice for the race about my tire management."

I laugh at this. "You must feel so relieved."

"I feel like this weight has left my chest," he says, tapping his front with his hands. "I don't know if it's going to help on the track, but something has shifted. Plus, more than anything, I think I might have got my best friend back."

"Oh," I sigh. "I'm so proud of you for going."

"Yeah, that's what Stavros said too." He lets out a light laugh. "Turns out people can forgive if they care enough."

"I wish you'd told me last night."

"Sorry. I was kind of distracted last night," he jokes, letting his hand brush mine as we stroll down the tarmac.

I quiet, wondering if he's talking about us now, but I don't want to ask. Matt doesn't make me wait long. "I saw you in the bar with Jack," he says.

"Oh, shit," I say quickly, stopping immediately to turn to him.

"You're really bad at pretending we're just chatting," Matt laughs, turning me by the shoulders and giving me a light push to walk.

"Quit trying to shock me, then!" I protest.

"Eyes on the track, driver. They can see us, even if they can't hear us."

A murmur of excited voices from people heading out for the night, the muffled sound of music coming from the clubs, and the dinging and trilling of slot machines fill the air. Just a few meters to either side of us, the clang of workers fixing the grandstands and the distant roar of road cars taking their detours a few feet across.

I want to jump in and reassure him, for what it's worth, that I did not invite that meeting. Jack found me as though he'd been following me, honestly, mere minutes after I'd sat down.

"It really, truly wasn't what you think," I whimper.

"I know that," he says calmly, evenly. "I heard you both."

"Oh?" *Oh!* "Really?"

"I was behind a plant pot." He looks at me and gives a shy smirk. "It doesn't matter. I get why you talked to him. I know how he deceived you. We all need people to let off steam with. People we think we can trust."

"I . . ." I want to run, hide. Oh god. What did I say? I rack my brain trying to recall a conversation during which I was so focused on saying nothing printable that I can barely remember anything else. "He's awful."

"A soulless snake?" Matt says, laughing.

"I'm so sorry," I say again. "Matt, I need to be totally honest with you. So maybe it all makes more sense even if you don't forgive me completely."

"Well," he says, waving and smiling at fans who have gathered at the chain-link fence. "I'm going to forgive you, Coleman."

I smile ahead, trying not to make our conversation look too intimate. Trying to keep my cool as I clear my throat.

"I wish we could talk somewhere private," I mutter.

"We could. But I need to warn you, Jack the snake will probably want to do a follow-up story about some kind of romantic tryst between the two of us. And that, Chloe, is a very bad idea right when you're riding this high."

"I see." *Great.*

"Besides, there's nothing in the world I prefer more than walking a track with you, even if it looks like we're just friends." He tips his head toward me and looks directly at me now. "Even if I want so much more."

I feel warmth flow through every cell in my body. "Really?"

"More than you know. But this will do for now, Bug," he says.

We walk again a little farther, until we hit the first turn and we're off the main beat. The crowds are a little quieter off the main strip, but we're still visible.

"Okay, where did you get to with your sorry-ass explanation?" he says teasingly.

I look across at him, and he is trying hard to fight a grin. "It's not funny," I say.

"Sorry," he says, looking left and right, checking all the time for people taking photos, making sure we're standing far enough apart.

"When we were brought together for Arden, I *did* have a very bad reaction—I didn't want to work with you. I was angry because I felt you ran out on our friendship. I was hurt. I didn't want you around, and I let those feelings burst out of me to someone I thought I could trust, and shouldn't have. But I'd known him so long, and he knew our past, and it felt okay."

"I know," he says gently.

"I didn't provide all those quotes about Stavros, you know that, right?"

"I do."

"But it doesn't excuse me talking to him at all. I can't even remember what I said. He asked me if you'd been in touch and I don't remember what I said. I was so tired and he was walking me to my room because I couldn't carry all my things and my dinner . . ." My voice trails off.

"It's all true," Matt says. "I was gutless about Stavros. But I've faced that part of myself now. Thanks to you."

He glances back at me, and he frowns, his eyes dark and serious, suddenly.

I look up, feeling a rush somewhere between pleasure and shame. I feel like I'm bungee jumping into the abyss and Matt is my rope. Unreliable. Untested. Dangerous. And yet, I want to jump. I wish I could jump.

"We need to focus on your career," he is saying now. "You were right all along. This can't happen. At least for now."

The warmth I was feeling cools in an instant, as the truth settles inside me, and the ache returns.

"I know," I say, forcing the words out.

"For now," he says again. "While you're the boss, and you're building your career. I'm not going to drive forever." Matt moves to take my hand, but then thinks better of it and drops his hand to his side.

"Chloe, I love you. I think deep down I've always been in love with you. You're the complete package—smart, tough, funny, caring, beautiful, and the only person I've ever truly felt myself around. So when I say this can't happen right now, that doesn't mean I don't want it to. I just want you to have your shot—really have it. Because it's what you deserve."

I look up into Matt's face, the sun almost completely set and the Las Vegas lights shining in his eyes now. If I could go back in time to teenage me, she wouldn't believe this moment. Adult Chloe is barely comprehending how far Matt and I have come—from enemies to friends to lovers and so much more.

"I love you too, Matt. You have no idea how much I appreciate you looking out for me. You did when we were kids, and you're doing it now. It's one of the many reasons I fell, and have fallen, for you." We get as close as we can to each other without looking suspicious, which makes me want him more. The electricity between us is charging. I back off and keep walking so I don't ruin everything we're trying to protect.

"We'll figure this out, Bug. Believe that."

"I'm not even sure Barry is going to keep me on after what happened, though. In fact, I'm pretty sure I'm gone if we don't get a result this weekend."

"Pressure," Matt says, grinning.

"I've done as much as I can. It's up to you and Noah now."

"I can talk to Barry," he says. "Your work with the sponsors was apparently excellent."

I am about to tell him exactly the tone of those conversations, and about the offer from Haas, but now is not the right time.

I glance over at him. "What are you going to say?"

Matt smiles. "That you're the best team principal I've ever worked with, and if you go, I go."

"Subtle as a V-8 engine."

"Besides," he says, sighing, "you're kind of a hot commodity right now. At my expense, of course."

I laugh, just as Roger comes spiriting back in our direction, followed by Noah, who has clearly lost control of two greyhounds who want nothing more than to run.

"Hey, buddy," says Matt, crouching down as the dog races toward us and curls up between his legs. He slips a finger under the collar as Noah arrives, panting with the lead clutched in his hand.

"Shit, he's fast," Noah says, doubling over.

"Speaking of which," I say, looking at my watch. "We got two hours until qualifying, and you two need to get back."

"Yes, boss," says Noah, saluting. Then he stops and looks between Matt and me. "You two old bastards made up yet?"

CHAPTER 28

Matt

Las Vegas Grand Prix
Race Day

Barry is shouting down the phone at me as I rush into the paddock, late. But no one will be mad after my incredible qualifying run yesterday. I'm starting eighth today. A huge improvement, and Arden's first top-ten start on the grid.

"Matt, we've always been straight up with each other. Word is you're going to retire?" Barry is beside himself.

"Not today, Barry." I nod hello to a couple of old Rossini colleagues as I walk through the gates, absorbing the camera flashes of the waiting photographers.

"Well, you can't walk out on all we've built," he says.

"All *Chloe* built," I correct.

"I'm mad as hell at that girl."

"That *girl*?" I say, raising an eyebrow, as I look toward the direction of the paddock club.

"I gave her a shot! *I* did! You think Red Bull would ever hire a woman?" he says, exasperated.

"You hired her because you needed the PR," I say, almost laughing. I want to put him out of his misery, but on the other hand, it would be nice to hear him grovel. "And by the sounds of the results of the sponsor meet-and-greet the other night, she did a lot better than me."

Barry falls silent. "I don't want Chloe to go. I like her. She's spirited and smart and I have no idea what the hell she's talking about most of the time."

"Thaaaat's better, Barry," I say.

"But I don't think I'll have a lot of choice in that. I heard Haas have been sniffing around."

"Proving my point even more." *Good for Chloe.* After this race, I'm going to Brackley. I know she'll be back there too with her family, and we can catch up properly there without fear of prying eyes. Today, I have to think about finishing high up in the single digits. A fifth or even a fourth. That's my goal.

"Listen, Barry. I'm going up to the paddock club to do some press."

"You are?" he says, sighing heavily with relief.

"Chloe made me. I'm only doing ten minutes, but I'll be there."

"Oh, thanks, Matt."

"If we do good today, you have to make me a promise you'll keep her on. And if the numbers work, I'll sign too, for next year. But, Barry. That will be it for me. You've got a great young driver in Noah, and we'll have all next year to attract another big name. But I think I only have a year left in me."

"You're going to retire, then?"

"I think so," I say.

"You *are* getting old," he mutters. "What idiot buys an expensive old hen who doesn't lay eggs?"

"Fuck off," I say, laughing as I hang up.

■■■■■■■■■■

The Las Vegas night is alive with energy as I line up on the grid, the city's neon lights reflecting off the asphalt. I take a moment to absorb it all, thinking only of Chloe as we head out for our warm-up lap.

"Matt Warner, back out for Arden in what has been a roller coaster of a first few races with his new team," I say, imagining the commentary in my head. "Surely, though, they've got to produce some real results with the upgrades and turn all that enthusiasm for Chloe Coleman and Matt Warner into actual results."

Just a few months ago, I was recovering from that crash, filled with fear and uncertainty, deep in therapy, ready to retire out of grief.

Now I'm standing on the brink of something, with this amazing team by my side and Chloe at the helm.

"You've got this, Matt. Stay focused." Archie's voice is in my ear, grounding me and focusing me ahead. I picture Chloe in her little Arden team polo, headphones on, chewing gum, hovering behind.

It must be easier driving.

The crowd roars. My heart thumps.

The lights go out, and like waking lions, the cars roar to life, accelerating into the first corner. I get a solid start, holding my position in eighth as we speed through into the next straight. It's a solid first five laps, in fact, as I hold on to my place, trying to keep the gap between me and the Williams under one second.

Soon, the race settles in for its fifty laps, and the tension eases.

"McLarens have pitted," Archie says.

"Next lap?" I ask.

"Yes, we're sticking with plan A." Two tire changes. Mediums, then softs for speed at the end.

"Okay," I reply.

"Just breathe, Matt. You're doing great," Archie's steady voice reassures me.

At the halfway point, I'm running in fourth, battling fiercely with one of the Red Bulls. The Rossinis are ahead, their pace relentless. As I approach the section near the Bellagio, that touch of understeer takes me off track, and my heart stops.

"Shake it off, Matt. You're stronger than this," I tell myself, gripping the wheel hard and forcing myself to refocus.

"Box this lap, Matt. We need a perfect stop." I pull into the pit lane, and the Arden Racing crew springs into action. I turn my head to see Chloe standing at the pit wall, just across the way, looking back at me. She's glowing. Pink cheeks. Nervous excitement. She waves and then pumps her fist in encouragement. "Go, Matt," she mouths.

The car is up, tires off, new ones on. It feels like a heartbeat, and the car is ready to go. "Two point nine seconds! Incredible stop, guys!" Archie shouts.

I glance into my rearview to see Noah following into the pit, just behind me.

"Tell Noah he's doing great," I say, before pulling out of

the pit lane and rejoining the race just ahead of the Williams, in seventh. I've lost a few places, but I can do this. Soft tires. Great track conditions. I have this.

I think of Chloe, and the way she looks at me, her warmth, her sharp mind, *her belief in me*. I want to deserve it all.

Ahead, I spot the second Williams, and when his car spins and veers briefly out-of-bounds, I am able to fly past. Sixth place.

Then I see one of the Red Bulls pitting and I hit the throttle. I'm not sure how far behind I am.

"Will they exit the pit ahead of me?"

"Yes, but it will be close."

But then, a stroke of luck. The Red Bull suffers a slow pit, 3.1 seconds. Those tenths are just enough.

"Jammed the left rear tire. Matt! Push now!" Archie urges. I press the accelerator, my heart pounding, as I blast out past the pit exit just as the Red Bull is released.

"Can I keep pushing?"

"We're moving to plan B."

"No second stop? Will the tires make it?"

"Yes, but you're going to have to defend, Matt. Wait for my instructions to push."

"He's right behind me," I say.

"He's one point three seconds behind you. Not in the DRS zone yet," says Archie. "You got this. Fifth fucking place!"

Fifth place? Chloe said fifth place would be enough.

I begin defending, keeping my car on the tightest lines, moving to block the Bull, who makes several attempts to pass but fails. Ahead, I can see the McLaren. If I could get in front of that, I'd be in fourth.

Fifth isn't enough. I'm hungry; I feel it like a fire in my belly. Like an animal coiled and poised to attack.

My radio crackles. Archie knows. It's sixth sense.

"Don't do it, Matt," he says. "Tires won't last."

I picture Chloe behind him, a smile on her face. She would want me to try, I know it.

With just five laps to go, I make the decision. "I'm going for it," I say, determination flooding my voice. I line up behind the McLaren, looking for any opportunity to pass.

I pull in directly behind him, my bumper just inches from his. It's risky. Fifth place would do. Every muscle in my body is tensed. Then, I think of Stavros.

Thoughts in my head start to swim. I see Stavros and me standing on the edge of Lake Como, diving in together. I see him trying to teach me how to ski, pushing me down the mountain, where I crash in a jumble of limbs and sticks, and he doubles over, beside himself with laughter. I see the two of us drunk, covered in champagne after another impossible podium one-two for Rossini. Stavros is grinning at me, his dark floppy hair in his eyes, that goofy smile on his face. I see *him*. I miss him. A new thought emerges.

I'm not thinking about the crash.

The clarity comes in an instant, and I close back in on the McLaren, our bumpers almost kissing. It's a super-risky move, but I dive down the inside, and while we jostle for place around the next two corners, I emerge in front.

I'm in third fucking place behind the two Rossinis.

"Yes, Matt! That's it!" Archie cheers in my ear. "Hold position, you risky bastard."

"Where's Noah?" I ask suddenly.

"P six, Matt."

"Holy shit!"

He's not too far behind me, driving an incredible race. A surge of pride—Noah's first time with points in his career. "Well done, Noah," I mutter to myself.

Let's bring it home.

The Rossinis are too far ahead, but I hold firm, the adrenaline pumping through my veins. Each corner is a battle to stay calm, keep my focus, drive this tin can across that line. The crowd's roar grows louder as I approach. Someone sets off a green flare. I see the British and American flags draped over the grandstand.

"I'm back, motherfuckers!" I shout into the radio.

"Matt. Jesus fucking Christ, the mouth on you," says Archie, laughing.

Chloe's voice comes through the radio. Well, first it's a chuckle, and her joy radiates down the line into my ears. "Don't screw it up now, okay?"

"Sure thing, boss. Anything else?"

"Yeah, bring me that podium."

"I'll see what I can do," I reply, feeling a cocky grin spread across my face as I eye up that checkered flag, watching the team climbing the chain-link fence between the track and the pit to cheer me home. And I finally feel it again. That fire in my belly as I cross the line.

It's relief that hits first, and then right behind it, tears.

A cathartic, quiet sob as I take my victory lap, slowing down so Noah can catch up and drive alongside. He raises a fist and pumps it into the sky, before flying off ahead of me. I know what they will be saying.

What a story here at Las Vegas tonight. The two Ardens side by side, in what is surely the Cinderella story of the season. Who needs first place when you can drag a team from the bottom to the top in just five races. I'd bet my house on Coleman getting a contract extension into next season and beyond.

I know what we just did. I grin through the tears, my vision blurred, unable to wipe my eyes until I get this damn helmet off. I can hear Archie and the team celebrating in my ear, but my mind is already looking forward. Tonight, I proved something to myself. But I slow down and take in the moment, hoping this will be just the beginning for this team.

I pull up into the third-place slot in the pit and leap into the arms of the cheering team.

CHAPTER 29

Chloe

As Matt pulls into third place, he yanks out his steering wheel, pushes out of the car, and stands on top pumping his fist. I watch him rush to the team and leap into their arms. Celebrating third place like it's first is my new jam. This was a victory beyond our wildest dreams.

I glance across at Jasper, who smiles his toothy grin back at me, slow-clapping with a cigarette dangling from the edge of his lip.

"Gonna go tell your boyfriend he did good?"

"The *whole team* did good," I mutter, my cheeks hot.

"Your secret is safe with me, kid."

I blush hard and want to protest, but Jasper waves my embarrassment away. Is there anyone who doesn't know something went on between Matt and me? I wonder. "Wanna talk to me about next season?" he says, grinning.

"You'll stay?"

"Fuck yeah. We've got a couple of Rossinis to beat." Then he grins.

Just then I feel the heavy thud of a hand on my back and turn to see Barry beaming at me. "Well, well, well."

"Happy, then?" I say, seeing the strain his grin is putting on those round cheeks.

"I'm happy," he says. "I suppose we need to talk about next year."

"Next year," I say tentatively, balling my hands into fists. "I've got the plans ready, if you want to see them."

I feel the curl of the two dogs around my legs and instinctively reach down to rub their heads. Ginger licks my hand, and Roger sniffs my ass and I laugh.

"Looks like they want you to stay," says Barry, looking out at the crowd. "Hey! Look at that!" I follow his pointing finger to where I see a few fans in black and green, one of them holding a sign with a cartoon picture of Ginger and Roger that says, GO UNDERDOGS. Barry's face almost explodes with pleasure, the smile reaching the crinkles in the corners of his eyes, his arms out wide as he moves forward to get a closer look.

"Underdogs no more!" I shout, enjoying watching Barry finally get some recognition, as he walks out with the two greyhounds and the handful of supporters go wild.

The press conference is packed as Matt and the two Rossini drivers file in. The room springs to life as cameras swing around in their direction, and to my delight, they turn their lenses on Matt, who grins at the room. The smile is almost cocky. A twinge of that playful arrogance that every fan used to love, or love to hate.

I follow behind, not in some ridiculous green pantsuit this time, desperate to show the world how serious I am, but in my Arden kit, my two race engineers beside me, jostling with the press for a spot to watch Matt seize his moment and shine.

"Matt, hell of a drive. How does it feel to grab your first podium of the year?"

"Like a shrimp cocktail. Good, but I want the main course," he says without hesitation, pointing to the next reporter. Laughter fills the room.

"Hi, Matt. Sky Sports. What a drive. It feels like Arden has come alive. Want to share any insights?"

"You'll need to ask the team principal," he says, pointing at the next raised hand.

Archie nudges me and grins. It is a nice thing to do, keeping my title front and center, giving the credit to me.

"The car has had incredible speed through the straights. Did it take you by surprise how much the upgrades have impacted the performance?"

"No. Because Chloe Coleman oversaw them, and Jasper Cox came on board to refine them."

I bite my lip, beaming with pride.

"You seem to be a big fan of your team principal," jokes the next reporter.

"Aren't you?"

More laughter ripples round the room.

"No one is asking the other drivers a single question," Archie whispers to me. "Look at them."

My eyes shift from Matt to the two Rossinis, who are starting to look a little annoyed by the lack of attention. *Holy shit.* This is better than I could have hoped. The story should be the podium one-two for Rossini. But it isn't. Arden is the story. Matt's third-place comeback is the story.

He glances across at me, catching my eye, and he tips his chin toward both me and Archie.

And then I hear a familiar voice.

"There's a rumor in the paddock that you and Coleman are more than old friends. Care to comment?"

Jack Sheppard.

I watch Matt's face remain completely impassive.

"No," he says.

"No, you don't care to comment, or no, it's not true?"

"No, it's not true. Can someone get this dickweed out? I want to talk racing."

All the faces of the press now turn their attention to Jack, who squirms in his seat.

"You want to talk racing, or do you want to fuck off?" Matt says, all his old bravado surfacing at exactly the right moment. Jack's face hardens. He looks furious, which gives me silent pleasure. But the damage has been done, and if Matt isn't careful his fiery response is going to elicit more rumors.

Calm down, Matt.

"You're both from the same town. Has that *special* closeness helped?" says another reporter, this time from the *Daily Mail*. They won't give a shit about racing. They'd love to break this kind of scandal.

A few photographers turn their lenses on me, and Archie nudges me and starts laughing. I follow suit with a confused chuckle, like *What the hell are they talking about?*

"No," says Matt firmly. "That's an inaccurate report and undermines the incredible story of this woman who has fought and clawed her way to the top. I didn't know sexist reporting was still in. C'mon, guys."

A lie. A bald-faced and very necessary lie that he delivers perfectly. I hold my breath, as Jack shrinks further into his seat.

Matt is saying too much.

"You're both single, right?" says another.

"The only thing that interests me about Chloe Coleman is her vision for the team. And frankly I'm bored now. Next question."

The denial couldn't be more concrete. And while I let out my breath, relieved that he's thrown cold water on it, a part of me aches. I know what he's doing—he's protecting me. But still, my stupid heart feels rejected all the same. I force a smile and stare ahead.

"You clocked the fastest lap today and were voted the FIA driver of the day," another reporter says. "How does it feel to be back?"

"Aww. Did you miss me?" he quips, as the press conference returns to focusing on Matt and his race.

I feel Archie's hand grab mine and squeeze it, and I turn to him. "He had to say all that," he whispers.

"I know," I say, nodding slightly, needing that encouragement. "I know."

My turn. By the time I'm due on that stage for the press conference, I saunter up there, my nerves steady. Next to me, Rossini's team principal. I glance across at him in acknowledgment and nod my head, trying my best not to look too smug, or too proud, or too arrogant.

"Congratulations today," he says, before leaning in and whispering, "Now the real work with Matt begins."

"Meaning?"

"You'll see," he says, leaning back in his chair and looking out toward the sea of reporters. "He's a fucking handful."

I roll my eyes. Like I don't know Matt. Like I can't handle that ego. Like he doesn't listen to me. Fuck this. I'm not going to play like I'm lucky to be here anymore. I'm not going to be grateful anymore. I'm not going to make myself smaller or meeker or whatever the hell these people want.

I look back out into the room and see Matt, standing with those forearms crossed, staring hard at me, a look of pure pride etched across his handsome face. Now we're sharing a secret. A joke. And this time, I'm in on it.

"Chloe, congratulations. In seven weeks, five races, you've taken Arden from the bottom of the pack to the top. How does it feel?"

I hesitate. I want to say something short, tough, and arrogant back to the reporter. I want to play like these men do, coolly commanding the room, keeping my cards close to the vest, but a part of me wants liberation from that.

"I'm thrilled. It's been a lot of hard work, and at times I've hid in the bathroom, or screamed into my pillow, but here we are. We fucking did it."

It's messy and personal. But it's me.

And the press seems to love it.

"Hugely relatable," says the next journalist, grinning. "Whose idea was it to bring Jasper in?"

"Well, mine. But we're a team that believes in second chances."

They like that one too. Turning to Rossini's team principal for a response: "What did you think about the appointment?"

"Formula 1 is about consistency at the highest level. At Rossini we look for extraordinary talent, but we also look for professionalism, loyalty, and the ability to maintain that level past a handful of races."

A murmur around the room. Holy shit, he must be rattled.

"Is that why you let Matt Warner go?"

My eyes widen as I wait for the response.

"He's thirty-four. We needed to move on from someone whose career was ending," he says, pointing to the next person. "And of course, his crash showed bad judgment. It was a career-defining error that cost us both drivers."

The journalists turn back to me.

"Any response, Chloe?"

"Haven't we all had moments in our life where things go wrong? Catastrophic things? I know I have," I say, smiling, looking directly into the eyes of the press in the front row, one by one. "I think real sportsmanship, true greatness, comes from our ability to endure the mistakes, learn hard, forgive ourselves, and rise. Matt Warner had a terrible crash, impacting his best friend. I'm sure you can imagine the agony it's caused him, and how difficult it's been to come to terms with. Can Matt maintain this level? I think so. As his team principal, I'm rooting for him, and we'll give him all the support he needs."

I glance at Matt, hoping it wasn't too much, but he smiles back at me, and so does Archie.

"This is a more confident, eloquent Chloe Coleman. Are you feeling on top of the world right now?"

"I am," I say, beaming.

"And what about next year, are you signing with Arden beyond the season?"

"You'll need to ask Barry Arden. I wouldn't want to have to let me go, would you?" I say, the press enjoying this. "But seriously. Most teams in F1 run like a business. Results based and ruthless. Arden is like a family. We stick by each other, even if we don't always get along.

"So yeah. I'm going to stick with the dogs, if they'll have me."

Outside in the hallway, I see Barry surrounded by press, his energy big and wild as he crows about the future of the team and how he always knew that Matt Warner could turn things around on the track. Matt and Archie and I head off down the hallway, leaving him to his perch.

But then I hear Barry say something that takes me by surprise. I stop and turn.

"Look, Chloe Coleman was a big risk for Arden," he says. "But she inspires that team. She trusts her team. She's a star. And I'm going to tie her up for as long as I can, so I can piss off to the Canary Islands with my two dogs, safe in the knowledge she doesn't need my fucking input anymore. *And probably never did.*"

I turn to Matt, and I grin. "I guess I'm staying," I say. "Thanks for that."

"It was all you," he says.

Archie coughs.

"It was everyone," I say quickly.

We keep walking to the end of the corridor, pushing through into the lot as we make our way back toward the garage. As we approach the entrance, Archie says, "Guys, I gotta split early. I have something I need to do."

"See you in Qatar!" I say, waving him off.

"He wants to *do* his girlfriend," says Matt, grinning.

"Really?" I say, chuckling, as we stay outside the garage in the quiet of the hall.

"I think so," Matt says, as the door closes behind us and we are completely alone for a moment. "We should probably go back to the hotel," he adds. "It's almost one a.m."

"Yeah, you're probably right."

The tension of the past few days finally melts away, and the realization of my achievement sinks in. I watch Matt catch his breath, and then his eyes land on mine, as the silence falls. I look down the hallway, pricking my ears for the sound of any of the strategists or pit crew, but most are long gone. The few who remain are in the garage. There is nothing but the banging of gear and the sound of rolling crates as the garage is stripped.

"Why so serious?" Matt says, searching my eyes. "You did it, Chloe. Enjoy."

We stand there staring into each other's eyes for a moment, Matt searching mine intensely, his pupils large, his jaw flexing. The sounds of the garage grow faint as I concentrate on my breathing.

"I'm just thinking about what you said at the presser.

About us," I say, my heart clutching instantly, the wave of sadness crashing in to clear out any jubilation or joy I felt just moments ago. "Thank you."

"I did what had to be done," he says, shrugging.

"It breaks my heart a little, though," I say, clearing my throat. I smile, put my hand on his shoulder, before leaning in to kiss him on the cheek.

"I'd do it again," he says, reaching out his hand and putting it on my cheek. I turn my face to kiss his palm.

"That's so mean," I say, pretending to frown.

Matt tips his head upward and breathes out. Then he locks eyes with me, his gaze darkening, as he leans in slightly, pushing me back into the hallway wall so I'm pinned. I bite my lip, my knees weakening as I feel the full weight of him against me.

"We should go meet the team at the club," I say. "They'll be waiting for us."

"Yeah. I just need one little thing first," he says, leaning in closer, his nose touching mine, forehead falling against mine.

"But you said . . ." I begin playfully, as he kisses my cheek, his breath hot, the smell of sweat and champagne in his hair. I pretend to recoil a little, smiling, my cheeks warm, my heart pounding. But I love that smell. That is the smell of our victory.

"Listen, Bug. I know what I said." He buries his face in my hair. "I wish it could be any other way."

A thought pops into my head, and suddenly I have the answer about us I've been searching for.

"We're only talking about waiting for a year or so, right? I mean, there are surely a hundred ways to have an affair that no one finds out about. Burner phones. Adjoining hotel rooms?"

Matt stares at me incredulously, then breaks into a wide, almost childlike grin.

"Overcoats and fake noses?"

"I'm serious!"

"You think we could sneak around for a year or so and hide this? Impossible." He kisses my forehead, checking to make sure we're alone, before we're both laughing at the craziness of it all.

"You know what? I'll take that challenge," I say, pulling back to look at his face, and then leaning in, hesitating slightly, and putting my lips against his.

"Secret meetings in the driver room?" he says breathlessly.

"Dirty motorway motels, tucked away, far out of the city," I reply, my hands hovering near his waist.

"I could get a fake girlfriend," he replies.

"So could I," I say, as his warm mouth hits the base of my neck. "Keyla might do it."

"Fuck, you're perfect," he says, running his hand up my body to cup my breast on top of my shirt. "I could never resist you. I can keep a secret for the time being."

"Our secret."

"Except Archie has pretty much figured it out."

"And I think Barry has known for ages. . . . Still, we emerge in fourteen months, just as you retire, and I'm established as a successful team principal. Successful enough to survive a sex scandal."

"Then you'd really know you made it," he says, laughing into my neck.

"We have enough people around us who we trust."

Matt pulls back and looks at me. "You're not being serious, Chloe. Right?"

"Why not?" I ask, running my hands down his arms, his muscles flexing at my touch.

"Because it's mad?" he counters.

"It isn't mad," I say, my smile softening. "It's what I want. And I think we'd be hard-pressed to do this any other way, Matt."

God, I want him. I'll take him anywhere I can get him. No one is here, but someone could come at any moment. . . .

"It's either that or you leave the team, and you're not leaving the team," I say, as Matt reaches beside me to open a door. It's a broom cupboard. He looks at me and grins. "I'll let you go eventually. A year. Maybe two."

I close my eyes as he kisses my ear, guiding me into the small space. He gives me a soft, lingering kiss that tells me everything I need to know.

"So, you're quietly mine?" he says, his eyes a little misty.

"I always was," I say, leaning forward and shutting the door behind us.

EPILOGUE

Chloe

London
One Year Later

"You look hot in red," he says, a hand on my thigh as our limo snakes its way through central London. I rest my head on his shoulder and smile. The dress is Valentino, long, strapless, figure-hugging at the bodice, with a soft silk skirt that moves like water.

"Are you *sure* you're not nervous?" he asks.

"For the hundredth time, no. I'm not nervous," I say, reaching down to adjust the straps on my pumps. "I mean, I'm nervous about my first red carpet in six-inch stilettos, but no, I'm not nervous about what we're about to do. We're ready."

Matt smiles, reaching for my hand and pulling it into his lap. His palm is clammy as he squeezes my fingers. I realize *he's* the one who is nervous.

"It's going to be fine."

"Are you sure?"

"Matt, I just took Arden to the top in my second season

as team principal," I remind him. "I don't need anyone's permission to be dating you. I do not give a damn."

He laughs, squeezing my hand again. "You've come a long way, Bug."

I really have. I believe in myself now. And so does everyone else.

"I guess I'm about to retire," Matt says, turning his head with a grin. "So, I don't need to care what people say either."

A cough from the front of the car. "We're nearly there," our driver says, catching my eye in the rearview mirror. "Want me to do a lap?"

"No. We're ready."

"Anyway, we have to be," I say, turning to Matt. "There's only so long we could ask Archie, Keyla, and Barry to cover for us."

"Don't forget poor Noah," he says, laughing.

"The Sexiest Driver of 2024? British *Vogue* cover model? Who could forget him?"

Matt gives me a look. "Who here *hasn't* been on the cover of British *Vogue*?"

I feel a flutter in my belly as the car pulls up outside the hotel for the FIA Awards. I never dared to imagine that Arden would be the most improved team of the year under my stewardship, two years running. That we would get two wins this year, multiple podiums, and third place overall. That I would have the F1 world at my feet, and finally feel like I deserve everything. And Matt, my Matt, is here on my arm, supporting me, pushing me, and loving me.

The car stops and a long red carpet stretches ahead from the street into the foyer. I bite my lip and breathe out to steel myself.

Our driver slips out of the front seat and moves around to open our door.

I look over at Matt, just needing one more confirmation that he's ready before jumping off the cliff. "Once we do this, we can't go back. Everyone will know that Chloe Coleman and Matt Warner are a couple and . . ."

The door is about to open, and the photographers turn their lenses on us right away.

"We're ready," he says, gently placing his hand on my lower back. "And I love you, Bug."

I turn to him, just out of view of the cameras. "I love you too. They're gonna see the ring, though, Matt." I grin, still unable to believe it.

I lift my hand up to his, the simple diamond dancing in the light, and he takes my fingers gently and kisses the ring. "Fuck it. Let's go."

Then all hell breaks loose as the door opens.

Matt steps out first, and the scrum of photographers and fans come alive. He waves cheerily before turning to offer a hand to me. I step out of the car and then focus all my attention on standing in these damn heels.

Matt doesn't let go of my hand as he leads me slowly up the red carpet, and together, hand in hand, we pose for photos.

"Matt, is Chloe your date or your team principal?" says a reporter from Sky Sport.

Matt turns to me, and our eyes meet, and we smile at each other.

"Both," he replies.

"Well, technically, just his date," I say, "since Matt is retired now."

"Is that confirmed, Matt? You won't return next season?"

"I guess it is now," he says, squeezing me playfully. "But yeah. I'm going to work with Barry Arden to build his new Rookie Driver Academy."

"Are you two a couple now?" asks a reporter, thrusting her small microphone under Matt's nose.

"You don't want to know about the academy?" Matt pretends to look offended, and we take a few more steps toward the door. *Nearly over.*

"How long have you and Chloe been together?" shouts another.

"Too long," I reply, pulling a face, and the scrum laughs, as Matt tugs me closer to the door. I look through the glass entrance and I can see Stavros and Archie standing in the lobby, cocktails in hand.

"Wait. Is that an engagement ring?" I hear, and Matt turns to me and laughs.

"Thanks, everyone," I say, waving as we push through the revolving doors and into the safety of the lobby.

"We did it," I say. My hand is still in his. I pull him in and kiss him on the lips. Outside, the camera flashes go wild as they try to get a picture through the gaps in the milky glass.

"We did," he says, moving his hands around my waist. "No more sneaking. No more hiding. I can't wait to show you off to the world for the rest of our lives." He places soft kisses on my neck, completely unfazed that we're out in public. A new feeling I adore.

I pull his face back playfully and give him a mock-scolding look before wrapping my arms around him, looking deep into his hazel eyes.

"You're going to drive me crazy, Matt Warner."

Acknowledgments

Oh boy, writing this book was a wild ride, and I couldn't have done it without a lot of support.

First up, my brilliant agent, Hattie, who somehow keeps believing in me even when I send panicked emails. You are magic. To my editors, Ashley and Tara, thank you for your wisdom, patience, and for gently guiding me away from my worst instincts (like adding yet another subplot or several new characters). You made this book so much better, and I'm forever grateful.

To the team at Putnam, marketing, publicity, design, sales. Thanks so much for all the hard work on our FIFTH book together.

To my friends and family, who have endured my many spirals, cheered me on, and reminded me to take a break every now and then, thank you. Extra love to Carolyn, to whom this book is dedicated, for lending her ear and encouraging me to keep going through some darkish times in the past few years.

To my fellow authors, you know who you are. Your pep talks, venting sessions, and general chaos-absorbing abilities have saved me countless times.

To my friends at Red Bull, but especially Wayne, for helping me to turn from F1 newbie into bona fide fan. I'll never forget the 2021 race in Abu Dhabi, and the buzz in the Red Bull office on Monday after Max won his WC. Leaving Red Bull has allowed me to branch out my obsession and support other teams (hello, Oscar and Charles), but I'll always have Team Red Bull in my heart.

And, of course, to the F1 girlies reading this. If you've made it this far, thank you from the bottom of my heart. Thank you for picking up this book, for spending time in this world, and for making all this worthwhile.

With endless gratitude and probably a glass of wine,
Lizzy x

A Conversation with Lizzy Dent about *Drive Me Crazy*

In your own words, tell us what *Drive Me Crazy* is about.

Drive Me Crazy is set in the high-stakes, drama-fueled world of Formula 1. It kicks off with Chloe, a newly appointed female team principal handed the impossible task of reviving a failing, ragtag team. On the same day, she's lumped with a surprise gift: Matt Warner, her childhood crush and a troubled but brilliant driver who will be her new number one. There's tension on the track, heat off it, and sparks flying in all the wrong places. Think *Drive to Survive* . . . with shagging.

This is your first foray into the Formula 1 (F1) / sports romance subgenre. What inspired you to write this story?

My time working at Red Bull was an absolute catalyst for my love of F1. Before I started there, I'd watched a few races over the years. I went to the Abu Dhabi Grand Prix with CNN and had spent time working on a film shoot with World Champion driver (and major hottie) Jenson Button, but nothing prepared me for the excitement of working for Red Bull at the height of F1's rise in popularity. I developed content around Motorsport, and it was there I got deep into the backgrounds of the teams, how they work, and what, literally, drives them. After race weekend, everyone would gravitate around the kitchen for a debrief. The passion. The WhatsApp groups. It was infectious!

Who are some of your favorite authors currently writing sports romances and did any of their books influence your writing for *Drive Me Crazy*?

I enjoyed *Cross the Line* by Simone Soltani. Also, it's been out for a while, but I really highly rate the Chasing Daisy series by Paige Toon and *Off the Grid* by K. Bromberg. My absolute favorite sport series (though it isn't a romance) is Beartown by Fredrik Backman. Benji, my number 16 forever. <3

Your previous book, *Just One Taste*, was set in Italy, and this book spans locations like Singapore, Texas, Mexico, Las Vegas, and Brazil. How do you choose the settings for your stories and what role do these diverse locations play in your storytelling?

F1 is all about the exotic locations and legendary tracks. I wanted to set the story in the second half of the season (after the summer break), when the pressure starts to build, and those locations had to match the real calendar. Vegas was a setting I was keen to include since it's a street circuit through one of the liveliest cities on the planet. I know it's also a new-ish (since 2023) and somewhat controversial circuit, but I couldn't resist the lure of the spectacle. For me, though, the Brazilian Grand Prix was key. There's just something electric about Interlagos: the history, the energy, the fans. And, of course, Ayrton Senna. His legacy looms large over the sport and over Brazil, and that passion felt like the perfect backdrop for some of the book's biggest emotional moments.

As a devoted F1 fan and former development executive at Red Bull, did you draw inspiration from any F1 drivers when developing Matt's character?

Matt is a mixture of Carlos Sainz Jr., Mark Webber, and all the best bits of F1 notorious playboy James Hunt. I wanted someone who had *lived*, because a lot of the current F1 fan favorites are very young. And, yes, Noah is basically based on Oscar Piastri.

Considering the secretive nature of Chloe and Matt's boss/employee relationship, is there a romance trope you find most enjoyable to write? If so, why?

I always enjoy a thrilling secret romance. It's fun to write because you get to dig into that push-pull of wanting something you really shouldn't have. If you've ever had one, you know!

Many F1 romances often depict female characters in stereotypical roles within the racing world. However, *Drive Me Crazy* sets itself apart by showcasing a female team principal. What motivated you to place a strong, independent woman at the forefront of a story about a sport typically dominated by men?

I wasn't going to write this unless the female character had a seriously senior role in F1. I admire women like Susie Wolff, who's now running the F1 Academy and pushing hard to open doors for young women, and Hannah Schmitz, who's one of the best strategists in the sport.

But the reality is that F1 is still male-dominated from the top down. Female team principals are basically nonexistent. That's why I wanted Chloe to be a team principal, not a token female in motorsport but someone leading from the front, making the hard calls, and learning the power of the position she's in. Fiction has a way of creating space for possibility, and I hope this book adds to the noise that's already building for more women in top jobs in F1.

There are many intimate moments between Chloe and Matt in *Drive Me Crazy*. How do you approach writing these steamy scenes between love interests in your novels to ensure they are both authentic and engaging for your readers?

I think chemistry is everything. The steamy scenes in *Drive Me Crazy* aren't just there for heat—they drive the emotional narrative. Both Chloe and Matt are guarded in different ways, and the physical intimacy forces them to confront the feelings they've been trying to ignore.

This is definitely the spiciest book I've written, and that came with a bit of trial and error. The challenge is always making sure the sex feels earned, not just hot, and specific to *these* two people and the emotional chaos they're going through.

Throughout *Drive Me Crazy*, Chloe grapples with imposter syndrome but ultimately recognizes her rightful place alongside her male peers. What do you hope readers, especially women pursuing careers in male-dominated fields, take away from Chloe's experience in the novel?

I hope Chloe can be an inspiration and remind people that you can still be figuring things out, even when you're supposed to have it all together. F1 is opening up more and more every year, and it won't be long before we have some more big breakthroughs in the top jobs.

I love sports, and having worked at both Red Bull and Religion of Sport in the last few years, I've really enjoyed getting close to athletes and seeing how hard they work. I love watching women's sports (across the board) grow and grow. What Ilona Maher is doing for women's rugby, or Caitlen Clark for basketball, or seeing the Matildas' breakthrough during the FIFA World Cup is so inspiring.

What are you working on next?

A few different things. TV projects and another book. Maybe I'll write Noah's story since readers keep asking for it! 😉

Discussion Questions

1. *Drive Me Crazy* is a whirlwind romance set in the high-octane world of Formula 1. Are you an F1 fan? If so, do you think the book accurately portrays the atmosphere and intricacies of the sport? Did you notice any Easter eggs that nod to real-life F1 players and drama? If you're not a fan, what did you learn about F1? Do you think you'll start following F1 after this read?

2. Chloe and Matt have a complicated history that makes working together at Arden Racing all the more tension-filled and exciting. If you were Chloe, how would you have reacted to seeing Matt all those years later, and in a professional setting no less? If you were Matt, how would you have handled your surprising romantic feelings for your childhood friend turned team principal?

3. If you were part of an F1 team, which job do you think would best suit your skills—first or second driver, team principal, engineer, or a different role? Why?

4. What was your favorite scene in the novel and why?

5. *Drive Me Crazy* has a colorful cast of characters—from the Arden teammates to the competition and talent that Chloe and Matt encounter as they advance in the season. Who is your favorite side character and why?

6. Why do you think Chloe and Matt are drawn to each other? In what ways do they push each other to grow, not only as individuals, but in the sport as well? Do you think they needed each other to finish the season in the position they did? Why or why not?

7. Chloe and Matt each have a strong determination to prove themselves in this highly competitive, cutthroat sport. How does this character trait drive their decision-making when it comes to their romance, career development, and personal lives? Have you ever felt the need to prove yourself in a job or relationship? If so, how did that affect you and the people involved?

8. What do you think is the most important aspect of a romantic relationship? Do you think Matt and Chloe have that? Why or why not?

9. If you were Matt, how would you have reacted when you read the article? Do you think Chloe was in the wrong and/or a victim in this situation and why?

10. Throughout the novel Matt grapples with feelings of guilt and shame surrounding the devastating crash that landed his best friend and teammate in the hospital. How do you think you would have handled that situation if you were in Matt's position? What did you think about Matt and Stavros's reunion?

11. Were you satisfied with the ending? Would you have made the same decisions Chloe and Matt did at the end of the season regarding their relationship and careers? Why or why not?

TURN THE PAGE FOR AN EXCERPT

Olive Stone is about to spend four weeks in Italy with the most beautiful man she's ever hated.

1

London

FROM BEHIND THE front window of London's most pretentious bar, I watch as my late father's restaurant, Nicky's, starts to stir for the evening shift across the street. The head chef, Leo Ricci, spins the handle to extend the black canvas awning across the eight outside tables. The little neon door sign my mother gifted my father for Christmas twenty-five years ago blinks intermittently beside the black front door. I feel a stab of deep regret and sadness. And wonder why the hell no one got the damn sign fixed.

"Here you are, madam. The whiskey is served at a precise 65.35 degrees Fahrenheit," says the sulky waiter as he hands me a double malt in cut crystal, elegantly withdrawing a stylish metal thermometer from my glass. He then slides a small bowl of smoked almonds with powdered Himalayan salt on the window bar in front of me. I paint on a smile before I briefly look up from under my baseball cap to thank him.

His mouth sags. "Oh. It's *you*." He's so deliciously bitchy, I laugh.

"I'm not barred, am I?" I ask, raising an eyebrow playfully. "They haven't got a mug shot of me hanging behind the bar?"

"Just don't let my manager see you," the waiter replies, shrugging with indifference. "You're public enemy number one round here."

I chuckle as he leaves. I'm a food journalist at *The London Times*, a free but very widely read paper that circulates on the Underground. About three issues ago, I wrote a several-paragraphs-long hit piece targeting this place—Temp—in a story entitled "Is This Effing Satire?" I'd hated the self-consciously gimmicky idea that all drinks must be served at a particular temperature with a bespoke thermometer. So, you get your Chardonnay at 48.1 degrees, your rosé at 51.8, and your Chablis Grand Cru at 55.4. And everyone can *really* taste the difference, apparently.

Don't get me wrong, it is nice to do things "properly," but can we please be serious? This bar is frequented by bankers who only appreciate the quality of wine by its price. I also hated the way the proprietor, a software engineer turned bar owner, had talked down to my friend Ginny when she requested a cube of ice in her Sauv Blanc. *"We are not a dive bar, darling."*

"Olive!" Ginny and Kate arrive in a flurry of kisses and hugs. Ginny, an excellent interior architect with bouncy black curls, wide brown eyes, and a chic tan suit, and Kate, an ice-blond relationship therapist who exudes Scandi chic in wide-leg jeans and a designer sweatshirt.

"Why on earth did you choose this place?" Kate asks. "Didn't you call it a Tesla for oenophiles?" She drops her voice. "This *is* the tech-bro bar, right?"

"It's disruptive drinking for the biohack generation," I reply, mockingly serious. "Kendall Roy would love it."

"Sweet returns, bro," Kate snarls playfully.

"I hope that awful owner isn't here," Ginny says, glancing around the restaurant.

"I've not seen him. Yet," I say, tugging down my cap, just in case. Ginny eyes the cap, somewhat despairingly.

"You look . . . cute," Ginny says, touching my slouchy gray hoodie and attempting to admire the ends of my fuzzy outgrown bob. Ginny is the friend who cannot lie.

"It's grief-core," I say, laughing at her. "I look like shit, but I'm fine with it."

They pause, glancing at each other with concern.

"I'm fine! Sit, I'll explain," I say.

I wait for them to settle in their seats on either side of me, so we are three in a row, peering out the darkened window into the daylight like barn owls.

"So, I went to the estate attorney's office today and you're seriously not going to believe it," I say, pointing across the road to Nicky's, where chef Leo Ricci has taken a seat at one of the outside tables and is going through paperwork. A cute red-haired waitress with a sleeve of tattoos comes out and slides a coffee in front of him.

"Oh my goodness, Nicky's! That's why we're here?" Ginny asks, mouth open.

"He left you the restaurant?" Kate asks in breathless awe.

"He left me the restaurant," I confirm, still in shock myself.

"Do you get that hot chef with it?" Ginny asks, pointing at Leo, who at that very moment looks up in our direction. He can't possibly see us with the evening sun so low and bright in his eyes, so I indulge myself, staring as he runs his hands up through his dark hair, biceps popping as he rests them on his head for a moment before breathing out, eyes to the sky, and then returning to his paperwork.

"All of it, yes," I say, a strange sort of prickly feeling going up my spine before I pull my eyes from Leo.

My father died suddenly almost two months ago. I emerged from an underground bar and my phone sprang to life with seven missed calls and several text messages from both my father and a number I later learned was Leo Ricci's. When I saw the sheer volume of calls, I just knew. But the speed at which he went downhill was dizzying. Some run-of-the-mill infection one day, sepsis and death the next.

I feel as though I've been stuck in a state of shock, moving like a marionette through the responsibilities of being his only living relative. Go here. Sign this. Cancel that. Send this letter. Call the energy company. Call the energy company again. And *again*. Mum offered to help, but it felt weird having her reading through his personal effects; she'd just remarried, and Dad and she were divorced so long ago. I also felt it was right to try to protect his privacy, especially since he died alone.

Dry, sardonic humor is one way to get through the sudden death of a parent. Booze is another. I lift my whiskey to my lips and tip it back like I'm taking a shot.

"He *left* you Nicky's?" Kate says again.

"My god, Olive, when did you last even go in there?" Ginny says as her wine arrives, and she accepts it graciously.

"I mean, maybe ten years ago?" I say, feeling the heat of shame creeping up my neck as I say it. "Longer?"

It was definitely longer. I remember walking away and dramatically announcing I was never coming back. I was seventeen years old. That's just about fifteen years ago. I'd seen my dad since for a birthday here, a Christmas there. We messaged. But it was Mum whom I stuck with when things fell apart. She was the wounded party, leaving when she could take no more of coming second to Dad's obsession with Nicky's. I still bristle at the memory of Mum crying at the bottom of the escalators at Angel station as we stood there with our bags, heading to live with my aunt until Mum found another job and we found another home. It was hard to love him after that.

"Holy shit," says Ginny, eyes wide, face grimacing. After a long period of silence, she perks up. "But also, I mean, what an opportunity. It's yours?"

"Mine," I confirm.

"You *were* kind of born for this, Olive."

I sink into my seat, deflated by Ginny's misplaced excitement.

People romanticize hospitality. It often shows up in books or movies as a cutesy job for creative, homely types. It looks like freshly baked croissants in mouthwatering piles on a table covered with homemade jam in a pretty shop on a sweet high street with plenty of middle-class foot traffic. It looks like chalkboard menus and handsome staff in stiff linen aprons with leather ties, and bench seating decorated with thyme and rosemary in tiny silver pots. And always, a tired but tenacious owner who is busy—yes—but deliriously fulfilled and with plenty of time to fall in love.

What it *actually* looks like? Carnage. Like the scene of a crime. Bloody, sometimes. Chaos, always. Meeting the booze delivery truck at 6:30 a.m. and calling the rat guy and sneaking him in and out during lunch service. It's sticky kitchen floors and hungover chefs who are fucking the waitstaff and waitstaff who are stealing from the till. It's a mild coke habit if you're under thirty and a mild drinking problem after that. It looks like high blood pressure, heart disease, couch-surfing exhaustion. It's sixteen-hour days with no one in your life but the people you work with.

Don't get me wrong. My parents had it good for a long while. Nicky's was a classic family restaurant, a simple and easy-to-execute Italian menu with a modest but comfortable turnover. A very good turnover for a time, when my dad's TV cooking show aired. They had a rotation of competent chefs and enough staff who could steer the ship so we could go on an annual family summer holiday to Italy. A week in Sicily, staying with Dad's friend and mentor Rocco in Catania, and another week somewhere on the north Riviera with his best friend, Roger. We'd see Rapallo. Cinque Terre. Portofino. Sunshine, sunscreen, and of course, plenty of eating.

They also owned the property outright. Dad bought it long before the real estate boom in East London. And the restaurant was never just a workplace. It was our second home. I would sit at table 7 doing my homework while Mum ran the restaurant and Dad made slabs of olive focaccia in the wood-fired pizza oven. At our real home around the corner, I ate utilitarian cornflakes for breakfast, but in the evenings, I sat at the bar at Nicky's eating truffle linguine with sparkling water in a wine goblet. And my parents? They were happy. Really fucking busy. But happy. *And* in love.

It *was* pretty perfect, actually.

Until it wasn't.

"I'm going to sell it," I say. "Please don't hate me, but that building is freehold."

"Holy shit," says Ginny.

"Wait. What's freehold?" Kate asks.

"She owns the actual building as well as the business," Ginny explains, her eyes wide. "Christ, what's it worth?"

"I'd pay a lot of tax, but still, it's a life-changing amount of money," I say, feeling my cheeks redden. I'm really *that bitch* with an inheritance. The one time being an only child pays out.

"You really don't want to keep it?" Ginny asks, frowning.

"The estate attorney says it's practically a teardown. I'd have to mortgage it to renovate. The turnover is terrible, so it would be hand-to-mouth paying *that* back. I'd have to move in upstairs to avoid it being taxed as a second home. It's complicated. Plus, there's the small but obvious problem that I've not worked in a restaurant since I was sixteen years old." I try to laugh, desperate to keep the conversation upbeat, but the girls are more subdued, nothing but a simple *ha* from Kate.

"I think you'd be good at it," presses Ginny. "You've worked in *food* for your whole adult life, Olive. It's your literal job to know what makes a good restaurant. Plus, you're very warm, when you can be bothered." She nudges me in the ribs, and I smile, nudging her back.

"I could sell it and finally help my mum out, and still have enough to buy my own home, Ginny," I say, trying to get her on board. "That I'd own. Maybe even *outright*."

"*That* would be life-changing indeed," says Kate, nodding.

"The stuff of dreams," Ginny says, wide-eyed.

"Everything would be the same, but I'd be rent-free. Living in London. Can you imagine?"

"Yeah. You can, like, keep doing the job you hate," Kate says wryly.

"But rent-free," I say. I tip my head toward Kate. "Come on."

"You *do* hate your job," Ginny agrees. "You spent most of the last year complaining about it. Like a shitty boyfriend you wouldn't dump." I catch the look of agreement on Kate's face and realize I've been the subject of some *breakout* discussions.

"But look at it this way, I'd have a lot of freedom to find something else. Maybe I'll write a novel or something?" I say wistfully, as the girls both *Mm-hmm*, nodding in unison. "Which leads me to the catch."

"The catch?" Kate says, straightening up.

"Oh boy," says Ginny, reaching for her wine. I pause briefly to take a sip of my whiskey.

"My dad was in the middle of writing a cookbook, and he wanted me to finish it."

"Ohhhhh," Kate says thoughtfully. "I think that's sweet."

"I didn't know he was writing one," I say, and then stare across at the Nicky's sign again. "He always wanted to, you know. More than TV, he wanted to make a cookbook that sat on everyone's shelf between *The Joy of Cooking* and *Mastering the Art of French Cooking*."

"Aw, that's really sad he never got to finish it," says Ginny. "No matter how you felt about him, Olive, you *have* to do it."

"I know. He was due to go to Italy for a few weeks next month to do the final push. So, the accommodation is booked and paid for and I'd just need to get the flight."

"Well, this is like the perfect way to say goodbye to him," says Ginny; then she leans in, nudging me. "Perhaps you can put some of those regrets to rest?"

I nod. So many regrets. I regret missing those last seven phone calls, for one.

"Where in Italy?"

"Back to Sicily for the first time in more than fifteen years, then somewhere in Tuscany, and finally Liguria," I say.

"Oh Jesus. Can I come with?" Ginny says, clasping her hands together.

I spin the whiskey glass on the table as I analyze my feelings for the hundredth time. There are so many conflicting emotions I can't yet communicate to my friends. But the one I feel overwhelmingly right now is that I do not deserve this huge gift from my father. I feel shame at his generosity. I hardly saw him in the last ten years, tucking myself away on the other side of the river, blaming him and resenting this restaurant for the end of my parents' marriage.

I look up from my drink and across to Leo.

I should be where Leo is right now. I should have gone to culinary school just as we'd planned. Then I would have trained under my dad, preparing to eventually take over Nicky's when he was too old to descend the wine cellar stairs or too forgetful to take an order. A quiet part of me thought I'd eventually come back. The child in me also thought my dad would live forever. But he didn't.

When I walked away, Leo Ricci stepped into my place. Dad poured all that love and attention into him. They even went on holiday together, I'd learned. Leo worked beside him for nearly fifteen years, and now I'm supposed to swoop in and take the spoils? Be Leo's boss?

Does Leo even know?

I grimace into my empty glass. I *have* to sell it, and sell quickly.

"*Duck!*" Ginny shouts as she spots Temp's owner arriving in his three-piece suit with bright-white trainers and a trilby.

We sink our heads in unison; Ginny arranges the wine list

(which is irritatingly sorted by fucking temperature) to hide our faces.

"Well. A lot to process, Olive. But I think a few weeks in Italy doing this for your father will really be a good thing for you," Kate whispers from behind the menu, in her practical way.

"Sun. Sex. Sangria," Ginny begins.

"Sangria is Spain," Kate interjects.

"I'm sure you can get sangria in Italy," whispers Ginny stubbornly.

"We have to get out of here," says Kate, craning her neck. "Let's go sit in the Book Bar instead."

"Yes, let's go," I say, throwing a twenty-pound note on the table just as the owner spots me. "*Quick.*"

As we spill out onto the street, I pull them down the road and between two parked vans, out of the glaring view of the owner, who is waving a fist and yelling down the street. "You suck, Olive fucking Stone!"

"Oh my *god,*" I say, cringing.

I glance at Leo, who is on the phone now but looks up to see what the commotion is about. Ginny starts to laugh, but my heart beats hard in my chest, and I hold a finger up to my mouth to shush her.

"Tech bro is gone," whispers Kate as she peers around the van.

"Damn," I reply, panting. "I'm a serious liability."

"You're a very rich liability," Ginny reminds me, pointing back at Nicky's.

"Shit. I haven't finished explaining the catch," I say, following her gaze, and we all turn to get a better look back at the restaurant.

"He's a catch, all right," says Ginny, swooning at Leo.

"The thing is," I say, putting a hand on both of their arms as we peer around the van like a trio of comedy government spies. "Because I'm not a chef myself, and can't really do the recipe part of the book . . ." I take a deep breath and point across to Leo, who is about to head back inside Nicky's and begin the evening shift. "Part of the deal is that the hot chef over there—Leo Ricci—he has to come and do it with me."

"You have to spend a month in Italy with *him*?"

"My nemesis," I say.

About the Author

Photo of the author © Kerstin Weidinger

Lizzy Dent is the author of *The Summer Job*, *The Setup*, *The Sweetest Revenge*, and *Just One Taste*. She (mis)spent her early twenties working in Scotland in hospitality, and after years traveling the world making music TV for MTV and Channel 4 and creating digital content for Cartoon Network, the BBC, and ITV, she turned to writing. She currently freelances for Tom Brady's production company, Religion of Sports, developing sports documentaries for streamers. She lives in New Zealand with her family.

CONNECT ONLINE

LizzyDent.com

Lizzy.Dent